GOLDEN AGE

ALSO BY JAMES MAXWELL

GOLDEN AGE

THE SHIFTING TIDES, BOOK I

JAMES MAXWELL

47N⬤RTH

Published by 47North, Seattle

www.apub.com

Amazon, the Amazon logo, and 47North are trademarks of Amazon.com, Inc., or its affiliates.

ISBN-13: 978-1503948419
ISBN-10: 1503948412

Cover illustration by Alan Lynch
Cover design by Lisa Horton

Printed in the United States of America

For my wife, Alicia, with all my love

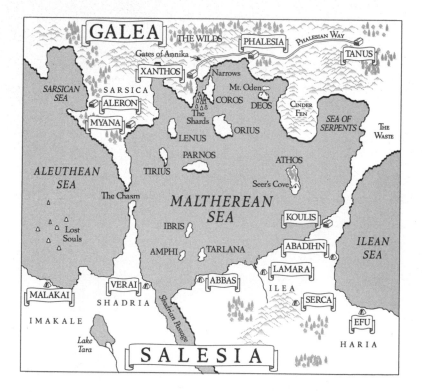

1

Roaring thunder crackled and boomed, rippling across the waters of the Maltherean Sea, bouncing from isle to isle. The sound climbed the cliffs skirting the shore of a heavy landmass. Arriving at a city nestled in the curve of a harbor, it rolled over the signs of civilization: mud-brick houses and towering temples of stone.

In unison, tens of thousands of people woke gasping with fear. The rumble was louder than any storm experienced in living memory. The heavens themselves were breaking; the sky would soon come raining down in pieces.

At a proud villa crowning a hill near the city's center, the thunder shattered the slumber of a young dark-haired woman.

Chloe's eyes shot open, her heart pounding in her chest. Lying on her back on her bed pallet, her gaze darted to the stone window where a thin curtain billowed in the breeze.

The window revealed a starry night sky, with not a single cloud in sight to obscure the firmament. This time of year, early summer, it rarely rained, and when she'd bid her father goodnight there hadn't been any sign of a storm. With the fading of the thunder she now wondered if she'd heard it at all. Perhaps the gods had visited her dreams and sent her a message to wake, for the cobwebs of sleep were now entirely banished.

Silence ensued. Chloe rolled out of bed and stood, her pulse still racing. Barefoot and naked on such a warm night, she rummaged in her clothing chest and swiftly wrapped a plain white chiton around her body, folding the diaphanous garment and fastening it with a copper pin. She exited her bedchamber, one of the many rooms in her father's sprawling villa, and walked down the hall to check on her younger sister. Having just woken, Chloe's long flowing hair was unkempt and she tucked a stray lock behind her ear.

Sophia lay on her pallet, wide-eyed and terrified. Just eleven, she was eight years younger than her sister.

'Chloe?' Sophia said hesitantly. 'I'm scared.'

'Hush,' she soothed. 'I'm just going to go and see. I'll come straight back.'

Evidently, despite the cloudless sky, the thunder was real. Frowning, Chloe went back through the wide hallway, stone-walled on both sides, and through the reception, the main communal space, with marble statues in the corners and low tables and stools scattered about. Exiting the reception and passing the kitchen, she finally reached the terrace, where a decorated rail framed a wide paved area. The villa comprised of two levels: an upper story for the family and a smaller, lower floor for the servant's quarters. The view from the terrace was unrivaled among all the homes in the city.

Finally, as she stood out in the open air, Chloe looked up at the sky.

Swathes of glittering stars returned her stare: the night was as clear as it had been when she'd retired. Bringing her gaze down, she saw a sliver of golden moon just above the horizon, the curling waves of the midnight sea revealed in its glow. She wondered if it appeared a little rougher than could be attributed to the breeze alone.

Chloe's brow furrowed as she turned her attention to the city below.

Her home, the villa of her father, Aristocles, First Consul of Phalesia, occupied a hill only a few hundred paces from the agora, the city's main market square and gathering place. Near the terrace where she stood, a stairway bordered by flowering shrubs descended to the cobbled stones of the streets below. From her vantage point Chloe could see the four temples that clustered around the agora, while two more grand structures nearby were the library, where the records were kept, and the lyceum, where the Assembly of Consuls met to administer the city.

Warm light glowed from braziers that rested against the temple columns. At this hour the agora would usually be deserted, but Chloe could see at least a dozen men, arms waving as they spoke frantically, but too far away for her to see much more.

Chloe's gaze swept past the agora and traveled upwards, to a place near the sea where a jagged cliff rose from the harbor's edge. At the summit, the highest point for miles, a large circular space could be seen from all quarters of the upper city. She felt comforted when she saw that the eternal flame burned brightly, reflecting from the tall marble columns of the surrounding temple. The huge torch on its pedestal cast flickering light on a golden chest the size of a large table, located half a dozen paces away, at the center of the paved plateau. The Ark of Revelation looked like nothing so much as an altar, which, in a way, it was.

An unusually large wave splashed against the shore, sending spray high into the air and drawing Chloe's attention once more to the harbor. The next wave was bigger still. It struck the small fishing boats lined up on the crescent shoreline and even threatened to drag at the bigger naval galleys. Fishermen and soldiers alike scurried down to the shore. Soon they were hauling vessels as high as they could above the tide line. Still more men, who'd barely taken time to dress, called to one another as they ran through the agora to the embankment, a sloped defensive bastion above the shore, where a diagonal stairway gave them access to the harbor below. Together they worked to save Phalesia's fleet from this strange thunder without clouds and waves without wind.

Chloe glanced inland to the densely populated township, and wondered where her father was. While the agora, temples, and villas of the wealthy were on raised ground above the harbor, the bulk of the citizenry lived below, within the walls guarding Phalesia's landward boundary. Her father had departed in the evening for a symposium hosted by one of the consuls who lived in the lower city. The rowdy symposiums always went until late, with wine consumed in quantity, but Chloe knew her father. He would come running at the first sign of trouble.

She decided to return to her sister's bedside. But as her hands left the terrace's stone rail, the thunder sounded again.

This time its power was overwhelming. It came from everywhere all at once, from directly overhead and from under the ground. The roar was louder than when Chloe had visited the great waterfall at Krastonias and boldly stood on a ledge beside the torrent, unable to hear her own voice no matter how much she shouted into the spray. Her thoughts vanished in primal fear as she clapped her hands to her ears.

The ground started to shake, and she fell to her knees.

The heavens rumbled around her, mingling with the crack and tumble of falling stone. The floor felt as if it was lifting underneath like a wild horse railing at its first rider. Rippling like the ocean, the ground bucked as she felt herself being raised and dropped repeatedly.

Chloe tried to stand but stumbled, barely managing to turn her body around to face her home. In front of her eyes three stone blocks fell from the walls holding up the tiled roof. Dust now filled the villa's interior; she heard a splintering crash of wood and tiles somewhere inside.

'Sophia!' she cried.

Chloe got to her feet, falling forward and clutching onto the wall as the ground heaved. Weaving left and right like a drunkard she plunged into the clouded reception, knocking into a table and then lurching the other way, grabbing hold of the kitchen's door-frame for support.

'Sophia?'

As her eyes readjusted to the darkness Chloe felt the trembling begin to subside. Suddenly she could hear nothing but the sound of her rasping breath, and then the roof overhead groaned, tiles loosened by the tremor, only the aged wooden beams holding them up. Ignoring the danger, she reached the hall and peered into the darkness. Approaching the first of the bedchambers, her own, Chloe's stomach lurched when she saw the damage ahead.

The ceiling at the back of the villa, where the bedchambers were located, had fallen in.

The area was now open to the sky. To her immediate left and right was solid wall, but going further into her own bedchamber revealed a ruinous mess. Clambering over the rubble, Chloe pushed her way past, heading deeper into the section where what had once been a ceiling lay in piles on the floor.

'Sophia!'

Chloe coughed, the air thick with dust. She could see that past the bedchambers the rest of the villa appeared to be mostly intact; it was only this area where the solid walls now held up nothing but themselves. She prayed she would find her sister unharmed. But when she finally reached Sophia's doorway and looked inside the blood drained from her face.

She couldn't believe that a moment ago she had paused in this same place to speak to her sister. The interior was now filled with stones, broken beams, and baked clay tiles. The cloud of dust was so thick that the light shining from the night sky overhead showed particles swirling and swimming like sea creatures.

She continued calling her sister's name and then, unbelievably, impossibly, she heard a thin voice wailing from under the pile.

'Sophia?'

Following the voice, Chloe threw herself at the tiles, scrabbling at the debris and tossing rubble to one side in frantic haste. She picked up a rectangular stone and lifted it with all her strength, then cast it away before grabbing another, tearing her fingernails in the process. She worked in a frenzy, her teeth gritted and every movement focused on freeing her sister.

Chloe knew that if another tremor came, whatever was keeping her sister alive, holding her safe from the weight above, would shift . . . and Sophia would die.

Time passed, stretching into endless labored breaths as Chloe wheezed and gasped. She choked on the dust. Her heart hammered in her chest. She prayed to the gods that the last of the quake was past.

She didn't know how long she fought against time and the prospect of another tremor before she saw a patch of pale skin and then a slender leg. With renewed vigor she lifted still more tiles and carried away the heavy stones, fighting the burning fatigue in her back and shoulders.

Chloe then saw what it was that had saved her sister's life at the same time as she saw Sophia's agonized face. A black wooden beam from the ceiling lay across the girl's chest. Two stones from the wall, bigger than those Chloe had encountered so far, leaned diagonally against the beam, creating a space that had saved Sophia from the devastation when the ceiling fell. There was a stone right next to her head. If it had fallen two inches further she would have been killed.

'Sophia! Look at me.'

Like Chloe, Sophia had dark hair, a wide mouth, and an upturned nose. In temperament Sophia was more carefree and she had dimples when she smiled. But now her face was filled with pain and, above all, terror.

'I can't . . . breathe.'

The beam that pinned Sophia down was as thick as Chloe's waist and long enough to span the entire width of the chamber. Chloe could try to lift it by one end, but if she did, it would add pressure to her sister's chest, and there was a good chance she would dislodge the two leaning stones from the wall, which were definitely too large for her to move.

Sophia whimpered as Chloe looked on helplessly, wondering what she should do. Her heart sank as she realized she could never free her sister alone.

'Sophia, listen to me. I need help. I can't do this on my own. I have to go but I will return.'

Sophia nodded weakly.

Still fearing that another tremor would come at any moment, Chloe left the chamber and clambered over the debris in the hallway to run back to the terrace. From the direction of nearby houses she could hear screams, cries for help, and the rough voices of men coordinating their efforts. The city's largest structures appeared mostly intact, with the temples lofty and indomitable as ever, but a plaintive wail told the story of at least one casualty. Revealed in the starlight, she spied several other houses with collapsed roofs.

Seeing movement close by, Chloe watched three scurrying figures descending the steps leading from the villa. She recognized the elderly household servants and was relieved all three were unharmed, but when she called and waved, try as she might, she couldn't get their attention.

She was going to have to descend the steps herself and find some strong men to come back to the villa to help. Her father was the first consul, and eventually she would find some soldiers who knew her and would come to her aid.

But the journey would take time, and there was no guarantee she would be able to find the help she needed. She didn't want to leave Sophia for so long. Even without another tremor, the rubble could shift. Chloe also didn't know the extent of her sister's injuries. Sophia needed help urgently.

Chloe closed her eyes and muttered a swift prayer to Edra, the protector of children. The gods were angry with Phalesia, that much was evident from the shaking of the world, but surely the goddess would spare an innocent?

She opened her eyes as she heard an improbable sound: a snapping and gusting, like wind in a sail. Though the sea breeze came from ahead, Chloe felt a buffeting wind on her back. She realized it was the movement of gigantic wings.

Her eyes widened as the faint shadow cast by her body changed: something huge was flying above and behind her.

Chloe whirled.

2

A strange mist cleared, revealing a man standing on the terrace a dozen paces away, where before the paved space had been empty. He wore trousers and a short tunic of soft deerskin over a frame that was tall and whipcord lean, with skin so pale it was nearly translucent. A narrow face displayed thinly arched eyebrows, a sharp chin, and a crescent-shaped scar on his left cheek. His eyes appeared dark in the low light, but Chloe knew they were brown flecked with gold, and that looking into their depths made her feel like a young child beside something ancient. Like all of his kind, he had silver hair, worn in his case to his shoulders.

'Zachary,' Chloe whispered.

The eldran must have left his home soon after the first thunder to have arrived so quickly.

'Chloe,' Zachary said with gravity. 'I came to see if your father needs me.'

'Please . . . Sophia is trapped. You must help.'

'Show me.'

Chloe grabbed his arm and rushed into the villa's interior once more, dragging him through the intact reception and leading him to the area where the roof had fallen in. When she reached the debris at the doorway to her sister's chamber she stopped.

'Sophia?' she called. 'Zachary is here! He's going to help!'

Barefooted, Zachary stepped lightly over the rubble and Chloe heard him speak with Sophia in low, soothing tones. He turned back to her.

'You can help her, can't you?' Chloe wrung her hands.

The eldran nodded. 'I can. But you know I will have to change.' He glanced up at the open sky where the ceiling once was and then turned to Chloe. 'You should go.'

Chloe drew in a deep breath before she finally nodded and retreated to the reception room. She clenched and unclenched her fists as she waited, her gaze fixed firmly on the hallway. The beam would have been heavy for four men to lift. She had to trust in him.

She could now only listen and imagine. Gray smoke suddenly poured out of the corridor. Zachary groaned, and as he did his voice became deeper. The groan became a rumble and then a gasping roar. Chloe heard moving blocks of stone and wished she could help, but knew she would only get in the way.

Still unable to help herself, as the mist cleared she moved forward to peek into the stone-walled passage. She caught a glimpse of a head, ugly and monstrous, with ears the size of soup bowls and a crescent scar on its left cheek. She saw muscled arms like tree trunks carrying a big stone as if it weighed nothing at all and tossing it to the side. Then the head ducked down once more and she heard more moving rubble.

Wishing she could enter further and see what was happening but knowing she should wait, Chloe tried to envision each sound. She fought her panic as she wondered if Sophia was badly injured.

There was silence for a time and she held her breath as she waited. She started to walk forward, scanning the corridor, peering through the dust. Her chest rose and fell as she approached the crumbled section and the doorway to Sophia's bedchamber.

Then Zachary appeared.

He had returned to his normal form, and he held Sophia in his arms. His eyes were wild and he was panting. When Chloe saw that her sister was awake and alert, bed linen wrapped around her body, she fought a sob of relief.

'Outside,' Chloe said. 'To the terrace. It's too dangerous in here.'

Soon they were in the fresh open air and Zachary was laying Sophia down on the stone, standing back while Chloe checked her sister, astounded to find she'd escaped with just cuts and grazes. Even so, Chloe had been instructed at the Temple of Aeris in the mysteries of healing. She wasn't satisfied until she'd checked every joint and her sister had recited the bedtime prayer three times.

'I must go and see if I can be of use elsewhere in the city,' Zachary suddenly spoke.

Chloe glanced up at him. 'What of your people?'

'It is your buildings of stone that are a danger, and we have none.'

'Zachary . . . If you must change again, do not forget who you are.'

Zachary nodded. He shook his head from side to side as clarity returned to his unfocused eyes.

'And thank you,' Chloe said.

Without a reply, Zachary left the terrace, darting down the steps.

Chloe fetched her bag of healing supplies and led her sister to the agora where she would be safe with the servants. She then rushed away to lend aid to anyone who needed her skills.

The rest of the night passed in a blur.

Much of the damage to the city followed the same pattern: dislodged tiles and collapsed roof beams with the occasional toppled wall. Everywhere she heard cries. Heading into the densely packed lower section of the city, Chloe set broken limbs, administered soma, and sewed gashes closed with needle and gut. She encountered too many cases where there was nothing she could do and left behind wailing wives and stunned children.

As she ran from house to house she saw eldren lending their unique abilities to help. A female giant worked tirelessly to clear the ruins of a broken house while a small boy watched from just a few paces away, too concerned for his family to be afraid of the monstrous silver-haired woman. Several times Chloe glanced up, hearing the sound of wings as furies wheeled overhead, scanning the city as the seven-foot-tall winged men searched the city for anyone needing assistance. Twice she even saw gray-scaled dragons, lithe creatures with wings the size of sails and muscles rippling under glossy silver scales. Her breath caught as one with a crescent scar on the side of its wedge-shaped head swooped close overhead; it could only be Zachary.

The great tremor was not followed by another but the consequences were plain to see. She passed a row of five bodies near the remains of two houses and blanched, muttering a swift prayer to Aldus, the god of justice, to grant them entrance to heaven.

Eventually Chloe was completely out of supplies and she realized it was now light enough to see. The sun climbed the mountains behind Phalesia to reveal a city that had been shaken but still stood. The night had passed. The worst was over.

Heading back to the upper city and climbing steps that felt as if they would never end, Chloe felt exhaustion in every limb.

But then as she approached the city's central square and its rim of civic buildings she heard a new chorus of cries, unmistakably shouts of fear.

People with wide eyes and pale faces ran back the opposite way, calling for soldiers as they passed. Hoplites with shield and spear sprinted in the direction of the agora.

Chloe started to run.

She skirted the Temple of Charys and reached the agora, an expansive square with paving stones in alternating shades of rose and brown. Wooden market stalls clustered near one side, while the tiered steps on the left-hand side had been turned into a makeshift infirmary.

A giant, fifteen feet tall, with silver hair and a crescent scar on his left cheek stood hunched in the center of the agora. Thick skin of tan-colored hide covered a frame of powerful musculature. His chest heaved and his brown eyes lacked the spark of intelligence, instead darting from side to side. Every part of his stance communicated the impression of a cornered animal.

As the soldiers of the city's guard arrived they moved to encircle the giant. The hoplites stood shoulder to shoulder, shield to shield, spears pointed at the heaving creature. Each man carried a sheathed sword at his side, ready to be drawn if his spear became unwieldy or was lost.

Chloe knew that eldren hated the sight of steel; the very presence of metal brought them pain. The giant roared at the prickly wall of iron-tipped spears.

As Chloe pushed her way forward she saw a man in leather armor and a blue cloak rush forward to stop her. Amos, the veteran captain of the city guard, cursed as she moved too quickly for him to catch her.

'Chloe!' Amos called.

'Call your men back,' Chloe said. 'How many did he save this last night? And you come at him with spears.'

Soon she was approaching the eldran, her hands spread in front of her as she spoke in a soothing voice. Zachary had been changing too much, shifting between the shape of dragon and giant depending on how he was needed. She prayed she wasn't too late for him to return to himself.

'Your name is Zachary. You are an eldran. This is just a temporary form, not your true shape. You live in the Wilds. Your wife is Aella.'

Chloe came closer still until she was within the reach of the giant's long arms. Despite the danger, she continued to speak softly, constantly reminding Zachary who he was. As she looked on, the wildness in his eyes began to clear.

Finally, gray smoke surrounded him. The cloud thickened and grew until the giant was completely enveloped by the mist. The vapor shimmered, wavering and flickering, like a mirage in the desert.

Then the mist cleared.

Once more Zachary was a tall, slim, pale-skinned man in deerskin. He straightened and put his hand to his forehead as he weaved on his feet.

'Chloe . . .' Zachary said. He shook his head slightly, fighting the wildness in his unfocused brown eyes. 'Did I . . . Did I hurt anyone?'

Chloe glanced at Amos.

'No.' Amos shook his head, speaking to Chloe rather than Zachary. 'He saved many. The rest of his people have left. No one was hurt.'

Zachary slumped and closed his eyes, before reopening them. The darting glance of an animal had left them completely. 'For that I am glad. I changed for too long.'

'Look,' a man said, pointing.

Chloe lifted her gaze. She frowned, then gasped. The eternal flame at the Temple of Aldus was extinguished. The flame always burned brightly through even the strongest storm, and despite the night's terror there had been no strong wind, with the thunder heralding a quake rather than a storm. Yet it had expired.

'It is an omen,' someone in the crowd muttered.

'We are being punished.'

'It is a warning.'

'Both the ark and the temple are safe,' Zachary said. 'That is what is important.'

Chloe saw more than one citizen glare at the eldran. Others regarded him with expressions of terror.

'And so is the city,' she said. Her voice rose as she spoke. 'Zachary saved my sister's life and worked tirelessly throughout the night to help our people. He did so for no motive other than the generosity of his spirit.'

'Thank you,' Zachary said. 'But now I must go. I cannot change again, so I must walk.'

Zachary stumbled out of the agora, heading for the lower city and the gates. The people made way, gazing at him fearfully, never taking their eyes away.

Chloe went to the nearby marble steps and sat down, exhausted. The lids of her eyes were heavy.

'Chloe.'

She heard Amos's voice, but didn't look up.

'Chloe!'

This time the voice was different.

Her eyes opened and she tilted her head to look up.

Aristocles, her father, First Consul of Phalesia, gazed down at her with concern. A skinny man with white hair balding at the top and perpetual lines of worry on his forehead, he still wore the

15

elaborate silk tunic he'd worn when he left the previous night to attend the symposium. Chloe stood up to embrace him.

'Father, you are safe.'

'Sophia? The servants?'

'The roof fell in at the back of the villa. Sophia was trapped but Zachary saved her.'

'She is unharmed?'

'Scared, but well enough. Will you see her?'

'There is nothing I would rather do, but I first must set the city to rights. Will you take care of her?'

'Of course.'

Aristocles looked up at the Temple of Aldus and frowned at the absence of the flame. 'This is a dark day,' he said ominously. 'A dark day for Phalesia indeed.'

3

Chloe leaned on the terrace guard rail and gazed out to sea. Waves rolled in one after another and she followed them with her eyes as the curling water broke on the rocky beach. Her eyes then traveled upwards, and above the shore, on top of the cliff, at the bay's closest end, she could just make out the flicker of the eternal flame at the Temple of Aldus, once more burning brightly. The golden ark below the torch's pedestal glittered in the sunshine.

The agora below buzzed with activity as citizens shopped and vendors hawked their wares. The workers had departed the villa earlier in the day, their repairs finally complete. The overseer had given Chloe his assurance that the work his team had done would survive the strongest tremor; even so, Sophia now shared Chloe's quarters; her own bedchamber gave her nightmares.

Chloe turned and saw Sophia limping toward her, although her younger sister couldn't seem to make her mind up whether to hobble her left or right leg. The servants and their father had been pouring attention on her, giving her sweets and checking on her several times a day. Sophia was enjoying their sudden indulgence.

'My bruises hurt,' she said as she approached.

'Which one is the worst?' Chloe asked.

Sophia lifted her chiton and pointed to a faint mark on her shin.

'No, I think it must be this one,' Chloe said, touching her sister's nose.

Sophia scowled. 'There's no bruise there.'

'Well then, why is it blue?'

'My nose is not blue.'

'It certainly is,' Chloe said gravely. 'As blue as your eyes.'

'It is not!' Sophia said with indignation.

'You had best look in the silver mirror and see for yourself.'

Chloe watched carefully as Sophia stalked inside and noted with satisfaction that this time her sister had forgotten to limp.

Sophia returned a moment later. 'I told you my nose is not blue.'

'I know,' Chloe said, pulling her younger sibling into a tight hug. 'I am glad you are well.'

Sophia squirmed but then turned serious when Chloe released her. 'Chloe . . . Why are the gods angry? Is it because of the eldren? What will happen to Zachary?'

Chloe frowned. 'What are you talking about? Where did you hear that?'

'I was with father at the agora and one of the consuls spoke to him, the fat one. He said that the gods are angry because we have allowed the eldren to live so close to our borders. He said they should all have been destroyed long ago.'

'Destroyed?' Chloe's eyes narrowed.

She knew the Assembly of Consuls was meeting at that very moment.

Turning away from her sister she gazed down at the lyceum, a long rectangular building of glistening white marble columns with a peaked stone roof.

'Don't worry. I'm sure Zachary will be safe.' Making a decision, Chloe lifted her chin. 'I have to go now.'

'Where are you going?' Sophia asked.

'To the lyceum.'

'But it's only for men—'

'All they do is talk,' Chloe said. 'Surely they've all seen a woman do that.'

Chloe changed her plain white costume for her finest garment, a chiton of pale blue silk that flowed like water. She fastened it with three copper pins in the shape of dolphins and put wooden sandals on her feet, then swiftly departed the villa. Her sandals slapped on the stone steps as she walked down the winding staircase, inhaling the scent of the flowering plants that grew on both sides, until she reached the bottom and made her way to the agora, now passing through streets filled with the stench of refuse.

Since the tremor a week ago, the city of Phalesia had nearly returned to its former self. As Chloe's father said, it could have been much worse, and almost all of the damage was confined to houses, while the city's defenses and harbor remained intact. The swift actions of the men who had laboriously hauled the boats of the fishermen and merchants up to high ground had saved nearly the entire fleet, with only a few war galleys caught in the surging tide in need of repairs.

Reaching the bustling agora, filled with folk dressed in a multitude of styles and colors, Chloe weaved through the throng, crossing to the far side to climb the marble steps that led to the lyceum. As befit a place where laws were made and trials conducted, a stern bronze statue of Aldus, the god of justice, stood tall and imposing outside. The god wore a long robe and carried two tablets in his arms. He appeared to be looking at the writing on the tablets but they were arranged so that only he could read what was inscribed.

The lyceum was the largest structure in Phalesia. A long building with an entrance in the shape of a horseshoe, it had no walls and essentially consisted of row after row of columns holding up the high triangular roof. In the center was a rectangular gallery, sunken into the floor in a series of tiers. The consuls sat on the lowest tier and the city's citizens seated themselves on the tiers above. Only one man was allowed to speak at a time from the central floor. No women were allowed to participate.

This was the first proper Assembly since the week-old wrath of the gods, and there were men on every level of the gallery, all facing the consul who was speaking, so that Chloe was able to reach the back of the crowd without anyone noticing her.

The crisp voice of round-faced Consul Nilus filled the air. As she stood on her toes to look, Chloe saw him turning at regular intervals to address all present.

'That the gods are angry there is no doubt,' he said in a voice designed to fill the lyceum. 'We must make offerings to all. Perhaps it is time to visit the Oracle at Athos, for we need to shed light on what we have done to bring such wrath down upon our city.'

Another consul, a heavyset old man with a gray beard, stood and waited impatiently to speak. Chloe recognized him as Consul Harod; her father said he was a troublemaker.

'I yield the floor to Consul Harod,' said Nilus, nodding at his colleague.

Harod moved to the middle of the floor, while Nilus seated himself on the lowest tier, gathering the folds of his white tunic in his lap.

'Offerings are not enough,' Harod's voice boomed. 'The gods have shown their displeasure. We cannot simply appease them. We must do more.'

A chorus of assent greeted his words. Chloe frowned. She had an idea what was coming next.

'The cause is clear,' Harod said, his full beard wagging as he nodded sagely, eyes roving over the gathered assemblage. 'The gods are angry because we have allowed eldren into our city.'

This time the voices of agreement were forceful. Harod waved for calm before he continued.

'This peace we have established with the strange ones is not a good thing. They turn wild when they change, forgetting who they are, becoming monsters that destroy our villages and eat our livestock. We have finally cleared the last of the serpents, dragons, and giants from the area. The last thing we need is more. Everyone knows what happened in the agora.'

Before Chloe knew what she was doing, she was moving. She pushed forward through the throng of men, resolutely heading down the steps. Ignoring their stares, she didn't stop until she reached the floor.

She saw her father, Aristocles, seated near Nilus, so astonished his eyebrows looked as if they were trying to climb to the top of his head. The gray-bearded Harod was stunned enough to forget what he was saying. Consul Nilus had his mouth wide open.

Crossing to the center of the speaking floor, Chloe pointed at Harod and she spoke loudly enough for everyone to hear. 'They only change if they must, and in this case they were changing to help us.'

'Clear the floor!' shouted a tall man on the third tier.

'Get her out!'

'Only when I've said what must be said,' Chloe called, turning narrowed eyes on the tall man who'd called out. He folded his arms over his chest and scowled.

Standing in the middle of the sunken floor Chloe spoke for all to hear and gazed out over the consuls around her. 'Zachary saved my sister's life. No number of men could have freed her without harming her, but Zachary did, and right now she is alive and well.'

She glared at gray-bearded Harod, who appeared unable to speak.

'The eldren saved countless more of our people,' she continued. 'Zachary knew the risk of turning wild, but he pushed himself to his limit, for us, and no one was harmed.' Chloe drew in a deep breath. 'I don't know if what happened was a punishment or an omen, but I do know one thing.' She spoke clearly with as much volume as she could now. 'It had nothing to do with the eldren.'

Chloe scanned the crowd. She didn't know if her words had had their desired effect. The citizenry appeared more stunned than anything, particularly the consuls, watching her in wide-eyed silence. Even Harod shuffled back to his seat on the gallery's lowest tier and sat down heavily. The consul next to him raised an eyebrow and Harod threw up his hands.

No one wanted to be the man to confront the first consul's daughter.

But then Chloe's father slowly stood, raising his thin frame and walking to the center of the floor. 'Please, daughter,' Aristocles murmured, speaking for her ears alone. 'There is a way these things are done. I must take no sides and then argue the course of reason. Letting me speak is the way to get the outcome you desire. A leader hears the opinions and then has the final word.' He raised his voice: 'Daughter, may I have the floor?'

Chloe nodded and her father smiled softly, indicating that she move to the side with his eyes. She left the floor's center but didn't sit with the other consuls, instead standing near the steps, her arms folded over her chest.

Aristocles looked down at the floor as if pensive, before raising his gaze to cast his eyes over the crowd. He somehow managed to look at everyone, even Chloe.

'We have heard impassioned arguments today. As your elected first consul I wished to hear the many opinions before revealing some new information that sheds light on our situation . . . and before imparting my own thoughts for your consideration.'

The mention of new information made many of the consuls frown. Consul Harod tugged his beard thoughtfully. Chloe had always known her father to be a gifted speaker, but she'd never been able to see him address the Assembly at the lyceum. With just a few words he had seized control of the dialog, while making his potential opponents curious rather than combative.

Aristocles let the silence hang for a time. It was difficult to have conflict in a room full of silence. He gave the impression of a thoughtful man who had pondered at length and was now prepared to share his wisdom with his peers.

'I have visited with the priests and magi from all the temples,' Aristocles said. 'All concur. We are not being punished by the gods, we are being warned. The thunder with no clouds and the tremor in deepest night, followed by the extinguishing of the eternal flame at the Temple of Aldus . . . this is no punishment but an omen. We are being warned of terrible danger.'

Chloe saw that every citizen's eyes were now on her father; every consul leaned forward, eager to hear his words. Aristocles felt the same way Chloe did about the eldren, but he hadn't needed to mention them once in order to bury the notion that the gods were somehow angry that he had shown a hand of friendship to their race. Instead of confronting Harod's emotional rhetoric directly, Aristocles had given them what they wanted: an answer.

'Phalesia is in danger,' Aristocles repeated with the utmost gravity, tilting his head back to include even the men on the highest tiers. 'This is a warning we must take seriously. You now ask yourselves: From where will the danger come?'

A sudden commotion interrupted the first consul's next words. On the high steps the crowd stirred, jostled by a newcomer. A bare-chested sailor in coarse trousers pushed through the crowd, clambering down the steps to get past those he shoved aside in his haste. The sailor was panting and had evidently run directly to the lyceum as fast as he was able.

'First Consul!' the sailor wheezed, reaching the bottom of the steps and placing his hands on his hips as he fought to regain his breath. 'I come from the harbor. We've been on patrol.' He drew in a deep breath. 'There's a ship!'

4

The consuls all stood and came forward; any decorum that usually existed at the lyceum had long departed.

'Ship?' Consul Nilus said, his round face looking quizzical. 'What ship?'

'A warship, Consul,' the sailor said.

Aristocles addressed the crowd. 'This Assembly is adjourned.' He made a swift decision. 'Someone fetch Amos and the city guard.'

Chloe looked at the consuls who were close enough to hear her father's request. The sailor was exhausted, and every one of the onlookers was at least fifty years old.

'I'll go,' she said.

Her father nodded, and Chloe turned to race up the steps, fighting against the push of those trying to get closer to find out what was happening. Finally she emerged into fresh air and began to run, bounding down from the lyceum to the agora and then sprinting down the series of paths to the lower city.

The barracks were both lodging house and training ground for the men in the Phalesian army. An arched entrance opened directly onto the training ground, with a sandy floor providing room for even horses to train with space to spare. A row of buildings at the back provided storage for food and weapons, a communal mess, and sleeping chambers for the resident soldiers. Those who had homes in the city generally saved their coin and stayed with family, but the guards who called the barracks home had the cost of food and board deducted from their wages.

She found Amos bent over a basin as he washed dust from his face and neck. He didn't see her at first, and she thought, not for the first time, that the crags on the weathered skin of his face would have made him recognizable among a crowd of hundreds. She wondered if he'd once been handsome; it was now impossible to tell. But he was brave and loyal, and had a reputation as a skilled warrior as well as a respected leader. He wore his dark hair short and she couldn't remember ever seeing him out of uniform.

'Captain,' Chloe said.

He glanced up, surprised to see her.

'A warship has been sighted. My father says to bring as many men as you can quickly gather to the embankment.'

Ever the professional, Amos simply nodded. 'The men are in the mess. We'll come immediately. Tell your father.'

Chloe ran back to the embankment, where the seaward side of the agora dropped down to the shore in a sloped defensive bastion. She was soon standing beside Aristocles and the other consuls as they watched the strange ship approach.

Her first thought was that it was obviously damaged. It listed to the side and appeared difficult to maneuver as it navigated the harbor and headed for a bare patch of shore at the small bay's far end. The sail was down and it was moving through the water by oars alone, while to Chloe's eyes the mast was at a strange angle. The tide was coming in and pushed the ship almost into the rocks at the headland, before a burst of speed from the rowers nudged the vessel past danger.

Chloe's next thought was that it was undoubtedly a warship. Though the ship was a galley, it was unlike any galley she had ever seen. Oars jutted out on both sides, more oars than she would have believed possible to fit into a ship of its size, and she realized that it actually had two rows of benches, one row on top of the other. Each tier was open at the side and she saw rowers moving back and forth in laborious unison. Above the top level of rowers was a deck that formed a roof above their heads.

Soldiers stood on the top deck: leather-armored marines, swarthy men with spears and triangular shields. An eye was painted on either side of the warship's prow, which curved out in a bowsprit and then back under the water in an iron-tipped ram just below the waterline. The ship flew a strange flag, a solid orange circle on a field of yellow.

Her final thought was that she'd never seen such a large warship. It was at least eighty feet long and must have employed well over a hundred men in its service. It made the Phalesian war galleys, presently pulled up on shore, appear puny in comparison.

'Back! Everyone back!' Chloe heard Amos's voice.

The crowd moved back from the edge of the embankment to let the soldiers gain access to the set of narrow steps leading down to the shore. Each hoplite looked resplendent in his short skirt of leather strips, leather breastplate, and leather helm, while Amos's helm was made of shining steel, crowned by a crest of horsehair dyed with indigo. Captain Amos and his subcommanders all wore blue cloaks, and Chloe counted ten units in total, which meant that a hundred men were soon assembling on the beach under the captain's direction.

Finally, Amos turned back to face Chloe's father, his head tilted back and legs apart as he looked at the embankment high above and waited for orders.

'It must have been damaged in the same event,' Consul Nilus whispered.

'Who are they? What flag is that?'

Chloe watched as the warship left the deep water to enter the lighter blue of the shallows. Phalesia's harbor was a crescent-shaped beach of smooth white stones with headlands and cliffs at both ends. It was large enough to easily accommodate Phalesia's entire fleet but not immense, its size making for easier defense, for any enemies would have difficulty making a secret landing.

'Captain!' Aristocles called down to Amos. 'Move to intercept their men as they disembark, but greet them with civility before you bring their leader to me. Respond to force in kind.'

'At once, First Consul,' Amos said.

The captain led his men along the beach until they were ranged above the high-water mark, showing discipline as they formed up one after the other, turning to wait in a wide phalanx. Chloe watched the warship beach itself before the rowers jumped out the sides, plunging into water up to their waists. They hauled the vessel higher and higher, timing their movements to a coordinated grunt.

Finally, with the warship hauled above the tide line, a ramp marked with regular steps slid down from the top deck. With long practice the dark-skinned rowers leaned the gangway up against the pebbled shore.

A solitary man left the upper deck to descend the ramp. He was too far away for Chloe to see much of his features, but she gained an impression of a warrior's physique contrasted with opulent orange robes.

Captain Amos went down to the end of the gangway. He removed his helmet to offer greeting as the newcomer reached the land. For a time they spoke together.

Amos then called out to one of his officers, evidently instructing them to wait as he led the foreigner along the beach, toward the steps to the embankment, while the rest of the soldiers remained to watch the warship.

Chloe saw her father exchange glances with the other consuls before speaking. 'Consuls,' he said, 'come.'

Aristocles walked to stand at the top of the embankment steps that led down to the shore. There were so many consuls that it took time for them to get into a semblance of order, but finally they stood in a mass vaguely resembling a half circle, ranged around the first consul at the midpoint with Consul Nilus at his side.

Moments later the newcomer and Amos crested the embankment steps and Chloe now had her first good look at the stranger. He was swarthy, with olive skin darkened by exposure to sun and sea. A curled beard glistened in the light and she guessed it had been oiled, along with his hair, a heavy mop of dark locks. His upper lip was also mustached, but unlike his beard it was neatly trimmed. He had black eyes and faint scars on his face and hands; Chloe's initial impression of a warrior was confirmed. Amos was not a small man and had an athletic build that reminded Chloe of the statues of the gods. Yet the foreigner was bigger still.

He cast his eyes over the city before turning his attention to the assembled gathering as he came to a halt in front of Aristocles. Chloe watched as her father waited with a face like stone. It was a tactic she had seen him employ on more than one occasion and it could make men tremble. She didn't know if the stranger even noticed. Instead he neither bowed nor smiled; he simply started to speak with a thick, rolling accent.

'I am Kargan, captain of the bireme *Nexotardis*. The earthquake damaged my ship.' He spoke the last in a growling voice, as if it was an insult that offended his pride. 'I need to make repairs.'

'I bid you welcome,' Aristocles said. 'I am Aristocles, First Consul of Phalesia, and this is Consul Nilus. Behind me is the Assembly of Consuls, those who administer the city of Phalesia and its environs.'

Kargan nodded slowly. He looked from face to face, examining the consuls arrayed in front of him. He appeared perplexed. 'Where is your king? Summon him, that I may discuss arrangements.'

Aristocles cleared his throat. 'I am first consul. In the first instance, you shall speak with me.'

'Eh?' Kargan raised an eyebrow, but then gave a dismissive wave. 'No matter. I intend to pay for all materials, though we have supplies and will not be requiring much. I will also pay for the use of your harbor and beach.'

Aristocles gazed out at the wounded warship. 'Your men are no doubt weary from your journey, which judging by the state of your vessel has been a harrowing experience. We can discuss arrangements when you have seen to their well-being.' He spread his arms. 'I extend an invitation for you and your senior officers to dine with me . . . and Consul Nilus, of course, tonight at my villa.'

Kargan grunted. 'I will need to secure the safety of my ship, but then I would welcome it.'

Without another word, Kargan turned away.

Consul Nilus spoke for the first time, clearing his throat before calling out. 'Before you go . . .' He was momentarily at a loss for words. 'Who are you?'

Kargan made a surprised sound, frowning as he faced Nilus. 'We are of Ilea, from across the Maltherean Sea. I serve Solon the sun king, who rules his empire from his capital Lamara, the city I call my home. Surely you know of Ilea? Our empire covers most of Salesia, from the Shadrian Passage in the west, to the city of Efu in the east.'

Kargan didn't appear to care about the consuls' reaction one way or another. He gave a short bow and then spun on his heel, heading for the narrow steps and the harbor shore. Amos glanced at Aristocles and then scurried to keep up with the stranger.

5

Chloe readily agreed to her father's request that she prepare food for the foreigner's welcome feast. While the servants were passable cooks, if the event was especially important, she often handled both the cooking and serving of the meal. As she worked in the kitchen she felt nervous, but she was curious about this man, Kargan, and his homeland across the sea. If she could help her father deal successfully with a nation that commanded such powerful warships, she would consider the night a success.

Sophia came over, carrying a large ceramic bowl colored black and gold and decorated with a scene of two men hunting stags on white horses. She showed Chloe the pile of fruit inside. 'I discarded the bad figs.'

'Well done,' Chloe said. 'Could you arrange the cheese, bread, and olives on the big plate over there?'

Chloe herself was grinding wheat with a mortar and pestle. The dish wasn't big enough, and she tipped the coarse grain from the mortar into a larger bowl before starting to grind more.

Her father poked his head into the kitchen and scanned the room. He nodded with satisfaction when he saw Sophia arranging the cold foods and noted hot coals in the cooking hearth, with smoke departing through the hood above.

'You look worried,' Chloe said. 'You should rest. Everything here's under control.'

Aristocles came forward and pulled her close, kissing the top of her head and smiling down at her fondly. 'My beloved child . . . Where would I be without you?'

She looked up at him and saw moisture at the corners of his eyes. She never knew when his thoughts would turn to her mother. People often said that with every passing year Chloe was growing to look more and more like her.

Leaving a hand on her shoulder, Aristocles turned to Sophia. 'I just need to mention, Sophia, this man is foreign and unused to our ways.'

'I will be your dutiful, doting daughter,' Sophia piped from the other side of the room.

Aristocles smiled, but it didn't touch his eyes. He truly was concerned.

'Father . . . Who are these people?' Chloe asked.

Aristocles paused before speaking. 'Ilea is across the Maltherean Sea.'

'Further than the isle of Athos, where the Oracle lives?'

Aristocles nodded. 'Further than Athos. Ilea is on the Salesian continent. I know little of their king, Solon, but word is that in the past years he has swallowed his neighbors into his empire. He is a powerful ruler.'

'This man, Kargan,' Chloe said. 'Is he powerful also?'

'That remains to be seen,' Aristocles said. 'We must ask many questions and answer few.'

Hermon, one of the servants, a stooped old man who had tutored Chloe in childhood, came and bowed to Aristocles. 'Consul Nilus is here, Lord.'

'Show him in,' Aristocles said.

Moments later Chloe heard her father in the reception as he spoke with his plump colleague. 'Nilus, how good of you to come.'

'Is he here?'

'No, not yet.'

'Any idea how many companions he will bring?'

'My message specified no more than two.'

'Tell me, Aristocles, what is our strategy?'

Sophia called out from the kitchen. 'Ask many questions and answer few.'

Chloe frowned at her younger sister, but Nilus laughed. 'An excellent idea,' he said, coming to the door of the kitchen. A plump man with curly black hair and a round face that was often red when he spoke, he was one of her father's rivals, but also a colleague and confidant who occasionally came to the villa to work with Aristocles late into the night.

Seeing Chloe, Nilus scratched at his cheek before speaking. 'Ah . . . Aristocles. Your daughter—'

'I will be a gracious host,' Chloe said. Her lips thinned. 'It was only when they started blaming the eldren that I had to say something.'

'You can't let them hurt Zachary,' Sophia said.

'Yes, well, it is a delicate issue,' Nilus said.

'I'm making one of mother's dishes,' said Chloe, changing the subject. 'Spiced meal cakes with pork sausages.'

'Excellent,' Nilus said. 'I do miss her cooking. The gods only know why fever strikes some and not others. She was a good woman, of that there could never be doubt.'

Chloe smiled sadly. 'Why don't you have father pour you some wine?'

'Excellent . . . Excellent.' Nilus looked around. 'Where is your father?'

'Nilus, come, our guest is here,' Aristocles called out from the reception.

Chloe and Sophia exchanged glances while they worked. Busy with the preparation of the food, Chloe listened to the conversation in the next room as she mixed the coarse flour she'd been grinding with salt and dried oregano.

'Lord Kargan, you have brought no companions?' Nilus was asking.

'There are none on the *Nexotardis* with my status,' Kargan's gravelly voice replied.

'Please, take a seat,' Chloe's father said. 'Let me pour you wine.'

'Where are your servants?'

'I have sent them away for the night. My daughters will be preparing the food and serving.'

'It is a great honor,' Nilus said.

'Your women are allowed to share the same quarters as your men? You have them serve your food?'

'I am sure many of our customs are different from yours,' Aristocles said smoothly. 'If you wish, I can recall the servants, if that would make you more comfortable.'

'Bah,' Kargan grunted. 'Your house, your rules.' There was a pause. 'Tell me, is this the palace you provide for your king?'

Chloe added water to the flour mixture and proceeded to make flat cakes. After using up all the mixture, she went to the fire and checked the coals were low enough, and that there was space in the stone bed for all the cakes to fit.

'This is not a palace. It is my villa,' Aristocles said.

'I must agree with you,' Kargan said. 'This is no palace.'

Chloe heard gulping and then a clunk as someone set a goblet back down onto the table. 'More wine!' Kargan called. 'Oh,' he said, 'I forget you have no servants.'

'Put these on the hot surface near the coals,' Chloe quickly instructed her sister, indicating the meal cakes. 'Then bring in the cold platter.'

Chloe left the kitchen and entered the expansive reception. The room was artfully arranged, with no evidence of the recent disturbance to Aristocles' home. Marble statues of Aristonias and Nestor, two of Phalesia's democratic fathers, occupied each corner, while along the stone wall were fine ceramics and low stools and tables.

The three men sat on angular recliners, spaced close together, and between them was a table the height of a man's knee. The room was big enough to accommodate twenty men, yet Kargan's dark eyes were scanning it dismissively.

As Chloe walked in she saw that he wore a flowing yellow robe of thick silk, fastened at the waist with an elaborate belt of woven orange thread covering leather. Hanging from his belt was a curved dagger with a jeweled hilt, the scabbard plain but fine quality. His oiled hair was tidier than before and his beard was now curled in a series of locks.

'Ah.' Aristocles cleared his throat. 'Lord Kargan, may I introduce my eldest daughter, Chloe.'

Chloe placed her hands together and gave a small bow, while Kargan glanced at her once and then looked away. 'More wine, Lord?' Chloe asked as she reached for the jug and refilled Kargan's cup, then pouring for her father and Consul Nilus.

As Chloe backed away, Sophia entered the room with the platter.

'And my youngest daughter, Sophia,' Aristocles said.

'It is my pleasure to serve you, Lord,' little Sophia said formally.

Nilus and Aristocles both smiled, but Kargan appeared bored.

'Come,' Chloe said to her sister under her breath. She led Sophia back into the kitchen, where the aroma of the spiced bread already filled the room.

After the girls' departure, Chloe heard the jangle of coin and then heard something thunk onto the wooden table.

'How much silver do you want for the use of your harbor?' Kargan said. 'We can buy our own materials and supplies at the agora.'

'Please,' Aristocles said. 'Enjoy the food before we discuss business. Surely it is a change from the fare you have on your ship?'

Chloe heard the sound of men eating. She went out once more to refill their cups and saw Kargan devouring figs and olives one after the other before she returned to the kitchen.

'These are fair enough,' Kargan said. 'I only eat and drink the best.'

'You mentioned your status earlier,' Nilus said delicately. 'What exactly is your status?'

'I am captain of the *Nexotardis* and admiral of the sun king's navy. I am Great King Solon's adviser. I have a military command also. Few in the sun king's court may call themselves my equal.'

'Please, tell us your story,' said Aristocles. 'How did your ship come to be damaged?'

Chloe added the sausages to a pot, along with some wine, thyme, barley, and fermented fish sauce. She rested the pot in the coals before returning to her place near the kitchen doorway, poking out her head to see if anyone's wine needed topping up.

'—appears that it struck your city also,' Kargan was saying. 'We were beached at the time and the waves threw the *Nexotardis* up onto the rocks. I sent the rest of our ships home while I searched for a harbor.'

Chloe entered the reception and refilled Kargan's cup. He ate while he talked, speaking in between mouthfuls of white cheese and gulps of red wine.

'The gods are angry,' Nilus said.

'Not my area of expertise,' Kargan said with a shrug. 'I command the sun king's ships.'

'What were you doing on this side of the Maltherean Sea?'

'Trading with the Sarsicans. Then we were heading to the Oracle at Athos to make an offering.'

'We trade with Sarsica,' Nilus said. 'Wine, barley, ceramics, leather, tools . . . I wasn't aware of any trade between Sarsica and the Salesian continent.'

Chloe and Sophia cleared the dishes, as invisible as servants to the big man with the oiled beard and mop of dark hair. Then Chloe had to attend to the pot on the cooking hearth, stirring the stew and then turning over the meal cakes. The delicious aroma made her mouth water, but the men would have their fill before the women. When Aristocles was alone he was never so formal, and they all dined together. But Chloe knew this night was important. She didn't like to imagine what a mass of warships like the *Nexotardis* – biremes, she remembered the word Kargan had used to describe his ship – could do to Phalesia's proud fleet.

Finally, Chloe brought the steaming pot to the central table while her sister set down another plate with the spiced meal cakes, along with bowls and spoons.

Aristocles looked at Chloe gratefully and Nilus made appreciative sounds, but Kargan growled, ignoring Nilus's last comment about trade.

'This is not the banquet I was expecting. When I saw how many of your men in expensive tunics were there to greet me I was sure a table the length of your agora was going to be required to fit them all. I thought to myself: this king has many advisers. Despite his simple garb he must be a powerful man. Your city is wealthy. You asked me my status, Aristocles. What is yours?'

'Lord Aristocles is the first consul,' Nilus said.

'And what is a first consul?'

'Our consuls are elected by the citizens,' said Nilus. 'We then elect one of our number to be first among us.'

'Elect?'

'We vote by speaking out in favor of one candidate or another. The man chosen by the most citizens is elected.'

'Hmm,' Kargan muttered. 'Strange system.'

'It has served us for longer than living memory,' Aristocles said. 'Every man's voice is heard.'

'Even the slaves?' Kargan asked incredulously.

'No,' Nilus harrumphed. 'Of course not the slaves.'

Aristocles interjected. 'We see kings as tyrants, something to be abhorred. If a single man becomes too popular, too powerful, we send him away as an emissary to somewhere like Sarsica until his influence has waned.'

'But in the name of Helios,' Kargan spluttered. 'Why?'

'Long ago Phalesia was ruled by a strong tyrant, a good king, you may say,' Aristocles said. 'But he in turn was followed by a weak son, who was then succeeded by a ruthless despot. Men with ideals formed a secret cabal to overthrow the mad king before he led the city to ruin. During their struggle, they couldn't agree on who should be king next, so they deferred the problem until the tyrant was gone, instead making decisions by vote. After they succeeded, the system stayed.' There was obvious satisfaction in his voice.

'But how can there be order?' Kargan persisted. 'If any man can lead, what is to prevent chaos? There are always more commoners than nobles, but nobles are the only men with the breeding and education to be trusted with power.' His voice became firm. 'Let me just say that if I see any sign of your system taking root in Ilea, I will personally lead a division of my best men to cull these ideas before they spread. I am glad we have the wide sea between us.'

Aristocles bit off any retort. All Phalesians were proud of the Assembly of Consuls, and Chloe knew he would be itching to take up the argument, but he was also wise enough to put diplomacy first.

'What of your king, Solon?' Nilus asked. 'Please, tell us about him.'

'Solon is beloved of the sun god Helios and has taken Ilea into a new age.' Glancing in from the kitchen doorway, Chloe saw Kargan puff up his broad chest. 'Our armies are huge; our warriors are the strongest. The sun king takes tribute from Shadria, Sarina, Haria, and the isles of Ibris, Amphi, and Tarlana. In Lamara I can buy the finest goods. Our new biremes expand our influence every year.'

'We may also be interested in trade,' Nilus said, looking up to meet Kargan's eyes.

Kargan shrugged. 'It remains to be seen if trade is possible. I don't intend to remain long, only until I've made repairs to the *Nexotardis*.'

'We will help in any way we can,' Aristocles said. 'And we wish you to feel welcome while you are in Phalesia.'

'As I have said many times, I will pay. I do have one condition, however. Nobody is to set foot on the *Nexotardis*, nor wander too close. Understood?'

'That is acceptable,' Chloe's father said.

'Good.' Kargan frowned at his cup. 'Is there no better wine in this house?'

'Chloe,' Aristocles called. 'Fetch the Sarsican red.'

Chloe went out to the terrace and descended to the villa's lower level, quickly finding her father's best wine in the cellar but missing the conversation until she returned.

'—offer I would like to make,' Kargan said as he downed his cup and Chloe refilled it from the new amphora, before moving on to the two consuls. 'There is a temple,' he continued, 'high on the peak above the waterfront. A flame burns on the plateau, shedding light on the columns. In the middle of the summit is a chest of gold.'

'The Temple of Aldus, yes,' Aristocles said.

'I asked one of your people and he said the chest is solid gold. Is that true?'

'The Ark of Revelation is a sacred relic,' Nilus said.

'Hmm,' Kargan said, his eyes suddenly intent. 'What is it?'

When Aristocles and Nilus both hesitated, Kargan glanced up at Chloe, meeting her eyes for the first time. 'Girl?'

Chloe looked at her father, who nodded. 'My daughter studied at the Temple of Aeris,' Aristocles said. 'Chloe, tell our guest about the Ark of Revelation.'

She set down the amphora before speaking and took a deep breath, suddenly made nervous by the foreigner's stare.

'This is a story known not only in Phalesia, but in all the Galean nations, from Tanus to Sarsica.'

Chloe faltered when she saw a smile creep up on Kargan's face, flushed with drink.

'Lord Kargan . . .?' Aristocles asked.

'It is nothing,' Kargan said. 'Merely her accent. It sounds foolish on your men, but from a woman your speech is strangely attractive.'

She glanced at her father, who looked as if he was trying to frame a response, and then back to Kargan. The Ilean waved impatiently for her to continue.

Chloe went on with determination. 'Long ago, the first men prayed to the god Aldus, asking him to make humans supreme of all creatures.' Kargan frowned, but thankfully didn't interrupt. 'Aldus consulted with the other gods and an agreement was reached. The gods gave us mining, and taught us the use of gold, silver, copper, and iron, elevating us from the beasts.'

She drew another breath before going on.

'But the gods made their own demands in return, by way of a pact. Led by Aldus, god of justice, they said that in return for their gift of knowledge we had to abide by ten laws, which Aldus wrote on tablets and put inside a golden ark.'

'What are the laws?' Kargan raised an eyebrow.

'Aldus said he would not tell us the laws, but that they were self-evident. Anyone who could live by them of his own accord would be granted entry to paradise on his death.'

Kargan finished his cup of Sarsican wine in a gulp, refilling it himself. He became expansive, gesturing as he spoke. 'And this is the ark on the cliff? Surely you must have opened it by now.'

'No,' Chloe said. 'The pact states that if the ark is ever opened the wrath of the gods will come down on us all. Those already in the lands of paradise will be ejected, and none will be granted entry again. The knowledge to use metals would be taken away from us, and we would once more become as the beasts.'

'The nature of the laws is a source of constant debate among our magi,' Nilus explained.

'I still think you should just open the ark and find out,' Kargan said. When his words were greeted by expressions of horror, he laughed. 'Ah, this wine is better,' he said. 'I will tell the sun king about what I see here. You mentioned trade, First Consul. What do you offer?'

'Copper. Olive oil. Honey. Wool. Ceramics. Timber.'

'What of iron? What is the quality of your weapons?'

In a sudden movement, stunning them all, Kargan sat upright as he drew his dagger from the scabbard at his waist and laid it on the table. 'This is our best work. Show me your sword,' he met Aristocles' eyes.

Aristocles hesitated, creases forming on his brow, but finally he nodded. 'Chloe?'

Chloe went to her father's chambers at the back of the villa, by far the most sumptuous private quarters in the house, passing the new work the builders had just finished on the ceiling. She retrieved her father's scabbarded sword from an ornate wooden chest and returned to the reception, holding it out in both hands for her father to take.

'Draw it and lay it on the table,' Kargan said.

The whisper of steel sounded as Aristocles unsheathed the weapon, revealing a bright, well-oiled blade with an edge kept sharp by the servants. The hilt of her father's weapon was plainer than Kargan's dagger, but it was as good a sword as silver could buy.

Kargan spent time comparing the two weapons. He lifted the sword and carried it out to the terrace, making some practice swings, while the consuls swapped bemused glances. Returning a moment later, he laid the sword back down next to the dagger and ran a finger along the edge of both blades. He balanced the sword on a finger to find the center of gravity and then rubbed his chin as he looked across the table at Aristocles.

'This is a fine sword. The steel is good quality. Where is it made?'

'It comes from Xanthos,' Aristocles said.

'Xanthos?'

'The neighboring kingdom to the west, located between Phalesia and Sarsica.'

'Hmm. It seems I have much to learn, but I am only here for a short time.' He picked up the sword again, looking sideways along the steel, with his eye close to the blade. 'May I have this?'

Stunned, Chloe waited for her father to react. Nilus opened his mouth, then closed it.

'You may,' Aristocles said tightly.

'Tomorrow we will talk about payment for the use of your harbor. Your gift will ease negotiations.'

Kargan replaced the sword in its scabbard and then, straightening, he bowed to the two consuls of Phalesia.

'I bid you good night.'

He left with a slight weave in his step, having put away a pro-digious amount of wine.

Chloe's father let out a breath.

6

Bright sunlight sparkled off the waves, strong rays that poured from the rising sun and lent growing heat to the morning. It was a good day for sailing.

Dion, youngest son of King Markos of Xanthos, felt his spirits soar as the small sailing vessel skipped over the waves, riding the peaks one after another, the sail pocketing the wind and making the boat's timbers groan like muscles stretched by a sprinter at the Games.

He pulled the rope that traveled from his fingers to a rounded cleat, smoothed from friction, and then to the boom. As he hauled the sail closer in with the wind coming across his beam the boat leaped forward.

He heard a familiar grumbling voice nearby.

'If the narrows are truly blocked we are going too fast. Slow down, lad.'

'Of course, Master Cob,' Dion said with elaborate respect. He grinned and tightened the sail still further.

The sailing boat heeled in response, listing hard to port. Dion clambered across to put his weight on the starboard side. 'Move across,' he said to his companion. 'We can still get more speed out of her.'

'In the name of Silex, why is it we need such speed?'

'We have a big day ahead of us.'

'Our task is simple. We confirm the fishermen's reports that the narrows are blocked, and then we return to Xanthos.'

Dion ignored Cob, instead looking ahead to check their course. The boat was sailing with the looming mainland cliffs on the left and the lower but still imposing heights of the isle of Coros on the right. As the boat sped along, the passage became slimmer and the opposing cliffs grew closer. The air smelled of salt and sea and even on the higher gunwale cool water splashed his face.

Soon they would be at the narrows, the place where the cliffs were at their closest. It was the only sea route between Xanthos and Phalesia. Well, there was another, but Dion wasn't ready to talk to Cob about that quite yet.

Glancing back at Cob, he saw the old man with his hand on the tiller, glancing up at the jagged black cliffs and grimacing. He was stunted and bald, a full foot shorter than Dion, and were it not for his aptitude with boats Dion wasn't sure what the old sailor's place in the world could have been.

'Just like me,' Dion murmured to himself.

In his full growth of manhood, twenty years old, Dion should by now have been commanding regiments in his father's service. His older brother Nikolas was not only heir to the throne, he was commander of Xanthos's powerful army, with King Markos now too old to lead the men.

But Nikolas and Dion were as unlike each other as two men could be. There was nothing wrong with Dion's strength or agility, but the handling of swords and shields had never come to him, no matter how hard he'd tried. Despite staying up late into the night in the practice ground, hacking at dummies and getting instruction from anyone who would teach him, the sword simply fell out of numb fingers when he tried to make a strike, and the shield dropped every time he took a blow. Still he persisted, and then his older brother suggested archery.

To Dion's surprise, the handling of a bow came as naturally to him as breathing. He practiced in secret, developing his skill until he could hit the center of a target at seventy paces nine times out of ten. His brother was proud, and together they arranged a demonstration for their father.

But in Xanthos, archery was not considered a suitable skill for a king's son. The army's strength came from the coordinated phalanxes of hoplites, working together with shield, sword, and spear. King Markos didn't even stay long enough to see Dion's proficiency before he forbade further practice.

The young Dion could no longer entertain a position in the army.

But Nikolas intervened again. He took his younger brother to Cob and asked the old man to teach Dion the handling of boats. Despite the fact that Xanthos had only a small fleet made up mostly of fishing vessels, trade by sea between Xanthos, Phalesia, and Sarsica was increasing year by year. A nation needed wealth to pay the men who worked in the army and fit them with armor and weapons.

Sailing came to Dion even more swiftly than archery. He knew he had finally found his path in life. In a nation preoccupied with the land, where mining and farming were the main occupations after soldiering, and where athletes competed at the Xanthian Games in swordsmanship, wrestling, javelin throwing, and running, Dion instead loved the sea.

And in his time trading and traveling, as crewman and rower, purser and occasionally captain, he had come to a startling conclusion. The future of the Galean continent would not be decided by hoplites alone. It would be determined by control of the ocean's shifting tides.

'Look,' Cob said, pointing.

Dion saw that the cliff ahead, on the port side, leaning over the narrows, was newly broken. The earthquake that had taken place over a week ago had opened up a seam in the peak, and the protrusion had evidently splintered from the cliff and tumbled into the water.

'We need to get closer,' Dion said. 'See if there is anything we can do to clear it.'

'Clear it?' Cob snorted.

Dion smiled and then the smile fell, his forehead creasing as he devoted his attention to examining the water ahead. The narrows had always been more of a blessing than a curse, for on the other side of the passage was a clear run to the harbor of Phalesia, which meant that any enemy arriving by sea first had to pass Xanthos's neighboring nation's fleet. He considered the sense of security Phalesia provided a mixed blessing, however, for it gave his father, King Markos, little incentive to develop his own fleet. Boats were for fishing and trading, according to Dion's father, and little else.

He finally let some rope drift through his fingers, barely registering the friction on his calloused hands. The sail slackened and the small boat slowed as he approached the place where only sixty feet separated the island of Coros from the mainland.

'Be ready to turn,' Dion instructed.

As often happened, the order was met by a muttered curse, directed at his back.

Dion peered into the water ahead, but still the narrows appeared clear. The tip of the cliff must have fallen somewhere, but now that steep rock walls rose on both sides the boat was in shadow. The wind picked up sudden strength, gusting the vessel forward and dangerously close to the place where the gap was smallest.

Then he saw it.

It was directly ahead, a huge boulder with a jagged spear for a point, completely submerged under the water, but with the knife's edge just under the surface.

The razor-sharp rock, newly broken, was just a stone's throw in front of the boat.

'Turn!' Dion cried. 'Quickly!'

He released the rope and pushed the boom out as far as he could, a trick that used the wind to initiate the turn. Staring back with wide eyes, he saw Cob had the tiller hard around. The boat began to turn.

But still its motion continued. Six feet became five, then four. The point of the boulder disappeared under the boat as it completed the turn.

'Pull on the sail, you fool!' Cob cried.

Dion grabbed hold of the trailing rope on the boat's bottom and hauled, at the same time holding the boom so that the wind would catch the sail as soon as possible.

The vessel started to move and then she was sailing away from the blocked narrows. Dion let out a breath, then grinned.

'Well the narrows are blocked, that's for certain,' he said, looking back at Cob, whose square face was red. 'No trading vessels will make it over that.'

'Good,' Cob grunted. 'We can go home now.'

'Cob . . . We had to get that close.'

'Why is that?'

'I needed to see the boulder for myself to see what we can do to clear it.'

'Lad, what in the name of Silex are you talking about?'

'We have to remove the blockage,' Dion said seriously. He hauled the sail in to lend speed to their journey, taking them away from the narrows and back toward Xanthos. 'It effectively blocks our trade with Phalesia.'

Although there was a direct land route between the two cities, via the pass called the Gates of Annika, the Xanthian side was rocky and mountainous and had to be crossed on foot, with horses led by the reins. Runners with messages traveled on land, for it was generally swifter. But transiting a boatload of goods that was easily moved on sea would be impossible on land.

'You understand, don't you? If there is something we can do, we must do it,' Dion said.

'What we have to do is return to your father and tell him the reports are true. Then we can talk about clearing the passage.'

'Father is a soldier, not a sailor.'

'Aye, lad. But he will care when the silver stops flowing.'

Dion saw the first sights of Xanthos come into view as they rounded a headland. Crumbling fishermen's huts could be seen on the rocks back from shore, and then in the distance the city itself came into view on the vessel's starboard side.

The sight of the approaching city lent urgency to Dion's voice. 'Cob, I have an idea how we can clear the narrows.'

'How? There's a huge boulder in the way, under the water. It will take weeks to move it. Perhaps months.'

'There's a quicker way. But we'll need to enlist the help of Lord Aristocles.'

'The first consul? Dion . . . You know your father wouldn't approve of you making an unsanctioned visit. And what can Aristocles do?'

'Phalesia needs the trade as much as we do. He might enlist the help of an eldran. They're on good terms. A serpent could move that boulder.'

Cob pondered for a moment as the city on their right came to dominate Dion's vision.

Unlike Phalesia there was no raised bastion over the wide bay, instead the top of the sandy beach climbed to grass and the occasional stretch of rock. The city of Xanthos spread wings around the grass, back from the beach. A narrow inlet like a scar in the middle of the harbor divided the city into two halves, the larger left side filled with workshops, tanneries, markets, and a multitude of single-storied houses with roofs of baked clay tiles. The bulk of the citizenry lived in this residential quarter, while the smaller half was home to the Royal Palace and the lofty Temple of Balal, the war god, in addition to half a dozen smaller temples.

A wooden bridge spanned the sandy-bottomed ravine dividing the city, which was filled with water only at the highest tides. Xanthos was a narrow city, built around the curve of the shore like a thin crescent moon. The agora in the residential quarter was far smaller than the square in Phalesia.

But the difference was more than made up for in the size of the Royal Palace.

Three levels high, the palace was tall and grand, with walls of white stone and crimson pennants flying high above. The three tiers were built one on top of the other in order of decreasing size, giving the middle and upper levels broad open terraces filled with gardens.

The architecture of Xanthos was sturdy rather than fanciful, with stout walls around the palace and an even stronger wall guarding the city's landward side. Rather than the columned temples and multitudinous statues of Phalesia, the people of Xanthos lived in a city that spoke of their nature as miners, farmers, and, above all, warriors.

The largest structure in Phalesia was the lyceum. In Xanthos it was the Temple of Balal, where the soldiers of an army three times the size of Phalesia's worshipped daily. Made of fitted white marble stones with broad steps leading to a wide entrance as high as three men, there was no way to mistake the god it was devoted to, for just outside the temple of the war god was a colossal bronze statue of an armored hoplite warrior wearing a crested helmet, standing at the ready with shield and spear.

'All right, I will entertain the idea that a powerful enough eldran could move that boulder,' said Cob. 'But even so, how do you plan to sail to Phalesia with the passage blocked?'

Dion met the older man's eyes and smiled.

7

'Oh, no.' Cob shook his head. 'Not that.'

'Come, Cob. You taught me everything there is to know about sailing. You're up to the challenge, aren't you?'

'I have never done it, lad. And nor have you.'

'Some of the fishermen do it all the time.'

'And some of them don't come back to their wives at the end of the day and are never seen again.'

'I know you, old man. You are eager to try. I can tell.'

'What makes you so certain of that?'

Dion indicated the harbor of Xanthos with his chin. Soon they would pass by the city altogether. 'You've already agreed, else you would have turned us into the harbor rather than taking us past.'

Cob growled. 'If I turned this boat, with the two of us working against each other, we'd capsize. The route through the Shards is a secret, to be reserved for emergencies.'

Dion's smile became a frown. 'Cob. This is an emergency. You know my father. If we go back to Xanthos we'll never get another chance to try. And you know Peithon. He'll advise against anything involving the eldren.'

Cob slowly nodded. 'You have the right of it there.' He looked up at the blue sky, still washed with a hint of gold after the recent dawn. 'But what of provisions? We don't have enough food and water for a full day's sailing, and Phalesia would be at least that.'

Dion was at the midpoint of the boat and able to move more freely than Cob, who couldn't take his hand from the tiller. Glancing down until the stumpy old sailor followed his eyes, he moved aside the bunched-up sailing cloth with his foot.

He revealed a large skin filled with water, flatbread wrapped in cloth, and two sealed jars. One jar he knew was filled with olives and the other with dried goat meat. The thought of the food made Dion's stomach rumble as he once more covered the supplies with the sailcloth to ward off the worst of the sun.

'You planned this?' Cob spluttered.

'Well, I didn't just wish the supplies here.'

Cob proceeded to sink into one of his moods, so Dion left him to it. He knew the old man well enough to know he was eager to test their combined skills against the Shards; he was like Dion in that once he started sailing he never wanted to return to land. But Dion also knew Cob well enough to know that if Dion had mentioned the plan prior to leaving, he would have sought permission from King Markos or Nikolas. The old man would stop sulking when the danger began.

Dion recalled the route as he left Xanthos behind, following the isle of Coros at his left while the rocky mainland grew distant.

'Go right at the Spire of Kor to the Great Shard,' he muttered. 'Follow the Coros cliffs, then left of the Twins.'

The directions sounded uncomplicated. He had spoken to more than one fisherman who had said that navigating the Shards was simple, provided one knew the way. The only caution he'd been given was to use oars rather than sail, for the wind was unpredictable and some of the turns were tight.

This boat wasn't made for rowing; the oars were to be used only if something went wrong with the sail. Dion decided not to mention what the fishermen had said to his older companion.

Both the wind and the sea increased intensity as the boat approached the Shards. The series of jagged rocks was the reason that Xanthos had little to fear from an enemy navy, for they stretched across the entire channel until both Coros and the mainland fell away and the open sea began. Even sighting the Shards from a distance would strike fear into any captain. It was the route through the narrows in the opposite direction that was the official path to Phalesia and the open sea beyond.

Yet with the narrows blocked, one of the risks that made Dion so determined was that more vessels would start to take the hidden path, and that the secret route through the Shards would become known. There would be no Phalesia to protect Xanthos from raiders then.

Dion thought again about how the sea was the future. He decided to try breaking the silence with Cob.

'Xanthos needs a real navy.'

Cob turned his gaze away from contemplation of the sea. 'I will let you be the one to argue that out with your father.'

'We shouldn't just rely on Phalesia to protect us and give us the leavings of their trade. We need ships coming to Xanthos too, from Sarsica and Lenus, and from Orius, Tirius, and Parnos.'

'And how will we make them visit Xanthos?'

'We'll build our own ships and go to their cities. Much of what they consider Phalesian produce actually comes from us. When they see what we have to offer they will come. Surely Father knows that an army costs silver, and the more silver we have, the better an army we can maintain?'

'If I were Phalesian and you were a consul, you would have my vote,' Cob said. He moved the tiller to adjust the boat's course, shading his eyes with his hand. 'Right at the Spire of Kor,' he muttered.

'There it is!' Dion pointed.

It was a hundred feet ahead, a tall plume of solid rock, twisted like a potter's mistake.

'Bleed a bit of speed, would you?' Cob asked.

'If we slow too much we will lose steerage.'

'Lad.' Cob spoke in a tone that Dion had rarely heard him use. Looking to the rear of the boat, he saw the old sailor regarding him with gravity. 'I let you have control before because this is your father's boat and you know what you're doing. But if we're sailing the Shards, despite the fact that every fool knows it should be done with oars, I will be the one in charge.'

Dion met the man's eyes and held them, then nodded. 'Understood.' He opened up the sail to allow the wind to brush past rather than pocket it.

'Too much, a bit more on.'

Following the order, he pulled in the sail a touch.

'Good. Well done, lad.' Cob scratched at the stubble on his chin. 'Have a look down.'

They were now approaching the Spire of Kor, and Dion had been fixated on the sight of the strange formation looming larger with every passing moment, but when he stared down into the water he gasped.

Rather than looking at a sandy ocean floor, such as existed in the harbor of Xanthos, or one filled with a carpet of smooth white stones, as in Phalesia's bay, under the water here there was nothing but a field of jagged black rocks.

Dion was a capable swimmer and diver and knew that the water magnified what was below, but even so he had to suppress a shudder. Experience told him the rocks were at least a dozen feet under the small boat's keel, but they still appeared far too close for comfort. Some were the size of his hand, others as big as the boulder that had sheared off the cliff back at the narrows. There were different types, with rocks that were smooth and worn by the passage of time, akin to the approaching spire, but most were sharp and jagged.

Cob took them to the right of the Spire of Kor and Dion knew that the next part of the course was to travel straight on to the Great Shard. He saw it in the distance, hazy on the horizon, and realized there must be a fair margin of error in the route.

'On the sail,' Cob said. 'We'll make speed now.'

They were well into the Shards and Dion saw more rocks that would challenge the Great Shard for its name. They poked like the tips of spears above the water, more of them on the side of the mainland than could be seen in the direction of the isle of Coros. The path they followed was clear, though, and there was a wide swathe of unbroken water to their left and right.

Dion's heart had been racing, but now he felt calm. Xanthians had been using this passage for generations. They would make it safely through and then with a wind like this it would be plain sailing the rest of the way.

'Wildren!' Cob suddenly called.

Dion glanced back at his companion but the old man didn't seem alarmed, merely pointing at some distant rocks, flat-topped and slightly angular to the sun.

Squinting, Dion finally saw them, half a dozen large man-sized shapes with their upper bodies out of the water, sunning themselves and evidently presenting no danger.

'Oh,' Dion said. 'Only some merfolk.'

He looked for their scaled tails but the water was breaking on the rocks and he couldn't make out much more than the silver hair and bare torsos of both males and females.

'We should still keep an eye on them.'

Dion continued to watch the distant merfolk as the boat sailed past, heading for the Great Shard. 'Hard to think that once they were eldren, little different from you and me.'

'Eldren are nothing like you and me.'

The merfolk continued to ignore them. Dion thought about the times he'd felt primal rage or animal hunger overwhelm every other emotion. Was that what it felt like for an eldran when it turned wild? He vowed to ask his mother when he returned to Xanthos. Unlike some others, she could always be relied upon to discuss the eldren and their strange abilities with calm and reason.

An axe blade of black rock jutted out of the water ahead, as tall as the tip of the sailboat's mast. He had seen the Spire of Kor from a distance before, but he'd never seen the Great Shard. He couldn't believe how huge it was.

'Left or right of the Great Shard?' Dion asked.

'The direction is simply: "Right at the Spire of Kor to the Great Shard. Follow the Coros cliffs, then left of the Twins."'

'I suppose that if we turn in the direction of the cliffs of Coros we will be left of the Great Shard?' Dion asked hopefully.

'Makes sense to me,' Cob said. 'This is going to take us across the wind. Are you ready?'

Cob pushed at the tiller, sending the vessel heeling as he turned it across the stiff breeze. The dark silhouette of the isle of Coros was a mile away, but with the wind now gusting and a new sail set the boat grew swifter with every passing moment. It rocked up and down on the waves, but despite the wind it was a fair day with no chance of a storm. Dion never experienced seasickness and he smiled, patting the boat's gunwale as it met each wave head on.

Spray splashed his face, welcome and cooling in the growing heat of the day. The two men covered the next stretch in silence, crossing the channel to Coros in a surprisingly short amount of time before they changed tack again, following the cliffs. Dion kept an eye out for the Twins; he had no idea what they were supposed to look like.

'There!' He pointed.

The two waist-thick fingers of stone had initially appeared to be one, the distance between them barely six inches. They were tall and nestled together at the waist and the top, like two confidants sharing a secret.

'Left of the Twins.' Cob grinned. 'Look how much room we've got. At least two hundred feet between the rocks and Coros.'

Dion whooped with him as they shot through and then they were free. They tacked one last time, and then it was clear sailing all the way to Phalesia.

8

It was late afternoon by the time Phalesia became more in Dion's vision than just a landmass in the distance. He had never sailed from the southern tip of Coros, but both he and Cob were experienced at traveling by the sun and the currents, and when he entered the harbor and saw the Temple of Aldus on its tall summit, the highest point in the city, Dion felt a surge of pride at the successful transit.

He swept his gaze from left to right, comparing this city with his home. Phalesia was both wealthier and more populated than Xanthos, that was evident at a glance, but there was also a certain sophistication about Phalesia that Dion found it hard to put into words. The ceramics the city produced were artistic marvels, with pleasing shapes and stunning artwork no Xanthian potter could replicate. There were no less than four temples around the vibrant agora, and the other two huge civic buildings, the library and the lyceum, didn't even exist in Xanthos.

His homeland could rise to this level and higher, Dion thought, if only Xanthos had Phalesia's navy.

He dropped his gaze from the famed temple at the city's edge, crowning steep cliffs that plunged down into the water. As his eyes traveled to the right, away from the temple and marble columns, he took in the villas of the wealthiest consuls that occupied the hills near the agora, high above the unpleasant smells of the crowded city.

Dion's vision then came to the agora and the cluster of colonnaded temples on the surrounding high ground, each with peaked roofs and interminable marble steps. The market was as busy as ever, crowded with tiny scurrying locals, a riot of color from the swirling tunics of the men to the even brighter chitons of the women. On the seaward side of the agora was an embankment leading to a sloped wall that plunged to the stony shore.

Within the long curve of the embankment were villas, shops, and houses. Scores of fishing and trading boats were pulled up high on the shore below. The bay finally terminated in yet another set of cliffs, with a lookout tower located a dozen paces above the water's edge.

But it was the vessels that interested Dion. After taking in the approaching city, glowing rose-colored in the afternoon light, he turned to point them out to Cob.

'See the new Phalesian galleys? They're building them bigger to hold more cargo and handle stronger seas.' He pointed out a group of stout ships, fifty feet long, with a single large mast in the center and a smaller mast up front. 'I wouldn't want to face a score of archers firing from the deck.'

When Cob didn't answer him, Dion glanced back at his friend manning the tiller. He had his eyes fixed on something far from the Phalesian galleys.

'What are you . . .?' Dion trailed off as he followed the older man's gaze.

He wondered that he hadn't seen it at first, but it was at the extreme right side of the bay and he had been focused on the left.

'That ship is not Phalesian,' Dion murmured.

The Phalesian galleys were stout and strong, but they were small compared with the vessel that occupied its own private stretch of shore. Dion estimated that the length of the warship was at least seventy feet. It was beached far from the other vessels and rolled to expose one side, where swarthy bare-chested men were crowded so close together that Dion couldn't see what they were doing.

'Take us closer,' he instructed.

Both men were silent for a time as their boat approached the foreign ship. Dion revised his estimation of the warship's length, reckoning it was closer to eighty feet long, with a beam of about ten feet. It was nearly flat-bottomed, designed to be sailed during the day and beached at night, and although the central main mast was tall, he guessed that the power of the wind was intended to augment the oarsmen. The timber it was constructed from appeared to be pine.

'Have you ever seen such a thing?' Dion murmured.

'My guess is she is not from our part of the world. One of the Salesian lands, I'd say. Look at the one directing them.'

They were now sailing close enough to make out individual faces and Dion saw a man with a barrel chest and curled black beard calling out orders to the workers. The commander's yellow robe was unmistakably foreign, not the dress of Galea at all.

'She must have been damaged in the tremor,' Dion said. 'They are repairing her. By Silex, look at her ram!'

The ship's prow jutted out from above a painted eye, and Dion guessed there would be another eye on the other side. The prow curved inwards and followed the bow, where she would carve the waves, before curving again below what would be the waterline and spearing forward in a ten-foot-long bronze ram.

He thought about the damage such a weapon would inflict on another vessel. Suddenly he understood the full import of what he was seeing.

A foreign warship had come to Phalesia. And despite Phalesia's sizable navy, this ship outclassed the Phalesian vessels in every way. The thought filled him with dread.

'Take us closer still.'

The black-bearded commander was now staring at their small boat and glaring at its two occupants, his arms folded in front of his chest. Undeterred, Dion continued his assessment of the warship, feeling dwarfed by the monstrous rudder, which was as tall as the sailing boat's mast.

It had three decks, two for the rowers, open at the sides with scores of holes for the oars, and an upper deck giving a roof to those below.

Dion realized the simplicity of the design and wondered that it was only now that someone had thought of such a thing. He murmured to himself more than to Cob, 'A bigger ship is slower in the water, harder to move . . . makes it more difficult to increase to ramming speed. But more oarsmen create more power. So to keep the ship's length and beam the same we add another row of oarsmen, so that one is on top of the other.'

'It's a clever design.' When Dion glanced back at Cob he saw his friend was nodding as he spoke, but the wrinkles on his forehead showed concern.

'I count thirty ports for oars,' Dion said.

'Your eyes are better than mine. So two rows of fifteen oars each.'

'No,' Dion said. Cob's eyebrows went up. 'Thirty ports to a row. Sixty rowers to a side. That makes a hundred and twenty rowers in total.'

Cob whistled. 'Silex help us.'

'I think we've learned all we can here. But we need to find out more when we get to the city.'

Working together, Cob and Dion turned the sailing boat back away from the warship, following the shore as they headed for a place closer to the embankment steps. As he searched for a clear patch of shore where they wouldn't be in the way of the fishermen mending nets on the beach or the sailors scrubbing the decks of their galleys, Dion heard a voice calling out and glanced up.

A young woman was running out onto the rocky promontory on the harbor's left side, below the Temple of Aldus high above. She waved her arms as she ran, gesticulating wildly, but her words were lost on the wind.

'I think she wants us,' Cob said. 'She seems quite upset.'

Frowning, Dion nodded. 'We had best see what it is.'

The woman clambered down the rocks until she was close to the water, heedless of the splashes wetting the hem of her fine indigo chiton. She lowered her arms when she saw that the sailboat was coming over.

She had near-black hair flowing to her waist, her thick locks blowing in the wind. The dark hair contrasted with her pale skin and framed a triangular face, with an upturned nose and a wide mouth. Around her neck was a copper medallion, and as the distance narrowed to several feet Dion recognized the symbol of Aeris, goddess of music and healing.

The woman was pretty, but in a haughty manner that was heightened by her present expression of blazing eyes and set jaw.

Recognizing her, Dion thought she'd grown since he'd last seen her, some years ago. She would be nineteen now, he thought.

They were close enough to hear each other. Cob turned the sailboat so that Dion came alongside the rocks.

Chloe, daughter of the first consul of Phalesia, was furious.

'Get away from the Ilean ship!'

'Of course, lady,' Dion said. 'Should I draw away now?'

Chloe clenched her fists, uncertain whether he was mocking her. Dion could see that she didn't recognize him.

'Before I do, could you tell me something about it?' Dion asked. 'You said the ship is from Ilea?'

'We have an agreement. We are to stay away from it.'

'You have my apologies, Chloe, daughter of Aristocles. I am not Phalesian and was not aware.'

'Just stay away.'

Dion nodded gravely. 'You have my word.'

Chloe turned her back on him and climbed back up the rocks. As she moved from rock to rock, Dion smiled at the damage she was wreaking on her chiton. Evidently she valued her father's agreement with the Ilean shipmaster more than she valued her clothing.

'Come on,' Dion said to Cob. 'We need to land.'

'I'm surprised she didn't recognize you.'

'A king's son.' Dion grinned. 'Arriving on a derelict sailboat with a stunted old man?'

'Derelict?' Cob patted the boat fondly. 'She's a good girl. I'll award you the stunted part, though. But tell me, why didn't you explain who you are?'

'I wanted to see what she would say about the warship. And I would prefer to announce myself to Aristocles on my own terms. Preferably without her around.'

Cob chuckled, shaking his head.

'Do you mind waiting while I find the first consul?' said Dion. 'I might be a while.'

'I can find lodgings in the city if need be.'

Dion began to take down the sail as they approached a patch of pebbled beach. 'I have to see if Aristocles will help us clear the narrows. I also have to find out what I can about that ship.'

Dion climbed the narrow steps leading up the sloped bastion from the harbor. The way was unguarded and soon he was making his way through the agora.

He turned to look back at the sea one last time, then found his gaze drawn to the summit of the cliff and the golden ark with the eternal flame burning brightly at the Temple of Aldus. There was only one approach to the temple, a series of precarious steps carved into the stone, leading from the top of the embankment and curving left and right as they wound their way up.

The sun was sinking in the west, melting into the horizon. Even so the agora buzzed with activity as he navigated the market stalls, passing cloth sellers displaying lengths of wool dyed a multitude of bright hues: orange, scarlet, emerald, and turquoise. The smell of rosemary and baking bread wafted from a vendor serving three consuls in white tunics. Phalesian ceramics stood on the alternating pink and brown paving stones, each jar, plate, or vase decorated with a unique scene, from daily life in the city to depictions of the gods. He paused to examine a stunning design of children at play, each boy or girl running around the circumference of a wide bowl, but moved on when the seller noted his interest.

As he headed deeper into the marketplace the Temple of Aeris loomed ahead, each spaced column as wide as the stoutest tree. He watched citizens come and go with regularity, making offerings for the health of loved ones. He then returned his attention to the agora as a priestess of Edra slinked past, her gauzy chiton revealing tantalizing female flesh and her eyes lined with kohl. She gave Dion an appraising look, but he simply smiled and nodded and she turned away, looking for customers elsewhere.

Although the Temple of Helios was the farthest from the agora, it was as busy as always. Dion fingered the silver medallion with a trident in a circle that he wore on a chain around his neck. The shrine dedicated to his personal deity, Silex, the god of fortune and the sea, was down in the lower city; he doubted he would have time to visit.

As he wondered how he would find the first consul, his gaze traveled over the several hills dotting the city's upper level, crowned by palatial residences, the homes of the wealthy. He knew one of the villas was the home of Aristocles, but he didn't know which.

The market ended halfway into the agora, and now on his right there were steps leading upwards to the library and the lyceum. He had once visited the library and was awed by the thousands upon thousands of clay tablets, astonished that with nothing more than the simple act of reading he could find out the price of wheat on the day he was born.

He paused and rubbed his chin as he looked at the lyceum and the bronze statue of the god of justice just outside. Shaking his head, he continued walking. His father the king would be angry enough that he had visited Phalesia, let alone announced himself to the consuls.

Looking around, scanning the hilltop villas and the merchants' homes below, he could see occasional signs of the recent tremor. It had evidently struck Phalesia much harder than Xanthos, but already men were repairing the buildings. The sight reminded him of his task. He knew that clearing the narrows would be worth risking his father's ire.

Then Dion saw someone he knew. A stocky man in leather armor with a weathered face of crags and wrinkles was walking toward the market. He had an athletic build, square jaw, and dark, somber eyes.

'Captain,' Dion said warmly.

Amos frowned for a moment, then smiled as recognition lit up his visage. 'Dion of Xanthos.'

'It's good to see you, Captain.'

'I'm not with my men. You can call me Amos. What brings you here?'

'The tremor. A piece of cliff broke off and now blocks the narrows. Our two nations are cut off from trade.'

Amos's eyebrows registered surprise. 'I was not aware. A dark night, that was. How fares Xanthos?'

'It appears the quake struck Phalesia harder.'

Amos nodded. 'We lost over a hundred souls.' His brow furrowed. 'And what do your magi say? Was it a punishment for deeds done, or an omen of darker days to come?'

'You know Xanthos. The priests of Balal are consulted above all. The signs point to war.' Dion gave a ghost of a smile. 'My mother says that Mount Oden erupted and caused the tremor, with the gods having nothing to do with it at all.'

'I won't criticize the queen, but no Phalesian doubts the gods are telling us something.' Amos frowned. 'Some here say it was a punishment for the growing acceptance of eldren, others that it heralds a great threat to our nation.'

'Whatever it was, my father and brother both train the men constantly.' Dion hesitated. 'The warship. Who are they?'

'Ileans from across the sea. Their ship was damaged in the tremor. I met their commander, a man named Kargan. He's paid the city for the use of the harbor and declares his intention to leave as soon as his repairs are finished.'

Dion sensed there was more. 'But . . .?'

'It's nothing.' Amos was pensive for a moment. 'Only that Kargan barely hides his contempt for our ways.'

'I suppose he's no emissary. To command a warship he must necessarily be a hard man.'

'The oarsmen are all slaves.' Amos shook his head. 'Not a back without the scar of the whip.'

Dion didn't mention the fact of the warship's obvious superiority to the ships of Phalesia's navy. He was a visitor here, and Amos was a military man.

'How is Nikolas?' Amos asked. 'I hear your brother has a son?'

'He's well, a proud father. The boy is now seven. He has yet to be given a man's name but he's a strong lad.'

'And your father?'

'The king is well.' Dion saw that before long it would be dark. 'Amos . . . Do you know where I can find the first consul? This isn't an official visit, but I need to speak with him.'

'He's praying at the Temple of Aldus; the first consul's been spending a lot of time with the magi lately. Come, Dion of Xanthos. I'll take you there.'

9

Amos led Dion back through the agora to the embankment. The wall dropped to the left as they followed the edge until they came to the cliff, and tilting his head back, Dion saw the flat plateau, a third the size of the agora, but his view was obstructed by the rock face and he could only make out some of the temple's columns. As they waited at the base of the steps that wound up to the summit – it would be impolite to disturb the first consul at prayer – the two men looked out at the warship.

'They call it a bireme,' Amos said. 'Named for the two banks of oarsmen.'

On the shore near their vessel several groups of Ileans sat around fires, plumes of smoke snaking into the sky. Their work was done for the day and the ship was no longer listing to one side.

'Have any of them taken lodgings in the city?'

'Not one. Kargan keeps a close eye on his men.'

'Did you get much of a look at their soldiers?'

Amos nodded. 'A dozen or so marines. They carry triangular wooden shields, spears, bronze and steel swords. Another six archers, although I'd say our bows are better.'

There was movement on the steps, and both Dion and Amos turned as they saw First Consul Aristocles descending alone. He was both thinner and balder than when Dion had last seen him, with white hair at the sides of his head where his scalp wasn't bare. His brow was furrowed, and he appeared lost in thought.

'The night of the tremor, the eternal flame at the temple went out,' Amos murmured. 'Yet the wind wasn't strong.'

Aristocles was panting by the time he reached them. In unison, Dion and Amos both bowed.

'First Consul,' Amos said. 'Dion, son of King Markos of Xanthos, is here.'

'First Consul,' Dion said as he bowed. 'I'm pleased to see Phalesia has weathered the night the ground shook and appears little harmed.'

'We are harmed, Dion of Xanthos,' Aristocles said wearily. 'Be sure of that. How fares Xanthos?'

'The city is well, as is my father the king. He doesn't know I'm here, but if he did I'm certain he would send his regards.'

'He's unaware that you are here?' Aristocles' eyebrows arched. 'Then why are you here?'

'I apologize, but my visit was hasty. The narrows have been blocked by a piece of cliff, fallen into the water. Until the passage is cleared there can be no trade between Xanthos and Phalesia.'

The first consul nodded abruptly. 'I have many things on my mind right now.'

'I thought perhaps the eldren—' Dion began.

'Enough about the eldren,' Aristocles interjected, scowling.

Dion immediately saw that he'd timed his arrival poorly. 'I can see you're busy, First Consul. I apologize for arriving unannounced. Perhaps we can discuss this another time.'

Aristocles ran a hand over his face. 'No, it is I who should apologize, Dion of Xanthos. I will speak with you, but now I must go and discuss an important matter with one of my fellow consuls. You will rest tonight at my villa and we will discuss what brings you here.'

———⌣———

Chloe was in the kitchen unpacking the day's purchases at the market with Aglea, a stout servant with white hair tied at the back of her head. As she unwrapped a hunk of goat's meat while Aglea added coals to the cooking hearth, Chloe's mind was elsewhere. She was worried about her father, who was brooding in the reception with a cup of red wine. He was more careworn than usual of late, and not for the first time she wished she was a man, so she could help him with his work at the Assembly.

She heard old Hermon speaking in low, respectful tones and then her father's louder voice. 'Ah, I had completely forgotten. Of course, show him in.'

A stranger's voice greeted her father and then Aristocles called out. 'Chloe? Come here. We have a guest.'

Chloe exited the kitchen and stopped in her tracks. The young man from the sailboat earlier in the day was looking at her and smiling. She had barely paid attention to him before, but she realized now that the tunic he was wearing marked him out as no common sailor.

He had short, unruly, sandy hair and tanned skin, with an oval face and sunburned lips. His square jaw was clean-shaven and his build was lean and athletic. Intelligent brown eyes sparkled as his smile broadened.

'Chloe, you remember Dion, King Markos of Xanthos's youngest son? Dion, my daughter Chloe.'

'Lady.' Dion gave a short bow.

'The last time you two met you were quite young, is that correct?'

'It was six years ago,' Dion said, still smiling. His expression was full of mischief; he was enjoying her discomfort. 'I was fourteen.'

'Which means Chloe would have been thirteen.'

'I'm sure she doesn't even recognize me,' Dion said.

Despite herself, Chloe reddened, then she became angry, but she fought to keep her expression calm.

'She has certainly grown,' Dion said. 'Your daughter has become a beautiful woman, First Consul.'

'I do remember you,' Chloe said tightly. 'You were always curious, if I recall correctly. But curiosity can cause harm, particularly when there are grave matters at hand.'

'Daughter!' Aristocles rebuked. 'What an odd thing to say. Dion, I apologize for any offence.'

'None taken,' Dion said lightly.

'Chloe, fetch wine would you? Actually no, have Aglea serve the wine. Come and sit with us. Please take a seat, Dion. We shall dine informally at the high table. I know you Xanthians don't object to breaking bread with female company.'

'I'm honored, First Consul. It's kind of you to invite me to your home.'

Chloe issued instructions to Aglea and then sat at the table, opposite Dion, who was looking out the window at the terrace. Aristocles sat at the head of the table and Dion at his right hand. Both men rose before sitting down at the same time as Chloe.

'Now, Dion, I know you said the city is well, but how did Xanthos truly fare in the tremor?'

'Many were frightened and still are, but we were fortunate. A few fallen stones . . . little more.'

Aglea came to pour the wine. Chloe drank to disguise her discomfort, for Dion's eyes kept turning to her before flicking back to her father. She sipped too much, and the tart liquid burned the back of her throat.

She started to cough uncontrollably. Both her father and Dion looked alarmed.

'Daughter?' Aristocles started to rise.

'No—' Chloe held up a hand. 'I'm fine. Aglea? Water, please.'

Some gulps of water soothed her chest, and as her color returned Dion once more grinned at her maddeningly.

Aristocles asked Dion about his family while Aglea served a cold meal of cheese, fruits, and olives, along with bread baked earlier in the day. Dion ate heartily but drank sparingly, praising Aristocles for the meal.

'I must also express my admiration for how quickly the damage to the city is being repaired.'

Aristocles nodded sagely. 'Soon enough it will be as if the tremor never happened.'

'The repairs to your own home are stout and strong.'

Aristocles frowned and then he chuckled. 'You have a keen eye. Yes, there was damage to my home. The stoutest walls are no protection from the gods.' He turned grave. 'My youngest, Sophia, was almost killed.'

Dion's eyes widened. 'First Consul . . . I had no idea.'

'You could not have known,' Aristocles said. 'Now—'

'One of the eldren saved her,' Chloe interjected. 'Yet some of the consuls speak as if they are our enemies.'

Aristocles sighed. 'Daughter . . .'

'Some are of that opinion in my father's court,' Dion said as he regarded her. 'My mother always said otherwise.'

'Enough of politics,' Aristocles said shortly. 'Now, Dion, tell me again what brings you here.'

'The narrows are blocked. I thought perhaps you might be able to enlist the help of one of the eldren. In serpent form, I believe one of them could move the obstruction.'

Aristocles rubbed his chin. Dion hesitated, then continued.

'But there is something else I wish to speak with you about, First Consul.'

'Go on.'

'The warship.'

Silence filled the room. From Aristocles' expression it was clear that the mere mention of it had struck a nerve.

'What of it?' Aristocles asked.

'A dozen more like it, arranged in a single force—'

'I am well aware of the danger.'

'First Consul, I don't presume to question you in your city. I simply want your advice. What should I tell my father?'

'Tell him that Phalesia survived the quake. And tell him that with the Ileans possessing ships as powerful as the one in our harbor, we may all need to look to our defenses.'

'You met the captain?'

Aristocles hesitated. 'He made no secret of his contempt. He also expressed a great deal of interest in the sacred ark.'

Dion rubbed his chin. 'It *is* gold. A tempting prize to have on display.'

'But a source of inspiration to the people,' Chloe interjected. 'A reminder to live a good life . . . a just life, according to a common moral code that binds us all.'

Dion nodded. 'It's important to Xanthos also. I thank you, First Consul,' he said gravely. 'That's all I needed to know.'

'Let's talk of something else,' Chloe said. 'You work too hard, Father.'

'Of course,' Dion said. 'The narrows?'

Aristocles looked at Chloe. She was reluctant to ask Zachary for still more help, but knowing he was always eager to maintain the peace between their races, she was sure he would agree.

Chloe nodded. 'We can send a swift rider to the Wilds.'

'Thank you,' Dion said to Chloe, his expression sincere.

He was looking so directly at Chloe that for some reason she felt herself break the stare and look down at the table, which had the effect of making her angry. When she glanced up and scowled at him his face turned puzzled.

'Dion,' Chloe said, eager to take the attention away from herself. 'Tell me, can you ever see Xanthos adopting our system of consuls?'

Aristocles' eyes lit up as he saw an opportunity to discuss his favorite topic, but Dion neatly avoided the trap.

'I am the second son,' he said apologetically. 'It's something better discussed with my father or brother. However, First Consul, I am a keen student of music and even in Xanthos we've heard that your daughter is a skilled player of the flute.'

Chloe scowled. 'It's late,' she said shortly.

The twinkle had now returned to Dion's eyes. 'That's a shame indeed.'

'Daughter, don't be rude to our guest,' said Aristocles.

Accepting the inevitable, Chloe rose and fetched the copper flute from the chest in her bedchamber. Returning a moment later, she unrolled the leather covering, picked up the flute and held it expertly, running her eyes fondly over the burnished red metal.

She placed the fingers of both hands over several holes before bringing the mouthpiece to her lips.

Despite Dion's entrapment, she wasn't nervous. She had played to far more important audiences than a king's youngest son.

She performed a soft melody that was as old as Phalesia, a sad song with slow notes that hung in the air and required a full breath to render. As she played her eyes were half closed, and she saw Dion look at first surprised and then appraising as the melody gained complexity.

The song traveled up and down the scale, faster now, like flowing water, but simple and soulful, a tale of tragedy that Chloe had seen make grown men cry.

The young man from Xanthos now gazed past Chloe's shoulder, staring out the window, in the direction of the deep blue sea.

Chloe thought Dion looked worried.

10

'Would you call this one a leviathan?' Dion asked Cob, surprised to hear his own voice shaking.

'Yes.' Cob was white-faced. 'I would.'

The serpent was longer than the warship back in Phalesia's harbor. A muscular length of rippling flesh clad in glossy silver scales, it swam with sinuous movements, undulating and writhing. It was entirely underwater and moved swiftly past the tiny sailboat, so that soon it was little more than a black shadow seen below the surface.

Dion felt pitifully weak and defenseless. 'I'm glad they're not all that size, then.'

'No, that is one of the big ones. A powerful one.'

Sharing the confined space of the narrows with the eldran, between the opposing cliffs, was a harrowing experience. When it first appeared Dion's heart had nearly stopped. Cob had swung the tiller so hard he had almost capsized the boat. Dion had to remind himself constantly that this monster was here to help.

The serpent's head thrust out of the water ahead, before plunging once more into the sea, and he caught a glimpse of a long, triangular head, almost reptilian, with a spiny frill behind the jaw line. Along its back an erect silver dorsal fin followed the creature's spine.

Dion watched its entire length bend and loop to follow the head into the water as it dived. The spiny dorsal fin ended and still its body continued, each diamond scale the size of a man's hand. Its girth was wider than the columns that held up the roof of the lyceum.

'By Silex,' Cob breathed. 'I would never wish to encounter a wild one of that size.'

From ahead, below the place where the cliff loomed over the narrows, a rumble from under the surface made the water shiver, like the ripples caused by droplets of rain. The noise was muted, but swirls and eddies told Dion there was movement.

'If anything can clear the narrows, this is it,' Dion said.

Cob didn't reply, but Dion heard him mutter yet another prayer to the sea god.

Dion stood in the rocking boat, holding onto the mast as he shaded his eyes. The sun was directly overhead so that even with the cliffs so close together bright light penetrated the confines of the narrows. The sail was lowered while they waited, and wondering what was happening under the water, Dion leaned forward, trying to see what the eldran was doing.

'Stop rocking the boat,' Cob muttered.

'I need to know if it is succeeding.'

'I'm sure it will let us know.'

'How? Do they talk when they've changed form?'

The old man pondered for a moment. 'I have no idea. I've never heard merfolk speak.'

The sun passed, creating instant shadow in the narrows and making it more difficult for Dion to see. He hated not knowing what was happening, and instead of trying to see the black shape under the water he tried to read the water at the place where the opposing rock walls were closest.

'Can you see the splashes about thirty feet from the left face? I think that's where it is.' He pointed while Cob frowned, squinting and shaking his head. 'You can see the splashes, can't you?'

'I'm trying, lad.'

'Look harder.'

Cob narrowed his eyes and peered at the water. 'Surely it has to come up for air? I saw no gills.'

The time dragged out. In his mind's eye Dion tried to see the serpent using its sheer size and strength to push away the boulder.

He was staring so hard at the sea in the distant narrows that he almost fell overboard when there was a sudden explosion in the water next to the boat. Gray skin and scales appeared out of nowhere. The water beside the boat erupted like a volcano.

A monstrous head shot out barely four feet away from the boat's gunwale. It lifted itself vertically into the air as water streamed from its sides, drenching Dion instantly in the torrent. The boat rocked precariously and threatened to tip over as the eldran regarded Dion with angular glaring eyes. The thin pupils were as black as night, surrounded by amber irises flecked with golden sparks.

Dion and the serpent looked eye to eye.

The frill was flattened against its neck, adding to the impression of a wedge-shaped head, all sharp and spiny, with two holes for nostrils and a mouth of curved white teeth. The eyes were surprisingly warm and filled with intelligence. Dion knew without a doubt that this creature was aware, in a way no beast or fish was.

There was a crescent scar on the serpent's left cheek and the occasional silver scale was mottled, as if it were old. When he thought that this creature, or another of its kind, had saved Chloe's sister's life, and that Chloe considered the eldren friends, Dion gained new respect for the first consul's daughter.

The leviathan regarded him and bowed its head slowly.

'What . . . What is it doing?' Dion asked Cob.

'I think he's telling us that he's done it.'

'How do you know it's a he?'

Cob shrugged. 'He looks like a he.'

Still standing and gripping the mast with a white-knuckled hand, Dion bowed to the eldran. 'Thank you!' he called.

The jaws parted and the serpent nodded again. The huge reptilian head slowly sank beneath the water.

And when Dion and Cob raised the sail and once more approached the narrows, the blockage was gone.

⌣

Dion and Cob sailed into Xanthos as the last vestiges of sunlight vanished from the day and flaming torches flickered on the beach to guide wayward fishermen home.

Dion was pensive; the two men had spoken little on their homeward leg. He always felt a little frustrated when he compared his home to Phalesia and saw only fishing boats pulled up on the shore and a grassy bank rather than an impressive bastion. Outside the city there were mines and farms, and inside the walls was a training ground and barracks larger than Phalesia's agora. The Royal Palace at Xanthos was far grander than any of the villas of the consuls and merchants. But any successful craftsman, merchant, or shipwright that Xanthos produced inevitably made the journey to Phalesia and never returned.

However, this time there was more to Dion's brooding. He was worried about the Ilean warship and what its arrival portended. What were Ilean vessels doing in Galean waters in the first place?

The Galean continent was a long way from Salesia . . . It was supposed to take five days or more of hazardous sailing to cross the Maltherean Sea.

If Kargan sailed away and returned with a fleet of biremes, what could Xanthos or Phalesia do about it? Were they in danger? What was the situation in Ilea? Was the sun king eyeing the continent across the sea, or was he too busy with trouble in his own empire?

One thing Dion knew was that the leaders of both nations were dangerously lacking in information.

As the sailboat headed for shore, he imagined what would happen if Phalesia's navy was defeated by an enemy that then sailed on to Xanthos. The three-storied palace was walled on all sides, but the surrounding city was walled only where it faced the land.

Attempting to banish his growing concern, Dion leaped over the gunwale as the boat approached the shallows, plunging into water up to his calves and wetting the hem of his short tunic. A moment later Cob jumped out and the two men grunted as they pulled the boat above the high-tide mark and demounted the mast.

'Leave me here,' Cob said. 'You have a lot to discuss with your father.'

'You go,' Dion said as he bunched up the sail. 'I'll set the boat to rights.'

'You're a good lad,' Cob said, clapping Dion on the back.

The short old man stumped away, leaving Dion to work alone. Just as he finished he sensed eyes on him and looked up.

Watching him from the high bank was a tall but overweight man with the heavy build of a past warrior who now rarely exercised. A rich white silk tunic left one shoulder bare, held at the waist by a navy cord, and he was the only man in sight wearing sandals so close to the water. Hanging from his neck was a silver medallion displaying two fish entwined: Silex, in his guise as god of fortune. Three thick silver rings decorated his fingers.

'Peithon.' Dion nodded as he gave the boat one final check and then walked up to the bank. 'Well met.'

Peithon was King Markos's closest adviser and master of both trade and treasury. Long ago he and the king fought side by side in the war against Tanus. Though his stomach had a paunch, his face was large rather than fat, with a long nose and extremely thick lips.

'Dion,' Peithon said. 'You've been gone much longer than expected. Where have you been?' He shook his head. 'Your mother has been hectoring the king incessantly. Others have confirmed the blocking of the narrows since you left.'

'The blockage is gone,' Dion said.

Peithon fell in beside Dion and the two men made the short walk to the palace. Two sailors in canvas trousers stood to one side as they passed, bowing while Dion nodded back.

'Gone?' Peithon asked when they were out of earshot. 'How?'

Dion hesitated, but there was no way to prevent what he knew was coming. At least it was here, away from the rest of his family. 'An eldran changed to serpent form and cleared it.'

'No.' Peithon shook his head. 'I don't believe you. Why would an eldran help you?'

'I traveled through the Shards to Phalesia. I explained the situation to Aristocles and asked that he seek their help.'

'Eldren,' Peithon almost spat the word. 'How can the Phalesians bear to even look at them? They are demon spawn, all of them. Eldren . . . wildren . . . it is all the same. The cunning ones are no better than the wild.'

'Where is Father?' Dion asked, changing the subject. 'And Nikolas?'

Dion didn't want to talk to Peithon about eldren any longer than necessary. A flyer – a fury – had killed Peithon's bride-to-be just weeks before their wedding day. It was a wildran, of course, an eldran that had forgotten who he or she was. But Peithon's logic was that if there were no eldren left living there would eventually be no wildren. It was a line that many city folk took in Xanthos, as well as Phalesia.

'Your brother is busy at the training ground. Your father is with him.'

'I have important news.'

'They'll be back soon enough. Your brother is anxious to see you. The magi have spoken. Nikolas's son is to be given a man's name and a materia.' Peithon opened his mouth and then he gave a slight smile. 'I just realized I should have let him give you the news himself.'

'Luni is to have a man's name?' Dion grinned. 'Nikolas and Helena must be pleased. When is the ceremony?'

'In a few days.'

The high stone walls of the palace loomed overhead; they were approaching the seaward side, where a guarded stairway provided a direct entrance to the middle floor. Even though he'd been gone only a short while Dion felt pleased to be home.

'I must go,' Peithon said. 'If the narrows truly are clear, there are merchant ships waiting to set sail.'

Dion's lips thinned. 'The narrows are clear, as I said. Before you go, where is my mother?'

'Balal knows,' Peithon grunted. 'Doing whatever it is she does. Until later, Dion. If I were you I'd prepare yourself for your father's words.' With a nod, the older man departed.

11

Two soldiers with spears made way for Dion as he approached the stairway. Climbing to the summit, he stopped for a moment on a wide terrace, a private retreat for the king's family, and inhaled: the smell of citrus always reminded him of home.

This place, on the palace's middle level, was called the Orange Terrace, named after the fruit-bearing trees growing out in the open air. Paved walkways weaved through the garden, spiraling from a central paved area in the balcony's center, where stone benches in a semicircle clustered around a basin filled with clear water. The royal council – consisting of Dion's family and Peithon – often met in the terrace's heart to discuss issues affecting the realm. It was a place where one could sit and gaze out at the sea while thinking deep thoughts.

Walking along the path under branches heavy with bright fruit, Dion left behind the circle of seats and continued to the archway that led to the interior.

The wan light of sunset plunged to something near darkness as Dion found himself in his father's high-ceilinged audience chamber, feeling the dry air pleasantly cool within the thick stone walls. A high-backed throne of polished oak stood on a dais at the far end, the only item of furniture in the room. Torches in sconces burned night and day, the flickering flames dancing on the tapestries lining both walls.

Dion glanced at the throne as he walked past; he'd never seen another chair that looked so uncomfortable. One day his brother would sit on that throne, looking down on his officers and courtiers. Try as he might, Dion couldn't imagine anyone but his father up there.

Leaving the audience chamber he passed through a connecting passage at the side and entered the banqueting hall. Low tables, high benches, recliners, and decorative amphorae were ranged along the walls, leaving the middle of the room bare. A huge woven mat, the biggest Dion had ever seen, filled the floor, displaying a pattern of red and white diamonds.

Dion's bare feet moved soundlessly on the fabric as he continued through the banqueting hall. The fading daylight shone from a smaller arch that led to the Flower Terrace. He was now squinting as his eyes adjusted after the near-darkness of the interior.

The Flower Terrace was smaller than the Orange Terrace and offered a view of the mountains rather than the sea, where even now the setting sun in the west was dipping between two distant peaks. Tulips, sunflowers, lavender, and cornflowers sprouted from pots arranged just inside the skirting wall. Though it offered a view of the thin strip of city below and the hills around Xanthos, the king preferred the orange grove and views of the sea on the palace's other side.

Dion had hoped to find his mother here; it was her favorite place, perhaps because it was often hers alone. After swiftly scanning and seeing the balcony was empty, he placed his hands on the rail and looked down from the height.

Directly below, outside the Royal Palace's lowest level, were separate structures for the stables and servant's quarters: squat, utilitarian buildings. Within the palace at ground level were the cellars, kitchens, armory, and strong room. A wall guarded the palace grounds and a barred wooden gate, currently open, was the palace's main entrance.

Raising his gaze, Dion saw the crescent of red tiled roofs of the residential quarter, although most of it was out of view, on the other side of the cleft in the harbor. Guarding it all, the main city wall was twelve feet high and two wide, holding the entire city in its embrace.

Behind the wall, farmland stretched to the west, on the left, and rocky hills rose on the right. A dusty road climbed the hills in the direction of the Gates of Annika, the pass that led to Phalesia.

If Dion's mother wasn't on the terrace, the next likeliest place was the highest floor, where there was a bedchamber for Dion, a series of rooms for Nikolas and his family, and a separate wing for the king and his wife, the queen. Dion's mother often had the entire level to herself, for Dion spent time away trading and Nikolas could generally be found at the training ground, King Markos with him. Peithon worked from his own villa, close to the palace, and while her husband was busy, Nikolas's wife, Helena, often spent time with her son at the home of her parents.

The distant peaks split the sun into fragments and a moment later the glowing orb dipped behind the mountains altogether. Turning back to the interior, Dion found the stairs to the uppermost level and began to climb.

He found his mother with her head bent over a copper basin filled with cloudy black water. Thea, Queen of Xanthos, had a rough woolen cloth on her shoulders, worn like a shawl over the white silk chiton underneath. She ran her fingers through her hair. An oily black substance coated them.

'Mother,' Dion said, smiling as he entered.

'Dion!' she exclaimed, turning her head to regard him with soft brown eyes while still keeping her long hair over the basin. 'I've been so worried about you. I would embrace you but I'm certain you don't want to be covered in dye.'

Dion's mother was a slight woman, with a narrow heart-shaped face and dimples on her cheeks. She carried herself with grace and was nearly as tall as Dion, although Nikolas and Dion's father both towered over her. She was King Markos's second wife – Nikolas's mother, the previous queen, had died in childbirth – but Dion's father doted on her.

'Mother, you barely look a day over forty.'

'You are a man, Dion. Don't expect to understand. Gray is not an attractive color in a woman. A queen must always look her best.'

Thea rinsed her hair in the basin and then scrubbed her head with the woolen shawl. 'How do I look?'

'The same as ever,' Dion said wryly. 'Although you might need a comb.'

'Come.' She indicated a stool nearby. 'Sit beside me while I follow your advice.'

Dion sat on the stool while his mother ran a long comb of polished wood through her tresses.

'I should be angry with you,' she said. 'You left with Cob and then last night when you didn't come home . . .'

'Do you know when Father will be back?' Dion asked, changing the subject. 'I have important news.'

'He and Nikolas will soon return. Your brother has news also.'

'So Peithon tells me. Little Luni is to be named. Nikolas must be proud.'

Thea smiled as she combed her long hair. 'You've never seen a prouder father. Your news – what is it? Tell me about your journey.'

Dion explained about the narrows, but refrained from mentioning the Ilean warship.

'Some of the Phalesians say that the gods caused the tremor because of the eldren.'

'As I've already told you, earthquakes happen,' Thea said, shrugging. 'Mount Oden is no doubt to blame – it's been rumbling for years. If you were to sail over to the island you'd likely see a plume of smoke rising from the volcano and ash on the ground.'

'An eldran saved the life of the first consul's daughter.'

Thea arrested the motion of her hand mid-stroke as she regarded her son. 'Is that true? The Phalesians should all be grateful then.'

'I'm sure the first consul is. But many fear them.' Dion hesitated. 'Mother . . . Why is it you don't fear them? You have better reason than any. Wildren destroyed your homeland. They slaughtered your people.'

Thea sighed as she resumed combing. 'I will never cease to be asked this question.'

'I'm just trying to understand. The eldran who cleared the narrows . . . the serpent form he took . . .' Dion let out a breath. 'I can see why they frighten people. They could be powerful friends. Or powerful enemies.'

'Friends is better,' Thea said. 'Remember: Wildren, not eldran, destroyed my homeland. The two are different, far more different than one human nation is from another. There are good and bad eldren, and good and bad wildren. We have all seen wild merfolk who pose no threat at all. But the thing that must be remembered is that wildren are animals. Once they pass the point where they have forgotten who they are, and are unable to change back, they are eldren no more. Some wildren pose a threat to humans and eldren alike and must be hunted down like all dangerous beasts. But to blame an eldran for what he may become – but almost certainly never will – is evil. Like people, all must be judged on their actions.'

'All I know is that the one that cleared the narrows did a good thing. But by Silex, it was huge.'

Dion paused as he remembered the huge reptilian head bursting out of the water. He had one more question for his mother.

'You said your people were close to the eldren. Why is it some can only change to merfolk, while others become great serpents? Why are furies somewhere between man and dragon, and ogres somewhere between man and giant?'

Thea was pensive for a moment. 'I don't know exactly, but I believe it has to do with their power. They can all change to three shapes, one each for sea, land, and air. But whether an eldran shifts to an ogre or giant depends on his innate strength. There are more who shift to the smaller shapes – merfolk, ogres, and furies – than those who can become serpents, giants, and dragons.'

'Do they change often?'

Thea smiled. 'I don't know. I would assume that, given the risk of becoming wild, they only change in times of greatest need. The eldren in the Wilds, most likely, live quite like you and me, although they spurn metal and walls of stone.'

Dion rubbed his chin. 'It seems we are better as friends, despite what Peithon says. There hasn't been a wildran attack in years.'

He suddenly heard the booming voice of his older brother, loud enough to roll up the stairs and reach his mother's chambers.

'Go,' Thea said, reaching out to squeeze his hand.

Dion reached the audience chamber just as his father and brother entered. They stood close, side by side, as Nikolas enthused about his latest training methods.

'With the additional cavalry on the wings, the longer pikes in the center, and small groups of archers arranged behind each phalanx, we would be able to prevent being outflanked while at the same time protecting our center,' Nikolas was saying.

'But we would need more horses,' Markos grumbled.

'I know. And horses are expensive. I'll speak with Peithon.'

Dion stood a dozen paces from the throne and waited for them to notice him. His older brother was the first to glance up and see him.

Nikolas was a burly man, six years older than Dion, with a thick torso and muscled arms and shoulders, his body sculpted by years of training with shield, sword, and spear. He had curly black hair and dark eyes framed by bristling black eyebrows. Half of his round face was obscured by his bushy beard and he was several inches taller than Dion. When he spoke his voice could carry to men standing at the far end of the training ground.

'Dion!' Nikolas cried. He opened his arms wide as he approached. 'Brother, did you hear? The magi have spoken. My son is to be named.'

'Congratulations,' Dion said, grinning at his brother's excitement. The two men embraced and Dion winced at the pounding on his back. 'I'm sure he'll make a fine warrior.'

'If the magus chooses iron,' Nikolas said, holding Dion back as he beamed. 'But he will. Balal will guide him to the right decision.'

'Dion,' King Markos said. He regarded his younger son with cold eyes. 'You expect to disappear and then return as if nothing happened? You were supposed to be gone for a few hours, not two days. You've worried your mother.'

Dion's father had once been as tall as Nikolas and he still had the frame of a born warrior, but age had stooped his shoulders and his left leg dragged when he walked. Like Nikolas, he had curly hair and dark eyes, but the king's hair was completely white. He had a broad, weathered face, with frown lines on his brow and a scraggly white beard. His voice was like gravel compared to Nikolas's boom.

Both men wore dusty tunics, with only the golden thread woven in their belts marking out their status.

'Father,' Dion said, 'I have news.'

King Markos frowned. 'We know the narrows are blocked. Others confirmed it after you left.'

'Yes, but there's more. Much more. What I have to say is important—'

'We need to wash and change,' Markos said. He looked pointedly at Dion's bare feet and tunic, its hem still wet from the sea. 'That includes you. I've told you not to walk around the palace like that. You look like a sailor, not the son of a king.'

'Father—'

'Later, Dion. We'll meet on the Orange Terrace to hear what you have to say. I will inform Peithon and your mother. I hope you have a good reason for your absence.'

12

Dion approached the half-circle of stone seats in the center of the Orange Terrace, seeing his father, mother, Nikolas, and Peithon already seated. The king now wore a purple toga with a golden rope tied around his waist, and like Dion, Nikolas and Peithon both wore clean white tunics. Dion's mother's straight dark hair glistened under the flaming torches on stout poles and she wore an embroidered silk chiton of pale blue.

Like all Galeans – Phalesian and Xanthian alike – all present had a medallion on a chain around their neck. Although most noblemen wore gold, both Markos and Nikolas wore iron, their amulets bearing the symbol of the war god Balal. Iron was the materia of warriors, miners, masons, and farmers – anyone who used metal tools in his work. As befitted her status as queen, Thea wore gold. Both Peithon and Dion wore silver, the materia of sailors and men of commerce. No one in the council wore copper, commonly worn by musicians, artisans, and healers, although Dion remembered seeing a copper amulet on Chloe, the daughter of Phalesia's first consul.

It was a clear night, as was often the case in early summer, and though there was no moon, the constellations in the heavens shone brightly. The warm sea breeze smelled of salt and the small waves crashing on the shore provided the only background noise, for the king had little love of music other than on festive occasions, when it was expected.

Dion was nervous. He had come to a conclusion regarding the Ilean warship, a kernel of an idea that would give him a chance to prove himself to his father. It only remained to see how his words would be received.

All eyes were on him as he approached and sat on the last remaining bench, beside Peithon and across from his mother. Nikolas and Dion's father occupied the two benches in the middle of the half-circle.

'Dion, begin,' Markos said without preamble.

Dion's mouth was suddenly dry as he prepared to address the gathering. Often away on trading voyages to the isles of the Maltherean Sea, he hadn't attended one of these council meetings in quite some time.

'First, the narrows. I discovered immediately that it was true. The tremor caused a piece of the cliff to break off, making the passage unusable.'

Markos scowled. 'You should have returned immediately. Between the blocked narrows and the Shards we're hemmed in, with no trade in or out.'

'Actually—' Peithon began.

Dion drew in a quick breath and interrupted. 'I took the passage through the Shards, following the secret route. Cob helped, of course.'

Nikolas whistled. He raised a bushy eyebrow and grinned at Dion.

'You went through the Shards?' Markos demanded. 'Why?'

'I went to Phalesia. I spoke with First Consul Aristocles.'

The king underwent a transformation. His eyes bulged, and when he spoke, it was through gritted teeth.

'Our alliance with Phalesia is fragile. Diplomacy must be handled with care. I've told you this before. You never listen, boy!'

'Father,' Nikolas said. 'Please. Give him a chance to explain.'

Dion swallowed. 'I know, Father. But I also know that we need the passage clear for trade to flourish. As you said – the sooner, the better. I'm sure Peithon will agree.'

Peithon spread his hands, the rings on his fingers reflecting the torchlight. 'It's not for me to say . . .'

'You had better explain yourself more convincingly than you have so far,' Markos interrupted, staring into Dion's eyes until he looked down uncomfortably.

'Perhaps he will, husband,' Thea said softly, smiling. 'If you let him.'

'After I saw the blockage, I had an idea,' Dion continued. 'I thought that perhaps an eldran might clear the passage. Knowing the first consul has friends among them, and would want the passage cleared also, I sought his help.'

'And what does he demand in return?' Markos growled.

'Nothing,' Dion said. 'He had other things on his mind. I assured him it wasn't a state visit; I made that very clear. I explained I had come of my own accord.'

'So he demands nothing?' Markos asked.

'He agreed to help,' said Dion. 'It worked. It's done. The passage is now clear.'

He leaned back, waiting for his father's reaction to the news, but the scowl didn't leave the king's face. Dion looked at his mother.

There was silence for a time.

'You did well,' Thea said.

'You sailed the Shards?' Nikolas murmured, shaking his head.

'Well, there we have it,' Markos finally said, half standing. 'I'm sure Aristocles will let us know the price of his help. I will think on it.'

'Father,' Dion said, holding out a hand. 'There's more.'

'What now?' Markos growled as he sat back down again.

'Is it Phalesia?' Nikolas asked. 'Did the tremor strike them badly? Do they need our help?'

'No,' Dion said. 'It struck them hard, much harder than it hit us here, but the eldren helped the city in its time of need.'

Peithon frowned and lifted his head to glare at Thea, who refused to meet his eyes. Both had endured tragedies from attacks by wildren, but Thea's equanimity and Peithon's rage were at complete odds.

'So you passed through Phalesia long enough to see that they don't need our help,' the king said. 'You incurred a debt with Aristocles. If you have a point, Dion, I suggest you make it. You said you had important news.'

'I do.' Dion took a deep breath. 'There was a strange ship, damaged in the tremor. It came to Phalesia for repairs.'

'Go on.'

'A foreign warship,' Dion said. 'But like no warship I've ever seen. It was eighty feet long, with two banks of oars, one above the other. It had a sharpened bronze ram, as long as a tree is tall.'

King Markos scratched at a small white scar on his cheek, looking pensive.

'Father, this ship makes the Phalesian ships look primitive, and we rely on their navy to protect us from attacks by sea. Aristocles met with the captain, a man named Kargan, who says he has many more vessels under his command.'

'Did Aristocles say where this ship was from?' Nikolas asked.

'Ilea, from the capital Lamara, where the sun king Solon rules.'

Nikolas spoke again. 'Did Aristocles reveal anything of the sun king's intentions? Is he looking to open up trade?'

'Aristocles is worried. This man, Kargan, gave his rank as admiral. He's arrogant and contemptuous of Phalesia. He expressed interest in the Ark of Revelation.'

Peithon's eyes widened. 'Interest?'

Dion hesitated. 'By interest, I mean desire.'

'But it is sacred!' Peithon exclaimed.

'That was explained to Kargan. Yet he persisted.'

'Do you think he's planning to return?' Nikolas asked.

Dion felt honored that his brother was asking for his opinion, rather than that of Aristocles. 'There's no way to say. They may return for trade, for war, or they may never return at all. The Salesian continent is far away.'

'Hmm,' King Markos said. He hadn't spoken in some time. 'I've heard rumors of this sun king and his growing power. Word is that he has subdued his neighbors. It's unclear whether he has his eyes on our side of the Maltherean Sea.'

Dion leaned forward. 'You and Nikolas have been building up the army. We're strong on land. But if Phalesia falls or becomes a satrap, subservient to the sun king's power, we'll be next, and we can't stand alone. We must develop a navy.'

The king put his hands on his knees and also leaned forward, jutting out his chin. 'Do you have any idea how much coin we would need to build a navy? With skills we don't have? How much time it would take?'

'The army requires a great deal of our resources—'

'All necessary,' Markos bit off the words. 'Our army is our strength. We are a warrior nation. A nation of the sword, the shield, and the spear. We worship Balal, the god of war, not Silex, the god of the sea. Bah!' He clenched his fists. 'Perhaps we were better off with the narrows blocked. Perhaps you have done us no service after all.'

'Father,' Nikolas urged. 'That wouldn't help our alliance with Phalesia. Nor would it help Peithon. We need trade, which means we need the sea.'

'What we truly need is knowledge,' Dion said. 'We are a smaller nation than Phalesia, and smaller by far than Ilea, but our future could be determined by the tide of events between them. Kargan of Ilea now has an insider's view of Phalesia's harbor, defenses, and governing Assembly. Whatever Aristocles and the other consuls learned from him in return, little was shared with me.' He looked from face to face. 'I think someone from Xanthos, one of us, should return to Phalesia so we may learn what we can, before the warship leaves.'

Markos grunted. 'And my guess is you think that someone should be you.'

'Nikolas is busy at the training ground, you have the kingdom to run, and Peithon sees to our trade. I want to be useful, and I truly believe this warship heralds danger.'

'What if the Ileans have departed?' Nikolas asked, scratching at his thick black beard.

Dion was prepared for the question. 'Father, you always said a good leader maintains initiative and acts decisively. A good warrior makes actions rather than reactions. If the warship has left Phalesia, I could follow in its wake. I could visit Ilea, posing as a trader. We need knowledge.'

Thea drew in a sharp breath. 'Across the Maltherean Sea? The voyage is too long, the dangers too many.'

'I could consult with the Oracle at Athos on the way, which would give the journey a secondary purpose. I know there are dangers—'

'Dangers?' Peithon cut in, arching an eyebrow. 'Have you ever spoken to a man who has beached at Cinder Fen? Surely you've heard tales of the Sea of Serpents?'

Dion set his jaw with determination. Ignoring Peithon, he addressed his father and brother. 'It is the longer journey, but I could sail via Orius and Parnos, missing Cinder Fen altogether. Navigating the sea is to me like leading warriors is to you. Let me do this. Let me use my skills to do something for Xanthos, the same way Nikolas does every day at the training ground.'

Markos looked uncomfortable. Dion was worse than useless with a sword, awkward to say the least with a shield. But in front of a father who valued the skills of a warrior, it was rarely spoken about so openly.

'Think about all we could learn,' Dion persisted. 'Their ship-building techniques. Their intentions. Their strengths and weaknesses. Even if danger never comes, the knowledge will help us. Trade on the Maltherean Sea is as important as the struggle to control it. Silver buys many swords.'

'I will think on it,' the king said, and Dion knew that was all he would get from him tonight. 'In the meantime we have my grandson's naming ceremony.' He paused, and then spoke decisively to everyone in the group. 'I will make my decision by then.'

13

Stools, benches, recliners, and bed-like sofas lay clustered around the banqueting hall, framing the walls and cluttering the interior but leaving much of the center bare. Tasseled pillows, embroidered cushions, and dyed linens covered items of furniture and were covered again by lolling occupants in opulent costumes. Fires roared in the six great hearths, filling the hall with warmth that was utterly unnecessary on an evening in early summer.

The forty guests wiped sweat from brows, laughed uproariously, ate salty food, and then called for more wine to slake their thirst. The aroma of roasting lamb and goat rose from the cooking hearth, an iron bed the size of a table, occupying a wall near the wide-open doors leading to the Flower Terrace. Two servants stood at either end, regularly rotating the two spitted beasts that sizzled over the crimson coals. The noise of loud conversation drowned out the music, though the two seated musicians with lyres played on regardless.

Dion sat on a bench near his brother, who drained his cup and then held it up into the sky to call for more wine. They were near the banqueting hall's back wall, which afforded them a view of the entire room. Nikolas had been saying something about the different lengths of a pike and the effect on tactics when he'd forgotten what he was saying, had his cup refilled, and now suddenly looked at Dion with an expression of alarm.

'Luni . . . My son. Where is he? The magus will come at any moment.'

'Nikolas,' Dion said, shaking his head and grinning. 'You're drunk. Look.' He nodded. 'Over there. Next to my mother. There's Helena, and your son next to her.'

'Good, good,' Nikolas said, smiling. He sipped again at the wine and his smile fell. 'What if the magus doesn't choose iron?'

'Everything will be well, brother,' Dion said. 'He's a strong lad, and waves his toy sword at anyone who comes near him. The magus will choose rightly. He'll make a fine warrior.'

Dion looked across the room at Nikolas's black-haired seven-year-old son, who was dressed in the naming gown, a special garment he would wear only today. The crimson tunic was oversized on his small frame and he looked overwhelmed by all the attention. Nikolas's statuesque blonde wife, Helena, was beside him, crouching and arranging the folds of his tunic as she smiled and spoke to Dion's mother. Thea chuckled as she assisted Helena. The women stood clustered in a group close to the empty center of the room and apart from the men. There was an air of expectancy to their posture; they were evidently nervous as they awaited the magus.

In contrast, Dion's father sat near the cooking hearth with his old comrades, paying the women little attention as he laughed and waved his cup with stabbing motions, evidently reliving some past battle. He made an overly ambitious swipe and nearly fell from his recliner, as inebriated as Nikolas. A servant scurried to help him up while the scarred soldiers with him roared and stamped their feet on the floor.

Peithon formed another group, in company with two of the city's richly dressed merchants and a burly old man with an iron necklace who oversaw the quarries and mines. They were deep in discussion, and the plump first adviser to the king was sober-faced as he prodded his palm with the tip of a thick finger.

'Tell my wife to come over,' Nikolas suddenly barked. 'I want to talk to my son again.'

'Leave them be,' Dion said, smiling as he sipped from his cup. 'He's as prepared as he'll ever be.'

'He soon won't be Luni anymore,' Nikolas said. 'He'll be given a man's name. How will he fare when they put a real sword in his hands? Will the other boys consent to his leadership?'

A servant bent down to refill Dion's cup. 'There's only so much you can do, brother. His fate is in Balal's hands.'

Nikolas turned a bleary gaze on his younger sibling. 'I sacrificed this morning and prayed at the temple.'

'Then you have done all you can.'

'Listen, Dion. When I am king I will help you build your navy.'

Dion smiled. 'You're drunk,' he said again.

'Truly,' Nikolas insisted. 'Peithon agrees that we need one. You have a place here, and a part to play. I will give you—'

'Hush!' someone called out. 'The magus is here!'

Gradually all conversation came to a halt, and the musicians in the corner ceased playing. Those standing near the stairs to the ground level parted.

A withered old man in a black robe came into view.

As the people around him drew back in sudden awe, he walked with slow footsteps taken laboriously, one after the other. All eyes were on him but his head was down and the cowl of his robe was over his head, so that only his sharp nose could be seen. His hands were clasped together, the white skin contrasting with the long black sleeves.

His breath rasped as he walked and shuffled. Finally, he came to stand in the cleared area in the center of the room and lifted his head. He pulled back the hood of his robe.

The magus wore a heavy black chain made of thick rings around his neck from which hung an iron medallion, the size of a dinner plate, displaying an embossed flame in a circle. Wisps of white hair crowned his wrinkled scalp and when he turned to cast his eyes over the assembled gathering his stare was intent.

The rug that usually covered the floor was gone, leaving the dark stone bare. The magus began to hum, a singsong chant that rose in volume as he took a piece of pale chalk and started to draw.

He drew a long white line, five paces in length, and then turned at a sharp angle to draw another, connected to the first. His chant now formed words, but they were in a strange language that caused the hairs to rise on the back of Dion's neck. The magus chalked a third line and then a fourth, until he had drawn a diamond in the middle of the banqueting hall.

Dion glanced at his brother, who now looked completely sober as he sat bolt upright and watched the magus at work. The magus moved to stand inside the diamond and lifted his arms.

His voice never ceased as his chant increased still further in volume. Dion heard the names of the gods interspersed in the chant: Balal, the god of war; Edra, the goddess of fertility and children; Aldus, the god of justice; Helios, the sun god; Silex, the god of fortune and the sea; Aeris, the goddess of music and healing; Charys, the goddess of wisdom.

The magus ceased his singing, and silence filled the room as he slowly let his arms fall at his sides. All eyes were on the stooped figure in black robes.

'I place the materia of gold,' the magus called.

Dion saw that in his hand he had a nugget of solid gold. He turned so that everyone in the room could see it, before taking five steps. He placed the gold on one of the diamond's four points, farthest from Dion and Nikolas. He then returned to the center of the room.

'I place the materia of silver,' he intoned.

The magus held up a piece of silver, the same shape and size as the gold. After displaying it to the crowd, he crossed the diamond and his knees cracked as he bent down to place the silver at the intersection opposite the gold, closest to Dion.

He returned to the center and called out again. 'I place the materia of copper.'

The magus reached into his robe and withdrew a lump of pure copper, the red color reflecting the flickering light as he showed it to the assembled gathering. He placed the copper at the intersection of lines on the diamond's right-hand side.

'I place the materia of iron.'

Dion sensed his brother tense beside him. The magus held out a nugget of black iron that matched the color of his robe, for he was a priest of Balal. He spent a little longer showing the iron to the group, before setting down the final piece of pure metal at the last intersection of points, on Dion and Nikolas's left.

Even though he was the boy's father, Nikolas wasn't allowed to participate in the ceremony in any way. Of course, over the last days, he had taken counsel with the priests, and given counsel to his young son. But anything might happen: Dion's experience at his own naming ceremony was proof of that.

The magus stood once more in the center of the diamond with the four materia at each point. The gold and silver were deliberately far from the center, whereas if the magus stretched out his arms, he could almost touch the more common copper and iron, at the diamond's closer points.

He turned slowly until he was facing Nikolas's son. 'Boy, I will now use your child name for the last time. Come to me, Luni.'

The onlookers held their breath as they waited for the boy to move. Dion smiled as he saw Helena give her son a slight push from behind.

Luni struggled with his costume but began to walk to the magus, staring the entire time in captivated fear at the old priest, who never ceased to appear stern and unyielding. The boy crossed the floor with hesitant steps as his parents urged him on with their eyes. Even Dion breathed a sigh of relief when Luni reached the center of the diamond and came to a halt beside the old man. Occasionally a parent had to intervene to take their child to the magus, but this wasn't considered a good omen.

'Child,' the magus called. 'We magi have called on the gods to choose for you the path that you will take in life.'

He looked at the tip of the diamond farthest from Dion. 'Gold will lead you to a life of leadership, nobility, charisma, and power.'

Dion couldn't help but wonder how often the magi chose gold for a peasant boy, whose parents would never be able to afford his necklace, let alone his round medallion.

'Silver is the materia of the winds of fortune and the tides of commerce.' The magus gazed at the nugget of silver.

'Copper stands for music and beauty, craftsmanship, and the arts of healing.' Dion could see why the copper and iron were closest to the magus and the boy beside him, for they were by far the most common metals chosen.

'Finally'—the magus turned again—'iron leads to the path of the warrior and the farmer, the mason, the smith, and the miner.'

Luni looked fearfully at his mother and then turned again to stare with confusion at his father. Nikolas struggled to keep his face impassive.

'The gods have made their choice,' the magus intoned.

He left the boy standing in the middle of the diamond and then stepped outside the lines of white chalk.

Walking with his slow shuffling steps, the magus now circled the diamond three times. The seven-year-old child now watched the magus; everyone else in the room was utterly still.

The magus stopped. He was standing outside the lump of iron.

'The gods have chosen iron,' the magus said, his thin lips creasing in a smile.

Nikolas was unable to hide a sigh of relief. Glancing across the room, Dion saw that the king was now standing, fists clenched at his sides, but he was beaming.

Yet the ceremony wasn't over. There was one final part for the child to play.

'I name you Lukas,' the magus said. His parents would have supplied the name, but it was the first time anyone else in the room had heard it.

'Lukas,' Dion mouthed. His nephew. He decided he liked the name.

'Come, Lukas,' the magus said, still standing near the lump of iron. 'Come to claim iron.'

The smile fell from Nikolas's face and he tensed once more. But his son knew what to do, and he walked to the magus, knelt at the corner of the diamond, and picked up the lump of iron.

Nikolas whooped as a resounding cheer filled the room. Helena wiped her eyes as she and Thea embraced. King Markos shook hands with the men around him.

'Lukas is a fitting name. The gods chose rightly,' Dion said as he turned and clapped his brother on the back.

'Thank you, brother.' Nikolas pulled him into an embrace. Dion felt prickly hair on his face as his older brother planted a kiss on his cheek.

'Go.' Dion laughed, pushing him away. 'Go to your wife and son.'

Nikolas lurched across the room to join Helena, who was impatiently waving a hand for him to come over. She had a necklace of tiny iron rings in her hands and together she and Nikolas fastened the chain around Lukas's neck; soon a circular amulet imprinted with the bull of Balal was proudly displayed for all to see.

As the parents united around the boy, Dion smiled. But then he felt a gaze on him and saw the magus's dark eyes looking at him from the very center of the hall. Their eyes met before the old man nodded.

Dion's smile faded as he reflected on his own naming ceremony.

He was now old enough to know that the magi and his family would have been discussing him behind closed doors. Even at the tender age of seven it was already clear that Dion wasn't a natural warrior like Nikolas. He'd somehow managed to cut himself on the dull edge of a child's sword and he'd always been afraid of large groups of hoplites, with their sharp spears ready to kill and steel helmets hiding their faces. He did have skills: he was good with horses and liked to ride; he was clever with numbers and could add, subtract, and multiply better than his much older brother.

Gold wouldn't have been appropriate, for it was Nikolas who was heir to the throne, and Dion didn't exhibit the natural charisma that would have made him the leader of other boys his age. Copper was out of the question: the last thing King Markos wanted was a musician or a craftsman for a son.

So the magi chose silver.

But when the magus circled the diamond and gave Dion his name, calling him to the silver, Dion wouldn't come.

It had been an awkward moment. Eventually, King Markos had picked up the newly named Dion and taken him to the magus.

With loud conversation now filling the banqueting hall as the musicians took up their instruments and the festivities resumed, the magus continued to stare. The silver chain, with its amulet bearing the symbol of Silex, felt uncomfortable on Dion's skin, as if it didn't belong.

14

As the night progressed, the guests became more raucous, until finally, in ones and twos, they begged their leave, departing after a final congratulation offered to the proud parents. Eventually only the royal family and Peithon remained, though the magus was still present, waiting on the king's permission to leave. They all sat in a circle of benches drawn up close together in the center of the room, the white chalk now smudged by countless feet crossing to and fro.

In a lull in the conversation, the old magus, seated a little apart, turned an inquiring gaze on the king. It was tradition that at the end of every family banquet would come a story for those still awake. Often the storyteller would be Markos or Nikolas, but on this occasion the king had requested that the magus honor them with a tale.

'Magus,' Markos said with a nod, 'I believe now is the time, should it suit you.'

The magus moved his bench a little closer to the circle. 'Which story would you like to hear, sire?'

The king turned to Nikolas and Helena, now seated together, with Lukas on his father's lap. With Nikolas's thick black beard and broad-shouldered frame he looked every inch the king-to-be, while the beautiful blonde woman beside him was the model of a future queen.

'Lukas?' Nikolas said, never tiring of using his son's new name. 'What tale would you like to hear?'

Warm and comfortable in his father's arms, his fear of the magus now somewhat diminished, Lukas spoke up boldly. 'I want to hear about King Palemon and the eldren.'

The magus tilted his head at the king.

'Very well,' Markos said.

The stooped old man cleared his throat and looked down, before casting his eyes on the people seated in front of him. The silence grew for a time, broken only by the faint crackle of the last embers in the hearths.

Finally, the magus spoke.

'Long ago, our people, and all other people, fought a terrible war with a race separate from our own, those we call the eldren. Where we are sometimes dark-skinned and sometimes light, the eldren are universally pale. Where we have brown hair and blonde, the eldren have hair of silver. Where we are strong workers, able to mine and shape metal, the eldren are thin and weak, and because they hate the touch of metal, they carry no steel or bronze weapons. But'—the magus let the word hang in the air for a moment—'they can change their shape.'

Lukas shivered in his father's arms, his eyes fixed on the magus.

The old man put out his right hand. 'On one side was the king-dom of Aleuthea, greatest of all human civilizations. We still see their monuments in Sarsica, and it is clear that there has been no people so advanced since. Palemon, King of Aleuthea, is said to have lived in a palace nineteen stories high. The golden rays of the Lighthouse could once be seen from as far away as Myana, the Sarsican capital.'

All present were silent while they digested the magus's words.

He then held out the other hand. 'On the other side were the eldren in their magical land, Sindara. Their king, Marrix, was the most powerful eldran who ever lived. All eldren are magically connected to the ultimate source of life energy, but Marrix more than any other. When Marrix changed shape,' the magus's voice became low and ominous, 'the whole world trembled.'

He now clasped his palms together and his thin arms tensed. 'Some say that King Palemon started the war in order to claim Sindara for his own, and others that it was Marrix who vowed to end the human race. In any event, the war was long and bitter. Multitudes died on both sides. Bodies floated along the shores of both the Aleuthean Sea and the Maltherean Sea, turning the shallow waters red.

'To do battle in the skies the eldren could become furies, men with wings like bats, and even dragons, huge reptilian creatures with wings each as big as this room. To fight in the sea they could become merfolk, men with tails like fish, and even serpents, monstrous sea snakes that could tear a ship to pieces. To war on land they could grow in size to become ogres, with the largest so big we call them giants.'

The magus started coughing and bent to pick up a cup at his feet; he was so old that the process took a long time, but Dion knew he wouldn't appreciate any help. He sipped and then resumed.

'If they could have changed for long periods the ancients would never have stood a chance. Palemon, king of Aleuthea, would have seen his proud kingdom laid to waste. But they could change for only short periods. For they sometimes went wild.'

Dion found himself falling under the spell of the magus's story. Aleuthea was gone now; the stories said the island nation sank beneath the sea a thousand years ago. But signs of the ancient civilization still existed, and he'd once seen a crumbled ruin on the edge of the Aleuthean Sea where there were obelisks so big that the Sarsican builders knew neither how they were cut nor erected.

'Seeking a way to gain an advantage over the humans, King Marrix made a magical horn out of a conch to recall the wild ones and bring them home. Blowing the horn brought all the wildren back to him, and if wildness was upon them they were reminded of their true selves and turned back. At the end of a terrible battle, when the human dead numbered in the tens of thousands and the fighting went on for so long that hundreds of eldren turned wild, King Palemon first heard its call. As he saw the wildren travel in the direction of the sound, he realized that the eldren now possessed a decisive advantage.'

'What did he do?' Lukas asked.

'Shh,' Helena hushed.

'In a daring raid, King Palemon went to Sindara, the eldren homeland, and stole the horn. He put it in an iron box so that it could never be reclaimed, for no eldran can willingly touch pure metal. Raging, King Marrix launched attack after attack, but he was reckless, and ever more eldren became wildren. His army grew smaller with every sortie.'

Dion thought about the wildren rumored to infest the Sea of Serpents. Were all of them former fighters in the war against King Palemon?

'Knowing he was close to victory, Palemon launched a great assault on Sindara. It was a mighty struggle, but he was finally victorious. Yet even in defeat Marrix could claim revenge, for after the war's end, Sindara became a wasteland, a place we now call Cinder Fen. Any promise the land had for farming and mining was lost, for many wildren were, and still are, drawn to Cinder Fen, the same way a horse returns to its stable.'

There was silence in the banqueting hall as the story reached its conclusion.

'King Palemon drove the remaining eldren into the Wilds, where they still live. Some also live in the Waste, closer to the Salesian continent. Palemon's last years, however, were not content. Disaster struck when the ocean rose, burying the kingdom of Aleuthea beneath the waves. But I will save that story for another day.'

The magus stood and bowed. 'By your leave, sire?'

'Thank you, magus,' King Markos said as he took a long draught of his wine. 'You may go.'

The old man shuffled out of the room, leaving the group of seven behind. The men were in varying states of intoxication: Markos was bleary and Nikolas was looking as ready to retire as Dion himself felt, but Peithon was swaying slightly as he stared down into his cup.

'All eldren should be eradicated like the vermin they are.' Peithon swished the red wine, spilling some on his expensive clothes.

Thea frowned. 'That wine you are so drunk on came from Phalesia, via the narrows that an eldran helped clear.'

Peithon's broad face reddened as he turned on the queen. 'What manner of woman are you, to preach peace with the race that destroyed your family?'

'Peace,' Markos said wearily, holding up a hand. 'Peace between my beloved queen, and my loyal companion and first adviser.' He turned to Dion's mother, whose pretty face was curled into a scowl. 'Wife, Peithon has fought by my side in many battles. And some of those battles were against groups of wildren. We lost good men. Peithon also lost his bride three weeks before his wedding day. Will you come to an accord with him?'

'Yes, husband.' Thea nodded stiffly.

Markos now addressed Peithon. 'Peithon, Thea is my beloved wife, whom I love. She has helped us find a path to a peaceful solution for living so close to the eldren in the Wilds. They now aid us rather than hindering us when we destroy the wildren who were once their kin. She is also your queen, and deserving of your respect. Do you see the wisdom in peace?'

'Yes, sire,' Peithon said. When the king looked away, Dion saw Peithon throw his mother a look of loathing.

'It is late,' the king said. 'We have had a long day. But,' he looked at Dion, 'I have said I would make a decision regarding my youngest son's request, and here it is.'

Dion sat up, his tiredness vanishing.

'Nikolas is the heir and commander of the army, as well as a skilled warrior, the best I have seen in my many years. He has a beautiful wife and a strong child, Lukas, my grandson.'

Markos nodded at the boy, who was now fast asleep.

'But Dion has yet to take on the responsibilities of his brother. Danger to the kingdom is ever present. A warship from Ilea has arrived at the harbor of Phalesia, our closest neighbor, and it may be the first of many. Dion wishes to prove himself, and I believe him when he states the importance of filling in the gaps in our knowledge. Dion will go to Phalesia to learn more of this vessel and its commander.'

Dion nodded his acceptance. He saw his mother looking at him with concern.

'But,' Markos said in his gravelly voice, 'if the warship has departed, Dion will return to Xanthos.'

Dion struggled to hide his disappointment.

'He will return to Xanthos unless Aristocles, First Consul of Phalesia, gives his blessing for a voyage to Ilea to be made – on behalf of both our nations. If such a thing comes to pass, Dion will serve at the behest of the first consul, placing himself under his leadership. It will be Aristocles who will be the one to decide if Dion should go to Ilea to learn about the sun king's realm across the Maltherean Sea.'

15

Aristocles walked barefoot along the pebbled shore. On his right the waves made a familiar hiss as the water crashed onto the small stones, while on the left the smooth wall of the sloped defensive embankment rose to a height of sixty feet. He wore a thick tunic of blue silk, holding it above his ankles to keep the hem from dragging.

He glanced at the group he had with him, also barefoot and finely dressed. Nilus and the other four consuls were arrayed around him, so that Aristocles led them all from the center. Round-faced Nilus's expression of jocularity looked a little forced to Aristocles' experienced eyes. The other four consuls smiled as they walked, much as they would as they made their way to any banquet or symposium where there would be flowing wine and loose conversation. But they also appeared to be keeping a close check on feelings of anxiety, with one consul fidgeting as he walked along the beach and another incessantly smoothing his hair.

The final member of the group was Aristocles' eldest daughter. She walked close by his side, standing tall despite her trepidation.

'You look beautiful,' Aristocles said to Chloe.

Chloe looked down at herself self-consciously. She wore a new chiton made specifically for this occasion, a gauzy garment of white folds that contrasted with her long near-black hair. It was bunched at the waist, tied with a golden rope, and left her arms bare. The neckline was low enough for the copper amulet bearing the symbol of Aeris, a cross with a double loop, to be clearly visible, but not so revealing as to be scandalous.

It was at times like this that she reminded Aristocles more than ever of his late wife. Like Chloe, she had been a dark-haired beauty. Like Chloe, she was never afraid of holding her own in the company of men.

'How long will we have to stay?' Chloe asked.

As they walked they passed fishing boats, colorfully painted vessels with horizontal stripes of yellow, crimson, and brilliant blue. The sun had set, falling into the horizon as they'd walked, and now the sky took on a purple hue. The breeze began to strengthen, flattening clothes to bodies, but it was a warm wind; the summer promised to be hot.

Ahead, Aristocles could see the unmistakable bulk of the unpainted Ilean warship, the *Nexotardis*, its outline horizontal at the sides but ingeniously curved upward at both ends. The bireme occupied its own piece of shore at the bay's far end and had been given a wide berth by the Phalesians ever since its arrival. The ship's repairs were finished now, and it looked fit and ready to depart.

'I don't know,' Aristocles said.

Sixty Phalesian hoplites stood on the beach, a careful distance from the warship, at their ease but standing close by as an additional precaution. Kargan had said he would depart with the dawn. The soldiers would stay until he left.

'Amos and his men are already here.' Nilus nodded in their direction. 'Chloe, if you want to leave early, have some soldiers escort you.'

For the first time, as they approached the bireme, Aristocles found himself close enough to read the lettering on her side. '*Nexotardis*,' he read.

'A strange name, and a strange people,' Nilus said. 'They insist we give their ship a wide berth, and then they invite us on board for a farewell banquet. I will never understand them.'

'What is important is that we understand this ship,' one of the other consuls said. 'This is our chance to see it up close.'

'Everyone, keep your eyes and ears open,' Aristocles said. 'Ask many questions and answer few.'

'And why invite your daughter?' Nilus was shaking his head.

'Kargan asked for a musician and suggested Chloe. I couldn't deny her existence, given the fact that he has met her.'

'Father gave me the option of refusing,' Chloe said.

Aristocles took in the sight of the bireme as they walked to the lowered gangway, little more than a plank with steps fitted at regular intervals. He'd seen bigger merchant vessels, but this was easily the largest warship he'd ever encountered. He looked at the spike of the bronze ram, prominently visible with the warship drawn up on the beach bow first. He tried not to stare too hard, but he couldn't take his eyes off it.

'Aristocles,' Nilus whispered. 'Face front.'

Aristocles led Chloe up the gangway, their progress made easier by the fact that they wore no boots or sandals. Reaching the top deck, open to the elements, he was confronted by a long space of planks worn smooth by the passage of countless feet, cleared for the occasion. The section of decking farthest from shore, behind the big mast, had been set up for a banquet. Cushions clustered in piles beside carpets woven with strange dizzying patterns. Swarthy bare-chested men in loose loincloths held small wine jugs ready to pour. Immense iron bowls used as braziers cast warm light, tended unceasingly by dedicated slaves, for the danger of fire aboard a wooden ship was obvious.

Kargan waited to greet the consuls as they crested the gangway. He wore the same flowing yellow robe and curved dagger at his waist he had worn on his visit to the first consul's villa. Aristocles could smell the sweet scent of oil in his black hair and curled beard.

'First Consul,' he addressed Aristocles, towering over the Phalesian. 'Welcome to the *Nexotardis*. And your daughter is here. Welcome, lady.'

'We are honored to have been invited,' Aristocles said. He cast his eye over the deck, seeing dozens of Ileans, all strangers. Some were obviously slaves, but he found it difficult to ascertain if others were marines, officers, or crewmen.

'First Consul, this is Hasha, the commander of my oarsmen. He will seat you while slaves bring refreshment.'

Aristocles followed the Ilean, a lean man with a hooked nose and curled mustaches, who led him to one of the carpets.

'We will sit in the manner to which we are accustomed in our lands,' Hasha said.

'Of course, I would expect no different.'

Aristocles made himself comfortable, following Hasha's example and arranging the cushions behind his back. Soon the other four consuls were also seated on the carpets, with Chloe reclining beside her father.

Aristocles saw that despite the presence of so many men on deck, Kargan had them in careful order, with the Phalesians in a section with the men he presumed were the senior officers and crewmen, while the rougher-looking Ileans were placed near the bow. The ship's crew displayed an astonishing variety of builds, from lean to squat, and skin tones from the darkest brown to a light olive color little different from the Phalesians. Some of the men had hooked noses while others had wide mouths and deep-set eyes. Aristocles guessed that they weren't all Ileans; the crew was likely drawn from across the Salesian continent.

The last glow of twilight had faded from the sky and a million pinpricks now shone in night's curtain above. Though the warship was drawn up on the beach, her stern, where Aristocles' group sat high on the upper deck, was in the water, and rocked gently from side to side. He glanced up when he heard a soft patter that became a rumble and saw a man with a drum between his knees, tapping a rhythm with his fingers that caused the heart to beat a little faster.

Remembering that he needed to learn about the warship's construction while he was here, Aristocles ignored the men and instead scanned the deck, running his eyes over the timbers and mast. But he realized swiftly that with the lower decks sealed by boxlike coverings placed over the hatches there was only so much he could learn. The mast was tall and as thick as a man's waist; it would have been a mighty tree in life. The oars were all down below. Kargan had risked little by inviting the consuls to this departure feast, for this beast's skeleton and muscles were all hidden from view.

Aristocles made a quick count and saw that while the top deck appeared crowded, with one hundred and twenty oarsmen alone – slaves, all of them, knowing the Ileans – only a small proportion of the crew was present. The ship would be crowded below decks.

He nodded as a slave handed him a wooden cup filled with wine, but Aristocles felt unsettled. It was strange to be feasting, while just a few feet below this very deck, over a hundred miserable souls huddled on their rowing benches, resting before their work began with the dawn.

'Now it is my turn to serve you wine,' Kargan's voice boomed as he seated himself near Aristocles, pushing aside one of the other consuls in the process.

And with those words, the banquet began.

The drum's rhythm and volume increased. Conversation became loud and laughter more frequent. The only light was the dim crimson glow of the coals in the iron bowls, illuminating faces with reddish tones, lending an eerie feeling to the festive mood.

Food came after the wine. Aristocles ate his fill – it would be rude to do otherwise – but then his heart sank as more slaves brought yet more food. It was Phalesian fare, sourced from the agora, and as good as anything Aristocles ate at his own table. Well-trained slaves handed out a cold assortment of olives, nuts, fresh and dried cheeses, flat bread, figs, roasted goat, pig ears, and smoked fish. Some unfamiliar spices had been liberally sprinkled over the meats, but Aristocles found the flavors surprisingly pleasant.

Kargan ate everything, and insisted Aristocles do the same. He drained his cup with every mouthful and waited expectantly, watching and scowling, his glare becoming ever more fierce until the first consul's wine cup was empty. It would then be refilled immediately.

Checking on his daughter, Aristocles saw that an Ilean officer was regaling Chloe and Nilus with a bawdy tale. Some of the humor appeared to be lost on the Phalesians, and when the Ilean laughed uproariously Chloe merely smiled, while Nilus looked bemused.

Kargan and Aristocles spoke of Phalesian cooking and Sarsican wine – the warship's commander said that for the banquet he'd gone to the market and asked the wine sellers to supply him with the same wine they sold to the first consul. They talked about the weather in Ilea and the places the wealthy went to escape the heat of summer. Aristocles tried to discuss music, but the mind-numbing repetition of the drums appeared to be enough for Kargan's senses.

'More food!' Kargan shouted.

The wine was taking its toll, and Aristocles was wondering whether the time was before midnight or after when Nilus leaned forward. 'How long will this go on?'

Kargan overheard him. He grabbed Nilus's upper arm and pulled him over, so that Nilus tumbled on top of the swarthy master of the *Nexotardis* in a tangle of white cloth.

'This is a real banquet,' Kargan roared into Nilus's ear. 'It will go on until the last star vanishes, of course. More wine for the consul!'

Nilus righted himself and rearranged his tunic as well he could given his unfocused eyes and the way his fingers kept grasping on empty air. His round face was bright red.

Still the wine kept coming.

Kargan started to dance with his men, performing a strange jig with arms spread and fingers clicking together in time to the drums. Hopping from foot to foot, shifting around a circle formed with four others, he started to sing with such gusto that Aristocles wondered if the entire city behind the harbor could hear him. The four other dancers knew the words and formed a humming chorus like the chant of a priest.

Chloe was now seated on Aristocles' left, and as the drums finally faded away Kargan again sat down heavily on his other side. Across from them Nilus's head was nodding as he struggled to keep awake. The symposiums the consuls and merchants hosted often went late, but never was such a quantity of wine consumed.

'Now,' Kargan said. He turned his dark eyes on Aristocles. 'I am asking you seriously. The sun king desires gold above all else. We have silver. How much do you want for the ark? Name your price.'

Aristocles stiffened and saw that Nilus was suddenly awake and scowling. He reminded himself that he was Phalesia's first consul and tried not to appear offended.

'It is not – and will never be – for sale,' Aristocles said. 'But if it's gold you want, we have many fine jewelers—'

Kargan barked a laugh and clapped Aristocles so hard on the back that he spilled wine over his tunic. 'I had to try.' He turned his head from side to side and frowned. 'Music! Where is the musician?'

'He fell asleep, lord.'

'Throw him overboard! The stars are still out!'

Kargan lurched as he stood up and then walked three steps to the rail, facing outward, then began to urinate noisily over the side.

'Perhaps we should make our way—' Nilus said.

'This banquet is not over!' Kargan rasped as he returned. He sank down again beside Aristocles. 'I nearly forgot! Your daughter plays the flute, does she not? Did she bring her instrument as I asked?'

When Aristocles hesitated, Kargan barked at Chloe, 'Play, girl.' He waved his arms to the people nearby. 'Quiet, all of you!'

Chloe unwrapped her flute and placed it to her lips. She commenced a bright melody often performed at feast days.

She had played for only a short while when Kargan put his hands over his ears and grimaced. 'Enough! Save my senses!'

Chloe winced and stopped playing. She wrapped her copper flute once more in cloth and stood.

'Girl, why don't you dance instead?'

Chloe gave Kargan a look that he barely seemed to notice. She walked away from the carpets and cushions, heading for the ramp and the shore.

'Chloe.' Aristocles tried to stand. His head was throbbing from the wine. 'Lord Kargan, I must protest—'

'Not so fast, First Consul.' Kargan clapped a hand firmly around Aristocles' shoulder. 'Not while the stars still shine. More wine! More food!'

Finally, the last star left the sky and the horizon began to glow. Aristocles, Nilus, and the other two consuls lumbered across a deck filled with lolling Ileans and made their way to the gangway at the bow.

Kargan saw them to the ramp and then clapped Aristocles on the back. 'I foresee good relations between our peoples, First Consul.'

'I wish you safe travels.' Aristocles struggled to make the words. 'And I must apologize for my daughter's hasty departure—'

'Bah,' he said. 'It is nothing. Girls her age are often headstrong, which is why they need husbands.'

'Well . . . It has been a pleasure . . .' Aristocles mumbled.

'Your soldiers will escort you back to the city. I saw a pair with your daughter earlier. She will be home and safe.'

Aristocles nodded, his attention consumed with the prospect of making it safely down the gangway. As he reached the pebbled shore where his fellow consuls waited, he turned back and ran his eyes over the warship one last time.

The Phalesian soldiers came to join the group and together they followed the shore back to the steps below the agora. Aristocles heard one of his stumbling companions cough as he was violently sick and his own stomach writhed in response.

When they finally reached the embankment they heard the blast of a horn and gazed back at the Ilean ship; the *Nexotardis* was already moving.

A multitude of oars hauled at the water, tossing it into foam with synchronized motions, sending the ship forward with astonishing speed. The sail went up.

'They're gone now,' Nilus said. 'Thank the gods.'

16

Dion picked up a bulging water skin, his muscles groaning as he carried it from the sandy shore to the large vessel rocking on the waves. He plunged into water up to his knees and handed the skin up to bald-headed Cob, who carried it to the bow and nestled it in the sheltered section with the other supplies.

His jaw cracked as he stifled a yawn; it was just after dawn; they were leaving early to catch the outgoing tide and give them plenty of time to sail to Phalesia. The water was warm on his legs and a sea breeze blew gently on his face, cooling his tanned skin from the already radiant sun. He wore a well-made white tunic suitable to both sailing and trading.

Dion made way for a wiry man twenty years his senior to get past and nodded. Sal, a longtime friend of Cob, nodded back, handing up still more supplies to the old man. As Dion headed back to the beach for more provisions he saw the last two men who would be crewing the twenty-foot sailing galley – his father's biggest ship – newly arrived.

'What orders?' a slim youth with his first growth of beard asked. Dion saw he had a scabbarded sword in one hand and a stuffed satchel in the other.

'Riko,' Dion said, clapping him on the shoulder. 'Glad you could make it. Get your things into the boat, and then help us load her up.'

'Not much in the way of provisions,' said the second man, Otus, a tall brawler with a broken nose.

'We're only going to Phalesia. If we're traveling further we can get supplies there.'

'Will we be there tonight?' Riko asked.

'No,' Dion said. 'The wind's against us. We'll have to beach tonight on the far side of the narrows.'

'Fair enough,' said Otus. 'Come on, lad.' He inclined his head to Riko.

Shielding his eyes, Dion saw his mother waiting on the grassy bank higher up. He looked for more figures but felt a surge of disappointment when he saw that she was the only member of his family who had come to say goodbye.

As he climbed the beach he felt sad. He hadn't expected much more from the king, but it was unlike Nikolas to let him go without a word of farewell.

'Mother,' he said, 'it's time to go.'

With her typical lithe grace, she came forward to embrace her son. 'I don't know if you are departing on a long journey or not. I wish I knew.'

She continued to hold him by the shoulders as he scanned the area, trying to hide his emotions but failing.

'Father . . . Nikolas . . . They're both busy?'

The queen nodded. Her manner was strangely distracted. 'You know how they are; it's always soldiers and fighting with them. They've had an early start at the bowyer's workshop.'

'Well, I'd best be going.'

'Wait . . .' Dion's mother continued to hold his shoulders.

'Why—?'

'Ah, there's Helena!' Thea said, finally letting him go. 'She must have come to say goodbye.'

Nikolas's tall blonde wife wore a silk chiton of deepest blue hemmed with gold. She was walking quickly, with a forced smile displaying even white teeth.

'Dion,' she said, 'you wouldn't leave without saying farewell to me?'

'Well, I—'

She pulled him close and kissed him on both cheeks, so that her soft hair tickled his face and he smelled her floral scent.

Dion saw Helena pass his mother a meaningful look, leaving him feeling puzzled.

'Have you loaded your supplies?' she asked.

He glanced back at the boat, seeing that the last of the sacks were nearly aboard – something that Helena could see for herself.

'Yes,' he said. 'Well, my men are waiting. Thank you both for coming down. Tell Nikolas and Father that I—'

'You can't go this instant,' Dion's mother interrupted. 'There's something I have to tell you.'

Dion frowned. 'What is it?'

'I . . .' Thea began uncertainly.

Then Helena visibly relaxed. 'They're here,' she murmured to Thea.

Following her gaze, Dion saw the big burly form of his brother approaching as he followed a path through the nearby trees, all dark hair and bristling beard. A moment later his father came into view beside him. Both men were walking with swift steps, their progress made slow by the king's limp.

'Thank the gods,' Nikolas panted, grinning as he neared. 'We had to twist a few arms, but we got here in time.'

'Nikolas, Father,' Dion said, smiling as a surge of emotion threatened to bring tears to his eyes. 'You came.'

The king halted beside his wife as Nikolas and Dion embraced, but then Dion realized his brother was holding something behind his back. 'What are you hiding?'

Nikolas ignored the question, frowning. 'Are you taking your bow with you?'

'Of course,' Dion said.

'Then throw it in the sea,' Nikolas said. He brought his hand from around his back and held out a large leather-wrapped packet, twice the length of his arm.

Taking it in both hands, Dion unraveled a corner of the cloth. When he revealed a length of polished wood he gasped. Unable to stop himself, he let the rest of the cover fall to the ground as he examined a length of curved wood. The composite bow was strung and ready to use, the workmanship finer than anything he'd seen before.

'It's your new bow.' Nikolas beamed.

'This is for me?'

'Father and I were having it made for your birthday, but we thought it better to give it to you now. The future is uncertain, and you never know when you'll be in need of a good weapon.'

Dion examined it with both hands. It was sleek, made of alternating pieces of wood and horn, expertly spliced with the connections so tight they felt completely smooth when he ran his fingers along the bow's length. It curved back on itself at both ends and was as long as a tall man's stride.

'It's beautiful,' Dion said, testing the draw. He had never owned anything so costly, nor held a bow so well made.

'I told the bowyer you spend a lot of time at sea and he took that into account in the construction. The string is silk – he said sinew or hide wouldn't deal well with the moisture. The different pieces are glued with gelatin from Sarsica and bound with deer gut.'

'Nikolas . . . How can I thank—?'

'I hope it serves you well,' Markos said. The old king had been frowning as he watched the exchange, and now he spoke for the first time. 'You're fortunate your brother is persuasive, Dion, for it cost as much as a set of armor.' He harrumphed. 'You have the offering for the Oracle at Athos?'

'Yes, Father.'

'If you end up crossing the sea, whatever you do,' Thea said, 'don't go near Cinder Fen. And remember, we want peace with the sun king.'

'Peace isn't always possible,' King Markos said.

Casting his eyes back down to the shore, Dion saw that his crew was inside the large sailing vessel and waiting, with the youth Riko waist deep in water as he held the bobbing ship, fighting the tossing back and forth of the waves.

'I'd best go,' Dion said to them all.

His mother embraced him again, and then, unstringing the bow and sheathing the weapon in its leather cover, he said goodbye to the assembled group.

He sensed their eyes on his back as he walked to the water and waded in, handing the packet up to Cob and then throwing his body over the gunwale to jump inside. The sail went up and the oars started moving in their slots.

Finally looking back at the bank, he saw that his father, brother, and Helena had left, with his mother the only one still waiting to see him go. He waved at her one last time, and wondered when he would next see her again.

Then Cob asked Dion if he wanted to take a turn at the tiller, and he forgot all about his family as the fresh wind sent a mist of spray against his cheeks.

The odor of stale sweat and salt-soaked timber overwhelmed Chloe's senses. She lay awkwardly with her ankles tied tightly with twine, her wrists behind her back, and a gag in her mouth. She had been stuffed below decks on the *Nexotardis* among the jugs and amphorae, water skins and sacks. Prone on a platform close to the bow, somewhere between the painted eyes, she had at least managed to turn herself around so that she could see the interior of the bireme.

The view from under the warship's upper deck contrasted sharply with the festive scene above. On a narrow wooden bench nearby, half a dozen swarthy soldiers with arms in slings and cloth bandages covering old wounds sat in silence. Wretched slaves slumped in the rowing benches. Blood stains old and new decorated the timber planking. In addition to the supplies, the hold where Chloe lay was stuffed with loot: sacks of jewelry and decorative chests sealed tight. Before the quake, Kargan had said his ship had been trading, but it was obvious his men had been in combat.

Chloe moaned and tried to cry out again and again as the night passed with terrifying speed. She kicked at the timber but no one came to save her. Tears trickled from her eyes and the twine cut into her ankles and wrists.

Then the worst happened. The hatches on the upper deck opened, sending in a puff of fresh air that was swiftly swallowed by the evil reek below. Men came down the ladders and barked orders. The slaves scurried as they left their benches and exited the vessel; soon she felt them hauling its bulk off the shore.

The bireme rocked as it wallowed in the water before the slaves returned and a whip cracked, sending them to their positions. Oars slid out and a drum began to beat, sending a pounding rhythm through the ship's interior, throbbing in time to Chloe's constricted wrists. She screamed and kicked, writhing and rolling, trying to free herself, but Kargan's men knew their business, and the knots were too tight for her to have any hope of freeing herself. Her nostrils flared and her heart raced as she hyperventilated, feeling her vision close in as she fought to get enough air into her lungs. The gag in her mouth, a tight ball of cloth, pressed up close against the back of her throat. It was held in place by a second length of linen tied behind her head.

The ship started to roll up and down as it carved its way through ever-bigger waves. Chloe felt the floor beneath her drop and then rise with each movement. She closed her eyes; the motion made her feel ill and disoriented, and she knew it would never stop.

After more than an hour she opened her eyes when she heard voices. Kargan stood nearby, regarding her. Despite there being two rows of benches, there was only the one central floor running the length of the ship, and the ceiling was low enough that Kargan had to crouch to look at her.

'Free her hands and legs, then bring her up to me,' he ordered.

Kargan couldn't have slept, yet the night appeared to have taken no toll on him, aside from a slight shadow beneath his black eyes. None of his previous humor was evident as he returned to the top-most deck.

A sailor cut through Chloe's bonds, then hauled her to her feet. With oarsmen moving back and forth at both sides, he led her to a ladder leading to an open hatch.

'Climb.'

She tried to grip the rungs but couldn't. Fire filled her fingers and she cried out in pain. Her limbs were little better; she could barely stand.

The sailor looked up at the open hatch, where another man beckoned, his arms reaching. Chloe felt herself lifted from underneath and the other man grabbed her arms. The sailor on the top deck hauled her up and sat her on the edge of the hatch.

'I . . . I can walk,' Chloe said.

He grunted and stood as she clambered to her feet. The bright light blinded her and the deck rolled, nearly sending her over the rail until yet another sailor caught her. Spying the mast, she gripped a hoop on the stout pole with one hand and waited for her eyes to adjust to the glare. High above her a square sail snapped in the freshening wind. The air was blessedly fresh, her senses freed from the sickening reek below.

'Hurry up!' She heard Kargan's voice.

He stood at the ship's bow, legs astride, easily riding the ship's listing rhythm. He had changed into long linen trousers and an open shirt that revealed his barrel chest, covered with a dense mat of dark hair.

A strong hand pushed her from behind and she walked to the bow, where a forked bench afforded space for two people to sit side by side. The bowsprit nodded up and down while, audible even on the topmost deck, the throbbing drum formed a countermelody to the splashes of more than a hundred oars.

Glancing over her shoulder, Chloe felt her stomach lurch when she saw that her homeland was little more than a flat gray line on the horizon. She knew that none of her father's ships was this fast. No one could catch her, and even if a captain could, no Phalesian warship working alone could challenge the bireme's power.

'Come,' Kargan said. 'Sit.'

Chloe lurched to the seat opposite. Her bowels clenched at the unceasing up-and-down, rolling motion. She had never enjoyed the sea.

'You want to know why I took you,' Kargan said. 'I have more than one answer to give.' He paused as he gazed back along the deck of his ship, and then looked up at the sail, finally nodding in satisfaction. 'I think the sun king will want to learn more about your people.'

'My father will see this as a declaration of war,' she said, glaring at him.

'I think not,' he said dismissively. 'Your consuls were afraid of me.' He shrugged. 'And perhaps war is what the sun king will want. If not, you can always be returned. Or ransomed.' He stared directly into her eyes. 'At any rate, your father is no king. A king would seek vengeance, no matter the consequence. But these consuls will advise caution. Such men always do.'

Chloe felt the seeds of doubt grow in her mind. She knew the way the Assembly functioned.

'Believe me, Chloe of Phalesia,' Kargan said. 'Your fate is now in the hands of the sun king.'

17

Dion climbed the series of stone steps cut into the cliff at odd angles. Some were larger than others and he had to be careful with his footing. The higher he ascended, the more conscious he was of the steep drop to the sea below.

He tried not to look down, instead focusing on each individual step. But his gaze wandered, and he occasionally looked out at the city, seeing a scene of strange normality at the agora and surrounding temples where one would instead expect chaos and turmoil.

Finally, the path leveled and he paused, gripping a nearby jut, and waited for his breathing and heart rate to return to normal. Tough shrubs lined both sides of the path ahead, which was short and led directly to the plateau.

He had never climbed to the Temple of Aldus before, and had never been so high. The cliff dropped away at his left and he fought off the dizzying sensation of vertigo as he walked along the path. Keeping his back straight and his eyes level, he approached the dozen columns surrounding the flat, circular space, and now that his footsteps were taking him away from the cliff he finally began to breathe more easily.

From his vantage point he could see the entire city of Phalesia revealed behind the plateau's far side. The evenly spaced columns held up no roof, simply providing a skirting fence for the sacred relics within. Even though it was near noon, the eternal flame was easily visible, burning fiercely on a stepped pyramid, nestled within a hollow at the very top. The spears of fire leaped and danced.

Six paces in front of the flame, at the temple's perfect center, the Ark of Revelation shone brightly, the gold shimmering under the sun's rays. Ornate and decorated with imprinted designs, it had a flat lid that was small compared to the chest. Strange, sharply angled symbols were arranged along the front, underneath lines of cursive text in a language Dion had never seen before.

Even though strong purpose had brought him here, he stopped in awe.

But he shook himself and intentionally tore his eyes away from the golden chest. He looked instead at the solitary man who knelt in front of the ark, his hands clasped together and his lips moving soundlessly as he prayed.

It was unthinkable to disturb First Consul Aristocles at prayer, but some things could not wait. Amos of the city guard had told Dion that Aristocles was so grief-stricken he was spending nearly all his time at the temple, praying to the gods and pacing, gazing out to sea in the direction his daughter had been taken.

Dion licked his lips and spoke. 'First Consul.'

Aristocles looked up in surprise. He appeared to have aged dramatically, though little time had passed since their last meeting. The white hair framing his bald crown was lank and the skin around his eyes was shadowed and sunken; he looked like he hadn't slept in days. He slowly clambered to his feet and turned to face Dion.

Dion walked forward to meet him, taking in the older man's grubby tunic and coming to the conclusion that Aristocles hadn't washed or changed his clothes since his daughter's capture. 'I've heard the news, and I wish to express my sympathy.'

'Dion,' Aristocles said listlessly, gazing at him with reddened eyes. 'What brings you here? What is so urgent as to disturb me at prayer?'

'My father sent me to learn more about the newcomers. He fears that more ships will come in the wake of this visit. I was to ascertain their intentions.'

Aristocles gave a sardonic laugh.

Dion continued: 'I believe my task is even more important now. Their intentions are clear. The Ileans are undoubtedly hostile. The fates of our two nations may hang in the balance. Yet, huddled in the mountains as we are, Xanthos is in the dark.'

'Yes, yes,' Aristocles said wearily. 'But my problems are nonetheless greater than yours.'

'Have you sent a rescue party yet?'

'I cannot.' Aristocles shook his head. 'The consuls fear any act that may lead to outright war.'

Dion was puzzled. 'Hasn't that already happened?'

'No,' Aristocles said. 'This could still be brushed off as a mistake, with both parties pretending misunderstanding, and any wounds soothed with silver and gold.'

Dion opened his mouth, then closed it. 'So what are you saying? What will happen to your daughter?'

The first consul sighed. He looked like a man in physical pain. 'I must pray that her captors treat her well and keep her safe. I tell myself that they wouldn't have gone to the trouble of capturing her if they intended her harm.'

'Surely the consuls are advising some response?'

'Many believe the day will soon come when the sun king's men will return demanding tribute and acknowledgement of vassalage. It stands to reason that any agreement would be conditional on return of my daughter. To this end they believe that it is time to start gathering gold.'

Dion's eyes widened with horror. 'They've given up? All because of one warship seizing a citizen, the daughter of the first consul? And Phalesia would give up its independence?'

Aristocles spread his hands. 'Nothing has been decided. A decision will take many days, if not weeks. It is not my choice alone.'

Dion met the first consul's gaze with an intent stare. 'What would you do?'

'It's not about what I would do. We are an Assembly.'

'Pretend you are king for a day.'

Aristocles coughed and turned his head away. When he again met Dion's gaze, Dion saw that the first consul's eyes glistened. 'I know my daughter. She would never allow herself to be any part of Phalesia's loss of sovereignty. She would toss herself into the sea rather than be a bargaining chip. I also know of this sun king, Solon, by reputation. If Phalesia gives him gold he will only demand more. Negotiation is not our best move.'

Dion glanced at the golden chest. 'Why not hide the ark? Put it somewhere safe?'

'We could never do it,' Aristocles said. 'It would send a message that we cannot defend our most sacred relic. The people would never stand for it. We consuls only have the power they give us.'

'Then you must launch a rescue mission,' Dion said. 'The longer you wait the smaller the chance of success.'

'If a Phalesian oceangoing vessel left these waters the Assembly would learn of it. Though every moment that passes takes her further away, I cannot order a rescue, not alone, not without the Assembly's approval. I am working on it, but it will take time. Until I can gather a vote, my hands are tied.'

Dion made sure Aristocles took note of his next words. 'I am not Phalesian,' he said, fixing the first consul with a firm stare.

Aristocles tilted his head. He stayed silent.

'My father has given me permission to travel to Ilea, posing as a trader from Xanthos.'

'To what end?'

'To ascertain the sun king's intentions and capabilities. To learn about these warships and their construction.'

Aristocles stood back and looked Dion up and down, his expression pensive.

'The sun king knows nothing of my people,' Dion continued. 'They wouldn't immediately connect me with Phalesia.'

'Speak plainly, Dion of Xanthos,' Aristocles said. 'What are you saying?'

'The sun king wouldn't suspect me of making a rescue attempt.'

'Your father knows of this?'

'I just arrived. He has no knowledge of your daughter's capture.'

'Why would you help me?'

'Because I believe a war is coming, with the Maltherean Sea as battleground. Because with your daughter hostage the likely outcome is that Phalesia will focus on ransom rather than gearing up for war. Because we in Xanthos need your navy and your men if we are to survive.'

Dion paused to let his words sink in.

'Alone, Xanthos cannot survive against the sun king,' he continued. 'The Ileans have shown their intentions. War will come. We need to get your daughter to safety, to take her out of the conflict. We need to prepare.'

Silence ensued, broken only by the wind whistling on the cliff top and the faint sound of waves crashing below. The glaring sun reminded Dion that time was passing.

'I will pray to the gods,' Aristocles finally said.

At that instant Dion caught fleeting motion out of the corner of his eye. His breath caught as he saw an eagle flying in an arc.

The great bird settled in the air, just a few feet from the edge of the cliff, where it hovered, watching them with intelligent eyes. The eagle spent long seconds simply regarding the two men, and then wheeled away. It flew swiftly away from the temple, in a direct path out to sea.

The two watchers followed the eagle's flight but it never changed course, becoming a tiny speck, and then vanishing altogether.

Aristocles' face was white.

'The omen is clear,' the first consul said. 'War is coming. Go, Dion of Xanthos. My prayers will be with you. Do your utmost.'

He spoke with ragged emotion as he gripped Dion's shoulders.

'Get my daughter back.'

18

The long warship traveled through deep waters that were a darker shade of blue than Chloe had ever seen. Mighty waves pounded at its bow, lifting it up before slamming it into the troughs behind. Sitting at the stern, where she felt the motion least, Chloe looked back toward her homeland, where the vessel's wake left a whitened trail.

It was the second day of travel, and the wake pointed directly to the island of Deos, where they had beached the previous night. Chloe could still see the island now, marked out by the triangular silhouette of Mount Oden. Her sleep had been filled with terror, not only because of the rough men surrounding her, but because of the rumbling volcano, its peak clouded by the black smoke it spewed forth.

No Galean would have chosen the volcanic island to beach on: Mount Oden was the home of the gods, and their whims could never be predicted. Children listened to stories that told of shipwrecked sailors being stranded on the island. Some stories ended with the traveler being sent home, traveling on a cloud. Other times the victim was changed into a goat or a horse.

Chloe's stomach growled, clenching itself painfully. Kargan's men had given her food and drink but she struggled to keep any of it down; she vomited the contents of her stomach whenever she had anything more substantial than a sip of water.

'Lady,' a voice said. Glancing up from pondering the sea, Chloe saw a ragged Salesian with pockmarked skin, crouched on the deck as he looked up at her. 'Here,' he said, holding out something. 'Grapes. From your city.'

She hesitantly took the proffered grapes. There were a dozen of them, green and fresh, still clustered to the vine.

'Eat them slowly, one at a time,' the Salesian said. He spoke with a stilted accent and his manner was fearful. 'It will be good for your stomach.'

'What is your name?' Chloe asked.

'Kufi, lady. I am a slave from Efu, in Haria.'

'Thank you, Kufi of Efu. Do you know where we're going?'

'To the great city of Lamara,' he said. 'Capital of Ilea.'

'Does your family live in Lamara?'

'My family is dead, lady. Killed when the sun king's army sacked the city. My brother and I both fought—'

Kufi broke off, his eyes widening with fear as he turned and saw Kargan approaching. The master of the *Nexotardis* ignored the slave as he scurried away.

'Good,' Kargan said. 'I'm glad to see you eating. The sickness will pass in time.'

Chloe felt her strength return as she ate the sweet grapes. She lifted her chin as she scowled. 'I want you to know that I will escape.'

Kargan chuckled. 'Have you been so fixated on what is behind that you haven't seen what lies ahead?'

He pointed with a thrust of his head and Chloe saw that they were approaching a landmass. A black escarpment formed a long line of spiked peaks as far as the eye could see in both directions.

She couldn't yet see the shore, but this place was dark and forbidding, with gray clouds clustering above while the rest of the sky remained blue.

'Cinder Fen,' Kargan said. 'Do you have the same stories of this place that we do?'

Chloe felt fear climb up her spine. 'It was once the homeland of the eldren,' she said, gazing at the looming cliffs that grew larger in her vision with every passing moment. 'Before they lost the war.'

'That's what the magi say. Do your wise men explain why it is the way it is?'

'They say the magic of the eldren has left it. Only wildren inhabit the area now.'

'The name says it all,' Kargan said, looking ahead with Chloe. 'Cinder Fen. Swamp of ash. Past the mountains is the heartland, though I have met none who have traveled there and made it home to tell the tale.'

Chloe shivered as chill fingers of cold air brushed her bare arms.

'We must beach overnight at the tip of the promontory, a place where our camp will be farthest from the high ground,' Kargan said. 'There will be wild ones all around. Count on that, Chloe of Phalesia.' He stood and looked down at her. 'Escape if the sun god wills it, but I wouldn't try it here.'

Kargan had obviously chosen the place where he would beach the *Nexotardis* well in advance. A finger of startlingly white sand jutted out from the shore, and he took personal command of his vessel, guiding the bireme to the extreme point, several hundred feet from the black rock faces and sheer cliffs. Gnarled black trees skirted the shoreline above the beach, somehow eking out an existence. The wind that plunged down from the mountains was cold, despite the expected summer heat. Inhaling, Chloe smelled the incongruous scent of char.

With the ship beached and the ramp out, Chloe saw that the dozen marines were once more armored, carrying long wooden spears and triangular shields in addition to the swords at each man's waist. They trotted down the ramp and encircled the bireme, facing the mountains, each man warily watching the sky and casting his eyes over the cliffs.

Kargan barked swift orders. The ship was only beached enough to hold her fast against the tide and the oarsmen would stay in their benches, ready to leave at a moment's notice. A sailor grabbed Chloe by the arm and led her down the ramp. With her feet on the crystalline sand, she gazed up fearfully at the mountains, where the darkening clouds swirled as if in the midst of an angry dance.

She was made to sit within the protective circle of the marines as the sun sank into the sea in the west. The soldiers never ceased watching as Kargan sent crewmen out to gather wood.

'Fetch one armful each and then return. If I hear a single man speak of gemstones, I will cut out his heart and feed it to him.'

Soon a growing pile of sticks formed within the circle of marines. Hasha, the lean hook-nosed overseer of the oarsmen who had initially sat with Chloe and her father at the banquet, smoothed his curled mustaches as he knelt and placed some coals from a clay pot under the wooden stack. Before long a fire blazed, and the sailor with Chloe guided her to sit beside it in the sand.

She saw the slave Kufi handing out rations. 'Is fire advisable?' she asked as he handed her a plain ceramic bowl containing bread, olives, and cheese.

Hasha stepped forward and kicked the slave, sending him running, then he seated himself beside her. 'Some of the wildren do not like fire,' he said conversationally. 'Our party is large and we will not have escaped their attention. It is best to use the flames to keep them away.'

'Will it work?'

Hasha shrugged. 'We did not come this way when we left Lamara. We will soon find out.'

Chloe realized she was suddenly ravenous: she tore into the hunk of bread, following it with some tart dried cheese. Away from the rolling motion of the ship, her stomach demanded sustenance to make up for the past days. Hasha ate as quickly as she did and then handed her a water skin. She swallowed mouthful after mouthful of sweet water until she thought she would burst.

'I suggest you get some rest,' Hasha said. 'We may need to leave at short notice.'

Without another word the mustached Ilean handed Chloe a patterned blanket and nestled himself into the sand, wrapping his body in his own covering. Chloe shuffled a little apart and tried to follow suit, but when she closed her eyes the rocking motion returned, making her feel queasy after eating her fill so quickly. She tried concentrating on the crackle of the flames but she was conscious of her vulnerability among so many strangers.

After attempting sleep as a growing chorus of snores drowned out the waves crashing on the nearby shore, she slowly opened her eyes. Kargan was across the fire from her with his hands on his thick stomach, eyes closed, mouth open and chest rising and falling evenly.

Chloe sat up.

With the soldiers in an outward-facing circle and the ship and shore behind her, she began to contemplate escape. Perhaps Kargan and Hasha's words were meant to frighten her into submission. She clenched her jaw. She had never let fear conquer her before.

At that moment lightning flashed in the smoky clouds hanging over the mountains. A dozen winged figures were suddenly visible as they flew across: shapes with the head and shoulders of men but with the rest of their bodies gnarled and reptilian. They were close enough for her to see bones in their outstretched wings. Both arms and legs were clawed appendages. Chloe made a small sound of fright, terrified they would turn and fly toward her.

These were wildren, she realized. She had never seen a wildran before. The thought that these creatures were as wild as wolves and were permanently in this form filled her with dread. She could believe the stories that said they would eat any flesh they could seize, with humans considered prey as much as goats, pigs, or sheep.

Feeling a hand pinching her arm, she saw Hasha sitting up and staring at her. 'What did you see?'

'Furies,' Chloe said.

'Are you certain?'

'Y–Yes.'

'Did they see us?'

'I don't think so.'

Another burst of lightning flashed, though there was no accompanying thunder. The sudden glow lit up the beach for a heartbeat and was gone immediately. The flicker revealed one of the sailors fifty feet from the camp with his ankles in the sea, his hands at his belt as he urinated.

Hasha shot to his feet. Chloe wondered what he was looking at, and then she saw them.

A hundred feet further up the shore, two tall ogres stood watching and assessing. Chloe had seen Zachary in giant form, but these were different in more ways than their slightly smaller size. The silver hair on their bony heads was thin and scraggly. Ragged animal skins hung from their waists. Bare chests revealed hairy torsos and a multitude of scars.

'Get back to the camp!' Hasha shouted to the man in the water.

The man looked back at them, confused, but another flash of lightning made him wheel with fright as he saw the wildren, spinning on his heel so fast he nearly fell into the water. He started to run.

Chloe heard another roaring voice and saw Kargan gesturing to the men. 'Close ranks! They fear steel – show it to them!'

Slaves began to throw more wood onto the fire and Chloe ran forward to help, tossing branches onto the flames until the fire roared. The soldiers clattered their spears onto their shields.

The next time the lightning flickered, the ogres were gone.

Chloe sat back on the sand and wrapped her arms around her knees. At any moment she expected dragons to plunge down from the skies, ripping men into shreds with teeth and claw as ogres attacked the camp in a raging horde.

But the next thing she knew, Hasha was shaking her and light was in the sky.

'Wake, girl,' he said. 'It is time to leave.'

19

The bireme left Cinder Fen as soon as there was enough light to see by, speeding across the water as the men of the crew did their utmost to leave danger behind.

Kargan ordered the pounding drum to set a pace twice the usual rate, and even as Chloe's heart went out to the slaves below decks, she felt relief as the mountains and the black clouds crowning them disappeared under the horizon.

Hasha came up to the top deck and bowed when he reached Kargan, whose hand was on the mast as he scanned the sea.

'Slow the pace, lord? Two slaves are not moving. Even the whip will not raise them.'

'Keep it up,' Kargan growled, never ceasing his exploration of the water. 'We are skirting the Sea of Serpents. Even the *Nexotardis* is not safe from a leviathan.'

'Lord, we will lose more slaves, and we have no replacements.'

Kargan finally turned his gaze on the master of the oars. 'Right now my eyes are on you, when they should be on the sea. Do you need to hear your orders again?'

'No, lord.' Hasha bowed, leaving Kargan to his work and returning below decks.

Her fears now heightened, Chloe moved back to the ship's stern, finding a place near the helmsman where she could be alone, her hands gripping the rail tightly as she inspected the dark blue water. Every darker patch caused her heart to skip a beat; every piece of flotsam made her jump. She took comfort in the fact that she wasn't the only one: every man on deck not fully occupied searched the water with anxious eyes. They were out in the open ocean now, so dark and deep that the sailors muttered among themselves and prayed to Silex for protection. The waves were half the height of the ship. Chloe realized she was so afraid of wildren that she had forgotten about the ship's sickening motion.

Kargan left the mast and traveled to the stern to speak with the helmsman, his booming voice loud enough that she easily heard his words.

'Take her three points to starboard. This is the longest run of our journey, and we need to get to Athos by nightfall, for if we miss the island altogether there's no land for leagues.'

The day passed with interminable slowness, the sun climbing the cloudless sky and hanging directly overhead as the slave Kufi gave Chloe some bread and dried figs. She tried to engage him in conversation again but he shook his head and moved away without a word.

Kargan finally allowed the drum to slow, and every man on the open deck sighed with relief, knowing they were past the greatest danger. As the dazzling orb of the sun fell toward the west Chloe moved her place to stay within the shade of the sail. Her chiton was thick and white, good for warding off the bright rays, but it left her arms bare and her pale skin was already burned pink. She hadn't changed her clothing since the banquet; the hem was dirty and the rest was sweat-stained.

She wondered what her father would be doing to free her. There were over a dozen powerful war galleys in Phalesia's navy – none strong enough to challenge the *Nexotardis* alone, but as a group they would make short work of the Ilean ship. The problem would be speed. Unless winds were exceptionally favorable, no Phalesian vessel could hope to catch the swift bireme.

Unless, Chloe thought, Kargan planned on spending a long time on the isle of Athos.

Her heart sank. It was unlikely. Although Kargan might have plans to make an offering to the Oracle, he would be anxious to return to Lamara after his long voyage and the delays caused by the repairs to his ship.

Thinking of the Oracle made Chloe consider the future, and she pondered her own fate as the day passed. The sun reached the low horizon, sending angular rays across the ocean in long shimmering tapers, and still they had yet to sight land. She thought about Lamara, a city she knew almost nothing about, only that it was the capital of Ilea and home of the sun king. From this city he ruled his empire, which now encompassed most of the Salesian continent. The names of these lands were all strange to her: Shadria, Ilea, Sarina, Haria . . .

Despite Kargan saying that Solon would want to know about Chloe's home, it was obvious that he had taken her on his own initiative.

What if Solon had no use for her? What if he tortured her in order to glean information? Chloe swallowed. She could be married off, beheaded, imprisoned, or given as a gift to the sun king's soldiers.

She fought down panic. She couldn't think like this. She had to escape.

As if on cue, Kargan came to stand beside her at the rail. 'We will stop tonight to make an offering to the Oracle at Athos and rest. Tomorrow night we will beach at Koulis, and we will have crossed the Maltherean Sea.'

'You worship the Oracle also?'

'Of course. The sun king honors the Seer. She is the most powerful of all the magi. For what is more powerful than foretelling the future?'

The sun had now completely set, leaving an afterglow that would soon give way to starlight. Kargan's voice was calm, but his ceaseless scan of the horizon as he searched for Athos betrayed his anxiety.

He suddenly breathed softly, a nearly inaudible sigh of relief. Peering ahead, Chloe saw a dark island rising out of the open sea as Kargan went to give further orders to the helmsmen.

'Land!' a sailor cried.

Athos was one of the most isolated islands in the Maltherean Sea, but it was also large and self-sufficient, beholden to no other nation. As the ship approached Chloe saw a dim blanket of pine trees covering the low ground – it wasn't a mountainous place – interspersed with the occasional patch of oak or cedar. Given the island's reputation as home to the Oracle, she was almost surprised to see that it was so wild; in her mind the isle and the temple were one and the same. Instead it was the sort of environment where one would expect to find deer.

Night descended as they skirted a headland and traveled along Athos's coastline, heading south, passing tiny coves and long sandy beaches, barely discernible in the starlight. Continuing to follow a long stretch of white shoreline with curling breakers pounding on the sand, Kargan took the ship closer to the shallow water, so that she lifted and fell with every line of waves traveling underneath her. Hearing the roar of the crashing surf, mesmerized by the white spray, Chloe hoped Kargan wouldn't attempt a landing, for the waves would throw the ship heavily forward, and she couldn't see how it could be managed without the bireme breaking up.

Then they rounded another headland and came still closer to shore, but the water here was calmer, and Chloe saw that they were heading into a narrow cove. The sudden calm filled her with relief as she realized they must be close to their destination.

The drum pounded as the oars crashed into the water, pulled the ship forward, lifted out, and plunged in once more. Kargan ordered the sail to be lowered.

Peering ahead, to where they would be landing on a strip of white sand, Chloe gasped, gazing for the first time at the sacred site.

The land here was treeless, devoid of any plants at all. Structures of fitted stone melded with the shape of rock and crag to create a place where the manmade and the natural collided. But there was also a third force present, something strange and ethereal, for there were flames everywhere, burning fires erupting out of the rock, the flames all different colors: blue, emerald, crimson, and gold.

Above the beach was a domed hill, shaped like a horseshoe that had been bent out of shape. It rose out of the ground a mile from shore, dominating the area around.

Tall monoliths were erected at various places along the top of the hill, facing the water, a spiked crown of smooth white stones. Each the height of five men, the one thing binding them all together was their precarious position. Chloe couldn't see how they could have been placed at such heights.

Stone temples were set snugly into clefts in the rock and crowned two of the tallest cliffs, but Chloe's eye was drawn to one place above all.

Set into the hill was a cave.

The black entrance, huge and craggy, formed a gaping maw that beckoned as much as it filled her with foreboding. Revealed in the flames, a snaking path of brilliant blue stone led down from the cave, between the fires, ending at a gap in a long stone wall that followed the shore. The message was clear: this path led to one place only.

Chloe tore her eyes away from the cave with difficulty.

Soon the ship was once more beached, the ramp pushed out, and a camp on the sand swiftly made. After eating by the fire, Chloe saw Kargan stand and look up at the wall.

Following his gaze she saw the silhouettes of two robed men standing by the path, just inside the gap in the waist-high stone. Kargan hefted a heavy chest in his arms and began to walk up.

Chloe followed.

She sensed the watching eyes of the soldiers but she hugged close to the tall Ilean as if following instructions, and with a wall cutting the shoreline off from any escape route no one moved to stop her. She fell in just behind the big man and with his attention on the priests he didn't notice her.

After climbing up the beach she soon felt grass beneath her feet, soft and pleasant. Kargan came to a halt just in front of the gap in the wall.

'Kargan, overlord of the *Nexotardis*, master of the sun king's navy and adviser to the ruler of the Ilean Empire,' one of the magi intoned. 'We see you, as does the Seer.'

The two magi were twins, identical in every way. Both had shaved heads and wore white robes belted with black ropes. They were so thin as to be emaciated, giving their features an angular sharpness, all bones and tightly drawn skin. They had sunken cheeks and deep-set eyes.

'I bring an offering from Solon, the sun king of Ilea,' Kargan said.

It was the first time that Chloe had seen him appear anything close to afraid. He bent down and placed the chest on the ground, unwilling to take a single step further.

'Your offering will ensure your night on Athos passes without danger,' the other magus said. 'We will pray to the gods for Solon.'

Kargan bowed.

'Tell your men that none may approach who does not have an offering for the Oracle.'

'I will.'

'And none may step onto the path who does not wish to consult the Seer. Will you step onto the path, Kargan of Lamara?'

Kargan bowed and took a step back. 'No—' He noticed Chloe for the first time. 'Girl, what are you—?'

Chloe had been thinking about her own uncertain future all day. Before she thought too hard about what she was doing, she had pushed past Kargan, made her way through the gap in the wall, and stepped onto the path.

Kargan grunted as he reached out, but his fingers clasped empty air. One of the magi turned his sunken eyes on Chloe.

'You have an offering?'

Chloe unclasped her copper chain. She removed the heavy amulet before returning the bare necklace to its place around her neck.

'I do,' she said, displaying the amulet.

'She must stay with me!' Kargan growled.

The magus closest to Kargan fixed his dark eyes on the bigger man. 'You have made your offering, and so we will ensure she is returned to you. But she has stepped onto the path, and now we will take her to the Seer.'

'I cannot—' he began.

'Do you wish to know the manner of your death?' the magus said. 'For I can tell it to you, Kargan of Lamara. There is no curse greater.'

Kargan shook his head. Relenting, he scowled at Chloe. 'I will wait here.'

'Come,' both of the magi said in unison.

Chloe's heart raced as she followed them up the winding path. She passed flames the color of sapphire that lit the surrounding rock blue, and crimson fire as red as blood. The path was wide and the two magi flanked her on both sides. Thinking about the threat they had made to Kargan, she suddenly felt terrified about what the Oracle would say.

The path continued for an eternity, and then the magi stopped in front of the cave.

'Enter,' the man on her left said.

Chloe walked inside.

The ground was now unpaved but nonetheless she felt smooth stone beneath her feet, sloping deeper into the passage. Water dripped down the rock walls of the passage at both sides, yet the floor was dry and the rivulets followed channels where the walls met the stone, trickling into the shadowed depths. The tunnel curved around sharp promontories but she could see by a fiery glow coming from somewhere ahead.

Taking turn after turn, Chloe saw the light growing brighter and brighter, and then after a final bend she put a hand to her eyes, blinded by whiteness.

Squinting against the glare her vision cleared, and she saw a pure white flame burning in the center of a high-ceilinged cavern. The fire burned without tinder. Chloe smelled a scent she had encountered only once before, when she had slept beside the rumbling Mount Oden.

A woman sat staring into the flame. Her back was to Chloe and all she could see was a hunched figure with pure white hair cascading down her back, stretching all the way to the ground. The woman wore a black robe with long sleeves that covered every part of her skin.

'Come, Chloe of Phalesia.' A sibilant voice bounced around the cavern, coming from everywhere at once. 'Place your offering beside me and then sit with the fire of the gods between us.'

Swallowing, Chloe stepped hesitantly forward and placed the copper amulet next to the woman. Without looking down, she circled the white flame and sat on the hard stone, across from the Oracle.

Chloe looked up.

The flame danced between them, rippling across the Seer's features so that they were hard to make out. Chloe gained an impression of surprising beauty: with startlingly green eyes, the Seer had the delicate features and noble cast to her face that Chloe had only seen before on the statues of Edra, goddess of love, fertility, and children.

'You offer the materia of copper,' the Oracle murmured. Reaching down without looking, she picked up the amulet and tossed it into the fire.

Chloe waited for the copper to melt, but it didn't change at all.

'Stare into the flame,' the Oracle said. 'Open your soul to the fire. Gaze and do not blink.'

Sitting cross-legged on the floor, Chloe gripped her knees as she focused on the white flame. Sweat formed on her brow and her heart rate increased as if a galloping horse was trapped in her chest. Her vision narrowed as she stared until she could no longer see the Seer; she felt she was floating in a sea of darkness, and nothing existed but the pure white fire.

'Close your eyes,' the Oracle instructed.

Chloe closed her eyes, and the feeling of floating free from her body became so strong that she began to panic. But she fought to remain strong and banish the fear. Her breath came in short gasps.

'The gods have accepted your offering. I now pronounce this prophecy.'

Chloe was desperate to open her eyes and see the face of the woman speaking to her as she revealed her future. Her consciousness floated in a void. She could concentrate on nothing except for the Oracle's words.

'You will kill a man you pity. You will desire a man you fear. You will wed a man you do not love. The gods have spoken. Open your eyes.'

Chloe opened her eyes, trembling with dread.

The fire had ebbed. The amulet in the flame was gone.

Chloe could now see the Oracle's face.

The woman's skin was blackened, as if the flesh had been pressed to hot iron. She had no eyes and shifted her head from side to side in the swift movements of the blind. The Oracle put her palms together in prayer. When she did, Chloe saw that her hands were withered and her fingers were like claws, with nails so long they curled back on themselves.

'You may now go,' she said in a rasping voice.

Chloe clambered unsteadily to her feet.

As she fled back through the cave, the words of the prophecy were burned into her mind like a brand on the hide of a beast.

You will kill a man you pity.

You will desire a man you fear.

You will wed a man you do not love.

Rather than bringing clarity to her uncertain future, Chloe felt cursed.

20

Gusts of wind came and went, ebbing and then returning in force, making constant work for the five men who crewed the twenty-foot sailing galley. Tall waves lifted the vessel up and sent it skittering down the far sides. Bursts of spray drenched the sailors, but the sun was bright and the day warm.

Dion manned the tiller, judging the approach of each wave carefully and fighting to keep the boat on course. A fresh flurry of wind pocketed the mainsail and just ahead of him Cob pulled on the rope with his calloused hands, hauling the sail closer still.

The seas were too strong for the oars but the other three crewmen – the youth Riko, the tall broken-nosed brawler Otus, and the wiry middle-aged Sal – kept themselves busy bailing water and following Cob's instructions with the headsail.

'Cinder Fen.' Cob nodded to the brooding landmass dead ahead. 'We'll be there before sunset.'

Dion recalled his mother's warning to stay away from Cinder Fen. But she hadn't known about the capture of the first consul's daughter, and it was by far the shortest course to Athos and then Ilea. Cob knew the terrain, and said that provided they found the jutting promontory affording them a camp a reasonable distance from the mountains, they would be safe. He had beached there three times before.

But wildren were always unpredictable.

As the wind freshened and came more steadily rather than in unpredictable squalls, Dion decided they were making good time. Their destination grew closer, revealing the different mountain peaks and the dark clouds hanging over them. A strip of brilliant white shore became visible.

'Take us no closer,' Cob instructed. 'We'll follow the shore from a good distance until we find the safe place.'

Suddenly Riko stood bolt upright, gripping hold of the mast as he stared out into the sea, white-faced. He shielded his eyes and scanned the water, back in the direction of their wake, his eyes roving wildly.

'What is it?' Sal asked.

When Riko said nothing, Cob roared, 'Speak, boy!'

'A—A serpent. I saw gray scales and a huge arching back.' He turned eyes filled with terror on Cob and Dion. 'I . . . I think I just saw a leviathan!'

'Silex, keep us safe,' Sal whispered.

'Are you certain? Which way?' Cob asked.

Riko pointed to the right of dead astern. Dion turned and stared as every man in the boat squinted at the sea.

'Keep her on course!' Cob growled at him. 'There are enough of us looking.'

Dion's skin crawled as he waited for another sighting. He continued to follow the shoreline, a few miles away.

The moments dragged by. The wooden beams of the boat groaned and he shivered, expecting the timbers to split apart as a serpent struck from below. Despite the old man's instructions he scanned the sea when he could, fighting to also keep the boat lined up against the ceaseless pounding of the waves.

Finally, after a long silence spent searching, Cob called out to Riko again. 'Are you certain, lad?'

'I . . . I think so,' Riko said. He still stood by the mast, clutching the stout pole with white-knuckled fingers.

'It could have been a whale,' Dion said.

'And if it wasn't?' Sal demanded. The wiry man, who had sailed these waters with Cob for half his life, was almost trembling.

'If we're sharing the sea with a leviathan, we need to head in,' Cob said. 'Before it's too late.'

'We should keep sailing,' said Dion. 'Cinder Fen is more dangerous than the open ocean. Everyone says to either camp in force or beach at the refuge. It will be safer farther up, on the promontory, as far as we can get from the mountains.'

'Turn us in.' Cob brought the full force of his glare on Dion. Despite his diminutive size, he could still be intimidating. 'If there's a serpent out there our safest option is to head for shallow water.'

'There's more sailing in the day,' Dion persisted. 'We have to—'

'You've never been to Cinder Fen, Dion. I have.'

'I'm with Cob,' Otus said.

'Take us in,' said Riko.

'Sal?' Dion asked the last man in the group.

'Cob's the best sailor I know,' Sal said, scratching the stubble on his angular jaw. He took a deep breath. 'He's also stayed alive long enough to grow warts.' He nodded to the beckoning shore, close enough to make out the breakers. 'I'm for getting us out of the water.'

Dion reluctantly nodded. He turned the boat so they were angling into shore while Cob let the rope in his hands run freely as their course altered.

Watching their approach, Dion saw that the beach here was narrow, leading up to a stretch of smooth rock before the ground became steeper, eventually becoming black walls and broken ridges like jagged teeth. Tilting his head back he saw that they would be landing just below a cliff taller than the peaks around it. Behind the vessel the sun was drawing close to the horizon, but the glow of late afternoon didn't touch the storm clouds gathered at the mountaintops.

'Sail down!' Dion called. The boat caught a wave and sped forward faster than he liked. 'Everyone out on my command! Stop her from turning and get her out before the water breaks over the stern and fills her up!'

Judging his moment, he finally cried out. 'Now!'

Every man in the boat hopped over the side and instantly was in water up to his armpits. The remorseless waves threatened to turn the boat but the crew took hold and hauled it forward. At the bow, Riko and Otus were in shallower water and had a good purchase. They almost ran as they pulled the vessel forward through breaking waves. Some water came in but Dion saw with satisfaction that they'd done as well as could be expected.

The five men grunted as they lifted the vessel, working to drag her up where the rising tide couldn't touch her. Soon the boat was high on the beach, tilted to the side due to the keel. Dion felt soft powdery sand under his feet as he scanned the cliffs ahead. Beside him Cob was staring up at the sky.

'Look,' Dion said, pointing. 'A cavern. Just above the sand, near the scrub.'

Cob rubbed his chin and glanced down at the boat. 'I'd prefer to stay close to the boat, ready to depart.'

'Stay here,' Dion said.

He ran along the beach while Cob cursed and called after him, telling him to be careful. He reached the bushes and came to a scooped impression in the cliff, not a deep cave, but sandy floored and sheltered overhead and at the sides. Staying only long enough to make a swift assessment, he sprinted back to the group.

'It's safe,' he said. 'And I have an idea. The wildren will see a boat on the beach, but if we take it into the cavern, there's little chance we'll be spotted.'

'As long as we haven't been spotted already,' Otus muttered.

'It's a good idea,' Cob said. 'Only one downside.'

Dion nodded. 'We'll have to take down the mast.'

'Makes it harder for us to flee in an emergency.'

'We can keep the mast inside the boat, and we still have the oars,' Dion said. 'What do you all think?' he addressed the group.

'A cave sounds better than spending a sleepless night watching the sky for flyers,' Sal said.

Otus and Riko agreed.

'Come on,' Dion said. 'Let's get it hidden as soon as possible.'

They were all strong sailors, accustomed to coastal trading where every night was yet another round of beaching at an unfamiliar place, and the boat was designed to be easily lifted. Soon they had the vessel well hidden inside the cave, with just enough room left over for the crew of five to stretch out and sleep.

'No fires,' Dion said as he looked out at the sea and saw it was growing dark. 'It's a warm night. We'll eat a cold meal.'

'Captain?' Riko's voice came from behind him. The youth's face was eager; his courage had returned now that they'd left the water. 'You know the stories. Can we look for gemstones before we leave? We can be careful.'

'No,' Dion said shortly. 'We stay in this cave and then leave as soon as we can see our hands in front of our faces. No man goes out, not until morning. Understood?'

Riko glanced at Otus and then nodded. 'All right.'

'Let's eat and rest. We have an early start tomorrow.'

Dion's dreams were disturbed by whispers, sounds of scuffling footsteps, and low voices at the edge of hearing.

Always a light sleeper, his eyes shot open.

A rumble came from a squat shape nearby; Cob was snoring as always. Sal lay near the old man, his arms folded to form a pillow as he slept on his side.

Dion sat up. It was dark in the cavern and the sky was clouded, but the moon was just over the horizon. The mouth of the cavern was wide, and with his eyes adjusted to the darkness, he swept his gaze over the interior. Standing, he looked at the rear, behind the boat.

With urgency Dion bent and grabbed hold of Cob's shoulder as he started shaking.

'Wha—?'

'Shh,' Dion hissed. 'Wake Sal. Riko and Otus are missing.'

Cob cursed and shot up, clambering to his feet and kicking Sal in the legs. 'Get up. Stay quiet.'

Dion grabbed his bow, placed near his head in case it was needed. Removing the leather cover, he flung the quiver of arrows over his shoulder, taking a solitary shaft and nocking it to the string.

He saw that Cob now held a small axe and Sal gripped a scabbard. Sal took hold of the sheathed sword and slowly drew it, the flat blade making a scratching sound that sent a shiver up Dion's spine.

Dion led his two companions slowly forward. Spreading out, they saw a double moon as the orb's reflection showed a wavering version of its original on the sea. They stepped cautiously down to the water's edge and scanned in both directions.

'There.' Sal pointed.

The two missing men were wandering along the beach, eyes on the ground as they searched for the fabled gemstones. The smaller form of Riko was closer to high rocky ground and Dion watched him lift his head and call to his companion. Otus came running as Riko crouched and then straightened, holding something out in his hand while they both inspected the stone.

'Riko,' Sal hissed. 'Otus.' Neither heard him. 'Can I shout?'

Dion looked at Cob.

'Too risky,' Cob said.

'Come on, hurry,' said Dion.

He started to run, but he was dragged to a halt when Cob grabbed hold of his wrist, arresting his motion.

Three black shapes plunged down from the clouds overhead, flapping wings growing larger in Dion's vision with every passing moment. Their path was clear as they descended on the pair of treasure seekers. Bent over the stone, neither Riko nor Otus noticed.

'Balal save us,' Sal whispered.

His heart giving a lurch, Dion registered the swooping figures and raised his bow, drawing the nocked arrow to his cheek. He chose a target, sighting along the shaft as he let loose at the birdlike creature.

The string hummed and the arrow whistled through the air as it left the bow. But the shot went wide, and the triangle of furies continued their plummeting raid. They were now just a stone's throw above the preoccupied men.

Dion aimed yet another arrow and took his first close look at creatures he'd only ever heard about second hand. Their legs and lower bodies were completely reptilian, with clawed feet and scaled leathery skin all the way to their torsos. Their heads were almost human: aside from the scraggly silver hair and wild eyes they had noses and mouths where they should be, although the jaws were enlarged, with long incisors. The scales rose to a varying degree on their torsos. The fury in the center had shoulders leading to normal arms, hands, and outstretched fingers, while the other two had reptile skin to their necks and wrinkled arms like birds, appendages closer to animals, with claws ready to rend and tear.

Outstretched wings spread from behind their backs, veined and ugly, with the bony framework clearly visible. It was as if as eldren they had been unable to completely change to dragon form, stopping somewhere halfway.

Sal and Cob now cupped hands over their mouths and screamed at the two men.

Dion loosed an arrow at the fury high on the left.

His aim was true and the shaft plunged deep into the creature's back, just below the wings. As the arrow struck, the fury screamed in pain and wheeled away. First Riko and then Otus looked up at the sky, showing the whites of their eyes as they saw the danger.

Sal and Cob ran toward them, weapons held high. They had only halved the distance when the fury with the arms of a man collided into Riko and wrapped him in a deadly embrace, instantly rising into the air with his victim held fast. The youth writhed but was lifted high into the sky.

Dion fitted another arrow as the last fury swooped down on Otus, hitting him hard with sharp claws outstretched. For a moment there was a chaotic tangle of man and creature and then a spray of blood accompanied the creature's cry of triumph as it flew once more into the air. Otus clutched hands to his throat and Dion saw that his face and throat were torn by long gashes. He fell to his knees and slumped, tipping over and sprawling on the ground.

The wounded fury spiraled away, flying raggedly. The other two had disappeared but Dion tracked the remaining creature and then loosed his arrow, striking it in the torso. It shuddered and then fell from the sky, landing hard on the ground nearby.

By now Cob and Sal had reached Otus but there was nothing they could do. Dion ran over to join them, scanning the sky. 'Riko could still be alive,' he panted.

Something large and flailing plummeted from the sky a hundred paces away. It struck the rocks with a sickening crunch. When the group of three ran to the huddled mass on the ground, Dion's heart sank as he saw that it was Riko. The youth's eyes were wide and sightless, blood covering his clothing. He had died before having his first shave.

'We can't stay here,' Cob said. 'We have to leave them.'

'They'll be eaten,' Sal said.

'So will we if we stay,' said Dion. 'We have to go. Quick. Back to the cave.'

The three men sprinted to the cavern. Dion wondered how long it was until dawn. They all threw their possessions into the boat and then exchanged glances, Cob still holding his axe and Sal his sword.

Then Cob looked out at the night and pointed with a trembling hand. 'By the gods,' he breathed.

A pack of huge man-shaped figures lumbered along the beach in the distance, dark silhouettes far too large to be human. They were following the shore, in a path that would take them directly past the open mouth of the cavern.

'They don't communicate, do they?' Sal whispered. 'They're no longer eldren. They're just animals.'

'Pack animals,' Dion said grimly.

'What do we do?' Sal looked at Dion.

'Only the furies saw us,' Cob said slowly. 'There's no evidence they're looking for us. This cave is defensible.'

'We can't take the risk,' Dion said. 'The three of us are going to have to manage the boat.' There was a giant in the midst of the ogres, five feet taller than its companions. The pack was coming closer with every passing moment. Dion met the eyes of each man in turn. 'Better to risk a leviathan than every wildran on Cinder Fen. We have to go. Now!'

21

'Cob, take the front on your shoulders. Sal and I will each lift a corner of the stern.'

'This is madness,' Sal muttered. 'We'll never carry it with just the three of us.'

'Got a better idea?' Dion growled.

'If the boat was on the shore in the first place . . .'

'The furies would still have come,' Dion finished. 'Get moving. Our lives depend on it.'

Each man went to his place and then Dion counted. 'On three. Ready? Lift!'

The open-decked boat had been placed with the front facing the beach. Groaning in unison, they lifted, getting it up into the air and then moving forward. Dion had a crushing weight on his shoulder but he knew that to stop would be to die. His back screamed for him to set the boat down but he set his jaw and kept moving.

'Watch your footing,' he grunted. 'Take slow steps. Move!'

Dion was on the left as they shuffled out of the wide gouge in the rock wall they'd called a cave and made their way over the precarious ground, bare feet stepping over sharp rock.

The pack of wildren on the beach saw them immediately and the monstrous creatures started a lumbering run toward them.

'They're coming!' Dion said hoarsely. 'Let's get off these rocks, but the moment we're on sand, we run too!'

He struggled to keep his attention on his task but his eyes kept going to the wildren. The giant opened its mouth and roared, desperate for flesh. It led the charge now, long strides pounding the ground. It ran faster than Dion had expected for a creature of such size.

'We're on the sand. Run!' Dion shouted.

They almost dropped the boat as they shifted into their own ragged sprint. The boat slipped off Dion's shoulder and stars sparkled across his vision as he lifted it back on. The beach began to slope toward the water.

'Last stretch!' Dion gasped. 'Nearly there!'

He looked over his shoulder and saw a mouth the size of a dinner plate open wide, displaying sharp black teeth as the giant roared again. There were seven in the group; he didn't know how he managed to count them but he did. Though no words were spoken, there was clear coordination to their actions. They were close enough for him to see individual scars on their bodies.

Dion's feet plunged into the water and the sensation was so unexpected that the boat slipped forward and none of them was able to hold it up any longer. It struck the shallow water hard, but the keel held, despite digging hard into the sand underneath.

'Get her off the bottom!' Cob shouted.

Working together they got the boat moving once more. Dion thanked the gods that the tide was coming in as a wave sent water underneath the hull, lifting up the vessel and enabling them to push it forward.

'Get in!' Dion cried.

Cob was short and already in water up to his armpits. With groaning effort, he managed to haul his body over the side. Sal followed a moment later.

Dion ran forward, pushing the boat ahead of him. He gave one final mighty shove and nearly lost his grip near the tiller, but Sal held out a hand and Dion threw himself forward, tumbling into the back of the boat.

He heard a series of unforgettable sounds: the crash of several sets of legs plunging into the water; the roar of the giant; the chorus of grunts from the ogres; bumping knocks of wood against wood as Cob fit the oars.

'The tiller!' Cob called with panicked urgency.

Righting himself, Dion saw that the tiller was hard against the stern. Cob had the oars going but with the tiller angled the boat would turn in circles. He grabbed at the pole and centered the steerage.

Waves pounded at the hull, pushing the vessel back to shore. Risking a glance behind, Dion saw snarling monsters now waist deep in the water, just a dozen paces from the stern.

But Cob had his jaw set and pulled hard at the oars. The light vessel rose over the crests of the waves and drew away from the pack of raging wildren. Looking back, Dion saw the creatures finally halt.

Their prey had escaped.

As the boat reached calmer waters Sal went up front to help with the oars. For a long time they rowed only to increase their distance from shore, and then both the oarsmen slumped in exhaustion.

They exchanged wide-eyed glances.

'Come on,' Dion said. 'Let's get the mast up.'

The sun had risen by the time they mounted the mast and fit the sail, running it up and finally setting the boat to rights. Dion pushed the tiller, turning the boat until they were once more oblique to the distant landmass, still too close for comfort. Wind filled the sail and the sea was calm, as it often was in the early morning.

The growing light banished some of the fear from the previous night. But they had lost two men, and Dion kept wondering what he could have done differently.

'We should never have brought Riko,' Sal said.

'It's bad luck to speak ill of the dead,' Cob murmured.

'He saw some whale and called it a leviathan,' Sal spat. 'We should never have listened to him.'

Cob suddenly released the rope in his hands; his fingers went limp. He stared down into the blue water, then raised his head to look at Dion. His expression was strange, a look Dion had never seen before on the old man's face.

'I wouldn't be so sure of that,' he said.

Dion looked down into the water.

An expanse of serpentine flesh was passing directly underneath the boat. The monster was as thick as the biggest tree and it revealed its entire length to Dion's eyes as it writhed and undulated, faster than the boat it was swimming beneath. The glossy silver scales went on and on, displaying a crest-like silver fin along its spine and a tail like an eel's, swaying back and forth to propel the body forward.

Dion's blood ran cold. 'Serpent,' he whispered.

'Where?' Close to the front of the boat, Sal's movements were frantic as he tossed his head one way and another, peering into the depths. 'Where?' he cried. 'I can't see it!'

'Under the boat,' Cob said calmly. 'We're dead men.'

Not being able to see it was worse than knowing where it was. The serpent was smaller than the one at the narrows. But unlike the eldran who had helped clear the trade route, this monster was wild.

Cob shook his head. 'Something has agitated the wildren in this area. Perhaps the eruption of Mount Oden. Perhaps the passage of the Ilean warship. Perhaps something else altogether.' He met Sal's eyes and then Dion's. 'Pray to the gods. There's nothing else we can do.'

Dion heard a mighty splash to his left, in the direction of Cinder Fen. He caught sight of a curled body, gone as swiftly as it had appeared. The sea heaved, creating waves where the serpent had plunged.

He reached for his bow and quiver.

The three men stared silently into the depths. Dion began to hope it had left.

Then he saw it again. This time he caught full sight of the angular head and spiky frill as it traveled under the ship. He prepared his bow. Once more it vanished from sight. Dion drew in a shaky breath as he waited.

The serpent's angular head suddenly shot out of the water a dozen feet away; in an instant it was heading directly for the boat and its occupants. Open jaws revealed incisors the size of daggers jutting either side of its mouth, yellow with extreme age. Remembering his experience at the narrows, Dion saw that this serpent's eyes were different. Wild. This creature wanted only prey.

Dion had the string against his cheek, anticipating the serpent's movement. As the head came forward, he released.

The arrow struck it in the very center of its eye.

Enraged, the serpent flung itself forward, passing through the sail, cutting a hole and stabbing into the water on the other side. A length of snakelike body came down on the boom, snapping it like a twig until the length of scaled flesh lay across the deck. The mast came crashing down.

The boat's timbers creaked.

Dion grabbed another arrow and shot at the middle of the serpent's body where he hoped to strike something important, but the arrow bounced off the tough hide. With the serpent's long body lying across the deck, he saw the head of the beast circle underneath the boat, blood streaming from the wounded eye and clouding the water as it looped around the vessel.

'It's trying to squeeze the boat!' Dion cried.

Spurred into action, Cob hefted his axe and swung with a strong overhead stroke at the scaled skin. His weapon bit hard, sinking to the haft, and the monster shivered.

The boat's timbers cracked. Water began to seep into the floor.

Seeing Sal too stunned to react, Dion nocked another arrow and stood tall, riding the boat's jolting motion as he waited for the head to appear. He suddenly saw it under the water, just a few inches below the surface, a dozen feet from the gunwale.

The serpent was so fast he knew he would have to lead the shot. In one smooth motion, praying for success, Dion drew and released.

The arrow jutted an instant later from the water, and this time the shaft was buried in reptilian flesh. The head rose to the surface, and he saw that the arrow had struck a soft part on the side of its head. The scaled body lying across the ship trembled again.

His chest heaving, Dion didn't take his eyes off the serpent. But the creature stayed motionless.

Dion turned to Cob. 'I think—'

Something smashed into the bottom of the boat, so hard that it knocked Dion clear off the vessel and tumbling into the water head-first. He managed to keep hold of his bow as he fell, but holding onto his weapon made it difficult to swim. When he finally surfaced and looked back at the boat he felt the blood drain from his face.

The creature he had killed was only a serpent. This was a true leviathan.

Its head was as big as the boat, large enough to swallow the vessel in a couple of mouthfuls. It raised itself slowly out of the water, slippery and scaled, the crest behind the triangular head fully erect. The wildran fixed a baleful stare on the boat's two occupants.

The leviathan opened its jaws and roared.

The deafening noise was the most terrifying sound Dion had ever heard. The teeth revealed in the open maw were the size of swords. Before Sal could react the creature arched its neck and shot down from the sky, snapping him in half with a single bite, spraying the wooden planking with blood.

Cob stood tall and held his axe in both hands. When the leviathan came for him he swung at the monstrous jaw but the creature dodged out of the way, faster than Dion would have thought it could move. Cob's return swing never came.

The serpent's huge mouth opened wide as it plummeted, swallowing the old sailor whole, together with a mouthful of splintered timber and surging water. The creature continued the movement to crash through the hull of the broken sailboat. The force of its passage created a swirling vortex of planks and rope as the vessel disintegrated.

Dion was sucked into the water behind its passage, together with the boat's remains. The paddle-like tail of the leviathan grew ever more distant. He clutched at anything his fingers could find.

22

Dion woke and saw scales.

He had arms wrapped around him, arms that kept his head above water and pulled him through the water with the smooth passage of a creature born to the sea.

His mind clouded and eyes stinging, recollections came back to him in a series of flashing images. The last thing he could remember was grabbing hold of a plank as his body was dragged down deep underwater. At some stage he'd risen to the surface and thrown his body on top of the wood, draping himself over it like seaweed on a rock. Exhaustion overcame him.

Sadness took hold of his heart when he remembered the deaths of his crew, eaten by wildren. Cob was gone. Dion was alone.

Now he was being carried in a strange embrace. He was on his back, head carefully raised out of the water. His body was angled so that he was looking at his feet, which were beneath the surface. Below his legs he could see scales.

The long tapering body under his own terminated in a fish-like tail. But the arms that held him had soft white skin and feminine hands. The tail swept at the water; the arms held him tightly.

Ever so slowly, Dion rotated his head.

Out of the corner of his eye he caught a glimpse of silky silver hair and pale brown eyes, a heart-shaped face with a small chin and pert nose. He tried to turn still further but her pink lips parted and she made a strange shushing noise, her placid face creasing slightly in a frown before returning to an expression of animal-like contentment.

Dion was in the arms of one of the merfolk.

He had heard tales of men being rescued like this, but never believed a word of them. It was always the female wildren – mermaids – who saved drowning sailors, taking them to land and safety. Even now Dion couldn't believe what was happening.

She swam on her back, holding him to her chest. Despite being so close to a wildran, rather than try to move, he was suddenly afraid that if he struggled she would leave him to die in the open sea, which was calm but showed a flat horizon with no sign of land in any direction. He hoped she knew where she was going; she seemed to have a plan.

He couldn't help but wonder what was going on inside her head. Did she think that perhaps he was one of her male kin, wounded and no longer able to swim? Was she intelligent enough to think of it as a good deed?

Feeling something entangled with his upper arm he stared dully at a length of curved wood, finally realizing it was his bow; he'd somehow managed to keep hold of it.

Dion laid his head back on her breasts and stared up at the bright blue sky.

Once more, weariness overcame him.

———◡———

'What do we do with him?'

'You ask the wrong question, brother. How did he get here?'

'He could have swum here.'

'From where?'

'A ship must have come into trouble somewhere near Athos.'

Dion was face down in the sand. Small waves broke over his legs; the tide was rising and he knew he had to move. But he was parched, desperate for water, and his head felt like a thousand hammers pounded against his temples. He groaned.

'He's stirring. Take that weapon away from him.'

'No,' Dion moaned.

He was powerless to prevent strong hands untangling his bow from around his shoulder. Opening his eyes and flinching from the glare, Dion saw an emaciated man in a white robe crouched on the sand, looking down at him. A bald crown topped his triangular head, which was devoid of excess flesh. Dark eyes regarded him from sunken pits.

'I have your bow,' he soothed, showing Dion the weapon.

'And it will be returned to you when you leave,' said another man nearby.

Eyes shifting, Dion saw that the crouching man had a companion, but he realized with shock that the two men looked alike in every way.

'Can you rise?' said a third voice from still further away.

Dion rolled and finally managed to push himself up onto his elbows. The third man was robed just as the other two. His face was the same. There was no way to tell any of them apart.

'Where . . . Where am I?' Dion asked hoarsely.

He tried to lick his lips but his tongue was dry. He needed water more than he'd needed anything in his life.

The crouching man closest to Dion spoke. 'You are at Athos. Not just at Athos, but at Seer's Cove. We are magi, devoted to the Oracle. How did you come to be here?'

Dion tried to speak but simply shook his head.

'He needs water,' said the closest of the standing magi.

'If we give him water, we are accepting responsibility for his well-being.'

'Then that is what we will do.'

'I am not certain this is the right course of action, brother,' the furthest magus spoke. 'He is not here of his own accord. He brings no offering.'

'Wait,' Dion croaked, sitting up and holding up a hand. 'I am here by choice; I simply met trouble on the way. Wildren. I want to visit the Oracle.'

'Where is your offering?' asked the suspicious magus.

Dion thought about the silver coins he carried, sewn into his tunic. He tried to recall everything he knew about the Oracle. 'Here,' he said, lifting up the silver medallion around his neck. 'This is my offering.'

'See?' the two magi regarded their wary companion.

'Give him water, then.' The last man folded his arms over his chest. 'He has chosen to step onto the path. The Oracle will know what to do with him.'

Dion tried to stand, but it wasn't until one of the magi returned with water that his strength returned enough for him to stagger to his feet. He swayed and put a hand to his head until the dizziness passed.

He was finally able to take stock of his situation.

The three magi stood around him, looking at him uncertainly. He was on a beach in a small quiet cove, and just above him a stretch of grassy bank led to a long stone wall. Through a gap in the wall he could see a paved path made of brilliant blue stone. A mile inland was a misshapen hill; the area in between the hill and the wall was dotted with stone temples and rocky knobs.

Aside from the grass in front of the wall, there wasn't a tree, bush, or shrub in sight. And fires burned on both sides of the path.

The flames flickered in a multitude of hues, from bright vermillion to warm gold. Green fires and blue fires burned on top of the rocks, though he could see no kindling beneath them.

White monoliths poked up from high points on the hill. The path curved like a snake and led to the dark mouth of a cave.

'You must now set foot on the path,' the closest of the three magi said. 'And you must not stop until you have entered the cave.' He gestured. 'Go. The Oracle awaits.'

Dion nodded. Taking a deep breath to steady himself, he began to climb, and was conscious of the magi's eyes following him as he passed through the wall and stepped onto the path.

He wondered what the Oracle would tell him about the future. Would she share what the omen of the tremor truly portended? Would she tell him whether there was coming danger for Xanthos? Would she tell him what he should do next?

He concentrated on placing one foot in front of the other and tried to ignore the strange flickering flames on either side of the path. Finally, he reached the mouth of the cave, and before his courage could fail him he walked in.

The cave wound back and forth, initially dark but growing brighter as he continued. Rounding the last bend, he saw that the white light came from a pure flame that filled a circular cavern.

A woman leaned forward; her body was obscured by a black robe but her white hair was so thick and long that it covered her back and formed a fan on the ground around her.

'Place your offering beside me and then sit opposite the flame,' the Oracle said in a soft, whispering voice.

Dion unclasped his chain to remove the amulet with the trident of Silex. He placed it on the cavern floor, beside the Seer, then refastened the chain around his neck. Circling the white fire, he settled himself and looked at the Oracle through the flame.

He saw her place her fingers on the amulet.

'You are . . . You are . . .' she said.

The Seer suddenly shrieked, a piercing sound that echoed through the cavern, shrill and filled with pain.

Dion frowned. He knew little about the Oracle, but he knew enough to know that something was wrong.

He heard footsteps and saw a white-robed magus rush into the cavern. He had the same sunken cheeks and deep-set eyes, but Dion didn't know if this was a new priest or one of the three men from the beach.

'Priestess . . . What is it?'

The Oracle had her head down but she now raised it as the white fire between them ebbed. Dion saw through the flames that she was a young woman, beautiful and pale, with smooth skin and an oval face. She gazed at Dion with piercing green eyes, revealing a troubled expression.

'This man . . . The materia does not respond to him.'

'What do you want us to do?'

'Take him away from me. He interferes with my abilities.' She moaned. 'I want him to leave.'

'Do you want us to kill him?'

'No,' the Seer said sharply. 'I cannot say that his future is dark . . . only that it is beyond my ability to see. Killing him could be a blessing to humanity, or it could lead us all to darkness. The gods decree that we do not seek to alter another's destiny without knowing the consequences are clear.'

Dion was confused. His eyes went from face to face. 'Please,' he said. 'I need to consult with you. Let me explain.'

'Tell me nothing,' the Oracle hissed. 'Nothing!'

'What do you want us to do?'

'I want him gone.'

'But, Priestess . . . He has no way from the island.'

'Then give him a boat.'

'Without provisions we would be killing him just the same,' the magus said.

'Then give him provisions,' the Seer said. 'I want him gone!'

The magus came and hauled Dion forcibly to his feet. He handed Dion his amulet. 'Come,' he said harshly.

'Take him!' the Oracle wailed.

Her voice followed Dion as he was hauled out of the cave. 'Take him!'

When Dion returned to the beach, unsure about what had actually just happened, he saw with surprise that there was now a small boat, bobbing in the shallow water, anchored to the beach with a trailing rope that led from its bow.

He couldn't believe his eyes. He had seen the magus with him make no communication with any other, yet here was a boat, evidently a reluctant gift to him from the magi.

'Your vessel is here,' the magus said after leading him down from the cave. 'You will find provisions inside, along with your weapon. The Oracle has given you a generous gift, but there is a condition.'

Dion turned and met his dark eyes.

'Never return to Athos. The gods are powerful, and the Oracle is their representative in the world of mortal men. Never return to Athos, on your life, and on your soul.'

'I understand,' Dion said.

He stepped slowly down the beach, leaving the emaciated man behind. Suddenly he couldn't take his eyes off the boat.

It was small, not designed to carry more than three men, but wondrously proportioned, sleek as a cat, rakish and lean. Its hull was decorated with alternating horizontal stripes of blue and gold and the unpainted timbers of the interior glistened in the sun, polished to reveal the beautiful grain of the wood. A solitary mast sprouted from her center and there was no line for a headsail, but the material of the white sail rolled on top of the boom appeared as lustrous as silk, and the mast was so tall that Dion knew the slightest puff of wind would send it leaping.

Sailing across the Maltherean Sea meant crossing the open ocean, and typically a vessel of this size would be far too small. But this boat was a gift from the magi of Athos. Dion would trust it more than he would trust a vessel three times the size.

'Her name is the *Calypso*,' the magus behind him said. 'She is yours.'

'I'm traveling to Lamara, capital of Ilea—' Dion began, preparing to ask the magus for guidance.

'Do not tell me of your quest,' the magus said, holding up a hand. He turned to depart, speaking over his shoulder as he left Dion alone on the beach. 'Just never return to Athos.'

23

The reddish land ahead grew larger with every sweep of the bireme's many oars until it came to dominate Chloe's vision, revealing rust-colored cliffs, rocky bays, and promontories that jutted out into the water like fingers.

The sea had changed color, becoming a pale blue similar to the hue of the sky, indicating a shallower depth. Kargan ordered the sail lowered as he took the warship into a wide bay that became a series of smaller inlets.

Soon, Chloe knew, they would arrive at Lamara.

They had spent the previous night beached near Koulis. Although they had never ventured into the city, remaining camped on the shore just below, she had gained an impression of white columned temples of glistening marble, and men and women wearing surprisingly Galean costumes. The palm trees and baked yellow walls had marked Koulis out as different from Chloe's home, but when she asked Hasha about it he explained that the city once saw itself as closer to the Galean nations than those of Salesia.

The sun king had dominated Koulis for several years, however, and yellow flags flew from the towers at the corners of the walls. Kargan had sent a trading party into the city, but kept Chloe under close guard. She had watched them leave enviously, trying to remember what it felt like to be free, but she hadn't complained when they returned hours later with fresh meat, fruit, barley, and bread.

She had crossed the Maltherean Sea, and she was now on the Salesian continent. Soon she would meet Solon, the sun king of Ilea. The thought filled her with dread.

Now, shielding her eyes as the *Nexotardis* headed for its home port, she saw a distant structure on a finger of land and realized it was a lighthouse. Sweeping her gaze in the opposite direction, she saw a second promontory with yet another lighthouse on its tip.

The *Nexotardis* passed between the two structures, miles apart from each other, and Chloe saw more ships ahead, traveling the same way: sailing skiffs and rowing galleys, merchant vessels with bulging bellies, and ramshackle fishing boats.

Another promontory divided the bay in the middle and Kargan led them to the right, following the other ships. Chloe saw that they were entering an inlet, the curling waves colliding with the rushing water of a mighty river. As they passed the central jut of land on the right, she shielded her eyes and saw a huge statue.

It was made of stone and bigger than the lighthouses she'd seen earlier. She recognized Helios the sun god, legs apart and arms at his sides, head tilted back to look up at the sky.

'The statue marks the start of the river,' a rumbling voice said beside her as Kargan joined her at the rail. 'You will see the city soon enough.'

The drum thrummed below the deck, so ever-present that the sound was now at the edge of her consciousness. The *Nexotardis* traveled on oars alone, blades lifting out of the water, sweeping back and dipping in again with endless repetition. There were now banks at both sides, sometimes showing yellow cliffs and other times broken shores filled with boulders.

Buildings appeared on the left bank, mud-brick structures with gaping holes for windows and roofs of stick and straw. Then Chloe saw a wall. It was dusty and red, as tall as the ship's mast and broad enough for men to walk on top. A hexagonal tower rested up against a cliff where the wall met the river, and for a time the wall hid the city within.

Glancing at the other bank, opposing the city, she decided that this was where the poorer people lived, for the huts were crude and crammed close together. Dusty streets marked out one block of huts from another, while on a hill behind she could see regularly spaced trees and fields of grain. There were no bridges; passage between the two sides of the river would be granted by ferryboat only. Every vessel on the right-hand shore was a fishing boat.

As they passed the wall, her attention turned once more to the left-hand bank and the main city.

'Lamara,' Kargan said. 'Capital of the Ilean Empire.'

Structures appeared as they passed the city wall. So many buildings that Chloe struggled to comprehend them all. Lamara dwarfed Phalesia, more yellow than white, perhaps less beautiful, but . . . huge.

The city followed the bank of the river for at least a mile. A series of tiers in the very center marked out a ziggurat, and on the highest level Chloe saw a walled palace, undoubtedly the home of the sun king. The sprawling edifice crowned the city, spearing the sky with tall spires, so thin that Chloe wondered how they didn't topple over. Like most of the buildings around, it was made of red brick, but she could see marble columns and the rust color was further broken by a multitude of yellow flags with orange suns in their centers, snapping in the breeze.

Below the palace was a confusion of two-storied residential blocks delineated by winding alleys and broad avenues. Chloe saw temples of basalt and marble statues, sprawling slums and grand villas. Palm trees clustered here and there, made ethereal by the dust.

'Look,' Kargan said, pointing. 'The bazaar.'

'Bazaar?' Chloe frowned.

'Market.'

She realized he was pointing at a rectangular square located somewhere in the lower city between the palace and the riverbank. Canopied stalls with tent-like coverings of every color imaginable crowded one next to another. Aisle after aisle filled the square, leaving no empty space uncovered. The bazaar of Lamara could have swallowed the Phalesian agora several times over.

As they drew inline with the palace the bank dropped away, curving in an arc of sandy shoreline. Chloe realized it was the city's harbor. She couldn't believe the number of vessels drawn up on the shore, a number that must be approaching a hundred.

Seeing the sun king's fleet, she felt fear stab her stomach. Over half of the vessels on the shore were biremes, all of them as large and powerful as the *Nexotardis*. The powerful warship that had so concerned her father and the other consuls was just one of many.

Kargan stayed with Chloe at the rail, appearing to enjoy her awe and consternation at the sheer size of the city. His men knew what to do. In moments he would be home.

Scanning the harbor, she saw soldiers and sailors guarding the ships and scrubbing the decks. The beach sloped up until it joined the buildings facing it. A sailor exited a hut on the shore, two steaming bowls in his hands, handing one to a friend.

Kargan had a hint of a smile on his face as he regarded her, as if he were waiting for something. Chloe frowned, and looked back at the harbor.

Then, somewhat distant, but so large it couldn't be real, she saw something that took her breath away.

It rose from behind the red buildings, erected on the land further upriver, within the city walls but far from the palace. It was a mountain . . . but a mountain made by men, perfectly proportioned, triangular-faced on all sides. It was the biggest structure Chloe had ever seen.

She rubbed her eyes. She could see shining golden blocks the size of houses piled one on top of the other, describing how it had been made, with each level slightly smaller than the one below. Strangely, two thirds of the way up, the glistening faces ceased and the levels became naked stone all the way to the summit.

The triangular mountain continued to grow bigger in Chloe's vision as they approached the harbor. Where the stones were clad, the mountain shone bright yellow in the sun.

'In the name of Aeris, what is that?'

'It is the pyramid,' Kargan said.

Chloe couldn't take her eyes off it. 'Who built it?'

'Slaves.' Kargan laughed. 'It was built with the pitiful lives of wretches.' He looked at it for a while before sobering. 'Solon built it.'

'What is it?'

Kargan's expression was now grave. 'It is the sun king's tomb,' he said softly.

'And is that . . . Is it covered with . . .?'

'Gold,' said Kargan. 'Pure gold.' He hesitated. 'It might help you to know: the sun king is dying.'

Chloe looked at Kargan's face. He was deadly serious.

'The magi say there is a cancer inside him, robbing him of breath, causing him to cough blood. He visited the Oracle at Athos to seek the Seer's wisdom. The Seer did not tell him what he wanted to hear. She said he doesn't have long for this world, and that he would be dead by the end of the thirty-first year of his reign. When he pressed the Seer, asking what he could do, she said there was only one thing: prepare his soul for the afterlife.'

Kargan was pensive for a time.

'When he returned to Lamara he consulted the priests of all the gods. But only the prayers of the priests of Helios the sun god were answered; only they gave Solon the solution he sought. The sun god says that building this pyramid will assure the great king's passage through the gates of Ar-Rayan to the next world. It must be the tallest structure in the world, and it must be clad in gold. Solon has scoured the continent for gold. You will not see golden jewelry on the women here. Yet his tomb is not complete.'

'What year is it?' Chloe asked.

'It is the thirty-first year in the reign of Solon the sun king.'

He and Chloe both gazed at the distant golden pyramid.

'This year is his last,' Kargan said.

———

Chloe looked back at the *Nexotardis* one final time as Kargan's marines formed an escort for the pair, leading them up from the harbor to the dusty streets of Lamara. Her journey had been an ordeal, fraught with peril, and she still had the prophecy of the Seer burned into her consciousness.

Her greatest trial was still to come.

Led by Kargan, her escort led her away from the harbor along a broad avenue with tall buildings on both sides. These people knew their city, yet the route veered and twisted; there was no clear plan to the streets. She plunged through the bazaar, overwhelmed by the scent of strange spices, stench of refuse, odors of cooking, and sweaty, swarthy masses of hawkers and thronging city folk. The escort kept her moving, clearing the crowd ahead, but it nonetheless took an eternity to exit the bustling marketplace.

Beggars leaned against walls on every street corner. A skinny one-armed Ilean tugged on Chloe's sleeve, but was swiftly repelled by a blow from a soldier's triangular shield. Children with faces pockmarked by disease hid fearfully from the group, tucking themselves into doorways and raising their arms to ward off blows that never came. The soldiers knocked to the ground an old man leading a donkey who didn't hear them coming. Glancing over her shoulder, Chloe saw him wearily struggle back to his feet.

Their path twisted and climbed as they now entered a wealthy residential area, the quarter closest to the palace. The doors here were made of solid wood, barred against intrusion. Chloe was constantly in shade; the sun's rays couldn't penetrate the streets below.

She lost track of how many steps she climbed, and then suddenly she was in a wide, curving street, squinting and feeling bright warmth on her face. They followed the well-paved road, which skirted a high red wall, smooth and tall. The wall curved and their path curved with it.

Thinking constantly of escape, Chloe realized they were following the exterior wall of the sun king's palace. She took note of the height – as tall as three men – and the wooden spikes on top placed every few inches. It was designed to keep intruders out and prisoners in.

She saw an elaborate pillar ahead and then a matching post on the other side, a wide gap between them. A dozen soldiers stood just inside the palace gate, with leather skirts covering yellow trousers and matching breastplates over tunics.

A tall officer recognized Kargan and bowed. 'Overlord. You have been missed. We thanked the sun god when we saw the *Nexotardis* approach. The king of kings wishes to see you.'

'I have a prisoner,' Kargan said gruffly, indicating Chloe. 'She'll need to be readied before I present her to the sun king.'

'Should she be quartered with the women?'

'Until we know what Solon wants with her, that would be best.'

Without another word, Kargan strode imperiously into the courtyard within, his steps bold as he followed a wide path framed by gardens.

Chloe was now alone.

'Come, girl,' the officer said. 'Follow me.'

24

Chloe had neither weapon nor the skill to use one if she had. She was confused and in a strange place. She was determined to find a path to freedom, but for the time being, there was nothing she could do.

The officer handed her to another palace guard, who delivered her to yet another. He took her through an archway draped with a length of silk to obscure the interior. She passed through the gardens just inside the palace wall and then entered a long passage skirting a central courtyard filled with flowering shrubs. She crossed a high-ceilinged atrium that allowed light and air to flood the interior, before following a passage that veered twice at sharp angles.

She now stood outside another curtained entrance while her guard cleared his throat. 'Eunuch!' he called.

A wild-looking man with shoulder-length hair and pockmarked skin pulled aside the curtain.

'What is it?'

'A newcomer. See she is washed and made ready to present to the sun king, should he call for her.'

The tall man rumbled an assent and took hold of Chloe's hand. He was as big as Kargan. Attempting to free her hand would serve no purpose other than to anger him.

'Come,' he said. 'You stink, girl.'

He led her down the hall, past open doorways at both sides, to the very end, pulling another curtain aside to reveal bright sunlight. Chloe exited into a sunny courtyard, where ewers of water stood beside wide basins. Piles of cloth sat on stone benches. Small jugs lined the wall.

'Strip,' the man said.

Chloe swallowed. She scanned the courtyard, seeing a high wall on all sides, with the only doorway the one through which she'd just emerged.

'Hurry up. We're alone here. The curtains mark out the women's quarters. You're safe from prying eyes.'

Still she stood frozen.

'Look, girl,' he said in exasperation. Pulling down his loose trousers, he revealed an abdomen coated with hair that grew thicker as her eyes inadvertently traveled down. He thrust his hips out obscenely and parted the bush of black hair.

Chloe flinched as she saw a gash where his manhood should have been.

He pulled his trousers back up. 'They took it all. You have nothing to fear from me. Now take your filthy garment off.'

She removed first one copper pin and then another, shrugging out of the diaphanous chiton and letting it fall to the floor. The eunuch – she understood the word now – looked on impassively. She felt strange to be naked and standing out in the open in a foreign place. The constant sun of the voyage had tanned her limbs golden, leaving the rest of her body pale as milk.

'Come over here.' The eunuch led her to the nearest basin and without further ado splashed water onto her hair and body. 'The water has been in the sun all day. See? It is warm.'

Chloe nodded as she began to wash away the stains of the journey. The eunuch walked to the wall, bending down and grabbing a ceramic jug before reaching for a horsehair brush. He tipped oil from the jug over the hairs on the brush.

'Lift your arms,' he said.

As she complied, the eunuch started to scrub. His strokes were practiced and neither harsh nor soft, the oil lubricating the brush and foaming as he worked. Chloe turned when he asked and when she inhaled she realized the oil was scented; she recognized rosemary and lavender.

He finished by scrubbing her hair and then completed the ritual by upending a ewer over her head.

'Dry yourself,' he said, taking one of the piled cloths and handing it to her. 'Now come with me.'

'My clothes—'

'—Will be burned,' he said matter-of-factly.

Reaching the doorway and pulling the curtain to the side, he frowned when he saw she wasn't following.

'Did you not hear me, girl? You are in the women's quarters. Your lack of clothing will cause no comment.'

With a sigh, Chloe followed the eunuch back into the interior, dark and cool compared to the courtyard. He led her to one of the side doors and, entering, she saw a large room so expansive that if she threw a stone she wouldn't strike the far end. Frescos of flowers and naked children decorated the surface of every wall. Woven mats covered the floors. Latticed screens divided the area into a multitude of corner spaces, each having a bed pallet and chest. Young female slaves scurried past carrying jugs and baskets. Despite the eunuch's earlier words, they all looked at her curiously. She fought not to cover herself with her arms.

Then a slim boy with short dark hair entered from a hidden doorway at the room's far end, obscured by the screens. He was young, barely out of his teens, and held the handle of a jug in one hand.

Chloe stopped in her tracks. Her eyes shifted to the left and right, but there was nowhere she could hide.

'Master,' the young man bowed to the tall eunuch. 'Her place is ready.' He spoke with a soft, lisping voice. 'By the tulips, in the far corner.' He pointed to a place across the room.

'Good,' the eunuch said. 'Come and see me when your work is done.'

'Of course, master.' He bowed again.

Chloe felt better when he'd gone, though she wondered if he was also a eunuch. She supposed he must be, to be allowed in the women's quarters. He was obviously a slave. It disturbed her that anyone could maim a slave, and one so young.

She was led to a bed pallet no different from any others. The other pallets around her were empty; she had the place to herself. The eunuch pointed to the chest. 'Clothing inside. Dress yourself.'

He turned to depart, and even as she opened the chest and pulled out the first chiton she found, throwing it over her nakedness, Chloe reached out to touch his arm.

'What is to become of me?'

Behind the question, she was wondering how she might escape.

'You are a woman,' he said. 'Your place is here. Women are to be kept hidden.'

'Hidden?'

'Your attributes are beauty and the ability to bear children. You need to be secluded. Unlike men, you have no skills.'

'Wait,' Chloe said, biting her lip in desperation. The prospect of spending her life in this place filled her with horror. Without freedom of movement, and the ability to learn about this city, she would have no chance whatsoever to get away. 'I have skills.'

He shrugged. 'It is no business of mine.' He glanced at the white chiton she'd draped over herself like a bed sheet. 'You know how to clothe yourself?'

'Of course.' She scowled.

'Good,' he said. 'I have my duties.'

He stalked away.

Her heart filled with trepidation, she began to dress.

───────

Chloe sat on a wooden bench in a waiting room. Her thick, near-black hair was now combed until it shone, falling from her shoulders to her waist. Her copper amulet was gone, offered to the Oracle, but she still wore the chain of burnished red metal around her neck. Copper pins held the white chiton draped around her.

The youth had summoned her, handing her to a palace guard at the arched entrance to the women's quarters. She had been waiting for what felt like an eternity. Sweat beaded on her brow, though it was cool in the palace's interior.

Chloe knew she was about to meet the sun king.

The waiting room had guards at both ends. She could hear a rough, booming voice in the opposite direction to the way she had come. Finally, the guard on that side beckoned.

She felt her chest rise and fall as she followed him into the sun king's audience chamber.

The cavernous space was bright and airy, facing the harbor so that a cool breeze ruffled the patterned tapestries spread along the walls. White marble columns held up the ceiling and thick carpets rested snugly one against the other so that almost no part of the floor lay bare. At her right, wide windows allowed afternoon sun to pour through, while the left side displayed a series of arches leading further into the palace's interior.

Palace guards stood ahead of her, still and silent, framing the long rectangular space in the room's center. She recognized Kargan, standing in fresh clothing, facing a golden throne.

The room was sumptuous and exotic, filled with colors of yellow and purple. As she stepped forward and stopped, Chloe was almost overwhelmed by the sight of so much wealth.

'Keep your eyes down,' the guard whispered, standing behind her shoulder.

'—Raiding is a simple matter,' Kargan was saying, 'but complete conquest would be achievable. With a good harbor across the Maltherean, the rest of the world will enter our influence.'

'So you say,' a clipped, precise voice came from the throne. 'Where is she? I think it is time to meet one of these Phalesians.'

Glancing over his shoulder and seeing her, Kargan beckoned.

'Come, Chloe, daughter of the first consul of Phalesia,' he said.

Chloe felt her footsteps sink into the carpets as she walked over. She carefully kept her eyes on the floor until she stood by his side.

She finally looked up at the throne, a high-backed chair with arms in the shape of a lion's limbs, terminating in curled paws. Evidently the sun king wasn't yet desperate enough to melt his throne: it was made of solid gold.

Solon, the sun king of Ilea, who was said to have taken his nation into a new age of glory, was a tall man; even without the additional height of his raised throne he would look down his long patrician nose at anyone he spoke to. Black hair flowed to his shoulders and he had a sculpted, pointed beard. Piercing dark eyes looked at her from under thin arched eyebrows. He had smooth olive skin and his frame reinforced the angularity of his features – he was extremely lean.

He regarded her with a strangely feverish expression that was both hypnotic and fanatical. As the seconds dragged his visage shifted to sardonic amusement.

'Prostrate yourself,' Kargan hissed.

Chloe sank to her knees and clasped her palms together. She realized that this meeting of peoples could have an effect on the fate of her nation.

'Now bow,' Kargan muttered.

She bowed forward, awkward in the movement. 'Greetings, sun king. Were he here, I am certain my father, First Consul Aristocles, would give you his wishes for health and prosperity.'

'Rise,' Solon said. He frowned at Kargan. 'Do all her people speak like this or does she have a speech impediment? I can barely understand her.'

Chloe climbed to her feet and stood uncertainly. 'I have lived all my life in the one city, the place I call home, sun king. My people all speak as I do.'

'I can see, Kargan, that I cannot accuse you of preparing her words and actions. Not only does she not know how to behave in front of the king of kings, I address a question to you and she answers.'

'The women in Phalesia exercise many liberties, Great King,' Kargan said, scowling at Chloe.

She recalled the words of the eunuch. She had to do anything she could to get a modicum of freedom. If she were treated as other women, she would never escape.

'If you are so willing to speak, girl, tell me of your homeland,' Solon commanded.

'My . . . My homeland is a peace-loving nation—'

Solon interrupted her with a wry chuckle, holding up a hand. 'A peace-loving nation with well-trained soldiers carrying good steel, a sizeable fleet of war galleys, a defensible harbor, and stout walls on all sides. Unless, girl, you tell me my loyal servant Kargan is lying?' His amused expression vanished in an instant. 'Choose your next words carefully. The punishment for deceit is death by impalement.'

Chloe swallowed. 'Phalesia is peaceful but powerful. We have a city forming the nation's heart, but several villages give tithe also. Compared to many other Galean states, we are prosperous. We produce the finest ceramics in the world and our silver coins are used as currency from Tanus to Sarsica.'

She stopped there, but Solon nodded. 'Continue.'

'If you return me to my father there can still be peace and trade. We have wine, wheat, barley, marble—'

'What of gold?' Solon leaned forward, his penetrating eyes staring directly into hers. 'Is there much gold in your land?'

'We use silver for coinage—'

The sun king waved a long, delicate hand. 'Whip her.'

'Wait!' Chloe cried. 'We have some gold. Small items of jewelry—'

Solon held up a hand once more. 'Enough. I have no time for her dissembling. I tire.' He winced, and his shoulders slumped. With more time for inspection, Chloe saw dark shadows under his eyes. 'Kargan, you may leave, and the girl also. I will question her at another time to gain her view on the things you have told me.'

He gestured with his manicured fingertips and Chloe saw a guard coming for her. Kargan scowled again at her, leaving the room with angry strides.

As she was led away, she realized she had survived her first encounter.

———◡———

Chloe stayed by her pallet as she'd been told, but there wasn't much to do in the women's quarters. If she was to escape she needed information. She needed allies.

Deciding that she wasn't just going to stay in the one place forever, she ventured past the empty pallets and rounded the latticed screens, checking each corner, looking for someone whose plight resembled her own.

Yet this section of the women's quarters was empty. She wandered, about to give up hope, when she finally passed another screen and found the sole other occupant. She was a young girl, perhaps fourteen, struggling to get out of an elaborate silk robe.

'Here, let me help,' Chloe said.

The girl looked at her strangely but allowed her to assist. Like the women Chloe had seen in the streets she had black hair, but darker skin and high cheekbones gave her a more fragile beauty. Kohl lined her eyes and she had a circle of blue powder the size of a coin on each of her cheeks.

As Chloe disentangled the girl from her garment a sturdy woman in a brown tunic appeared and put a hand to her mouth. She sank to her knees and bowed her head to the floor, slinking along the ground until just two paces away. 'I am sorry, Princess,' the woman said. 'Your slave has done you disservice.'

'Be gone,' the girl suddenly snapped. 'Stand on the tips of your toes with your nose touching the wall until I come and fetch you. If you are not on your toes when I come, I will have the eunuchs whip you.'

Still prostrate on the floor, the slave turned herself around and didn't rise even as she slithered out of view.

'Who are you?' the girl asked as Chloe finished taking off the garment. She asked the question in a peremptory fashion, imperious but not rude. This was a girl accustomed to being obeyed.

Even so, her manner struck a nerve with Chloe. 'I am Chloe, daughter of Aristocles, First Consul of Phalesia,' she said, lifting her chin. 'And who are you?'

'I am Princess Yasmina of Shadria.'

'Why are you here?' Chloe asked. 'Are you visiting?'

'I am a hostage. Is that not that why you are here?'

Chloe bit her lip. 'I don't know why I'm here.'

'Then you are a hostage also.'

'The slave woman,' Chloe said. 'Why did she act like that?'

'Because I am royalty and it is the custom.'

Chloe wondered how she would steer the conversation to gain information. 'Do people treat you the same way in the city?'

'The city?' Princess Yasmina frowned. 'Since my arrival two years ago, I have never left this section of the palace.'

Chloe fought to contain her horror. She couldn't stay in the women's quarters all day, every day. Not if she wanted to have any chance of eventually escaping.

She would have to take some risks.

Lowering her voice, she asked the princess, 'Have you thought about escape?'

'Escape? How would I survive? And if I escaped, the sun king would avenge himself on my people. My presence here keeps my people safe.'

'I worry that by being here I'll prevent my people from being strong and standing up to the sun king,' Chloe said. 'I plan to escape.'

She heard a man clearing his throat. Turning, she saw the tall eunuch, watching her with Princess Yasmina. He was far enough away that she was sure he hadn't heard.

'Leave me out of your plans, please,' the princess murmured. She raised her voice. 'I thank you for your help, Chloe of Phalesia, and I bid you good night.'

25

Chloe spent the next days in the women's quarters. She tried to engage Yasmina in conversation but there was little common ground between them, and even when she persisted the imperious princess didn't warm to her advances. The once spacious apartments began to feel cramped and staid. As she paced restlessly, the passing slaves stared at her, puzzled by her inability to settle and calmly accept her fate.

The eunuchs brought food three times a day and there was a constant supply of fresh water. The exterior garden provided somewhere to get some fresh air but she was always accompanied. Chloe was well rested and had fully recovered from the journey.

She replayed her last encounter with Kargan and the sun king over and over in her mind. He had asked about gold, and when she had said Phalesia possessed just a few items of jewelry, he had become angry.

She had to protect the secrets of her home, but the Ark of Revelation was no secret. And evidently the sun king wanted it.

Just after midday on the third day, the summons came once more.

This time she didn't have to sit in the waiting room; the palace guard led her directly to the throne room. Kargan wore a different robe – a crimson garment belted with golden cord – but he stood in the same place as before. Guards still protected the golden throne. Archways behind revealed a sunny terrace with a stone rail.

There were differences, however. Courtiers stood on both sides of the throne: six swarthy men with groomed beards and flowing robes in a variety of materials and colors, apparently arranged around Solon in order of precedence. The breeze from the harbor was close to non-existent, and the day was hot and humid. Sweat beaded on Kargan's brow and Chloe's palms felt sticky.

Solon wore a robe of golden silk and a delicate crown of gold spikes on his head. His long dark hair was sleek as the pelt of a cat and his pointed beard was now curled in front of his chin. Chloe walked up to stand beside Kargan, before kneeling and touching her forehead to the ground.

'Rise,' Solon said.

Glancing up at him as she returned to her feet, she saw he was more at ease than before. He still gazed at her with strangely hypnotic eyes and he was still so lean that his face was made entirely of sharp angles. But he appeared to be less troubled. She figured it must be the ebb and flow of the pain caused by his illness.

Kargan, by comparison, looked uncomfortable, as if he wished he were anywhere else.

'Chloe, daughter of Aristocles,' Solon said in his curt, clipped voice. 'I have questioned Kargan at length and I believe I have learned all he has to tell. I will now ask you some questions, and I have asked that he remain present.' He didn't take his eyes off her. 'If your answers do not match with his, then we will have a problem. If I believe you are deliberately hiding information, then we will have a problem. If you are too brief, too meandering, too obtuse, or simply too stupid to understand what it is I wish to come to the heart of, then we will have a problem. Do you understand?'

'Yes, sun king,' Chloe said.

'If we have a problem, then blood will flow,' he said. 'I ask you again, do you understand?'

'Yes.' Chloe nodded, her heart racing and fingernails pressing into her palms. 'I do.'

With the lords of his court looking on, Solon proceeded to ask Chloe questions about Phalesia. He asked her about the geography, the region's natural resources, the produce of the workshops, and the system of governance via the consuls of the Assembly.

Chloe answered truthfully and succinctly. Despite the sun king's threats, she didn't volunteer more information than he asked of her, which meant she had to think swiftly to send his inquiring mind in directions that would interest him but wouldn't compromise her city. When he asked her about mining she emphasized Phalesia's lack of a gold mine rather than highlighting the steady output of the silver mines. As he asked her about the manufacture of weapons she spoke of the proud warrior tradition of Xanthos, remembering Kargan's interest at her father's dinner table. He kept her talking, and she kept her posture respectful and her expression earnest, but all the time she avoided answers that made Phalesia appear overly weak or temptingly wealthy.

When he asked her about the city's layout she spoke at length on her city's beauty and grandeur, elaborating on the proud temples and expansive agora.

'Yes, yes,' he said impatiently. 'But tell me more of the city's defenses. A bastion rises up from the shore, does it not?'

'We have a sloped wall guarding the city,' Chloe said. 'Climbing up to the city from the water means ascending one of two narrow stairways.'

'And the army . . .? How many soldiers does your father command?'

Chloe knew exactly how many men were under Amos's command. 'I . . . I am a woman, sun king. I know nothing of military matters.'

'Kargan?' Solon frowned at the overlord of his fleet.

'It may be as she says, eminence,' Kargan said. 'I know that the Assembly consists only of men, and that while women and men share meals together in the home, it's likely she has little involvement or interest in war.'

Solon nodded curtly. 'Then, girl, tell me of this ark.'

Chloe had been expecting this. 'The Ark of Revelation was a gift from the gods. It was not constructed by men.'

'But it is a chest of solid gold, the size of an ox cart?'

'Y—Yes, it is gold. But to defile the ark would bring down the wrath of the gods. It must always reside at the Temple of Aldus.'

'This Aldus is not a god we worship in Ilea,' said Solon. 'We share Helios, the sun god, most supreme and mighty of all, and it is in honor of Helios that we build the golden pyramid. I fear Helios, as all men must. But I do not fear your god of justice.'

'It is sacred,' Chloe spoke up, knowing she was taking a risk. 'Inside the ark are the laws that a man is weighed by when Aldus decides whether to grant him entrance to heaven.'

'Then why not open the ark and discover the laws?' a lord with a wide golden belt around his girth asked.

'Because to know the laws is not the intention of the gods. A man must choose his path and develop his own moral code. He must rely on himself and the words of the priests to discover what the laws are.'

Glancing at the six courtiers, Chloe saw they all had puzzled expressions on their faces.

Solon's voice increased in volume as he addressed the entire room. 'I am the sun god's representative in this world and any justice is mine to dispense. Are there any here who disagree with my words?'

When silence was the only reply, the lean king nodded.

'I will take this ark for the gold it is made of,' he stated. 'As my soul prepares for the coming journey, I grow closer to the sun god, who now speaks through me. I decree that we have nothing to fear from the false god Aldus. Our decision is now whether to ransom this girl for the ark or to seize it by force, adding another nation to our dominion in the process.'

Chloe felt a shiver along her spine at the sun king's words.

'Kargan,' Solon addressed the big man, standing impassively with his legs apart. 'You advise attacking Phalesia with speed, before alliances can be made and defenses strengthened.' The king's dark eyes swept over the group of lords. 'Others among you advise leaving the far side of the Maltherean Sea to pursue its own destiny while we expand and consolidate our empire here on the Salesian continent. There is only one other option.' Solon turned to Chloe. 'Girl, would your people trade you for the ark?'

'No,' Chloe said, refusing to let them make the attempt. 'They would not.'

'So we should attack your homeland? Kargan tells me the ark alone will make the effort worthwhile.'

'I do not want you to attack my homeland.' Chloe hung her head as she said it.

Solon tugged on his pointed beard. 'I will think on the best course of action. The pyramid is near completion. We will soon have gold foil covering three quarters of its surface. Phalesia is far, but the prize is assured.'

'King of kings . . .' Chloe said, looking up to meet his gaze. 'What is to become of me?'

As he framed a response, she waited for the words that would decide her fate.

'You have pleased me,' Solon finally said. 'And any son you bear may be useful if we expand across the sea. You are of noble birth.

Are you not being treated in the manner to which you are accustomed?'

'I have no desire to be secluded.'

'You would rather risk your life and honor in the world of men?'

'Yes.'

'Why?' Solon frowned.

'I have many skills,' Chloe said. 'I gain fulfillment from employing them.'

'Skills? What skills do you have?'

She chose her words carefully. This was her one chance to gain some freedom of movement. 'Writing,' she said. 'Music. Crafts. I am a skilled weaver. I can shape metal into jewelry. I assist with ceremonies.'

'You are a priestess?' a short bald man in an orange robe asked.

'No,' Chloe said. 'I trained at the Temple of Aeris, but I'm not a priestess.'

She could see that all of the men were curious about her life, so different from the lives of women in Ilea.

'And what did they teach you at the temple?' the same short man asked.

Chloe had a sudden flash of inspiration. She realized she might have something to offer the sun king, something that would give her the opportunity to go out into the city.

'I learned the wisdom of healing,' she said, her eyes on the sun king. 'I know many medicinal plants and healing techniques.'

Solon leaned back and once more tugged on his beard. 'Healing?'

'Yes, king of kings.'

'My magi tell me I have a cancer. The Oracle at Athos tells me I do not have long for this world. Can you heal me?'

'I can ease your pain.'

'The magi say that the pain is my soul gradually slipping through the jagged gates of Ar-Rayan to the next world.'

Once again she chose her words carefully. 'Your magi are correct,' she said. 'But there are potions I can give you to ease your passage.'

'Lord—' one of the courtiers protested.

Solon held up a hand. 'How can I trust you?' he asked Chloe.

'You hold my life in your hands. Your power threatens my homeland.'

His brow furrowed. 'I will seek the guidance of the sun god.'

Chloe clasped her palms together and gave a small bow.

Solon glanced to his left, looking out the open windows at a clouded sky. 'I must pray now. Leave me. All of you.'

———

The tall eunuch – Chloe had yet to learn his name – fetched her from the women's quarters just a few hours later.

'Dress for the city,' he said. He nodded toward the clothing chest. 'Cover yourself in a shawl.'

Throwing the thick material over her shoulders, she followed him to the curtained entrance to the women's quarters, where he handed her over to two palace guards. Soon she was heading to the palace's main entrance. Chloe tried to memorize the layout and locations of the guards as she followed her escort, in case she needed to come this way when she made her escape.

Passing through the main gate and heading out into the city, she wondered where the guards were taking her as they traveled with purpose through the narrow alleys and winding streets, passing through wealthy residential districts and following the steps down to the lower city.

She had come through the bazaar when she first arrived, but she now saw that she was heading in the opposite direction. Houses gave way to workshops and then to strangely deserted streets. Then, as they passed through a gate, Chloe saw that they were now in a district of temples.

Priests in yellow robes walked past with stately steps, never the type to hurry, something that was much the same in Lamara as it was in Phalesia. Columned entrances led into the dark interiors of temple after temple. They followed a broad boulevard until she saw a group assembled at the very end, where the ground dropped away in a cliff.

She saw Solon standing beside a priest in ornate white and yellow robes. A dozen soldiers stood a respectful distance away. He was gazing down from the cliff at the land below.

As she drew up to him and saw the object of his attention, Chloe's eyes widened.

The golden pyramid was on a dusty plain, lower than the ground around it, so that it was even larger than she'd originally thought. Slaves now swarmed over it like flies on a piece of meat, scurrying under the direction of bare-chested overseers with whips. Scaffolding surrounded the stones close to the pyramid's peak. Although the afternoon wasn't bright, with gray clouds overhead, the golden slopes of each face nonetheless glistened. Chloe wondered how much gold she was looking at. She'd worked with gold foil before and knew it could be beaten until it was thin as a blade of grass. Regardless of the thickness, in the history of the world it was surely more gold than had ever been assembled in one place.

'King of kings,' one of the soldiers in Chloe's escort said. 'We have brought her.'

Solon turned as she bowed. He was so lean and tall that he towered over her. Up close, she could see that his eyes were sunken, with gray skin underneath.

'Behold, Chloe of Phalesia,' Solon said, gesturing to the pyramid. 'This is the gateway to the afterlife. Helios has spoken. The pyramid must be completed before my death.'

'Sun king,' Chloe said hesitantly. 'Could you not still enter without it? Don't people enter paradise without a pyramid?'

'Are you a devout person?' he asked.

'Yes, sun king. But I worship Aeris, goddess of music and healing. I don't understand . . .'

'There is one belief we share: when a man dies his deeds are weighed. I am the ruler of a great empire. I have taken Ilea into a new age. I have done good deeds and I have done things that may be considered cruel. I must never show weakness. It is no easy feat to unite five nations into a single empire.'

'Perhaps if you atoned . . .'

'Atoned?' he asked, curious.

'It means to make a change. To do good deeds in order to restore the balance of one's life and gain entrance to heaven.'

He barked a laugh. 'It is an interesting idea. But I prefer to deal with absolutes. This guarantees my entry and I can continue to be the ruler I must be, suppressing rebels and building a civilization that will stand the test of time. I have brought peace and wealth to almost all of Salesia. If I let that fall into chaos because of soft-heartedness and weakness, would that not weigh against me?'

Chloe gazed at the pyramid. She tried to count the bare stones, but soon gave up; all she could see was that, while there were more surfaces of gold than those unclad, there were still many remaining. 'But will you ever have enough gold?'

'There are nations in the east still unconquered. There are tributes I await. There are places across the Maltherean Sea, places like your Phalesia.' He suddenly looked exhausted by so much speech. 'Enough. The gods have spoken to me. Slaves!'

Chloe frowned as she saw slaves coming forward, each carrying an item in his or her hands. She realized what the items were as they placed instruments onto a mat on the ground nearby. She saw lyres and trumpets, tambourines and citharas, with an astonishing variety of each. Some were big and some small; there were instruments displaying fine workmanship while others were ancient relics.

'The gods have revealed a way to test your skills and your training. You listed music as one of your talents. Take your instrument and play. If the sun god is angered here, in this place, we will know.'

Chloe knew she wasn't being given a choice. She scanned the assortment until she found a copper flute, a little larger than she was used to, but not dissimilar to her own.

'Play,' Solon instructed as she crouched to pick it up.

Chloe straightened, swallowed, and put the mouthpiece to her lips. She began to play.

The first notes were uncertain and Solon frowned, but then she found her rhythm. As she had done so many times before, she made herself forget about where she was, playing for herself alone. Closing her eyes, her chest rose and fell as she played a song of her own devising, moving up the scale to find the key she felt most accustomed to with the unfamiliar instrument.

Each note bled into another as she used a breathing technique she had learned at the temple to make continuous sound without interruption. Her cheeks ballooned as she used a last puff of air at the end of each breath to inhale the next, evacuating the air in her cheeks to eke out the music while she expanded her chest.

Finding her key, she moved into the 'Ballad of Aeris', a song about the goddess's love for the heroic warrior Korax. When Korax died defending the Temple of Aeris in Sarsica from the ravaging of northern barbarians, Aeris tried to bring him back to life but his wounds were too dire even for the goddess. Her heartbreak was evident in the low bass while the trickling away of his blood formed a sad lilting melody of high notes.

Chloe opened her eyes as she approached the end of the ballad. She saw that Solon was watching intently, his expression thoughtful but giving nothing away. The dark clouds overhead had continued to gather, casting the pyramid in shadow.

Without halting, she continued on to the 'Tragedy of Aleuthea', a complex song describing the sinking of the great king Palemon's civilization beneath the waves. It was at the limit of her skill to execute the dancing trills and low throaty rumbles. Without the words, she had to tell the story entirely with the flute, hearing the stanzas in her mind but conducting them with her instrument.

Still Solon merely watched, and now Chloe made up the melody as she went, eyes once more closed, her fingers working furiously on the flute, combining mournful low notes with bright trills, adding a repeating coda to her song and weaving it through. She slowed and then filled the air with a series of long, slow, drawn-out notes in a minor scale.

Finally she let the music fade away and opened her eyes. As she took the flute away from her lips the clouds parted and the sun shone directly through the gap, striking the glittering pyramid's facets where one side met the next. The diagonal line formed by the meeting point flared with golden fire.

Chloe forgot all about the music as she stared in awe at the glistening gold, so bright her senses could take in nothing else.

Solon nodded. 'The sun god has spoken. It is a good omen.'

He didn't look at her; his eyes were on his tomb. Chloe felt suddenly drained.

'I will give you your chance. You will be assigned a bodyguard. Each night you will be confined with the women, but you may venture into the city to get the materials you need to make your potions. You may leave.'

He made no mention of the music. Solon continued his inspection of the pyramid, frowning at the places where the stone was bare.

26

Dion had sailed through two days and two sleepless nights, determined not to return home in failure. His vision wavered as he kept the *Calypso* on course, trimming the sail and sending the incredible vessel leaping over every crest.

When he sighted land, he knew he had finally crossed the Maltherean Sea.

But finding Lamara was another task altogether. He knew that if he headed directly south from Athos he should strike the coast higher than the city, and should be able to travel, hugging the shore, until he came to the sun king's capital. Yet he was worried, for he had little knowledge of what he was actually looking for.

He passed the third day scouting inlets and rocky bays, brow creased as he looked for the signs of a city. His only encouraging thought was that Lamara was reputed to be huge, and must therefore have fishing and trade vessels leaving and returning to the city in numbers. But as the day wore on and the sun passed the sky's midpoint, beginning to fall back down to the horizon, he wondered if he'd missed Lamara altogether.

Then he saw a ship.

It was a distant merchant vessel, with a fat belly and wide beam, but he could tell from the set of the sails which way it was heading, and he followed the same course. Keeping a wide distance between them, he skirted the rust-colored coastline until the merchantman turned to head toward shore.

A wide bay opened up ahead, and when he saw a tall lighthouse at the extreme end of a promontory he felt his hopes rise. At the opposite end of the bay another lighthouse marked a safe passage between the two and now he saw more ships, all heading in the same direction.

He spurred the *Calypso* forward, getting every bit of speed from her that he could. Overtaking the merchant ship, he saw that the other vessels were all heading into a wide inlet. A gigantic stone statue appeared on the left bank and Dion recognized the sun god.

His spirits soared. He had come to the right place.

He now saw galleys and fishing boats, dozens of vessels returning to safe harbor before the day's end. Heading into a wide brown river, he passed tiny coves and the occasional shack. A huge wall rose ahead, the longest and tallest he had ever seen. He stood up in the boat, holding onto the mast as he peered at it, though the city behind was mostly hidden behind.

Dion decided not to venture closer; he would hide the boat outside the city.

He worried about the danger underneath the *Calypso* as he turned into shore and scouted an inlet, before changing his mind and deciding the place wasn't hidden enough. A second cove was worse still, rocks poking up from the water making the peril clear. Finally he found a little bay, curving in on itself, a mile or so from the high city wall. Scraggly bushes grew along the sides of a little stream with steep banks on both sides, a place he knew he would be able to hide his boat.

He dropped the sail and allowed the *Calypso* to gently coast to the rocky bank. Moments later he was out of the boat and pulling the vessel into the stream, shoving the bushes aside. He fetched his bow – the string was ruined, but the bow might still be serviceable – and a satchel with supplies. Placing them on the bank, he then resumed his work to conceal the painted hull, not content until the *Calypso* was well hidden in the cleft where a casual observer wouldn't notice her. He would be leaving the same way he came.

With his bow in the satchel, he climbed out from the bay until he was on open ground high above the river, looking at the indomitable city wall, with hexagonal towers at regular intervals along its length.

He reminded himself of his quest. He needed to learn what he could about this land, about its ruler, warships, and army. He had to find and rescue the first consul's daughter.

Back in Xanthos, Nikolas would be building up the army. His father, King Markos of Xanthos, would be trying to arrange a military alliance with Phalesia. Taking Chloe made clear the sun king's hostile intentions. He desired the Ark of Revelation. He was a war king, a ruler of conquest. He would return.

Back in Phalesia, the Assembly would be preparing to appease the sun king, which would only prove their weakness. Aristocles would be aware that his daughter's life hung in the balance, even as he tried to convince his people to prepare for war.

Dion started walking toward Lamara. On the way, he began to think how he might gain entry through the city gates.

In the end, nothing could have been easier.

He simply reached a dusty road, joining throngs of people of all description, and walked through Lamara's wide gates.

He had seen the ziggurat as he approached and marveled at the walled palace on the highest tier, evidently the residence of the sun king. A triangular peak in the distance, on the far side of the city near the river, filled him with bemusement as to its purpose. The massive city walls went on and on, yellow and ancient. Initially concerned, as his gaze took in the crowd entering through the gates, he realized what a cosmopolitan city he was walking into, the bustling heart of an empire.

Aware that he was staring at everything around him, Dion lowered his gaze and tried to walk with purpose as he followed the crowd onto a wide boulevard with two-storied brick houses on both sides. When the road forked he took the left fork, though he had no idea where it led. The crowd now thinned and he rubbed his chin as he stopped in his tracks.

'Lodgings?' a piping voice called from nearby.

He ignored the query as he tried to formulate a plan. Something tugged on the sleeve of his tunic and, glancing to the side, he saw a small boy looking up at him, grinning hopefully.

'Lodgings?' the boy said again.

He had a round face and eager smile – a small urchin with a snub nose and dazzlingly bright white teeth. He wore loose, dirty trousers and a tight vest. His brown eyes sparkled from underneath tousled strands of black hair.

'You need a place to sleep? You want something from the bazaar?'

Dion shook himself loose. 'Not interested,' he muttered.

He continued up the road and climbed a series of steps, deciding to try to get closer to the palace. Turning into an alleyway, he wrinkled his nose at a smoky stench and saw two youths huddled in a doorway, furtively passing a pipe between them. They were both stick thin; in another place Dion would have assumed they were deathly ill. One sighed with apparent exhaustion, slumping as he let out a stream of thick smoke while another leaned back and stared at the sky as if seeing deep meaning above.

The youth with the pipe looked up, saw Dion, and scowled, revealing a face with a feverish cast. Deciding to try a different path, Dion went back the way he came. Glancing over his shoulder, he saw that the youth had returned his attention to the pipe.

Dion climbed until he emerged onto another avenue, home to a small fruit market. His stomach rumbled at the sight of all the bright fruits and vegetables. The magi from Athos had gifted him with food, but he hadn't had a proper meal since leaving Xanthos.

He realized he was standing in the wrong place when the people shopping at the market scurried out of the way and a marching column of soldiers in yellow cloaks pushed through. Narrowly avoiding them, he inspected them carefully as they passed. They wore leather skirts over cloth trousers and leather breastplates above tunics. Each carried a triangular shield and a spear, with a curved sword at his waist, longer than the swords worn by the hoplites of Xanthos. These were professional soldiers, he saw. His brother's warriors were better armed, but the sun king's men marched in tight formation and their hands were scarred from regular practice.

Dion's bow was in his satchel but he had seen several Ileans with swords at their sides. He decided he would be safe to carry his bow openly, if he needed to.

Resuming his climb as he searched for the palace, he left the square and followed a steep road leading to a wealthy residential district. Heading up to the ziggurat's highest tier, he finally came to a tall red wall the height of three men. A wide road followed the wall, curving with it, and he knew he was skirting the exterior of the palace.

He traveled along the wall, looking for the entrance, noting the sharp wooden spikes at regular intervals along the top. He walked for a time but still couldn't see any gates. Rounding a corner, he stopped and stared as the ground ahead dropped away, revealing the lower city all the way to the wide brown river.

He struggled to take in what he was looking at now. He saw the residences of the nobility give way to workshops and then a broad boulevard with gates dividing it from the city. The section within the gate was evidently a temple quarter, but it was the immense structure between the temple quarter and the river that drew his gaze.

A perfectly proportioned pyramid rose from the dusty plain of the city's outskirts, but still within the guarding walls and towers. Although Dion had traveled in Phalesia, Sarsica, and the islands of the Maltherean Sea, he couldn't believe mere humans were capable of building such a thing. Only the worn obelisks said to be remnants of the vanished Aleuthean civilization rivaled it in size, but they were ancient, and this was new.

He could see slaves climbing scaffolding and huge stone blocks on platforms of wooden logs hovering in the air, work teams lifting them by means of pulleys. He suddenly understood the sun king's obsession with gold: most of the blocks were faced with shining yellow metal, set against the stone steps both horizontally and vertically, cladding the pyramid's exterior.

The sun king must have exhausted every treasury in his empire. Every ingot from every mine must have fed his lust for the precious metal. It was either the greatest folly the world had ever seen, or a creation of utter simplicity and beauty. No matter which it was, it demonstrated the sun king's power for all to see.

Dion watched for a time, seeing priests in yellow robes standing near the overseers with whips directing the work. As he looked at the intense activity he tried to come up with a plan.

He needed to spend time in the city, preferably somewhere he could watch the palace. No doubt its gates would be guarded, so it was probably for the best that he hadn't stumbled across them. He had a few silver coins sewn into his tunic, but he would need more if he intended to remain longer than a couple of days.

Dion turned around, and there was the young boy from the main city gates, watching and smiling as he hovered near a side street. He had his hands out, showing he meant no harm. The boy looked a little fearful as Dion approached, but he was bold and persistent, and stood fast.

'What's your name, boy?' Dion asked.

'Anoush, master,' he said, clasping his hands together and making little nodding bows.

'Anoush, I need a place to sleep. Somewhere not too expensive but close to the palace. I want a high room where I can watch the city.'

Anoush nodded enthusiastically, smiling so that little dimples formed on his round cheeks. 'The House of Algar. Please, let me take you, master. You will have very fine views.'

Dion wondered if he could trust him. Anoush was about thirteen, and although he was skinny his clothes weren't the ragged garments of a beggar, which meant that he was either a good thief or a resourceful guide.

'Where are your parents, Anoush?'

'Parents are dead, master. I am an orphan. I came to Lamara when I was six. I know the city well. I can help you with anything you require.'

Dion rubbed his chin. 'We'll start with lodgings and take it from there.'

'Come.' Anoush took Dion's hand and started to lead him down the side street. 'It is not a long way. Come, come.'

The House of Algar was well located within the nobles' quarter, not far from the palace. The roofs in the area were crowded close together, each building either leaning against the next or joined

215

together, making the alleys a maze of twisting pathways. Dion saw a three-storied terraced house with a set of cleanly swept steps leading into a dark, cool interior. It was on the same side of the palace as the city gate and he nodded approvingly; he may need to make a swift exit. There was nothing to mark it out as a guesthouse other than a representation of a man lying on his back carved into the stone near the entrance.

'The House of Algar,' Anoush said proudly. 'Come.'

'Wait,' Dion said. He hesitated. 'Can I trust you, Anoush?'

'Yes, master.' The boy nodded.

Dion unpicked the three silver coins from the rough pocket sewn on the inner hem of his tunic. He showed them to the boy. 'Will these be accepted here?'

Anoush frowned. 'Strange coins.' He held out his hand. Dion placed a Phalesian silver coin into his palm. The boy bit onto it and examined the imprint of an eagle pressed into one side to demonstrate that the coin was solid. 'Good silver, though. Algar will accept them, but if he says he will not I can change them at the bazaar.'

'How much should I pay for the room?'

'Algar will ask for one of these silver coins, for one week's lodging.'

Dion smiled. 'But how much should I pay him?'

'Less than that.' Anoush grinned.

He finally made a decision. 'Anoush'—he put out his hand—'the first of these coins is yours. I want you to be my guide. I need my money changed and I need fresh clothing and a razor.' After giving the boy the coin, he indicated the composite bow poking out of his satchel. 'I also need to visit a bowyer. Can you help me with all that?'

'Of course!' Anoush beamed. 'I am the best guide in all of Lamara.' He looked down at the weapon and then up at Dion. 'Are you a warrior, master?'

Dion hesitated. 'Yes,' he finally said. 'I am a warrior.'

'Are you here to find work in the sun king's army?'

'I'm not sure.'

'Where are you from?'

Dion scratched the stubble on his chin. 'From one of the islands in the Maltherean Sea.'

'Which one? Ibris? Amphi? Tarlana?'

'No,' Dion said. 'Further than that.'

Anoush shrugged. 'Come,' he said. 'I will now take you to the bazaar. We will return to the House of Algar after.'

As Dion followed his new guide, he pondered the palace and the first consul's daughter, and wondered what his next move should be.

27

It was morning, rising heat filling the narrow alley as Dion waited in front of the House of Algar. He now wore clean clothing: strange brown trousers and a white tunic to his knees, the garb of Ilea. He had a quiver over his shoulder with a dozen sharp arrows inside, and the bow in his hand had been serviced the previous day. Anoush had proven his usefulness.

Hearing footsteps, he turned and saw a slight man with streaks of gray in his black beard exiting the guesthouse. Wearing expensive flowing garments of thick wool, Algar registered surprise when he saw Dion waiting.

'My friend, can I be of service?'

'No.' Dion shook his head, giving Algar a polite smile. The guesthouse's owner charged a premium for everything, even washing water. 'I'm just waiting for my guide.'

Algar lowered his voice. 'Save your coin. Please know I can arrange anything you require. For a mere two silvers—'

'I have everything I need, but thank you,' Dion interjected.

'I would not trust that boy too much.' Algar frowned. 'He is not a bad lad, but my prices—'

Then a small figure rounded a corner and came into view. Anoush grinned as he carried a steaming wooden cup and nodded to Algar before holding it out to Dion.

'Tea, master. For you.'

Smiling stiffly, Algar gave Dion a small bow before heading off down the street.

'What about you?' Dion asked Anoush.

'I do not like tea,' he said. 'But try it. You will like it.'

Dion sipped at the drink and wondered who could want such a hot drink on a baking hot day. Not wanting to offend the boy, he sipped until he drank to the bottom, then when he finished he was surprised to find himself feeling refreshed.

'See?' Anoush looked up at him hopefully. 'You like it?'

'It's good.' Dion smiled.

'I asked about the man Kargan for you,' Anoush said. 'He returned some days ago on the bireme *Nexotardis*. No one knew anything about a captive princess.'

Dion nodded. He hadn't expected Chloe's arrival to be common knowledge. 'You have done well. Here.' He gave Anoush three of the copper coins he'd received as change after paying for the room.

'You have already given me silver. It is too much.'

'Take them,' Dion insisted.

'Thank you, master.' Anoush hid the coins somewhere in his trousers. 'How can I help you today?'

Dion thought about his plan. Anoush had given him the idea. He needed time to learn about Lamara and for that he would need money. He had to find a way to learn about the sun king's fleet, for any attack would come from the sea.

'I want to enlist in the sun king's service.'

'In the army?'

'The navy.'

Anoush pondered for a moment. 'Come,' he said. 'We must go to the harbor. It is past the bazaar. Stay close to me, there will be many people in the streets. I will watch for thieves and beggars for you. Keep your money close.'

———⌒———

The harbor was a mile-long stretch of shore filled with beached vessels of all descriptions. It formed a natural curve in the river, within the city walls, and most of it was fenced off from the city by a long wall of vertical wooden poles.

Dion stopped for a moment, Anoush at his side, as he gained his bearings. Two soldiers guarded a gap in the fence leading to the naval section, where bireme after bireme rested side by side, so close together they were almost touching. An empty stretch of shore at the end would be where the marines practiced their skills. Past the cleared area two huge wooden vessels were under construction, covered by a confusing framework of wood. Sailors scrubbed decks and marines trained with sword and shield. Smoke rose from the corner of a long thatched structure and Dion guessed this was the mess.

Outside the fenced-off section were beached merchant ships and bare-chested men carrying sacks from various vessels to the paved area above the shore, assembling piles of goods of all description.

'You must go in there.' Anoush pointed to the guards standing at the gap in the fence. 'I will not be allowed so I will wait.'

'We can meet later,' Dion said.

'No, master. I will wait.'

Taking a deep breath, Dion walked down a series of steps to where the paving stones became sand and approached the two guards. Unlike the soldiers he'd seen the previous day, these men had wooden spears without iron points and carried lighter, smaller shields. They were both swarthy, with sleeveless leather cuirasses leaving muscled arms bare.

'What's your business?' the guard on the left said. He had a neatly trimmed beard and curly dark hair.

'I want to enlist,' Dion said.

The guard nodded his head. 'Go and see one of the captains.'

They made way and Dion entered, running his eyes over the multitude of warships and dozens of marines at training. He counted ten biremes and then made a guess at how many there were in total. Fifty . . . perhaps even sixty, he realized with wonder.

A bald man in a blue robe stood with his legs apart and arms folded over his chest as he watched two marines making stabs at each other with spears. Twenty paces away a pair of archers shot arrows at distant straw targets. Dion was relieved to see that the sun king's captains employed bows. If he was tested for his swordsmanship, he would never be accepted.

Dion walked over to the bald man, guessing he was a captain. 'I want to enlist.'

'Don't need anyone,' he said without looking. 'Find someone else.'

Turning away, Dion wondered who else he should approach. He shielded his eyes as he saw the shipbuilding sheds, where a stocky man stood directing some slaves.

Seeing an opportunity to learn about the warships' construction, Dion walked over, discretely watching from behind the stout, muscular man as he gruffly ordered the slaves to hammer wooden dowels through an expanse of planked flooring.

He decided that if Xanthos were to build a navy they would first need to make some of these sheds, sunken into the ground and stepped at the sides so that workers could access the vessel from all quarters. He saw that they would need a great deal of timber; but there were countless pine trees in the mountainous wilds near the

Gates of Annika. People would need to learn specific tasks: from cutting the planks into regular sizes to warping them so they would bend. Currently Sarsican or Phalesian shipbuilders built vessels for Xanthos. That would have to change.

He watched in fascination, then realized that the stocky man was looking at him. He also realized that the man was a woman.

'What do you want?' she barked.

Her hair was cut close to her scalp, a look that Dion had never seen on a woman and was so unfamiliar that for a moment he was stunned into silence. Exposure to the sun had bleached her hair near white and at the same time tanned her skin to a reddish brown.

'I . . . I'm here to enlist,' Dion said, finally finding his voice.

She proceeded to growl a series of rapid questions. 'What's your name?'

'Dion.'

'Where are you from?'

'A small village on an island in the Maltherean. You won't have heard of it.'

She grunted. 'What are your skills, Dion of No-land?'

'I'm a good sailor. I'm skilled with a bow. I can ride a horse.'

She scratched a white scar just under her right eye. 'Ever shot from a chariot, Dion?'

He frowned. 'No.'

'Can you drive a chariot?'

Dion's frown became even more furrowed. 'No.'

'Not sure if you've noticed, but horse riding is about as useful to me as the ability to drive and repair a chariot.' She strode over and looked at the bow he clutched. 'Give it to me,' she held out a hand.

Dion handed it to her.

'Strange weapon,' she said. 'Nothing like what I'm used to.' She held it up at the sky. 'Short. Different materials shoved together. Doesn't look like much.'

She tested the draw and gave a slight sound of surprise, then handed it back. Her brows came together. 'Who did you steal it from?'

'I didn't steal it,' Dion said firmly.

'Your family rich?'

'Something like that.'

'Yet you somehow end up here in Lamara, looking for work in the sun king's navy.'

'Family feud,' Dion invented.

The stocky woman grinned. 'And it's clear you're not the one who inherited your father's wealth.' She changed tack. 'Have you ever hunted wildren, Dion?'

He thought about the fury he'd killed on the shore at Cinder Fen, and the arrow he'd placed in the head of the coiled serpent before its larger cousin arrived. 'Yes.'

'All right,' she said. 'I build boats as well as sail them, so I'm busy now, but come back an hour before sunset. Ask for Roxana. Everyone knows me.'

Roxana suddenly turned and swore as she saw something the slaves were doing on the boat. Considering himself dismissed, Dion began to walk away.

'Oh, and Dion?' she added.

'Yes?'

'Let's hope you're brave. The reason I need men is because I lose so many. But the sun king pays good bonuses for dead wildren.'

She grinned, and Dion left her to her work.

⌣

Dion's room was on the third story of the House of Algar. It was simple but clean, with a linen bed pallet stuffed full of straw for sleeping and a small chest for possessions. A thin curtain covered the window and the room was high enough to provide a view of the streets around the palace and block some of the city's noises and smells.

He spent the day watching from his window, wondering if the fates would smile on him and he would see the first consul's daughter. He examined passing groups of soldiers and countless women in shawls and veils, but when late afternoon came and he hadn't seen her he wasn't surprised.

He pondered time and again what Kargan and Solon would have done with her. Chloe would have been questioned, undoubtedly, and with such men questioning often involved torture. But would they torture the first consul's daughter? If they harmed her they would lose some of their negotiating position. Surely she would be in the palace, safe and well.

But he wasn't certain that their plans involved using Chloe as a bargaining chip. If all they wanted her for was questioning, or if Kargan had taken her on a whim with the sun king having little use for her, she could already be dead.

Dion abandoned this line of thought. He had to assume she was alive.

Realizing it would soon be sunset, he attempted to make his way to the harbor without Anoush to guide him. He was glad he'd given himself plenty of time, becoming lost until a tea seller gave him directions. He arrived at the naval yard just in time, as a radiant orange sun dropped to within a finger's width of the horizon.

Passing through the guards, he found Roxana standing close to the water's edge on a cleared patch of hard sand, directing slaves to place straw targets at set distances from a line of red rope. As Dion approached she gave him a short nod but continued with her work. Nearby he saw two other archers, both dressed in similar tunics and trousers, but carrying bows that were plainer and longer than his.

Away from the red line, a dozen armed marines watched with arms folded over their chests.

Dion shielded his eyes as he examined the archery range Roxana was preparing. The first thing he realized was that, intentionally or not, she had set it up so that the archers would be staring into the sun. The first target was at thirty paces, the second at fifty, and the third at seventy.

Breathing slowly and evenly, Dion began to pace, stretching his arms over his head and swinging them to loosen his muscles. He circled for a time before coming to a halt near the two Ilean archers. One looked at his bow curiously, but neither made a comment about his appearance: there were plenty of men in Lamara who could pass for Galeans, so unless they heard him speak, Dion barely stood out.

Dion saw that both men had kohl under their eyes, applied thicker than even the most brazen street harlot. Roxana came over with a cloth in her hand, black on the tip.

'Here.' She handed it to him. 'Use it, you fool. It will help your aim against the sun.'

Not about to argue, Dion took the cloth and rubbed the kohl under each eye in turn, before handing it to a waiting slave.

'All men – or women'—she grinned—'here to enlist, come stand behind the red rope. Everyone else, back!'

When she wanted to, she could bellow as loud as any officer in the army of Xanthos. It was a talent that would serve her well on the deck of an eighty-foot-long bireme.

'Dion? What are you waiting for?'

Realizing he was the last to step forward, Dion took a place in between the two other archers. Roxana walked along the line of three men, staring into each face as she spoke.

'I've chosen shooting into the sun because on the sea, the sun shines twice. Once in the sky and once on the water. You'll often be blinded. So if you feel like complaining about the test'—she gestured at the city with her thumb—'get away from here, I don't want you.'

She waited for a moment, but when no one moved, she nodded and continued.

'The sun king pays archers well, but you have to provide your own equipment. If you fail this test you can still apply to fight with spear – you'll be paid less but your armor and equipment will then be loaned to you. There's no place in the sun king's navy for paid oarsmen. War has been good to the king of kings. We have plenty of slaves.'

Roxana ran a hand over her short bleached hair as she paused to take a breath. Dion fixed his gaze on the closest of the round straw targets. At thirty paces, he could make out the individual bands. If he wanted to learn more about the biremes and their construction, and to get the money he would need in the coming days, he had to strike as close as he could to the target's center.

'Nock your arrows. I will tap you on the shoulder and then you will draw and release. I'll be judging how swiftly you release after I tap you – speed and accuracy are both important.'

Dion's quiver was at his feet. He bent to pick up an arrow and fitted it to the string.

'We start with the closest target. Failure to strike at thirty paces means you're out. I take only the best.'

Roxana circled behind the archers and tapped the man to Dion's left on the shoulder.

The Ilean archer drew the string to his cheek and held it for a breath. A moment later the arrow whistled through the air, plunging into the straw target halfway between the center and the circle's perimeter.

Roxana grunted. 'Passable. Faster next time or you're out.'

Dion sensed Roxana moving, but he kept his attention on the target, allowing his eyes to unfocus as he waited for the instruction to shoot.

He felt a rough clap on his shoulder blade, and in one swift movement he pulled back on the string, sighted along the shaft, and released.

Lowering the composite bow, he whispered a curse as he saw that while he was closer than the man to his left, he was three inches from the center.

The third archer loosed his arrow a moment later and struck the target an inch closer than Dion's arrow.

Dion frowned. He had to do better.

'Next target!' Roxana cried. 'Fifty paces!'

The extra distance meant Dion struggled to focus on the target's center. He spoke a prayer to Silex in his mind, the familiar words calming him.

Roxana pounded the archer on Dion's left on the back almost before she'd finished speaking. The Ilean pulled and held for a long time as he struggled to regain his composure. Finally releasing his arrow, he clipped the edge of the target but missed making a solid strike.

The archer sighed.

'Loose more quickly and strike the final target properly or you're out,' Roxana growled.

Dion forced himself to breathe evenly. He squinted into the bright orange sun made hazy from dust. The target wavered.

'Draw!' Roxana bellowed in his ear, at the same time slapping him on the back.

The unexpected sound shocked him into drawing without thinking and loosing in less time than it takes a man to clench his fist. Dion's heart raced as he peered ahead to see the strike.

He soundlessly thanked his brother for the gift of the composite bow as he saw that his arrow had struck the circular target in the dead center.

'Well done,' Roxana said.

She clapped two meaty hands on the back of the final archer. He fumbled as he drew and his shot went wide, the shaft skittering along the hard sand of the beach as it lost its energy.

'Not even close,' she said. 'You're out.'

With slumped shoulders the man on Dion's right scowled at his two fellows and left.

'Final target! Seventy paces!'

Even Roxana seemed to know that distracting tricks weren't fair at such a distance. She tapped the archer on Dion's left gently on the back. Knowing he had to be swift to be accepted, the Ilean drew smoothly and sighted in a heartbeat before loosing.

But his arrow struck the ground just in front of the target.

'You're out.'

Dion's pulse was racing. As he bent to pick up another arrow his arms felt tight and his shoulders sore. He looked down at the ground – squinting into the sun made his eyes water.

The tap on his shoulder came an instant later.

Dion pulled and sighted, loosed and lowered. The watering of his eyes made him look down before he'd even had a chance to see where he'd made his strike.

He heard a roar of appreciation from the watching soldiers. Finally, looking up, Dion saw a white-feathered shaft sprouting from the center of the straw target. He lowered his bow as Roxana came to stand in front of him, her legs astride as she folded her arms over her chest and grinned.

'Congratulations, Dion of No-land. You have gained entry as a marine archer in the sun king's navy. The pay is two silvers a week, but acts of courage lead to bonuses starting at an extra silver. A dead wildran can buy a night with a woman even more comely than me.' Her gaze flickered to the onlookers; she grinned as a raucous laugh greeted her words.

With the test over, the crowd began to disperse. Turning suddenly serious, Roxana took Dion by the arm and spoke for his ears alone.

'Listen, Dion . . . I can tell you're new to the city. There's a warning I give all my men. Spend your money on women, drink, or even boys – it's yours to spend. But if you're offered tar of heaven, stay away. You might have noticed the wretches in the streets. Their lives are no longer their own. And if the sun king's soldiers catch them in the act . . .' Roxana shook her head. 'Understood?'

Dion remembered the group of hiding youths he'd seen with the pipe. He didn't know what tar of heaven was, but he had no desire to find out. 'Understood.'

'Good. Return tomorrow for orientation. Your real test will come soon.'

28

Chloe navigated the bustling bazaar, weaving around people in a bewildering array of costumes. Wealthy nobles stood encircled by private soldiers, given an enviable buffer from the heaving crowd. Old women in shawls glared at her as she pushed past; the locals, accustomed to the market, were unwilling to give ground to anyone. Strange sweet scents rose from stalls selling colorful spices, with bright powders and fragrant herbs displayed in baskets. The jabber of conversation and cries of hawkers created a cacophony of sound. The air was hot and sticky, so that she sweated in her chiton and wished she wasn't forced to wear a shawl over her shoulders.

Beside her at all times – stern and unyielding, never letting her out of his sight for a moment – was her bodyguard, Tomarys.

Chloe glanced over her shoulder; he had no difficulty keeping up. He towered over her, easily the largest man she had ever seen. He was neither lean nor stocky, but had broad shoulders and a heavy build, with muscled arms as big as Chloe's legs. He was brown-skinned and had whip scars on his shoulders, wounds she would never have the courage to ask him about. His face was broad, with thick lips and a wide mouth, a rounded nose, and deep-set eyes. Tomarys's black hair was tied behind his head with a leather thong.

He wore a brown leather vest, open at his hairy chest, and coarse linen trousers. She couldn't see any weapons, but it was obvious why he was a bodyguard. Her task of navigating the market was made infinitely easier by the man beside her radiating both strength and deadly grace.

Chloe finally had the freedom to enter the city, but she knew she could never escape Tomarys. Her only option was to befriend him.

'You are a eunuch?' she asked, looking up at him.

'Yes,' he grunted. 'All who watch over the women must be.'

'You are from Ilea?'

'From Lamara. This city is my home.' He scanned the bazaar, looking for threats. 'Stay close. There are thieves in this area. Thieves and worse.'

Chloe had already run out of conversation; she had a difficult task ahead of her if she wanted to learn more about him. Her thoughts instead turned to her purpose in the market.

She had gained some freedom, but unless she could ease the sun king's pain her liberty would be revoked. Intuition told her that Tomarys would never help her escape. But with freedom, an opportunity might come.

They passed the spice market and entered a section of ceramics. Glancing at the stalls and the countless varieties of jugs, bowls, plates, amphorae, vases, urns, and cups, Chloe decided that Phalesia possessed far greater skill with pottery than the nations of the Salesian continent.

'Tell me about your family,' she said.

'My father is dead. My sister cares for my mother. My brother is a slave working on the pyramid.'

'A slave?'

'He incurred debts he could not pay. I hope to buy my brother's freedom. Why are we here?'

Chloe realized they would soon be at the end of the bazaar. 'I'm looking for something.'

'If you tell me what you are looking for I can help you.'

She hesitated, but she realized she wouldn't find what she needed without help. 'I need to find the soma flower.'

Tomarys suddenly stopped, gripping Chloe by the upper arm as he stared down at her. 'You don't mean to obtain tar of heaven?' He shook his head. 'It is outlawed by decree of the sun king.'

'No,' she said. 'I only want the flower. Among my people, it has been used for generations to ease pain. It is safe if prepared correctly, I assure you.'

Tomarys released Chloe's arm, but continued to scowl at her. He wasn't convinced.

'Please, trust me,' she said. 'The tar and the flower it comes from are different things.'

He shook his head once more.

'Tomarys, the sun king will no doubt have someone taste any medicine I give him. I have no wish to be killed.'

He rubbed his chin. 'You follow the goddess of healing?'

'Aeris is my personal deity. I studied at the temple.'

'You are certain?'

'I am. I don't want the tar, only the flower.'

He finally nodded with reluctance and led her back the way they had come, turning into a thin path between a cluster of stalls until they were in a hidden section of the bazaar. This area was seedy and ramshackle, with beggars sitting against the walls and skinny youths standing lookout. A street urchin weaved around them, almost circling, his eyes appraising as he inspected the newcomers, assessing the potential for threat. But Tomarys, despite his appearance, was unarmed, and Chloe posed no danger.

Tomarys waited for the boy to nod, and then led Chloe to an old man with pockmarked skin and a hooked nose, standing outside a wooden hut and drinking tea.

'Tell him what you want,' Chloe's bodyguard instructed.

'I want soma flowers,' Chloe said.

'You want tar of heaven?' The old man looked at Tomarys and then back to her. 'Show me your coin.'

'I don't want the tar,' she said. 'I want some of the flowers.'

'What for?' He looked down his hooked nose and scowled. 'It is the tar you want.'

'Just the flowers,' she insisted.

He scratched at his cheek as he considered. Finally, the old man nodded. 'Wait here.'

She glanced at Tomarys, seeing that he appeared surprisingly nonchalant, but wondering if it was an act. Her instincts told her that she needed to be wary. She felt comforted by her escort's towering presence.

The old man returned, emerging from behind the shack and beckoning. 'Follow me.'

The pair fell in behind him. The hut covered the approach of a narrow lane, with high stone walls on both sides. The pockmarked old man continued to beckon them forward, into the boxed alley.

'This is a dangerous place,' Tomarys muttered. 'We should go.'

'You serve me?' Chloe tilted her head to look up at him.

'I do. I must protect you. I must also keep you close, and never let you out of my sight.' Tomarys's voice became deeper, a rumbling growl. 'But girl, do not think we are friends. I will do my duty and no more. If you try to escape, I have orders to recapture you, or kill you if I must.'

The lane was long and curved, so that it was hard to see what they would find at the other end. Eventually, they saw light. The old man had now vanished, and a boy who couldn't have been older than seven stood waiting for them.

'Two silvers,' he said.

Tomarys took a pouch from his belt and counted out the coins, handing them to the boy.

'Wait here,' the boy instructed. Leaving them still a dozen paces from the alley's end, he exited and soon vanished.

'I doubt we'll see him again,' Chloe murmured.

'Look,' said Tomarys.

The boy returned. Glancing around him, looking past the two figures to see if anyone lurked behind them, he handed Chloe a leather pouch.

She started to open the pouch.

'Not here,' the boy hissed.

She opened it anyway. Within were two plump flowers, somewhere between fresh and completely dried, with petals closed. Noting the purple-yellow coloring and pale green stem, Chloe nodded.

The boy departed without another word.

'Back to the palace,' she said.

'I hope you know what you are doing,' Tomarys muttered.

29

It was late in the women's quarters as Chloe sat cross-legged on her bed pallet, with only the light of a few flickering torches to see by.

Tomarys slept nearby on a woven mat, lying on his back as his chest rose and fell evenly. He was covered in just a thin linen sheet, but at least the night was warm. He'd told her this was an improvement compared to his last sleeping quarters.

Given her bodyguard's reactions, Chloe had decided it would be best if she worked at night. Tomarys had fetched a mortar and pestle on their return, and one of the flower pods was still in the pouch, hidden under the pallet.

The other was in the bowl-shaped mortar on her lap. Keeping her movements quiet, Chloe used the pestle to grind the bulb, working over the broken bits of plant again and again. She recalled the instruction she'd received at the Temple of Aeris in Phalesia and knew that the finer the particles became, the more surface area would be exposed to allow the pain-relieving agents to be extracted.

She worked the pestle tirelessly, her muscles becoming sore as she turned the flower pod into an unrecognizable cluster of fine hay-like particles. Finally deciding she was finished, she set the bowl beside her bed pallet. Before retiring, she checked the pouch with the last flower to remind herself it was safely hidden.

Then Chloe lay on the pallet, staring up at the ceiling.

She closed her eyes and went to sleep.

———

Chloe woke suddenly, certain that she'd been sleeping only for a few hours, her senses groggy and sleep in her eyes. Something had hold of her ankle.

The room was dark and the night still and quiet. Tomarys crouched over her; he had his hand on her foot and had been shaking her.

Sitting up, she saw that there was another man present, a slim Ilean in a plain white tunic, standing with his back at an angle to her, eyes averted. Wondering at his posture, Chloe realized he wasn't supposed to be in the women's quarters. To bring him here, his need must have been urgent.

'What is it?' Chloe whispered.

'I am Carin, one of the stewards. The king of kings is in terrible pain,' he said. 'The magi cannot help him. He has asked for you.'

Chloe rummaged in her chest and quickly threw a garment over her sleeping shift as the robed man spoke.

'Of course,' she said. She picked up the bowl full of crushed soma flower and moved until she was facing the steward. 'Take me to him.'

Tomarys followed as the steward led her out of the women's quarters to a part of the palace she'd never been to before. Passing through the silent courtyards and carpeted corridors they stopped at an ornate archway. Two palace soldiers stood guard outside.

'Enter,' the steward said to Chloe. He indicated Tomarys. 'He can wait here.'

Her heart pounding as she held the bowl in her hands, Chloe walked through the doorway.

She entered a huge bedchamber dominated by a four-poster bed with the mattress held above the floor by a frame of wood and cloth strips. Barely taking in the tapestries and carpets, the windows facing the harbor and the luxurious bed linen, Chloe's gaze went immediately to the man lying on his back on the bed.

Solon was on top of the tangled linen, eyes wide open as he wheezed. He wore a silk robe on his lean frame and had both hands over his sternum.

A magus in yellow hovered near the bed on the far side, turning his dark stare on Chloe as she entered with the steward behind her. Beside him she recognized one of the lords from the throne room, a short bald man in an orange robe.

Knowing she must project confidence, she turned to address the steward. 'I will need an empty cup, a jug of very hot water, some fine silk, honey, and lemon.'

'Wait,' the magus said, talking to the steward rather than Chloe. 'She could be preparing a slow-acting poison. She is a foreigner. She is not to be trusted.'

'Lord?' the steward addressed the bald man.

He thought for a moment. 'Bring what she needs. But fetch a slave also.'

When the lord nodded for her to proceed, Chloe made an inspection of the sun king. Despite who he was, she felt sympathy for the obvious pain he was in. Solon's wide eyes followed her movements as she checked him over and he winced at regular intervals. She felt gently around his throat, making the magus tense when she had both hands around his neck, and checked the color of his hands. His circulation was good, and his glands weren't swollen. His face had none of the yellow discoloration of jaundice. The shadow around his eyes was the result of fatigue and pain.

The problem was evidently in his chest, and Chloe found herself agreeing with his magi's assessment: he had a cancer, a malignant growth inside him. It was advanced, she decided. The magi, priests, and priestesses from the Temple of Aeris said that such cases always meant a painful but imminent death.

Completing her inspection, she saw the steward returning with the items she'd asked for. He'd brought a slave with him, an old man with a loincloth bunched around his waist.

'He is the best I could find at short notice,' the steward said. 'A night worker. I found him scrubbing floors.'

'Please, place the items on the table there.' Chloe pointed.

She soon busied herself preparing the tea of the soma flower, adding the plant matter from the bowl to the jug of hot water.

'What is it that you are making?' the magus asked.

'Tea,' Chloe said.

'What is in it?' he persisted.

'A flower, prepared in a special way.'

'What flower?' he asked in exasperation.

Chloe knew she had to let the tea steep for a time. She hesitated as she saw the magus come over to watch, hovering at her shoulder. 'The tulip.'

'Tulip?' He scowled. 'I would know if tulips had uses other than in a poultice.'

'It must be selected with care,' Chloe said, examining the swirling contents of the jug. 'I must select a single bulb out of hundreds. Certain features mark out a bulb that possesses the power to ease pain.'

'I want you to show me how you make it,' the magus demanded.

'The process is simple. I've ground the closed flower pod and now I'm making this tea. You've seen me do it.'

'Let her continue,' the bald lord in orange robes instructed from the other side of the bed. 'The king of kings is in pain.'

The magus grunted.

Chloe made a filter out of the fine silk, doubling it over on itself. She glanced around the room, seeing that the steward was busy pressing a damp cloth to the sun king's brow. 'I need someone to help me.'

'I will,' the lord said. He came around the bed and the magus made way for him. 'What can I do?'

'Hold this cloth over the cup. Mind your hands, the water is hot.'

Chloe poured the tea over the cloth in small portions until the cup was full and sodden plant matter had gathered on the silk. Seeing that enough liquid remained in the jug for another cup, she returned the soma flower clinging to the silk to the jug, scraping it off with her fingertips, loath to waste any of its potency.

Finally, she trickled honey from another jar into the cup, then dropped in a wedge of lemon. The last two ingredients were purely to disguise the taste.

'It's done,' she said.

Reaching around Chloe and the lord, the magus took hold of the cup and turned, beckoning for the old slave to come closer.

'Drink,' the magus said. 'A good swallow or I will have you impaled.'

Glancing fearfully at the onlookers, the old slave tipped the cup back, drinking a third of the contents in a single gulp.

While the magus and lord waited, Chloe kept her expression neutral. She saw that the steward had brought a second empty cup and with a nod at the lord to help her again she prepared the additional serving.

When she was done, she returned her gaze to the room. With nothing to occupy her attention the wait dragged out. The old slave looked from face to face. The tension had gone out of his stooped shoulders. He looked like a man contentedly preparing for bed.

'How do you feel?' the lord asked.

'I feel . . .' He cleared his throat. 'I feel fine.'

'We should wait longer,' the magus growled.

At that moment the sun king began to writhe, waving his arms about as he clutched at his chest and then reached out to grab hold of the steward's arm. He coughed, a wracking, shuddering cough that hurt Chloe to hear. He continued for what felt like an eternity and then blessedly stopped, his skin so pale he looked like death. The steward touched a cloth to his lips and Chloe was almost surprised to see there was no blood.

'We can wait no longer,' the steward said.

'I agree,' said the lord in orange robes. He nodded at the magus. 'Give the cup to the steward.'

Solon leaned forward slightly to swallow the tea, his bony throat swelling and contracting as he gulped it down. The steward tilted the cup back until every drop was gone.

The king lay back once more. Every set of eyes in the room was on him.

His color slowly returned.

The sun king's lips parted. He spoke, his voice strengthening with every word. 'Better . . . So much better.' His eyes were slightly glazed. 'The pain. It is still present, but my soul's passage through the jagged gates is made easier.'

A sleepy smile crossed his face. The magus frowned, but the steward looked relieved.

'The girl,' Solon murmured. 'Bring her to me.'

The bald man took Chloe by the elbow and led her to the sun king's bedside.

'What can I do, king of kings?' she asked.

'Your skills have made me better.' His smile drifted; he looked as if he would soon fall asleep. His eyes closed as she waited, but after a moment they opened once more. 'I would grant you a small boon for your service.'

Chloe held her breath. She knew the soma flower brought feelings of contentment. She may not get this chance again.

She wondered what she should ask for. She tossed away idea after idea. She couldn't ask for anything too big. Even if he granted her request, he may take it away the next day. She couldn't ask for alternate sleeping quarters, nor the freedom to roam the city unaccompanied. She couldn't ask to be returned to her homeland or for the sun king to cease his desire for the Ark of Revelation.

In the end, she realized, there was nothing she could ask for herself.

But she could help another.

'My bodyguard, Tomarys, has a brother working as a slave on the pyramid.'

'Mmm.' Solon nodded, close to drifting away.

'The work is dangerous. I would ask that you free the slave, or find him safer work somewhere else.'

Solon glanced up at the lord in orange robes and nodded. 'See it done,' he said.

'I will, sire.'

The sun king's eyes finally closed, and Chloe was taken from the room.

30

Dion couldn't believe he was actually part of the crew of an Ilean warship. No amount of examining a beached bireme, or even a vessel under construction, could have given him the level of knowledge he was accumulating by sailing on one. The warship's name was the *Anoraxis*, and it was a thing of beauty.

Dion and the other marines that formed the complement of soldiers under Captain Roxana generally remained above decks, but he was free to roam wherever he wished, and had already explored the vessel from top to bottom. He had inspected the twin tiers of rowing benches and assessed the length of the oars. After speaking with the master of the drum he had learned about the various tempos, from the slow rate used to bring the warship into safe harbor to the galloping rhythm used only when employing the sharpened bronze ram.

The big main sail that hung from upper and lower crossbeams fastened to the mast supplemented the power provided by over a hundred oarsmen. Halfway along the upper deck, the mast plunged through the two lower levels all the way to the vessel's hull. But where a sailing boat of this size would have had a deep keel, the bireme's draught was shallow, enabling it to be easily driven straight up onto a beach to unload soldiers on an unsuspecting enemy.

Soon after leaving Lamara the captain had tested the crew by performing maneuvers. Roxana had them turning one hundred and eighty degrees, all while instructing a slave that he wasn't allowed to take a breath. When they'd completely turned around the slave was gasping, but he'd held his breath the entire time. The arc they had covered was no wider than three ship lengths. Dion couldn't believe what he'd seen.

Roxana could sail the *Anoraxis* directly into the wind if she wanted to. She could alter its speed faster than any galley even close to its size. The captain's intimate knowledge of the vessel and its construction gave her respect with the crew, despite the fact she was a woman.

Now Dion stood close to the bow, gazing ahead and scanning the horizon. He had his bow in his hand and a full quiver of arrows on his shoulder.

The *Anoraxis* was hunting wildren.

It was one creature in particular that they hunted. A serpent had been destroying fishing boats and devouring the contents: not just the catch but also the crews. The *Anoraxis* scouted the Maltherean Sea near the isle of Ibris, two days sailing from the coast of Ilea. It was the last place the wildran had been spotted.

Dion heard heavy footsteps on the wooden deck and Roxana joined him in scouring the sea. He glanced at her, taking note of the sun-blasted skin and short hair. She had an expression he knew well. It was the face of someone only truly happy at sea.

'Nothing yet,' he said.

'Really?' she grunted. 'I thought perhaps you'd seen our prey but hadn't found the right moment to tell me.'

Dion smiled. 'She's a beautiful ship.'

'Got any more questions? The others only want to talk about the women they'll buy with their bonus.'

'They give the bonus to the entire crew?'

'No,' Roxana snorted. 'Only to the man who makes the kill. They all think it's going to be them.'

'What if it's the *Anoraxis* that makes the kill? That ram looks sharp.'

'So it is. And you're right; more often than not that's how we do it with serpents. I get the bonus in that case, and I get to decide how it's shared out. If'—she gave him an evil grin—'I decide to share it at all.'

'I do have one question,' Dion said.

'What now? You still want to know if it could take less than a year to build a bireme? I told you: it's possible, but it would take more than just manpower and gold. There's one final ingredient.' She tapped the side of her head. 'Knowledge.'

'That brings me to my question,' he said. 'How did you get to be both shipbuilder and sailor?'

'Captain, you mean,' she growled, but there was no menace in it. She peered ahead as she spoke. 'I was a slave, apprenticed to one of the shipwrights. I learned things quickly. But why build ships and never sail them? The other captains talk about me. Say I'm too informal with my men. But as long as I have my own ship to command I'll do as I please, and I'm too valued to punish.'

'Are you wealthy?' Dion asked, unable to hide his curiosity. 'A shipbuilder must be prized.'

Roxana chuckled. 'I'm still a slave. I share a house with seven others.'

'Why are you here, then? Has Lamara always been your home?'

'No,' she said. 'I'm originally from Efu, in Haria. I sailed in the king of Haria's navy before Solon's conquest. Now I'm here, making and sailing ships for the sun king.'

'Why fight for Solon?'

She fixed him with a puzzled look. 'Besides Solon, who would have the resources to build ships? One day, I might even have the opportunity to build my dream.'

Dion thought he saw a spray of water in the distance, but decided it was just two waves colliding.

She glared at him. 'Aren't you going to ask me about it?'

Dion laughed. 'Please, I want to hear.'

'I want to build a trireme,' she said. Roxana had a wistful expression that appeared out of odds with her broad face and brisk manner. 'Like this ship, but with three rows of oars. Slightly longer, it would have to be, but with even more power and the same beam. Think about it. One hundred and eighty oars, all pulling the most deadly warship the world has ever seen.'

Dion shared her dream for a moment.

Finally, he spoke, choosing his words carefully. 'You would be given that opportunity in Galea. In Xanthos or Phalesia.'

She grinned. 'I thought you were from a tiny village on a tiny island with no name.'

Dion spread his hands. 'I didn't say it had no name. I simply said you wouldn't know it. I've spent time in Galea, across the sea. You would be given a villa in Xanthos.'

'I don't believe you—'

'Bahamut!' a sailor cried.

Dion was puzzled, but Roxana returned his look calmly. 'Sea serpent,' she said. 'Not as big as a leviathan, but big enough. This will be the wildran we're chasing.'

Half the crew and all the marines on the upper deck now rushed to the rails, scanning the sea, until another sailor pointed.

Dion saw a gush of water shoot into the air half a mile ahead of the *Anoraxis*. A moment later a humped sea monster with glossy silver scales plunged back down into the water, revealing a long tail at the end.

Roxana left Dion's side to take command of the ship, bellowing for the oarsmen to increase speed. The pounding drum below resounded as it increased tempo, thudding along to the rhythm of Dion's pulse. As he clutched his bow he remembered the serpent he had killed as it wrapped its length around the sailboat off the shore of Cinder Fen. His first arrow had bounced off the leathery hide. But his second had proven true: the creatures could be killed by arrows.

It was close to noon and the sea was calm, with little wind to create waves. The island of Ibris formed a distant landmass, further impeding large seas. The regular dip and pull, lift and drop of the oars hauled the warship ever faster through the water. Despite the breezeless day a wind now gusted against Dion's skin as he felt the thrill of the chase.

He thought again about the huge leviathan that had swallowed Cob, his old friend. In Xanthos the vessels that traded with Phalesia were at the whim of the wildren, but in Ilea, the wildren were actively hunted. It was a prospect only made possible by ships like these.

The serpent disappeared again for a time and now every man was peering into the water as well as scanning the horizon. Dion wondered if the creature would flee their approach, or would be bold enough to attack.

The question was answered when he saw a dark, sinuous shape speeding underneath the water. It was directly ahead of the bireme. The serpent was heading straight for them.

'Dead ahead!' Dion cried. 'It's under the surface!'

He nocked an arrow but the serpent was too deep. As the silver silhouette passed out of sight beneath the ship, deep enough to avoid the ram, he only saw that the creature was fat, and longer than the ship by half a length. White-faced sailors peered down, hanging over the rail as they wondered where it would next appear.

Making a guess, Dion raced along the open deck to the ship's stern. He stood on his toes as he leaned against the rail.

Fifty feet behind the vessel and slightly to port, a scaled triangular head shot to the surface. Dion immediately drew the bowstring to his cheek and sighted along the shaft, aiming for the soft skin between its jaw and the frill behind its neck. Releasing the arrow, he grabbed another from his quiver and loosed again.

The first arrow tore into the silver flesh just behind the frill but didn't sink deep. The second bounced off its skull.

More arrows filled the air a moment later as half a dozen archers fired together. The serpent plunged back into the water, thrashing its huge paddled tail in agitation.

'Turn us around!' Roxana roared.

Executing the turn at practice was one thing, but to be traveling so fast and then have half the oarsmen back while the other half continued to push forward made the vessel groan like a wounded beast. The *Anoraxis* heeled to the side and anything loose rolled across the deck.

The mast creaked alarmingly and Dion ran to the ropes holding the top of the sail to the upper beam. He knew the risk of the ship turning so hard while on sail: if he didn't act quickly the mast could snap. He unhitched one line after another, careful of his hands as the whistling rope shot away once it was unfastened.

'Get that sail down!'

Sailors ran to take over and with most of the work done he left them to it, earning a quick grateful nod from the stocky captain. He now ran to the bow as the chase began in earnest.

'Ramming speed!' Roxana cried.

With the turn complete, the drum increased to a beat so fast that Dion wondered how any oarsman could keep up with it. He heard a whip crack below and winced: a slave had just lost part of his skin.

'Where is it? Come on, men. Talk to me!' Roxana bellowed.

'Dead ahead, cap'n!' a sailor shouted.

The oars tossed the sea into white foam, leaving surging swirls in their wake. The marine infantry hefted their spears. Archers waited with arrows nocked.

The serpent shot out of the water ahead, nearly leaping in its haste, flying forward as its head again submerged.

'Two hundred paces!' Dion called back.

'Sail back on!' Roxana shouted.

He turned in surprise. It was a bold move, for the extra speed the sail gave them would come with a risk if they needed to turn at short notice.

He heard a snap as the sail once more climbed the mast. With the vessel at ramming speed, the bireme flew over the water, her prow carving the waves like a knife.

'One hundred paces!' Dion cried as the serpent reared out of the water, sending a cloud of spray into the air behind it as the thick reptilian monster plunged back into the sea.

Roxana ran to the bow and then back to the stern to give orders to the helmsman. The *Anoraxis* turned slightly to bring them into a direct line with the wide body of their quarry.

The head came up at seventy paces and Dion pulled his bow-string to his ear. He again aimed behind its jaw, and his experience on boats came to the fore as he calmly rode the motion of the vessel beneath him. It was a difficult shot, at the limit of his ability.

He released and watched as the string thrummed. Someone nearby cheered, and he felt a sudden surge of pride as the arrow struck home.

The serpent shivered and its entire body came to the surface and into the path of the warship. The head turned and wild eyes glared back at them.

A heartbeat later the sharp bronze ram of the *Anoraxis* met the creature's silver scales behind its head, the sea frothing into blood as it struck. Dion saw the wildran's body floating on the surface of the water as they passed. The bronze ram had almost completely severed its triangular head from its body.

Roxana came to the bow to join him.

'Well done,' she said. She clapped him on the back and grinned.

31

Chloe and Tomarys were once more in the bazaar, but this time she'd asked her bodyguard to take her directly to the hidden section at the rear. They passed droves of beggars, and numerous cloth sellers trying to attract them with rolled lengths of yellow silk. But it was earlier in the day than their last visit, and the crowds were comparatively thin.

The going was made even easier by the imposing man who walked at Chloe's side. Tomarys still wore his leather vest and brown trousers; she had seen him in nothing else. Despite his towering height he walked with athletic grace. Even though he was unarmed, many people who would have intimidated or pestered Chloe drew back when they saw the man with her, averting their eyes and walking away.

'Chloe . . .' Tomarys said. It was the first time she had heard him use her name. 'Now that we are away from the palace . . . I must thank you. For what you did for my brother.'

'It was nothing.'

'No.' Tomarys turned and stopped in his tracks to look down at her. He gripped her shoulders with both hands. 'It was not nothing.

In another few weeks, perhaps a month, he would have been dead. Pyramid slaves suffer a fate worse than any hell.' He spoke forcefully, with passion. 'Fed worse than animals. Whipped until the skin slides off their shoulders. Dozens of bodies are thrown into the river every day, where they are eaten by the crocodiles.' The tall man's wide mouth spread into a smile. 'Now my brother tends horses in the stables. The money I was saving to buy his freedom will now be used to pay healers to look after my mother. If my mother's health improves my sister will be able to find work in the bazaar. And I have you to thank.'

Tomarys looked at his hands clutching Chloe's upper arms and released her, suddenly embarrassed. 'I am sorry, lady.'

'It's fine,' Chloe said with a smile. 'Shall we continue?'

He nodded, and followed her as she walked to the gap between the stalls leading to the decrepit square behind. A half-dozen beggars sitting in a semicircle on the floor stared up at the pair. Chloe's gaze instantly went to the hut where they'd last found the old man drinking tea, but there was no one there. She knew that behind the shack was the long narrow lane where the boy had given them the soma flowers. She wondered what to do.

Chloe had managed to ease the sun king's pain, but he had soon finished all the tea she could brew, despite her admonishment to eke out the medicine over a period of time. Now, just a few days after her last visit to the market, the sun king had given Tomarys silver and asked her to make more.

As soon as possible after being charged with her task, Chloe had left for the market. If she'd waited long enough for the magus to hear that she was buying more flowers he might have insisted on going with her, which was the last thing she wanted.

She had to buy more flowers. And this time she needed to find more than two.

'We should not spend long here,' Tomarys cautioned.

251

Scanning the area, Chloe wondered if she should look inside the shack. Slowly, she walked closer to the shadowy opening and called out. 'Hello?'

Tomarys walked forward to stand slightly in front of her, holding her back with an arm, as they both spied movement inside.

The old man with the pockmarked face and hooked nose slowly emerged. He was licking each greasy finger in turn as he walked toward them, making grotesque sounds of enjoyment. He stopped in front of them and wiped his hands on his coarse brown trousers.

'I remember you,' he said. 'What do you want?'

'We need more flowers.'

He shook his head. 'I have tar of heaven. That is what I will bring you.'

'No,' Chloe said. 'I already told you last time. I need flowers. Many more.'

He looked up at Tomarys and then at Chloe, regarding her with heavy-lidded eyes. 'You have money?'

Chloe nodded.

'Wait.'

The old man turned and walked around the back of the hut. Chloe and Tomarys waited. The time wore on.

Chloe started to walk forward, peering around the side of the shack until Tomarys pulled her back. They continued to wait.

Finally, after such a long time that even Chloe was about to leave, she saw movement. The seven-year-old boy who had given her the flowers last time came forward, beckoning.

'Come,' he said. 'This way.'

Following him they came to the back of the hut and saw the narrow alley. The boy skipped ahead and then turned around, continuing to wave them forward.

'Let me go first,' said Tomarys.

The tall, muscled bodyguard entered the alley with Chloe just behind. Once again they followed its interminable curve.

One moment the boy was just ahead, the next he suddenly put his head down and ran.

There was a sound of running footsteps from behind. Chloe started to turn. A man's arm went around her neck.

He held her up on her toes and she felt sharp steel pressed to her throat. She couldn't see his face, but she could smell his rancid breath. Tomarys stood looking at her, half a dozen paces away, trapped in the middle of the alley. Chloe saw another man approaching behind him. He carried a long curved dagger and was as lean as a pole, with a narrow face and a diagonal scar across his nose.

Tomarys stood with his back to the wall, Chloe held captive on his left and the second attacker on his right.

It had all happened in an instant. Chloe's heart pounded in her ears so loudly that for a moment it was all she could hear. Fear clutched hold of her stomach; she forgot to breathe. Finally, she gasped. But she was terrified that the slightest movement would cause the sharp steel to cut her neck. Her chest rose and fell with an irregular rhythm, short gasps followed by great heaves as her lungs forced her throat to bring more air.

Chloe felt the blood drain from her face as she turned pleading eyes on Tomarys. Her toes barely touching the ground, she was trembling.

'Give my friend the silver,' the assailant with his arm around Chloe's neck hissed to Tomarys, 'or she dies.'

Tomarys's eyes shifted as he looked from man to man. He was penned in the alley with opponents on both sides. His gaze suddenly shot to the right and Chloe saw a third brigand standing back, arms folded over his chest as he watched.

Making peaceful motions with his hands, spreading them out so they could see he was unarmed, Tomarys spoke. 'My pouch has only copper.' He moved slowly to touch the leather vest. 'The silver is in here.'

'Get it.' Chloe's captor clutched her harder, making her yelp as he pushed his knife harder against her throat. 'Hurry up!'

'There is no need to harm her,' Tomarys said. 'Here.' With his right hand he reached into his open vest.

Faster than Chloe had thought a man could move she saw him bring out something small and triangular. He made a flicking motion with his wrist. Steel flashed through the air, on a direct path for Chloe's head.

The grip around her neck melted away and she heard a gurgling sound. A moment later the brigand behind her crumpled.

Tomarys hadn't stopped moving. His left hand reached inside the other side of the vest and he took out a small silver throwing knife.

The whipcord-thin man charged, his curved blade held high in the air.

Tomarys weaved around him and pulled his attacker's extended arm forward, sending the man crashing to the ground. As the last of the attackers realized what was happening and ran forward to help, Tomarys crouched and tossed his knife. It struck the third brigand deep in the center of the chest. With a cry of pain the man sank to his knees and then fell to the side. Blood welled on his clothing and his eyes, staring directly at Chloe, began to glaze.

Turning his attention back to the scar-faced swordsman on the ground, Tomarys walked forward and saw that the sword had fallen out of the man's hand. He was scrabbling on the ground, reaching for it. Tomarys stamped on his wrist and Chloe winced as she heard a sickening crunch. The swordsman rolled and moaned, staring up at his assailant.

Tomarys bent down and gripped him around the throat. He took the man's shoulder in his other hand and grunted, his thick muscles bulging. With an expert twist, he broke the swordsman's neck.

Finally, Tomarys strode to Chloe, staring past her shoulder and nodding in satisfaction when he saw there were no more attackers.

'Are you hurt?'

Chloe tried to speak but choked. She tried again. 'No.'

'Good. Keep an eye out.'

She turned to the body behind her and saw Tomarys pluck his throwing knife from where it was embedded deep in the brigand's eye. He wiped the blade of the triangular weapon on the dead man's clothing and then returned it to his vest, before retrieving his other blade from the chest of the other assailant.

The struggle was over in seconds. Chloe was still trembling.

She looked away from the body at her feet as she watched Tomarys returning the last of his knives to his vest.

'Look out!' she suddenly cried.

A newcomer ran at Tomarys with sword held high. He must have been hiding around the curve of the lane. Tomarys was unarmed and crouched on the ground. She knew he would be killed.

Glancing up and seeing the danger, Tomarys shot to his feet and spun on his heel as the sword speared the air where he'd been a moment before. His hand was suddenly on the hilt of his enemy's sword, and then as Chloe watched wide-eyed she saw the point come around until it was in the air. The swordsman cried out in pain.

And then the sword was in Tomarys's hand.

He didn't hesitate to strike, thrusting in a practiced way that told Chloe this wasn't his first time holding a sword. He pushed hard, bringing the blade up into his opponent's chest, holding grimly until he yanked the weapon out. Blood gushed from the man's mouth and Tomarys stood back as he fell face forward, sprawling on top of his friend.

Tomarys threw down the sword and turned to Chloe. 'We need to leave. Now.'

Taking a deep breath to steady herself, she shook her head. 'We can't.'

'Did you hear me? This is their place. More will come.'

'Tomarys, we can't go. I need the flowers. Please,' she implored. 'I need your help.'

He hesitated, aware that every second was precious. 'All right. Come.'

Stepping past the four bodies, Chloe followed him to the end of the alley, where previously they had seen little more than an opening. They came to a crossroads, an intersection between four lanes, where sunlight overhead revealed a small square and a row of rickety shacks against the longest wall.

Tomarys entered the first of the huts and came out a moment later, shaking his head. 'Roof fallen in.'

'That one,' Chloe said, pointing to the most structurally sound of the huts.

This time she followed close behind him as he entered. She knew she'd come to the right place when she saw tables with strips of tar drying on leaves. Tomarys looked at her inquiringly.

'Keep moving,' she said.

At the back of the shack she lifted the lid of a large ceramic urn. Inside were flower pods, dozens of them. Chloe searched the dark interior until she found a sack. Her heart raced as she tossed pod after pod into the sack while Tomarys stood guard outside. She'd only half filled the sack when he called out. 'Voices. Quick. We need to go now.'

He held her by the arm as they left the way they'd come.

They made the journey back to the palace in silence.

32

The long warship passed the southern lighthouse and then the statue of the sun god before following the river to the harbor. The thudding of the drum was slow and stately; the oars plunged into the water with a walking pace. Roxana was giving the slaves some respite after the frantic chase. Behind the vessel was a rope, and attached to the rope was a long reptilian body.

Two days had passed since the hunt. Dion was looking forward to a decent night's rest when he returned to the House of Algar. Though the room was expensive, and there were simpler lodgings close to the harbor, he still had to find Chloe.

As the *Anoraxis* approached the shore, heading for a narrow stretch of beach between two other biremes, Roxana joined Dion at the rail.

'So tell me, Dion of No-land, where did you learn to shoot a bow like that?' She turned an inquiring gaze on him.

'My father was a great warrior, and my brother follows in his footsteps,' Dion said. 'I tried, but I could never use a sword.' He shrugged. 'So I learned archery. I practiced for years. My brother helped me get instruction from the best archers and I became good.'

'Did you make your father proud?'

'No,' he said. 'My father thinks archery is for commoners.'

The words were out of his mouth before he could take them back, but Roxana only grinned. 'Well at least I can make use of your skill.'

Dion sought to change the subject. 'The wildran's corpse,' he said. 'What do you do with it?'

'We'll be able to make leather and lamp oil, though the flesh is rancid.'

He nodded and scanned the deck. 'I should lend a hand.'

Dion felt her eyes on him as he left, but then the vessel was beaching and everyone on board was busy as they gathered all the equipment and supplies on the upper deck before disembarking and hauling it onto the shore.

With their work done, Dion waited with the other marines as they formed up with firm sand under their feet.

Roxana came and looked them over. 'Well done, men. You've earned your pay. Return to your billets and come back tomorrow morning for practice. Archers, I saw some of those shots go wild. I want you to work until you strike targets at fifty paces nine times out of ten. Soldiers, not all wildren we hunt are serpents. Hone your weapons. I want each of you to spar with every other marine in our group. Dismissed.'

The marines dispersed and Roxana issued instructions to the master of the oars and the other officers. Dion started to follow his companions up to the city, when a gruff voice called his name.

'You still have an interest in shipbuilding?' Roxana asked.

Dion felt a thrill rise as he nodded. 'I do.'

'Then follow me.'

She led him to the sheds at the harbor's far end, where he had first met her at one of the biremes under construction. He once more saw the supports holding the vessel in the air over the tiered depression in the ground. It was late afternoon, and the workers had gone for the day, meaning that the two of them were alone.

'Understand anything about carpentry?' she asked.

Dion smiled. 'Not much.'

'Know what a mortise and tenon joint is?' When he didn't respond, she continued. 'Imagine you're trying to fit two pieces of wood together at an angle. You need something strong to hold them together; a few wooden dowels aren't enough to do the trick. Come.' She walked down the outside of the ship, weaving around the supports, until she came to the ribs on the hull. 'See here? The wood fits seamlessly together. The best way to understand it is to think of the parts of a man and woman.' She grinned. 'We shape the end to give this plank here'—she touched one of the horizontal pieces of what would become the deck—'a tooth . . . an appendage . . . a man's knob. Whereas this rib here'—Roxana slapped the wood—'we gouge so that we have a hole. Understand?'

Dion ran his eyes over the warship, and now that he was looking, he could see where every joint had been carefully fitted to connect one piece of timber to another. 'How long are the teeth?'

'At least as long as what you have in your trousers.' She chuckled. 'Sometimes a lot longer.'

'Where do you get the timber?'

'The pine comes from central Salesia. We also use oak for extra strength.'

'How is the wood warped?'

'Heat. We soak the timber then bend it over iron.'

The more Dion learned, the more there was to learn. The carpenters in Xanthos would know most of what Roxana was telling him. But to make one of these ships, a bireme, would require intimate knowledge of stresses and forces, combined with precise measurement and, most of all, experience.

'The hull is built first, completely finished before we work on the decking and the interior.' Roxana looked at the vessel proudly. 'She's given a shallow draft not just so we can beach her, but also so she's agile and can turn quickly.'

'How far away is this one from completion?' Dion asked. He could see that the hull was close to finished, although much of the exterior planking still needed to be laid over the ribs.

'Another six months,' she said. 'At least.'

Roxana frowned as she walked along the vessel's belly, dodging around the supports and examining the work. 'I need to speak with the overseer,' she said. 'No more forays for a time. It looks like I'm needed here.' She glanced back at him. 'Dion . . . If you want to, you can help here for a time. No extra pay, though.' She smiled.

'I'd like that.'

'Come back tomorrow. You deserve a rest.'

Dion nodded. 'I'll see you then.'

She grinned. 'Aren't you forgetting something?' He frowned. Roxana's smile broadened. 'Your bonus. Go visit the paymaster. Ask at the mess, they'll tell you how to find him.'

⌣

Dion was surprised to find Anoush waiting for him outside the fenced-off area, hopping from foot to foot. The boy's round face broke into a beaming smile as he saw him emerge.

'You killed one? I saw you come in. You got a bonus, yes?'

'I did.' Dion smiled.

Anoush followed him as he entered the city. 'Anything you need, master? Anything I can do for you, anything at all? You need a woman? You need new clothes?'

Dion tried to discourage him, but the orphan continued to follow as he skirted the bazaar and climbed to the upper city, entering

the wealthy quarter around the palace. He climbed the main boulevard that would take him to the guesthouse, a wide street with
steps at regular intervals. Well-dressed Ileans in flowing robes passed
him on both sides while the occasional signboard above an entrance
marked jewelers and dressmakers.

Dion absently scanned the street ahead. Two sun priests chatted as
they walked in the direction of the palace. An old merchant argued in
front of his shop with a scowling noble. Further still, a huge man – one
of the biggest men Dion had ever seen – walked alongside a dark-
haired woman in Salesian clothing with a blue shawl on her shoulders. Despite her fine clothing, she carried a rough hemp sack.

'Anoush, I—' Dion was in the process of telling the boy that
after he paid Algar, there wouldn't be much money left in his purse.

But when Dion saw the distant woman he stopped in his tracks.
He then began to hurry.

'What is it, master?'

Quickening his steps, Dion almost broke into a run as Anoush
scurried to keep up with him. He passed the people arguing and
weaved around the two priests. The street forked and the woman
and her escort took the right fork toward the palace.

As they turned, the big man looked directly at Dion, who
shielded his eyes, pretending to be searching for someone. The tall
man's eyes dismissed him and the pair continued.

The young woman's face was in profile for the briefest instant.
Dion saw pale skin and an upturned nose. He took note of the flowing dark hair to her waist and her slim figure.

Dion immediately knew he was looking at Chloe, daughter of
Aristocles, the first consul of Phalesia.

Taking the right fork at the top of the boulevard, he continued
to follow.

The next street was short and opened out onto the wide road
that skirted the wall of the sun king's palace. The warrior kept close to

Chloe as they walked; without a doubt he was there to guard her and ensure she didn't escape. Dion knew that if the man turned around he would see him, and his suspicions had already been raised.

'Who are they, master?'

'Hush,' Dion said, waving his hand behind him. 'Stay quiet.'

Dion ran plan after plan through his head but discarded each in turn. Chloe and her escort were a hundred paces ahead and would soon be at the palace gates. He had his bow, but it was an impossible shot. Even a well-placed arrow might not finish off Chloe's grim-looking warden.

He finally hung back as the pair approached the gates to the palace, putting his back to the wall as they passed the guards and entered.

Chloe looked well and unharmed, but she was under guard. She was now gone from him.

'What is it, master? Do you know her?'

Dion thought furiously. He couldn't be in several places at once. Until he had a plan, he couldn't jeopardize his position with Roxana.

'Anoush.' He crouched, looking the boy in the eyes. 'I have a task for you. I want you to watch the palace. Be careful not to be seen, but get to know everyone who goes in and out of those gates. Can you do that?'

Anoush nodded vigorously. 'Of course.'

'If you see that woman again, give her a message. Tell her that the curious sailor is at the House of Algar.'

He made Anoush repeat the phrase and nodded. 'Good. And follow her. I want to know where she goes.'

'Yes, master.'

Dion handed Anoush one of the silver coins he'd been given by the paymaster. 'Are you sure you can do this? Do you need more money?'

'It is too much,' Anoush said. 'Thank you, thank you. I will begin watching right away.'

As the boy scampered away, Dion pondered as he returned to the nearby guesthouse. Algar asked him for more money after his absence, taking most of what he had. He wondered if he should get cheaper lodgings, but his instinct was to stay close to the palace.

He had found the first consul's daughter, and she was apparently allowed into the city. Anoush would keep watch for him. Dion now wondered how he would deal with Chloe's guard . . .

33

Chloe sat on her bed pallet, grinding one of the flower pods, her eyes unfocused as she thought about something else altogether.

She shivered as she relived the fight in the tight alleyway. She remembered her terror and helplessness; she'd been completely incapable of defending herself.

She never wanted to feel that way again.

Tomarys sat with his back against the wall nearby, his broad face inscrutable as ever. He watched her for a time as she worked, before looking away.

Chloe frowned as a sound filled the air: the staccato rhythm of footsteps. Both she and Tomarys glanced at the thin slit high on the wall that was the closest window. The din was rising from outside the palace. Many men were marching. It grew in volume until it became a thunder of clumping feet.

'What is it?' Chloe asked Tomarys.

He tilted his head. 'I do not know. Do you wish me to find out?'

'No. I'll find out.'

She set the bowl on the ground near her bed pallet – the sack of pods was hidden safely underneath – and rose to her feet. Since first speaking with Princess Yasmina, further conversation had been difficult, but Chloe was persistent, and the constant sound of marching provided her with an opening.

But the princess was gone. The open chest beside her bed pallet was empty, not an item of clothing within. Her bed was made, crisp and fresh. The princess's place in the room was now like just like any unoccupied corner. It was as if she'd never been there.

Chloe wandered nonetheless, peering around every lattice screen and scanning the walls, empty except for the murals of painted flowers. She asked two or three slaves as she passed, but they only shook their heads.

She tried with another slave girl sweeping the floor. 'Do you know where I can find the Princess Yasmina?' The girl shook her head, looking fearfully at Chloe, turning away as she resumed her work.

Perplexed, Chloe left the expansive chamber and ventured out into the hall. She walked directly to the eunuch who had taken her clothes when she first arrived. He stood just inside the curtained main entrance to the women's quarters, scowling as she approached.

'I can't find the Princess Yasmina,' she said. 'Do you know where she is?'

'I know.'

When he didn't elaborate, Chloe frowned. 'Tell me.'

'Her brother in Shadria is raising a revolt against Ilea. Though her father claims no part of it, the sun king considers the family to have broken their bond. Her head has been sent to her father in rebuke.'

Chloe put her hand to her mouth. She remembered the imperious princess, barely into her teens, so certain of her superior station and so reluctant to discuss escape.

'Did she . . .?' She swallowed. 'Was it quick?'

The eunuch spoke impassively. He took no pleasure in it, but nor did he soften his words for Chloe's benefit. 'The king of kings is angry. Her eyes were gouged out and ears and nose sliced off. Only then was she beheaded. Ilea sends a strong message to her family in Shadria.'

The eunuch turned as a palace guard came to the entrance. He held the curtain aside as the soldier looked within.

'The king of kings asks for the girl.' The soldier nodded his head in Chloe's direction. 'Come,' he said. 'Do not keep him waiting.'

⌣

The guard escorted Chloe to Solon's personal quarters. His color was good and he showed none of his prior weakness, as he stood tall, arms raised as a steward slipped a long shirt of glittering metal rings over his head.

He dropped his arms as she entered and regarded her with his penetrating gaze.

'Chloe of Phalesia,' he said, speaking with precise syllables. 'I have a rebellion in Shadria. The leader of this rebellion, the brother of the late Princess Yasmina, is trying to build an army in the great desert in the south. He has seized gold that was on its way back to Lamara. It was going to be sufficient to complete my pyramid.' His voice lowered to a soft growl. 'I need it back.'

'You must go yourself, king of kings?' Chloe asked.

'This I must do. Until my last breath, my commanders will know that I lead.'

'Then I wish you success.'

He smiled without mirth. 'I am sure you do. It is to your own best interests, and that of your homeland, that I am successful.'

The rest of his threat hung in the air. If the sun king couldn't regain his gold, he would need to find some elsewhere. The golden ark in Phalesia, melted, molded, and beaten thinner than the finest silk, would cover hundreds of the pyramid's stones.

'I need to know,' Solon said. 'Can you make enough of the tea for the journey?'

She saw a chance to get some important information. 'How long will you be away for, lord?'

'Either the rebels will flee before we can catch them, or we will destroy them to a man. In either case, I hope to return in two weeks, perhaps three.'

She nodded. 'I can make you the tea. But you will need to sweeten it yourself with honey and lemon. It will use up most of my stock, and there are few of the tulips I need in the city.'

'The taste will not concern me.' He waved a hand, then was pensive for a moment. 'I am pleased with you, girl. And you have proven yourself trustworthy. While I am gone you may continue to go to the bazaar to find the things you need. I will make sure your bodyguard has silver.'

Chloe bowed.

The sun king dismissed her with a nod and the guard escorted her back to the women's quarters. As Chloe reflected on Princess Yasmina's fate she sat on her bed and asked Tomarys to fetch the materials she needed: hot water, silk, and several jugs.

With the sound of marching soldiers filling the city outside the palace, Chloe thought about Tomarys and wondered if she could somehow immobilize her bodyguard and escape. She even considered somehow making him drink some of the tea, but discarded the idea. Not only would he be a difficult man to incapacitate, but she didn't like the thought of hurting him. He had saved her life, twice over if she added the fact that he'd helped her obtain more soma flowers to appease the sun king. He was her only friend in this terrible place.

Continuing to grind, Chloe considered making the tea too strong, but she knew that if Solon fell into a deathly slumber after drinking the liquid her head would roll.

She needed Solon to live. And she hoped he regained his gold.

———

Hours passed, and the heat of the day slipped into warm evening and then the cool stillness of night.

Chloe had delivered her medicine. The sun king was gone and his soldiers with him. The ensuing silence was almost eerie in comparison.

Sleeping on his side on his mat near her pallet, Tomarys's eyes slowly opened. 'It is late. You should sleep.'

Chloe sat cross-legged, staring at the murals on the wall; she hadn't even tried to sleep. Dark images swept through her mind: the knife pressed to her throat and the bloody fight . . . Princess Yasmina's horrific fate. The girl had done nothing wrong, but she had been given one of the worst deaths imaginable just to send her family a message. One moment she had been a young girl living in a strange version of captivity, the next moment men were holding her down and cutting out her eyes, slicing off her ears and nose. Chloe felt ill just imagining it.

Again her thoughts mingled and shifted like a flurry of leaves under a tree. She touched her fingers to her throat and imagined the knife going in, cutting into her windpipe and jugular vein. She wondered what it must feel like to know that with the agonizing pain would come certain death. Loss of breath. Inability to speak. Lifeblood gushing out onto the dust. Darkness closing in.

'Lady?' Tomarys said. He sat up. 'What is wrong?'

'Tomarys,' Chloe said, speaking softly, turning to gaze at him intently. 'Solon is gone for a time. Will you help me escape?'

He shook his head sadly. 'Regretfully, I cannot. I have family who would be made to suffer.'

'What if we could escape with them too?'

'My mother is sick.' He hung his head. 'She would never survive a difficult journey.'

'I understand,' Chloe said. She knew she couldn't ask so much of him. 'But . . .' She took a breath, releasing it in a long sigh. 'Would you help me in another way?'

'What is it?'

She clenched her fists as she thought about her helplessness, looking at each of her hands in turn. 'We haven't spoken about it since, but back in the alley I was almost killed.'

Chloe once more looked directly into his dark eyes.

'I grew up with soldiers. I used to watch them at practice, and the captain of my father's guard is a friend. When I saw you the other day . . . I have never seen another move like you.' She swallowed. 'Tomarys, I want you to teach me to fight.'

He frowned, his expression more puzzled than anything. 'But you are a woman.'

Chloe set her jaw with determination. 'Then they won't expect me to fight back.'

34

A week passed with no further sightings of Chloe, while Dion spent his days building ships with Roxana at the harbor. Anoush came to him at the end of every day and gave him a report. Meanwhile Algar demanded more money. Dion's supply of coin dwindled until he had just a handful of coppers left.

Despite the boy's promise, Dion knew Anoush couldn't watch the palace all the time. Dion contributed where he could, watching the streets near the palace until late into the evening. He knew that Chloe was inside, and that Solon had taken his army to Shadria and would be gone for weeks. There would never be a better time to free her.

But there was the issue of the huge warrior by her side. Dion knew he would have to kill the intimidating guard who was her escort. Once the man was dead and Chloe freed, he would take her to the *Calypso* – he had checked: the boat was still safely hidden outside the walls – and flee.

But then duty called. Reports came in that a wildran, a giant this time, had emerged from the mountains high above the village of Nara on the island of Amphi. It had killed a goatherd and his family, devouring its victims one by one.

Captain Roxana summoned the crew of the *Anoraxis*.

Dion knew it would be at least another week before he returned to Lamara.

Tomarys led Chloe to a dilapidated structure in the shape of a wheel, on the outskirts of the city's poorest quarter. As she found herself at one of several entrances tall and wide enough for a giant to pass through, Chloe tried to fathom what it had once been.

She followed the tall warrior into the shadowed interior, walking along dusty passages long disused, staying silent for fear of disturbing old ghosts. Dust particles filled the air in Tomarys's wake, swirling over each other, reflecting the few rays of light that made their way into the passage. She smelled wet stone as she heard faint dripping echoing through the corridor.

A cavernous opening beckoned ahead and she emerged into bright light. She shielded her eyes as she climbed steps to her left and joined Tomarys, where he waited for her approach.

She realized she was in the interior of the wheel, standing on one of many seats that also doubled as steps. All around her, to the left and right, ahead and behind, as well as on the wheel's other side, were tiers of the steps, stretching from the high circular perimeter all the way to the bottom.

The floor was a circular space guarded by a partly fallen rail. Tomarys began to walk down to the floor, having no difficulty despite the steps' uncommonly large size, and she hurried to follow. He reached the rail and pushed some loose timbers aside to enter the sandy floor. Chloe followed him to the middle, joining him in the epicenter.

'What is this place?' she asked. Her voice was instantly swallowed by the void.

'The Arena. Not so long ago, in the time of Solon's predecessor, men fought here to entertain the people of Lamara. It is now abandoned, but one day it may come to be used again.'

'Fought? In battles?'

'A better word is bouts, but yes, you could call them battles.'

'To the death?'

'To the death,' he said grimly.

Chloe examined the sandy floor, almost afraid to find old crimson patches but unable to prevent herself looking. As far as she could see it was just sand.

'Why here?' she finally asked.

He raised his arms and gestured to the open space. 'It is a good place to fight. No one will hear us or see us.' He smiled, but then the smile faded away. 'Are you sure you want to do this?'

Chloe nodded. 'I'm sure.'

'Then for now, watch, listen, and learn.'

She clasped her hands behind her back and waited in the center of the floor, Tomarys standing opposite her.

'The first lesson'—Tomarys held up a single finger—'and the most important of all, is thus. The seeds of victory are sown before the fight begins.'

'So it's best to prepare,' Chloe said, nodding. 'Better armor, better weapons, more training, more practice, good leadership—'

'Girl,' Tomarys interrupted, scowling. 'I told you to listen, not to talk. Today I am the master and you the student. Understood?'

She reddened. 'I understand.'

'Yes, all of those things are important, but any fool'—he glared at Chloe—'knows that it pays to be prepared. We can take the lesson further. The seeds of victory are sown before the fight begins . . .' He rubbed his chin. 'Think about this. Two men face each other. One has a sword. The other is unarmed. Both are prepared. Who will win?'

'The man with the sword.'

'Ah,' Tomarys said, holding up a hand. 'But . . . The man with the sword has prepared himself to face an unarmed opponent. He attacks . . .'

He glanced around and then his eyes settled on the rail. Walking over he broke off a piece of wooden rail as thick as three of Chloe's fingers, hardly showing any effort at all, and returned.

'He attacks.' Tomarys lunged with the three-foot-long piece of wood, skewering an imaginary enemy. 'Confident of victory against his unarmed foe. But . . .' He dropped the makeshift sword and faced the other direction. 'His opponent pulls out a concealed knife.' He reached into the hidden pocket within his vest and pulled out one of the short triangular throwing knives. 'And slashes the hand holding the sword.' Tomarys swept his arm down. He then straightened and looked at Chloe. 'We all know who wins the fight. But what is our second lesson, which is really an extension of the first?'

Chloe's brow furrowed. 'Being prepared means having hidden surprises?'

'Close,' Tomarys said. 'To sow the seeds of victory before the fight begins, we must play with expectations.'

He returned his knife to the sheath in his vest.

'I appear to be unarmed. My vest is open at my chest, which further enhances this image, but both my knives and my vest were carefully chosen to fit together. I want people to think I do not have a weapon.'

He took off his vest, laying it on the sand, revealing a giant, hairy torso, and white whip scars across his back and shoulders.

'But, in addition to this deception, I am also skilled without a weapon, using my hands and elbows, head and feet.' He made swift striking motions with the parts of his body he'd named. 'A potential attacker sees a big man, but big men are often slow. He sees an unarmed man. This gives me an advantage over a man with a sword. I play with his expectations. I cause him to be overconfident. I shape his tactics, before the fight begins.'

'But wouldn't you just rather have the sword? Many men carry swords in the streets of Lamara.'

Tomarys's eyes lit up. 'Another lesson. With two swords in play there is twice the danger you will be killed. Reality is not like the stories. Many fights end with both men taking blows.'

Chloe hadn't thought about it, but it made sense. A sword or knife was designed to slice. Wounds would often be deep. Even a victor might suffer a bleeding artery, or leave the battlefield with a deep cut that could become infected. Even if he suffered only minor wounds, his strength would be sapped, making him less able to achieve victory against a second opponent.

Tomarys picked up his wooden stick, holding it out to demonstrate, his left side toward Chloe. 'A man comes at me with a sword.' He made a thrust. 'There is one sword in play.' He turned around. 'I take that sword off him.' He reached out and pretended to be seizing a man's wrist, rolling his body until he had taken the sword from the first man. 'There is still one sword in play. Mine.'

Chloe finally understood. She nodded in appreciation.

'If I spend my time learning how to take a sword off a man, while my enemy spends his time training to be the perfect swordsman, I will win every time, for I will be the one with the sword. Understood?'

'I understand. So why the knives?'

'Throwing knives.' He bent to retrieve his two knives from their hidden sheaths inside the vest and handed one to her. It was almost entirely blade, with a rounded hilt displaying a hole in the middle. 'Be careful. It is sharp enough to shave with.'

Chloe touched her finger to the edge, almost cutting herself.

'I can get them out quickly. They are silent. I can strike from a distance. And still I appear unarmed.'

He looked around and rested his eyes on a thick vertical supporting stump holding the rail.

'Perhaps we will start here. Come.'

They moved until they were facing the stump, about ten paces away.

'Hold it like this,' he instructed, holding his knife between thumb and forefinger. 'The hilt is thin and rounded so that it glides out of your hand. Try to strike that post.'

Chloe took a deep breath and, holding the knife in her right hand, brought it over her shoulder, then swept her arm down. She released as her arm was extended in front of her. The knife shot through the air but went wide, missing the post.

She climbed over the rail to fetch it and returned a moment later.

'Not bad,' Tomarys said. 'Next time stand like this, facing front, with your left foot in front, and about an arm's length between your left and right.' Chloe moved to copy him. 'Your heels should be lined up, but your feet are angled.' She shifted. 'Both knees are bent, especially your front. Aim at the height of your chest, so that you are making a clean throw in line with the release. Move like you are holding an axe, and you want to chop off a branch between you and the target. As you swing, release when the point of the knife is exactly on the target. Snap your fingers together. After releasing, do not stop your swing – go on with the movement. Follow-through is important. Now try again.'

Copying Tomarys's stance, following his instructions, Chloe drew her arm back and down.

The knife plunged into the stump, quivering with the impact. She turned a surprised gaze at Tomarys.

'Well done.' He grinned. 'But keep control of your breathing next time. Take shallow breaths. At this stage, hold your breath if you must. Let's try again. When you are striking every time, we will increase the distance.'

Chloe made one more strike and then two misses before she began to get a feel for it. Tomarys walked over to her and adjusted her position, his strong arms surprisingly gentle. When she made three strikes in a row, he nodded.

'Good,' he said. 'You have a natural talent.' She looked to see if he was jesting, but his expression was sincere. 'Before we increase the distance, I have one more lesson.'

Chloe let her arm fall to her side as she turned to watch, ears open to every word.

'Our fourth lesson. As well as proper preparation, setting our enemy's false expectations, and being the man – or woman – with the weapon, winning means choosing the right moment. You want your enemies to be distracted. Then, when you take action, be bold. Be strong. Be confident. Nothing is more powerful than the warrior who will achieve his objective or die trying.'

Chloe wondered if, when the time came, she would be up to the challenge. She vowed to herself that she would be strong.

'Let us increase the distance. Come, Chloe, show me what you can do.'

Fifty miles away, on the shores of the isle of Amphi, Dion lay sleeping off his exhaustion after yet another harrowing battle against a wildran.

He rolled and mumbled in a restless slumber. His nightmares were filled with roaring giants and shrieking furies, thrashing serpents and savage dragons.

In his dreams he was in Xanthos, but all the people were various forms of wildren. Ogres roamed the agora and merfolk swam in the harbor. He was standing on the Orange Terrace outside the Royal Palace talking to his father, but Markos was a giant, a crown on his lank silver hair. Peithon was a coiled serpent, incredibly long, wrapped around the palace. Two furies that looked like Nikolas and Helena flew overhead, hand in hand. Everywhere he looked there were wildren.

Dion's eyes shot open, and for a moment he didn't know where he was. Remembrance slowly returned; he was far from home, on the Salesian side of the Maltherean Sea.

Leaving the circle of sleeping marines propped up around the fire, Dion walked down to the beach and stared into the water. He felt disturbed, although he couldn't place the reason why.

35

Peithon, first adviser to King Markos of Xanthos, master of trade and the treasury, stood on the balcony of his majestic villa, hands on the rail as he gazed out at the city below.

The voice of the overseer droned on and Peithon was fighting to keep listening. Instead he was thinking about his home.

After the Royal Palace, it was the most impressive residence in the city, but Theodotus, the richest merchant in Xanthos, had just commenced work on a villa that would make Peithon's home pale in comparison. Admittedly, the new villa's position, while high, was less desirable than Peithon's, which was both close to the palace and loftily raised from the stench of the poor. But what chafed most of all was that it would block the view he was currently enjoying. He could see it now – already the foundations had been laid and workers scurried to and fro as they erected the walls. He would be forced to watch as the first story went up, and then the second. The most skilled artists from Phalesia would decorate the exterior and design elaborate gardens. Statues would catch his eye whenever he looked from this vantage. People would remark on the residence of Theodotus where they had previously talked about Peithon's home.

Something the overseer said caught his attention.

'—going to halt work. I need a hundred pieces of silver just to keep going for another week.'

He was discussing the new harbor wall. It was barely a few inches high and didn't yet cover the length of the city's shore. Nikolas, the king's eldest son and heir, had pushed his father to erect it, but workers were expensive, as was stone.

Peithon turned to face the frowning overseer. 'You will get your coin when I have it.'

'Stopping work will set us back,' the overseer persisted. 'It takes time to assemble a crew and explain what needs doing to the team leaders.'

'Then don't stop work,' Peithon stated, spreading his hands.

'They are family men. They need to feed their children.' The overseer changed tone, his voice now inquiring. 'Perhaps, lord, you can provide some of your own silver, just until the king's money arrives? I heard in the city that you've just paid a sizable sum for an extension to your villa . . .'

Peithon's eyes narrowed. Heavyset but tall, he leaned forward and jutted a pudgy finger with a thick silver ring as he spoke to the overseer. 'Who am I?'

The overseer stammered, remembering his station. 'You are the king's first adviser.'

'And who are you?'

'I am a master of stone.'

'Well, I am master of stone, timber, food, wine, coin – the list goes on. There are many items that require my attention and that make demands on the treasury—'

Peithon's speech was interrupted when he saw one of his servants leading a slim man with neatly combed hair to the balcony. Recognizing Alastor, the king's chief steward, he decided to close the conversation.

'Tell your men to keep working. They will get their money when the king is ready. If they decide to halt, I will inform the king, and he will make an appropriate response. Do you understand?'

'Yes, First Adviser. But the queen said—'

'You spoke to the queen, rather than come directly to me?' Now Peithon was truly furious.

'She asked me about the progress on the wall,' the overseer protested.

'Everything comes by me,' Peithon spat. 'Everything. If you circumvent my authority again I will have you thrown out of the city. Your wife and children will go with you, and you will find yourself without a home, looking for work in a place where you have no friends.'

'Yes, First Adviser,' the overseer said mournfully.

'Good. Now get out.'

Peithon scowled at the overseer as he left, but then smoothed his expression and turned to face the king's steward.

'Alastor, my friend. What can I do for you?'

'Lord, you said you wanted to know about all messages that arrive for the king?'

'I do.'

'The silver . . .?'

Peithon's smile tightened. 'Is your news worth silver?'

'It is.'

'Follow me.' He led the king's steward into the villa's interior and retrieved a single coin from the ornate wooden box on a side table. He offered it, but when the steward reached out he drew back his hand. 'The news?'

'The news is from Phalesia. It is old, but we are only getting it now. The Ilean warship that was damaged in the earthquake . . .'

'Yes, yes.'

'Prior to the quake, as part of a larger fleet, the Ileans sacked three towns on the isle of Orius. They burned the houses, looted the temples, and raped the women.'

Peithon rubbed his chin as he murmured. 'Then, damaged in the tremor, they had the nerve to ask Phalesia for help.'

'The reports have convinced the Assembly. Despite the peace faction, they are preparing for war.'

Peithon mused, pondering these events, thinking about how it affected Xanthos and himself.

'The silver?'

'Here.' Peithon handed out the coin. 'You have done well. Keep this up and I will see you prosper. My position as master of trade is a very lucrative one. I am sure you understand.'

The steward hesitated. 'I have more news. But this is worth more than one silver. It involves you.'

Peithon frowned. 'How much?'

'Five silver.'

'If it isn't as important as you say . . .'

'Trust me, you will find it so.'

Peithon returned to the moneybox and counted out five silver coins, each bearing the impression of the eagle of Phalesia.

'Lord, I overheard the queen bringing up uncertainties regarding the payments from the king's treasury to the workers on the new harbor wall.'

Peithon kept his face carefully smooth, hiding his emotions. 'Go on.'

'It was difficult to hear. She said she has a witness, a merchant, who will prove the validity of what she says.'

Fear clenched his stomach but all he did was murmur. 'Who is the witness?'

'I do not know. The king saw me nearby and asked me to leave.'

Peithon forced a smile. 'Here is your silver. I am pleased you have brought this to my attention. Never fear, Alastor. This misunderstanding will be cleared up.'

'Lord.' The steward bowed and departed.

Peithon wondered if he had left any loose ends. He had carefully cultivated strong alliances with the merchants, who stood to benefit as much as he did from their arrangements. He murmured names and considered each man in turn. Who would betray him? Who would stand to benefit?

He decided it was time to see the king.

Peithon found the king and his queen out on the Orange Terrace, sitting on the stone benches and staring out to sea. Their heads were close together; they stopped speaking when he approached.

Markos smiled and stood, fixing a warm expression of welcome on his closest adviser. Although stooped, he still had the frame of a warrior, and there was no thinning of his thick, curly white hair. His matching beard covered his mouth but didn't hide the small scar on his left cheek.

Peithon remembered when the king had taken that wound, long ago in the war against Tanus. Once they had both been young men, strong and invincible, with the athletic builds of the world's finest warriors. Markos had been ten years Peithon's senior, but a strong friendship had grown. He remembered how close they had been then.

Now Markos's shoulders were hunched while Peithon's muscle had run to fat. Time had passed. This world was a different place.

'Peithon,' the king said. 'Please, sit with us.'

The queen didn't stand, nor did she speak or smile. Over time Thea had poisoned the king against Peithon, and she now had her husband's ear, whispering slurs against him, the king's most loyal companion. Peithon felt rage build within him, both at Thea and her policy of befriending the disgusting creatures who had robbed him of a bride, and at Markos, who appeared to have forgotten the strong bond they once shared. He suddenly wanted to hurt them, to make them acknowledge that he deserved to be more than a glorified merchant.

Peithon remained standing. 'King Markos, Queen Thea, I heard the news. The sacking of Orius was only the beginning, I fear.'

'Word travels fast,' Thea murmured.

'You won't sit?' Markos asked, returning to his seat.

'No, sire. It seems that I have many tasks ahead of me if we are to prepare for what might come.'

'Yet still no word from Dion,' Thea said, gazing out to sea. 'It has been weeks since he left on his foolish quest.'

'We all fear for him,' Peithon said. 'We must assume he is safe.'

'So what are your thoughts, Peithon?' The king turned his steady gaze on him.

'They are going to return to attack Phalesia. I have no doubt.'

The king's eyes widened with surprise at his conviction.

Thea frowned. 'All we know is that they raided Orius.'

Ignoring her, Peithon spoke to the king. 'The sun king's men slaughtered our neighbors, our countrymen – Galeans all of them – before making threats to Phalesia and seizing the first consul's daughter. We must send the army to help reinforce Phalesia's defenses. Our soldiers need to train with theirs, and our officers should advise the consuls in preparation for battle. Our allies need our help.'

'It would leave Xanthos defenseless,' Thea retorted. 'Who are you to advise the king on military strategy?'

'Now, wife,' Markos said, holding up a hand. 'Peithon is a warrior first and foremost. Just because we are old men with new responsibilities does not mean we have forgotten who we were.'

Keeping his expression sincere as his gaze turned from the king to his formidable queen, Peithon thought about how much he hated her. The king had needed a second son, he understood that, but somehow this woman with no people and no home had wormed her way into his graces. She had betrayed the memories of her countrymen, slaughtered by wildren, by refusing to take the fight to the eldren they once were. Eldren once fought humans for control of the world. They were just biding their time before the war began again. If he were king—

'Sire,' Peithon said, revealing nothing of his thoughts. 'The Shards protect our flank. Any attack from the sea must go through Phalesia to reach us here in Xanthos. Phalesia must be strong. Her navy and our army are all that will prevent our mutual destruction. We must combine our forces, sooner rather than later. The Ileans could arrive at any moment. The sun king is too powerful for either of us to face alone.'

Markos scratched his beard as he mused. Finally, he turned to Thea. 'I am sorry, wife, but Peithon speaks sense. I'll tell Nikolas to take the army through the Gates of Annika to Phalesia. We can always recall them if we have need.'

'The men will need supplies.' Peithon bowed. 'By your leave?'

'Of course,' the old king said.

Leaving the terrace and walking through the arched entrance to the king's audience chamber, Peithon glanced at the high-backed wooden chair that was the king's throne.

Peithon had made inquiries. Even working together, Xanthos and Phalesia would never be able to hold out against the might of the Ilean Empire. Challenging the sun king was foolhardy in the extreme.

He thought about the message he would send. He had a captain in mind who would make the journey for silver.

The king would send Nikolas and the army to Phalesia. Xanthos would then be a very tempting target for the Ileans.

The secret route through the Shards would soon be secret no more.

All Peithon had to do was keep the army away from Xanthos until the sun king's soldiers arrived.

36

The old arena was now familiar to Chloe; this was her fourth visit in as many days. She was no longer in awe of the empty seats, filled with ghosts of the past, watching savage combat and howling for blood. Instead, she now saw it as her training ground, the place where she transformed from a healer and musician into something else altogether.

'Come,' Tomarys said. 'I will crouch down, and you grab hold of my hair. People often use this to cause pain and immobilize an opponent, but I will show you how to take back control.'

She walked up behind him and with her right hand took a fistful of his dark hair, tied back behind his head with a thong. She grabbed it close to the root as hard as she could.

'Argh,' he grunted. 'That hurts.' She started to relax her hold. 'No! Do not soften. If a man takes you like this, he will not be gentle.'

She gripped hard once more.

'I will show you the move quickly, and then I will show it slow. Here it is.'

He slapped his hand down on hers, trapping her palm to the top of his head. He then brought his other arm into play and whirled.

Chloe felt a burst of pain in her wrist. If he'd used all his strength, he would have broken her arm.

'Did you see?'

'Not really,' Chloe admitted.

'Slowly this time. Take my hair again. Good. Now watch. I clasp my hand over yours. This takes away your power to yank hard, immobilizing me with pain. That is the first step. I then crouch, sinking lower. This removes still more of your power to pull my hair, while removing some of your leverage. Your arm is no longer strong in this position. It feels awkward, does it not?' He paused. 'We will stop here. This is the important part.'

Chloe examined their postures. Her hand still gripped his hair, but he had his right hand on top of hers. He had allowed his body to sink, meaning her arm was angled more than it had previously been.

'Now I still have one free hand. So I stiffen my hand like a knife. I bring my left hand behind my head, up and across. I place the knife between your hand and your wrist, where there is a joint.' He moved accordingly. 'Your arm is now mine. I spin, using the full force of my back and shoulders. I will do it slowly.'

He turned, keeping his stiffened hand against the joint of her wrist, still holding her hand clasped against his head. Pain grew in Chloe's wrist, even with Tomarys moving at a snail's pace.

'The assailant now wants only to be free of the pain. When I complete my spin, even if I haven't broken his arm, he will be nursing his hand. That is when I attack.'

Chloe nodded as he finished the spin until he was facing her.

'Your turn now. I am taller than you, so you do not need to crouch. I will come up behind you and grab the hair on the top of your head.'

He gripped Chloe hard, making her wince. She slapped her hand down, crouched so that she was moving into his body behind him, then brought her stiff left hand up, inserted it into the joint at his wrist, and spun into him. Tomarys had no choice but to let go as she whirled to face him. Even if Chloe couldn't break a man's arm, she could get herself free of such an attack.

'Good!' He smiled. 'We will practice it more over the coming days. I have one more movement to teach you. An easier one this time. Face away from me again.'

Chloe complied. Tomarys came up behind her and suddenly grabbed her right wrist. He twisted her arm up behind her back. She grunted at the sudden pain.

'Many people use this hold. It is extremely common, so it is a good one to know how to get out of. It is a matter of instinct. You want to pull away, but pulling in the direction your mind tells you to go in simply adds to the pain. Here is the key. As soon as you can – ideally surprising the man who holds you – turn in the direction of your free arm. The easiest way to remember this is to rotate and swing your free elbow at your enemy's head. As you turn, you bring your entire body to bear against the force of one man's hand. The hand being held moves away, reducing your opponent's leverage. The key is to use surprise. You are a woman, and surprise is your key advantage, for they will not be expecting you to have any skill or power. Try it now.'

Sure enough, when Chloe turned, the pain of the wrist twisted behind her back decreased rather than increased. She made a point with her elbow and freed herself as she whirled.

But her raised elbow didn't come close to touching her bodyguard's chin.

Tomarys grinned. 'Do not worry – my height is rare. Your elbow will likely strike a man's mouth, causing him a great deal of pain. If you are skilled, you could even strike his throat. We will practice that move in addition to the first. I will also teach you some basic swordplay. Remember, you only need to know enough to kill a man after taking his weapon.'

Tomarys looked up at the sky.

'Now, before we go, I have a gift for you. You wear a copper chain around your neck, but the chain is bare.'

Chloe's brow furrowed as he reached into the pouch at his belt and withdrew a heavy copper amulet. He handed it to her and watched to see her reaction.

The amulet of shiny red metal had the circumference of a large cup and was perfectly circular. Within the circle was an open child's palm, the fingers slightly curled so that the child held what appeared to be a sheaf of wheat. The sheaf had a narrow stem and was pointed at one end.

Chloe wondered how she should react.

'Tomarys . . . This is a fine gift. But I fear angering my deity. This is the symbol of Edra, goddess of love, fertility, and children. I worship Aeris, goddess of music and healing.'

'I know,' Tomarys said, his arms folded over his chest as he grinned. 'But the symbol of Aeris didn't suit my purpose. Examine it.'

'Wheat is the symbol of fertility . . . It appears I'm asking Edra's blessing to conceive.' Chloe looked up, perplexed, but smiling. 'Thank you, Tomarys. This is the first kind gesture anyone has made since I was first taken from my home.'

Accepting the gift, she unclasped the chain from around her neck and threaded the amulet through the little hoop at the top, before once more fastening the necklace. The amulet was a little large for Chloe's taste, and now hung below her neck, just above her breasts.

Tomarys's grin broadened as he reached forward and did something to the amulet. A moment later he showed Chloe the sheaf in his palm; he had completely removed it from the rest of the piece.

It was tapered and sharp on the underside. Chloe's eyes widened as realization dawned.

'It is a small throwing knife, made of bronze, rather than copper, for bronze takes a better edge. Practice with it as much as you can.'

He showed her how to place the decorated knife back in the child's open palm. Tomarys then glanced up at the sky again. He opened his mouth, hesitating before speaking.

'Listen, Chloe . . . I plan to get my family out of Lamara, but it will take some weeks. I want to leave the sun king's service and be with my family, far from here, and you should be with yours. I hope to be ready before Solon returns. For now, we need to bide our time.'

'Tomarys—'

He held up his hand. 'This is only possible because of what you did for my brother. He, too, wishes to be free.'

Chloe saw that the timbers of the dilapidated rail around the arena floor cast long shadows on the sand.

'We should leave,' Tomarys said. He smiled. 'Every day your skills improve. Perhaps one day it will be you who protects the weak from evil men.'

Chloe laughed aloud when she heard these words of praise from the toughest man she'd ever met.

The journey back was uneventful, with Chloe examining her new amulet as she walked. The usual beggars cried out to her when they thought they were out of her bodyguard's earshot. The stench of refuse and human waste rose from the sides of every street and alley of the poor quarter.

A particularly persistent street urchin came up and grabbed Chloe's chiton. 'The curious sailor is at the House of Algar,' he said, looking at her with wild eyes as she tried to fend him off. Tomarys sent him sprawling with a shove.

The words were so strange she assumed the boy must be taken by madness. She thought nothing more of the encounter.

The one stab of fear came when she passed the palace guards and wondered if they would take note of her new amulet; it would be difficult not to notice it. But as Tomarys said, sometimes the best hiding place was in plain sight.

They passed through unchallenged. Chloe was one step closer to freedom.

37

Dion was impatient for news as he helped the crew beach the *Ano-raxis* on the harbor shore. He had been gone for more than a week; at any moment the sun king could return.

After fulfilling his duties, he bid farewell to his captain and with his bow and quiver in hand left the harbor, heading out the gate to make his way into the city. Skirting the bazaar, following the now familiar streets to the palace quarter, Dion approached the guesthouse. He knew Algar would ask him for more money but the paymaster had told him to come back the next day to collect his wages.

Dion spoke to his well-dressed host, who grumbled but agreed to grant him another day. He then looked anxiously for Anoush and saw the boy sitting on a low wall near the House of Algar, munching on a handful of raisins.

'Anoush.' Dion frowned. 'Not watching the palace?'

'Master!' His eyes widened. 'You're back!' He leaped to his feet and ran over, tilting his head to look up at him as he hopped from foot to foot. 'I have news. I passed the girl your message yesterday.'

'How did she react?'

'I do not think she understood. I only had a short time to speak before the big guard with her knocked me away . . . But I am sure she heard me. She was confused, I think.'

Dion cursed as he looked away. If she knew he was here and that help might be coming, the knowledge could make his task easier.

'But there is more.'

Dion's eyes shot once more to the young boy. 'What?'

'She regularly goes to the abandoned arena in the poor quarter. She is probably there right now.'

'Alone?'

'No, the guard goes with her.'

'What is she doing there?'

'I did not follow them inside. I only saw that they came out again some time later.'

Dion's heart started to race. He had learned about Ilea and about the size of the sun king's navy. He had learned a great deal about the capabilities of ships like the *Anoraxis* and something about the way they were built. Chloe would have spent time with the sun king himself, and would know his mind.

All Dion needed to do now was to free Chloe and escape. The only obstacle in his way was her warden.

Dion's bow was in his hand and a quiver was on his shoulder. He spoke to Anoush with urgency. 'The abandoned arena. Take me there now.'

Dion crept along the wide passage, keeping to the shadows as he felt the weight of stone above his head, under foot, and in the walls on both sides. He saw bright light through a tall rectangular exit ahead and slowed his pace even further, placing one foot down before moving the next, anxious to move as silently and unobtrusively as possible.

Behind him Anoush hung back, fearful and hesitant. Now that he had led Dion this far, Dion waved the boy to stay in the corridor. He didn't want him getting involved in any conflict.

Dion took three more steps and then stopped just before the exit, where clouds of dust swirled in the bright rays of sunshine. He knew that as soon as he stepped forward once more the sunlight would blind him. He stopped and listened.

He heard voices, one male and one female.

Blood throbbed in his temples; he felt the tempo of his pulse increase, reminding him of the galloping rhythm of the *Anoraxis* at ramming speed. He heard the gruff notes of the guard's deep voice and the higher pitch of Chloe's replies. They sounded far enough away that he felt confident of exiting the passage.

He dropped to a crouch and squinted as he left the corridor. Dion saw that there was a wall in front of him and a set of steps heading up to the side. Keeping in the shadow of the wall he climbed the steps and peered around the corner.

Dion was halfway up the tiered gallery of a structure in the shape of a wheel. It reminded him of the lyceum in Phalesia, but the proportions were far greater than even that huge structure. There were seats doubling as steps that all faced a circular space in the center.

He saw two figures standing close together in the middle of the arena's sandy central floor.

The huge guard – tall and muscled, wearing a leather vest and brown trousers – stood at an angle with Dion looking mostly at his back. Near him and with her face visible in profile was Chloe.

His breath caught as he saw that she held a sword, pointed at the guard, who was unarmed. It appeared that Dion had timed his arrival perfectly; he couldn't have come a moment too soon. Chloe was making her own bid for freedom.

Dion left his hiding place. He was now exposed in bright daylight but Chloe's attention was entirely on the bodyguard.

Dion pulled an arrow out of his quiver and nocked it to the string of his bow. Knowing that a fast-moving shape draws the eye, he fought to keep his breathing deep and even, fighting the power of fear to remain steady as he descended, creeping down first one step and then another. He kept his eyes on his enemy the entire time. If he could kill this man his quest would be accomplished.

Dion circled around as he lost height, moving so that he would approach the tall warrior directly from behind. Chloe kept the tip of the sword pointed at her opponent as she said something to him; her attention was on anything but the gallery above.

Glancing back the way he'd come, Dion saw Anoush standing near the exit corridor, watching him with wide eyes. He made another wave to tell him to stay back.

He would need to make a good strike, firmly between the warrior's shoulder blades. Dion narrowed the distance to forty paces, and then thirty. He was now on level ground, standing in a gap in the decrepit wooden fence, with no obstruction between him and his target.

He lifted his bow. He drew the string to his ear and stilled his breathing.

He fixed his gaze on the big warrior's shoulders.

Dion prayed for a solid strike as he let the arrow fly.

———

'Keep the point always on your enemy,' Tomarys said. 'Think of the tip as a shield as well as a weapon, as long as you have the sharp end between the two of you, you are defending yourself. Angle it slightly higher, you do not want the sword to be horizontal.'

Chloe complied, but the sword was heavier than it looked. Holding the hilt with both hands, she lifted the point.

'Good,' Tomarys said. 'Now take a single step forward, leading with your front foot. Angle your body to the side so you are presenting a smaller target.'

Chloe followed his instructions and brought the sword closer to her opponent's chest.

'Now attack!' Tomarys said.

As Chloe was about to thrust, she saw motion out of the corner of her eye.

Time stood still.

The bowman was in Ilean clothing: white tunic and trousers, common dress she might see on any of Lamara's streets. His sandy hair marked him out as different, but there were many different peoples in the sun king's capital. He stood just outside the wooden rail girding the arena floor, where a gap in the broken fence enabled ingress.

He had his bow drawn, about to loose an arrow. Chloe knew she had the briefest instant to react.

She dropped the sword and ran at Tomarys.

His eyes widened with shock and surprise as she struck. Chloe hit him with her shoulder tucked in, shoving him forward. She felt the whistle of the arrow as it missed her head by an inch. Tomarys grunted, but although knocked back he stayed standing. Chloe's mad lunge meant she fell to the ground, tumbling onto the sand.

She rolled on to her back and saw Tomarys spy his assailant and make a swift assessment. The archer fitted another arrow and drew and released in a single smooth motion.

But Tomarys was aware of the attack now, and weaved as he ran directly at him. The second arrow flew past the big warrior's shoulder. Realizing he didn't have time to release a third shaft, the bowman dropped his bow and charged.

The two men crashed into each other and went down in a mess of flailing limbs. The archer got on top and smashed a fist into

Tomarys's jaw, but the bodyguard merely grunted and brought the heel of his hand into his opponent's chin.

The strike resounded like an axe splitting kindling. The bowman fell backwards and his eyes rolled. Tomarys shook his head to clear it and climbed to his feet as his opponent moaned, on his back and senseless.

Tomarys scowled and rubbed his jaw. He reached down and with his left hand grabbed hold of the archer by the throat, lifting him into the sky. The bowman's feet were now dangling and he gurgled as the bodyguard looked into his face.

As Tomarys held him high, squeezing his neck, he clenched his right fist and smashed it into his opponent's chest.

Chloe winced, hearing ribs crack. Another strike hit the bowman's face, near his eye.

Breathlessly, she managed to get to her feet as Tomarys pounded the bowman again and again. She saw that his face was turning red; his struggles were now pitiful. Tomarys was going to kill him.

In that instant, despite his foreign clothing, Chloe suddenly recognized him.

Her face drained of color.

Tomarys was beating Dion, prince of Xanthos, the second son of King Markos. He was the last person she expected to see.

The pieces fitted together. He had used the boy to pass Chloe a message in the street. He had seen Chloe holding a sword pointed at Tomarys. Dion had come here to rescue her.

'Stop!' Chloe screamed. She ran to Tomarys and pulled at the arm holding Dion by the throat. 'Stop! Don't kill him!'

Tomarys looked at Chloe and she saw the madness of rage in his eyes. But he let go, and Dion fell to the ground. He was barely conscious. His lip had burst, covering his mouth and jaw in blood. His right eye was puffed up and nearly closed shut. His fingers twitched as he lay prone on his side, the only sign that life was still in him.

'You know who he is?'

Chloe thought furiously. 'No . . . He must be part of the group that attacked us in the alley.'

Tomarys glanced down at him again. 'He chose the wrong people to waylay,' he muttered. 'I should kill him.'

'Tomarys . . . Don't. Let's just leave.'

He scanned the arena, looking for more enemies, but saw that his assailant had acted alone. 'This place is no longer safe,' he said. 'We need to leave. Now.'

Chloe nodded. She wondered if there was anything she could do for Dion, but any help she gave him would arouse Tomarys's suspicions.

She felt terrible leaving him this way, but once she'd saved Tomarys there was no other path before her. She was confused. Tomarys was her friend. She had no wish to see him dead on the ground with an arrow in his back.

They left the arena. Chloe glanced back once.

Dion still hadn't moved.

38

The sun king was back.

Solon had returned while Chloe and Tomarys were at the arena. Chloe was now terrified, for as soon as they returned soldiers took Tomarys away while more guards escorted Chloe to the women's quarters. Tomarys had been as confused as Chloe. Their manner hadn't been friendly.

She spent the night wondering what was happening. When she woke in the morning, her bodyguard's presence had been so constant that she felt strange not seeing him. The only information she got from the eunuchs was that the sun king had defeated the uprising in Shadria. She knew nothing more.

The day passed interminably. Chloe struggled to maintain her composure but couldn't contain the dark thoughts that kept bubbling to the surface. Had the sun king learned about her training sessions with Tomarys? Did he think that they had been spending too much time away from the palace? Was he planning to launch an attack on Phalesia?

A sudden fear clutched hold of her chest. She lifted up her bed pallet to look for the sack of flower pods.

It was gone.

Chloe hunted underneath and searched the area frantically. She heard a man clear his throat.

The wild-haired eunuch with pockmarked skin stood looking down at her. Beside him were two soldiers of the palace guard.

Chloe felt her breathing come in gasps as she stopped what she was doing and climbed to her feet.

'The sun king demands your presence,' one of the soldiers said. 'Come with us,' the other growled.

The first man gripped Chloe tightly by the upper arm as they marched her out of the women's quarters, through the corridors and waiting chamber, to the sun king's throne room.

Guards lined both sides of the rectangular space facing the throne. Behind it, a cool breeze blew in through the open doors leading to the terrace. The two guards stood on either side of her as Chloe glanced up at the man on the throne.

This time, she didn't prostrate herself, and no one asked her to.

Solon looked terrible.

He had lost more weight, even though only a couple of weeks had passed. His eyes were dark sunken pits and his cheeks were as tight as drums. He started to speak and then burst into a fit of coughing. When he finally finished, he touched a white cloth to his lips, and Chloe saw red.

'King of kings,' Chloe said. 'How are you?'

He placed a hand on his chest and winced, before straightening with an effort as he looked down his sharp nose at her.

'We took gold,' he said, 'but not enough.' His voice was still clipped and precise, but it was weaker than when they had last spoken. 'And now I can feel that the end is near. The Seer's prophecies always come true. This is the year I will die.'

'If there is anything I can—'

He held up a hand for silence. Chloe stopped. The sun king swallowed with pain and it was some time before he spoke.

'I need to speak with you about this very subject.' He nodded to a distant figure, and Chloe saw one of his magi come forward, the man's yellow robe indicating dedication to the sun god. As she recognized the dark-eyed magus who had questioned her when she first administered to Solon in his bedchamber, he handed Solon a sack, before bowing and withdrawing.

Chloe's eyes widened with horror as she recognized the sack, but she fought to remain calm. She had made it this far; she had to be strong.

'One of my magi smelled my tea and told me something that I initially did not believe,' Solon said. 'But on my return we searched your chambers and found these.'

He reached into the sack and withdrew a single flower pod, greenish-purple, with a circular crest on top.

'Tell me, Chloe of Phalesia, follower of Aeris, skilled healer,' he said, speaking in a low voice that filled Chloe with dread. 'Are these what the magi say they are? Are these things . . . flowers of bliss?'

Chloe tried to speak with a firm voice. 'They are a powerful medication for easing pain—'

'They are banned by law,' Solon said softly. He drew himself up on the throne, leaning forward, looming over her. His expression shifted from pain, to anger, to vengeful rage. 'You have had me drinking milk of the poppy!'

'If it eases your pain—'

'My pain—' he cried, and then broke off, coughing. He started again. 'My pain is merely my soul passing through the jagged gates of Ar-Rayan. We know what you have been doing. We know where you have been going to get these . . . things.'

He stood, stepping down from the dais and walked forward to loom over Chloe.

'Come,' Solon said.

With guards on both sides of her, Chloe had no choice but to follow. Solon walked to the terrace, passing through the archways and standing out in the open air. He turned and waited for her approach.

The terrace was a pleasant place, overlooking the city and the broad river, with colorful flowers in pots and a wide central basin filled with water.

It was devoid of people, and Chloe couldn't see what Solon wanted to show her. When she reached him he walked to the edge of the terrace and clutched onto the rail with bony fingers. Leaning forward, he looked down.

Chloe came to stand beside him.

There was a lower level of paved stones and spiky plants in gardens that she hadn't previously been aware of. It was far larger than the terrace, and she guessed it had something to do with the soldiers.

The wide space was revealed to her as she came closer to the rail, until she stood alongside the sun king.

She followed his gaze.

'No!' she moaned.

Tomarys was bare-chested and crimson blood covered his torso. His head lolled to the side, exposing his neck. Whip marks covered every part of his skin and his trousers hung in shreds.

His feet weren't touching the ground.

Looking down, Chloe saw a vertical wooden stake holding him up. It entered his body somewhere between his legs and traveled up through his insides, emerging from his mouth.

'I watched every moment of it,' Solon hissed. 'I made sure it went in slowly. Your betrayal was unexpected, but I understand it, you are my prisoner here. His, on the other hand, was not.'

Chloe couldn't look on, but nor could she look away. The only man who had shown her any kindness had been given the worst death imaginable. And it was all because of her.

'He told us everything,' Solon said. 'About your daily quests to find more flowers of bliss. He would not say that you planned to increase the dose to cause my death, but to me that is clear.'

Chloe realized that Tomarys had stayed loyal to her even in the face of unspeakable pain. He hadn't told his torturers about training her in the arena, or about his gift of the amulet that even now hung around her neck.

Then her breath stopped. She felt as if she would be sick. Chills ran up and down her spine.

Tomarys's head moved and he made a horrific gurgling moan. He was still alive.

'Dear gods!' she whispered. Tears ran down her cheeks and she stifled a wracking sob. 'Please . . . Dear gods!'

'Rest in the knowledge that you did this to him, girl,' Solon said, his low voice sounding somehow self-satisfied. 'His pain is your doing.'

'Please—' Chloe said. She turned her moisture-filled eyes on the tall man beside her. 'Please . . . Let me go to him. Let me say goodbye.'

Solon tugged on his pointed beard as he mused. He finally nodded to the guards on both sides of her. 'Take her down to him. Let her see from a closer vantage.'

Chloe was barely aware of being led from the terrace and back through the throne room. Her guards took her outside, near the palace gates, and down a set of steps. Her feet were leaden as she walked, horror in every tread. She passed through a section of palace more functional than beautiful and emerged out into the open once more.

She approached the impaled man and looked up at him.

'I'm so sorry,' Chloe said.

Tomarys couldn't speak; he couldn't even turn his head to look at her, but she knew he could hear.

Glancing up to where Solon watched from above, she pushed the guards away. She walked forward until just a few paces from her friend.

Chloe knew what she had to do.

She wrapped a hand around her amulet and looked down as if praying. With a click the small throwing knife came free.

Chloe prayed then. For the first time in her life, she prayed to Balal, the god of war, for her aim to be true. She prayed to Aeris to grant her this one act of compassion.

With her eyes fixed steadily on his exposed neck, she drew in a breath. Chloe's arm whipped down and she released the knife when the point was right on target.

The triangle of sharp steel flew through the air. It sliced into her bodyguard's jugular and then fell back to the ground with a clang of metal on stone.

Chloe watched, stone-faced and red-eyed, as bright, fresh blood pumped out of the man's neck, gushing in a torrent. Tomarys's head stopped moving. His body became entirely still.

She was dimly aware of shouting men, running forward and holding her fast. She kept her eyes on her bodyguard until they dragged her away.

Solon snarled. 'Throw her into one of the cells beneath the palace while I decide what to do with her.' He then called out again. 'My last gift to you, girl. I am assembling the navy. Do you hear me? We sail to war. Soon it will be your beloved father who writhes on the stake.'

39

'Dion, can you hear me?'

Dion heard Roxana's gravelly voice. He groaned and tried to nod, but nearly blacked out with the effort.

'He is very hurt,' Anoush piped.

'Really?' Roxana said, her voice dripping with sarcasm. 'I thought he was just nursing a hangover. Gods, look at your face, Dion. I've seen better-looking ogres. You said he got waylaid in the city?'

'Yes,' Anoush said. 'Bandits tried to rob him. I found him and got some men to help bring him back here.'

'But they didn't take his bow? First thing I would have taken.'

'Soldiers frightened them off.'

'Lucky for him. Or unlucky he got beaten before they came, I suppose. This city is more dangerous than hunting wildren, it seems.' She barked a laugh. 'Dion, if you can hear me, I've paid Algar from your wages. I've also given some coin to your'—she hesitated—'manservant. For healing balms and supplies. There isn't much left. Why in the name of Silex are you living in such expensive lodgings?'

Dion moaned.

'Look, I know it hurts, but give it a couple of days and you'll be all right. I've seen worse. Much worse. Hope you gave back as good as you got.'

Dion heard rustling.

'Boy, listen. There's not much you can do about his ribs. I'd say he's broken at least two or three. It'll hurt to laugh, so keep your jokes to a minimum.' She snorted. 'His head will clear. Put the poultice on his face, there, where it looks worst. Understand?'

'Yes, mistress.'

'Mistress? I like that. Look, I need to be going. You got all you need? Good. Tell him to come and see me when he's better. He can tell me the story then, over a mug of beer. My treat.'

Dion fought to open his eyes, but the effort was too great.

Darkness overcame his senses.

40

The cells beneath the palace were empty. Chloe had the entire place to herself. The guards had thrown her inside one of several identical windowless chambers and then closed a heavy door behind her. She'd momentarily seen their faces through the grill at head height, before they'd slid the bolt and left.

She guessed that only valuable or dangerous prisoners must be kept in this place. The sun king's captives would usually be either enslaved or immediately put to death. Although the copper chain around Chloe's neck remained, the amulet Tomarys had bought her was gone; the guards knew such things could be bought in the market. Still overwhelmed by horror – she had killed a man, a true friend – she spent hours trying not to be consumed by her ragged emotions. Even so, she wrapped her arms around her knees and whimpered, leaning back against the hard stone wall and seeing flashing images of Tomarys's suffering.

Finally, she fell asleep, huddled in the corner of her cell. She didn't know how long she slept, only that it was for a long time. Her lips were dry and her throat parched; she had yet to be given any food or water.

Sudden remembrance struck like a dagger in the heart. She saw the stake driven up through Tomarys's insides, emerging from his throat. She heard his terrible gurgling moan.

Chloe sobbed, but stifled it before it took hold of her. She had to be strong. She forced herself to look up and examine her surroundings.

It was dark, near pitch black; the only light came from the end of the corridor she'd entered through. The air was dry and cool. Standing and walking to the thick door, she peered through the window and counted six cells; she was in the cell closest to the door.

She heard movement – a soft tread of footsteps – and frowned, trying to locate the source of the sound. She then realized that her initial assessment was wrong: she wasn't alone after all. A shadowy face appeared, staring at her through the bars of the most-distant cell.

'You are upset, I take it?' a wry voice said. 'It has been a long time since I have had a companion here. I must say, I wasn't expecting someone like you. How old are you, human?'

The figure brought his face forward so that the barest amount of light touched his features. Chloe saw high cheekbones and sharp features. He was the last person in the world she expected to see.

'Zachary?' She clutched hold of the bars but then faltered. An eldran was looking at her, but he wasn't Zachary. 'Who are you?'

He was tall, even for an eldran, and despite his sharp chin his face was broad and strong. When he shifted his head Chloe saw that he was completely bald and that his left eye was missing, displaying an empty, wrinkled socket. She had never seen an eldran so visually striking.

'My name is Triton,' he said. 'You have heard of me? No?' He sounded surprised. 'I am the king of the eldren.'

'King?' Chloe was so surprised that she momentarily forgot about her own predicament. 'I didn't know the eldren had a king.'

He lifted his chin and spoke proudly. 'The blood of Marrix runs in my veins.'

With his movement Chloe now saw that he had a thin golden collar around his neck. She wondered at its purpose. Eldren weren't fond of metal, and could never willingly touch it.

'Who is Marrix?' The name was familiar, but Chloe couldn't place it.

'The last king to command all of the eldren. He died long ago, but his struggle is not forgotten. He led us, before most of my people turned wild and were lost to us. I have long ruled the eldren who live in the place you call the Waste.'

'Why are you here?'

'The sun king's armies advanced north of Abadihn and Koulis, seeking a route into Galea.' He shrugged. 'We stopped them.'

'You fight against the sun king?' Chloe realized she might have a potential ally, if she could ever find a way to free them both.

'We fought. But I was taken hostage and here I am. There is now an uneasy peace between us. My people will not fight while I am here.'

He brought up a hand as if to tug on the collar at his neck, but then stopped while still a few inches away, making a grimace of pain and bringing his hand back down.

'Why do you wear a collar?'

He smiled without mirth. 'I am not without power, girl. Without this collar around my neck I could change shape. Walls of stone would never keep me here.'

'Does it hurt?'

'The collar? Yes,' he said shortly. 'It hurts.' He was pensive for a time. 'Now who are you, girl? And why are you here?'

'I come from Phalesia, one of the Galean nations. One of the sun king's warships came to my homeland. I am the daughter of the first consul, and they took me prisoner. I was forming a plan to escape when I incurred the sun king's wrath. Now,' she said, echoing Triton's words, 'here I am. Solon now plans to lead a force to conquer my homeland.'

Triton frowned. 'There are closer conquests. What is it he wants?'

'He desires gold above all else. We have a sacred ark of gold—'

Triton swiftly leaned forward, his eyes suddenly wide as he peered at her, though he didn't touch the iron bars. 'Did you say an ark of gold? A chest?' His voice was urgent. 'What is inside?'

Chloe told the story of the tablets inscribed by the god Aldus, on which were the laws of morality that would grant a man entrance to heaven. 'It would be sacrilege to open the ark, yet Solon wants to seize it and melt it down for his tomb.'

Triton relaxed. He nodded sagely. 'I understand.'

'He plans to take the ark, and any other gold, and kill our leaders.' Chloe couldn't bring herself to repeat the sun king's threat to impale her father. 'He must be stopped.'

'He does, does he?' Triton's expression was pensive.

'Triton . . . Would your eldren help us against him?'

His one good eye met her gaze. 'If I were free, we would fight.' He once again nearly touched the collar, before allowing his hand to fall. 'Oh yes, we would.'

41

When Dion was finally well enough to think clearly, he was filled with anger.

In his mind's eye he saw Chloe push her guard to the side and his shot go wild. He had taken a great risk to free her. Why did she help her captors?

From now on, she was on her own. As soon as he could, he would return home to Xanthos. The first consul's daughter could remain a prisoner for all he cared.

He stood and looked around his small room. He wouldn't miss Lamara. When he returned to Xanthos he would tell his father and brother about the things he had learned in his time away. He would find the best carpenters and shipwrights and start working on warships to rival anything in the sun king's fleet. He would help Nikolas prepare strategies to prevent the sun king's biremes making an easy landing.

As Dion prepared to depart he swayed slightly but decided he was able to make the journey. He dressed and put his quiver over his shoulder, then took up his composite bow. He was just about to leave when he heard light footsteps outside, and a moment later the round-faced boy who had saved his life drew the entrance curtain aside. Anoush grinned when he saw Dion up and about.

'Master, you are well again. I have come straight from the harbor. Your captain gave me a message for you.'

Dion didn't expect to see Roxana again, but he nodded for Anoush to continue.

'She says that the sun king's navy is being made ready, and asks if you are fit enough to join her on a great expedition. There will be glory and plunder. The ships will sail to a new land across the sea.'

Dion's heart sank at the news. He thought quickly. 'Did they name the land? Did you hear the name Phalesia?'

Anoush frowned. 'No, that was not it. It was a different name.'

Dion's eyes widened. 'Xanthos?'

'Yes.' Anoush nodded vigorously. 'Xanthos. That is it.'

He wondered how it was possible. Why would Solon's fleet be sailing to Xanthos? The only route to the city's harbor would take them past Phalesia. The Shards blocked the only other channel.

'Are you certain it was Xanthos?'

'Yes, master. They are sailing for Xanthos.'

Dion clenched his jaw. He wondered if there was something he could do to help his people. With his quest to rescue Chloe at an end, he now had to put his homeland first.

He was known at Lamara's harbor. The guards would let him through. He had access to the sun king's fleet.

He knew he had no choice.

Dion reached into the pouch at his belt, wincing as even the slight motion reminded him there were places that still hurt, and took out the last of his money: a silver coin and a handful of coppers.

'Cup your hands,' he instructed Anoush. He spilled coins into the boy's palms. 'I need you to do something for me. I want you to go to the bazaar, quickly, and buy me some lamp oil. As much as you can carry. Get tinder also. If there's money left over it's yours. Go, lad. Now!'

Anoush nodded and left swiftly to do his bidding. Dion paced and made plans, feeling the time passing far too quickly for his comfort. He decided he would head for the harbor at the end of the day, when most of the crews would have left. He had to be clever as well as lucky if he was going to leave Lamara alive.

He ate some dried fruit and drank water, feeling his strength return. His brow furrowed as he tried to understand the plans of Solon and his naval overlord, Kargan. Roxana had told Anoush they were sailing for Xanthos . . .

But how was that possible?

Anoush finally returned an hour before sunset. He struggled to make his way up the stairs as he carried a heavy satchel over one shoulder.

'What is this for, master?'

'Anoush, I cannot tell you. The best thing you can do is to forget you ever met me. We might not see each other again.'

Dion took the satchel and put it over his shoulder. Peering inside, he saw a bulging skin and a bundle of dry tinder.

He left his bow and quiver in the room; if he could, afterwards, he would return to get them. He still hurt, but he could do this. Pushing aside the last remnants of pain, he summoned his determination as he crouched down and squeezed the boy's shoulder. 'Thank you, Anoush.'

Without another word, Dion left the House of Algar. He walked with purpose, heading straight for the harbor.

⌣

The guards at the gate let him through unchallenged, and Dion soon found himself walking along the sandy shore. Passing the lined-up warships, he saw bireme after bireme, with barely enough space between them for a man to walk. They were all drawn up on the shore with just a section of stern in the water. Some showed activity, sailors scrubbing the decks and mending sails. But most of the vessels were still and silent; their crews were done for the day.

Dion headed in the direction of the rectangular hut that was the mess. A hood on the structure's side funneled black smoke from the cooking hearth within. He saw a marine he knew and waved casually; Dion was just a man carrying supplies.

But inside, Dion's nerves ran ragged. He couldn't believe he was going to attempt this, but he could see no other option. He tried to keep calm, but his face was tight and drawn. He knew he still had a black eye and a swollen cheek. It didn't matter; he wouldn't be the only man in the sun king's fleet to have a wound or two.

He entered the mess and scanned the room. The hearth fire was kept constantly lit, banked up twice a day. He saw a few dozen sailors sitting around tables as they ate and he nodded to them. There were hundreds of lidded stone jugs – any fleet needed vast quantities of drinking water – lined up one after another against the wall. Dion picked up an empty jug and strode directly to the open hearth. Taking the tongs, he covered his movements with his body as he placed coal after coal into the jug. He replaced the lid to prevent the giveaway of smoke rising from the container.

Dion then carried the jug and satchel out of the mess. Glancing to the left, he saw the familiar stocky figure of Roxana in the distance, but she hadn't seen him and he ignored her.

Instead he walked along the row of sixty warships.

Selecting a pair of vessels roughly in the center, he passed along the narrow alleyway formed by the two hulls. He put the satchel and jug on the ground.

Dion returned to the mess, once again nodding to the men who glanced up at his entry. He stopped for a moment as he scanned the room, but then he saw what he was looking for: four buckets stacked one on top of the other. Dion grabbed the buckets and tried to stay calm as he returned to the hidden place between the ships.

He had to work quickly now.

Dion opened the satchel and took out the bulging skin. He divided half the lamp oil among the four buckets, so that each was nearly full. He then stoppered the skin and set it down on the hard sand near the jug.

One by one, he carried the buckets out into the open. He placed them at regular points along the line of ships, where they wouldn't be missed.

Dion scanned the harbor, but his careful, purposeful movements still hadn't attracted unwanted attention. He once more slipped between the two ships and took a deep breath to steady himself as he looked at the skin and jug.

Now he had to move as swiftly as he could, for the results of what he was doing would definitely be noticed.

He took the lid off the stone jug and looked inside, relieved to see the coals still hot and smoking. Facing the rippling brown water of the river, Dion reached into the side of the ship at his right, open to circulate air among the oarsmen. He had no tongs, so he tipped the jug to allow two coals to drop onto the wooden planking of the vessel's interior. He followed with tinder, placed around the coals. When he saw flames, he lifted the skin and poured lamp oil all over the area.

He then went to the ship on his other side, starting fire and pouring lamp oil there also.

Dion hefted the satchel onto his shoulder and left, nearly running, but fighting to keep his movements calm. He had the jug in his hand as he walked along the row, traveling until he'd passed half a dozen ships, and then ducking into the thin space between two more.

He started another fire and poured more lamp oil.

He left the area and continued to walk away from the crowded section, where there were few people who would see him.

Dion entered between two more ships and kept going.

42

Chloe woke after yet another sleep of exhaustion. She saw some flatbread and water just inside the doorway and realized the guards had visited her while she was asleep. She swiftly ate and drank in thirsty gulps, before climbing to her feet and gripping the iron bars of the grill as she peered at the distant cell.

'Triton?' she called. 'Are you there?'

She had spent hours speaking with him, deep in discussion. He had asked her about her home and she had questioned him further about his plans for revenge on the sun king.

But as she continued to call out, silence greeted her words. She tilted her head, perplexed. Somehow, the eldran king was gone.

Hearing footsteps, she saw a pair of palace soldiers enter the prison. One of the soldiers sniffed and made a sound of disgust.

'What time is it?' Chloe asked. 'How long have I been in here? What do you intend to do with me?'

'Quiet,' the guard in front grunted. 'Stand with your back against the wall.'

Chloe felt frustration course through her as she complied. The guard slid the bolt and then hauled the door open.

'Turn around and put your arms behind your back. Walk backwards until you reach me.'

Chloe followed the instructions and then felt a rough hand go around her wrist as her arm was twisted painfully behind her back. The soldier used his leverage to turn her around. Remembering what Tomarys had taught her, she let them handle her as they wanted; she knew she had to present the image of a weak, defenseless girl.

They marched her out of the prison, along rough corridors and through a hall filled with dozens of eating soldiers. Seeing that it was daylight – late afternoon, she guessed – she recognized something of where she was, and inadvertently glanced outside to the paved section with spiky plants. She shivered when she saw that the stake was gone.

She soon found herself climbing steps and then approaching the palace's main entrance. Crossing the courtyard, she took note of the external gates, located close to the entrance leading to the throne room.

The guard then twisted Chloe's arm further, making her gasp with pain. She pretended to collapse, making the two guards work together to prop her up.

The guard holding her wrist cursed. 'Walk, girl. Don't make us drag you.'

Chloe nodded as she grimaced. She drew in a deep breath and put one step in front of the other, carefully, walking like her father when he was trying not to appear drunk. The other guard grunted.

They led her around a corner and then down a corridor, finally approaching the throne room.

Chloe saw that all the courtiers were present. The short lord in orange robes who had been her ally when she'd first given tea to the sun king now scowled at her. The dark-eyed magus in yellow nodded smugly.

Then she saw something that nearly made her stop. Triton turned as he watched her approach, and he was unguarded. Revealed in the light, the missing eye made him appear ugly and sinister.

At Solon's right hand stood Kargan, arms folded over his barrel chest. His mop of oiled black hair and curled beard still didn't come close to covering his broad, swarthy face. He wore yet another sumptuous silk robe, this one yellow and white.

Chloe's gaze went to Solon.

He showed none of his previous pain, and although his eyes were still shadowed, they now burned with the strength of fanaticism. Despite his illness he dominated the room, his presence filling the space as he looked down from his throne.

Then Chloe realized something new. His golden throne was gone. He sat on a new throne, bigger than the last, but this time made of ornate ebony.

His throne had gone to feed the pyramid's hunger. He knew he was dying. Chloe was glad for it; she only hoped he died sooner. She couldn't believe she'd once felt sympathy for him.

'Chloe of Phalesia,' Solon said. 'The eldran king tells me you were trying to convince him to side with your people against me.'

'As I said,' Triton spoke in a soft voice, only glancing at her briefly, 'I am prepared to make a bargain. Inside the ark at Phalesia is something of great importance to me. I am prepared to fight by your side, king of kings. We will change for you, and dominate the air, land, and sea. As serpents we will neutralize the enemy navy and as dragons and giants we will wage war. In return, you can have your conquest, and you can have the gold. All I want is what is inside.'

Chloe's mouth dropped open.

Solon turned his gaze on her. 'Girl, you are here to demonstrate your continued usefulness to me. Consider this a test that may be your last. Guard, if I give the command . . .' He paused. 'Kill her.'

The guard who held Chloe's arm twisted behind her back put his free hand on the hilt of his sword.

'Now,' Solon said to her. 'Tell me about the approach to Phalesia.'

Chloe swallowed. 'There's a clear approach from the sea. The navy patrols regularly.'

Kargan spoke in his deep baritone. 'What about the approach to Xanthos?'

'Xanthos?' Chloe's brow furrowed. 'The isle of Coros provides a barrier around the harbor, with only one channel usable. You must pass Phalesia first. Our fleet protects Xanthos.'

'Is Xanthos not approachable from both directions?' Kargan persisted.

Chloe shook her head. 'The Shards protect the city – a stretch of jagged rocks in the other channel. They would tear any boat to pieces.'

'And there is no route through the Shards?' Kargan raised an eyebrow.

'No,' Chloe said. 'Not that I'm aware of.'

Solon nodded. 'Now, tell me of the land route between Phalesia and Xanthos.'

'There's a mountainous road. It climbs the hills outside Xanthos and travels through the pass, the Gates of Annika. After the pass the road is easier to travel. It drops gradually, passing through farmland, until it reaches Phalesia.'

'Chloe,' Solon said softly. 'There is one within the court of Xanthos who tells me of a passage through the Shards. He gives detailed directions. This man also tells me he has sent the army of Xanthos to Phalesia. The city is defenseless.'

Chloe drew in a sharp intake of breath.

Kargan spoke into the silence, directing his words to the assembled gathering. 'We could swiftly seize the city and move immediately to take the pass before they are aware. This would enable us to hold Xanthos while the fleet moves on to Phalesia. Two nations would fall to the sword of Ilea, without any opportunity for a drawn out, protracted siege. If,' he finished, looking up at Solon, 'this man's words are true.'

'He wishes to be king, a satrap under my rule,' Solon said. 'I see no reason to doubt him. If his information leads to the easy conquest of two lands, he can have what he—'

A soldier burst into the throne room. 'Fire!' he cried. 'The harbor is burning! Our ships are on fire!'

Kargan instantly ran to the terrace and returned a moment later. His face was filled with horror. 'It's true. By the gods . . .'

A din filled the room as some men ran to the terrace while others shot to the windows. A single voice rose above the cries of confusion.

'King of kings!' Triton called out. 'Remove this collar. Let me prove myself. I will change for you. Let me put out your fires.'

Thoughts visibly crossed Solon's face as he made a quick decision. 'Do it,' he said.

A soldier drew his sharp dagger and slid it between the collar and Triton's skin as the eldran king grimaced. The blade cut through the thin band of gold as it fell to the floor.

Chloe was overwhelmed by the chaos as Triton ran to the terrace, calling for everyone to clear the area. Smoke suddenly filled the air outside, a thickening cloud that shimmered, completely enveloping the eldran within.

Kargan growled, assembling soldiers behind him as he ran in the direction of the palace gates. Solon screamed for silence. The sound of huge wings pushing at the air came from outside, clearing the smoke so that for a moment Chloe saw the reptilian form of a silver-scaled dragon flying into the sky outside.

Despite the confusion, Chloe realized that she had to do something to warn the king and his family in Xanthos.

For they had a traitor in their midst.

43

Fires blazed on dozens of warships made entirely of timber. Sparks flew through the air, tossed around by the constant sea breeze. Masts came crashing down as the supports holding them crumbled into kindling. Every time he heard a crash, Dion felt a surge of triumph, for the longest pieces would certainly spread the flames from one ship to the next.

With flickers of firelight banishing the encroaching night, he ran along the line of burning ships, pointing men in the direction of oil-filled buckets and taking one himself, his face covered in soot as he tossed lamp oil onto flame, pretending to fight the blaze. Smoke filled his nostrils and burned at the back of his throat. The heat was growing so intense in the area that some of the sailors were giving up, heading to fend off the flames where the ships were still undamaged.

He'd thrown his satchel and the jug onto the last of the fires, leaving no evidence. He even threw some buckets of actual water onto a burning vessel, choosing an inferno he knew was past the point of saving. A sailor ran up and grabbed his arm, pointing at a ship that had so far escaped the fury. Dion nodded and pointed at the empty bucket in his hand while the sailor ran away.

All around him men were crying out to one another, with little cohesion to their movements. He saw Roxana pulling a few of the sailors together, organizing a crew to ferry water up from the river, with each man passing a bucket along the line. She saw him and waved, but Dion turned his head as if he hadn't seen her.

He had done what he could here, and he now had to flee the city and give warning to his family. Checking that Roxana's attention was occupied, he twisted his leg to the side and feigned a severe limp. Grimacing as he hobbled along, he headed for the exit.

He was just approaching the gate – now unguarded, for everyone was fighting the harbor fire – when he heard something new in the nature of the cries.

Despite his desire to get away, Dion looked over his shoulder. He stopped in his tracks, stunned by what he saw.

A winged dragon, a scaly monster with a missing eye and a wedge-shaped head, plunged down from the sky, landing on a patch of clear shore and shifting form even as it landed. The air around it wavered and mist filled the air. The gray clouds elongated and then dispersed.

Suddenly the dragon was a serpent, long and thick, a true leviathan. Wriggling like an immense snake the creature slithered into the water until it was fully immersed.

It followed the shore until it was abreast of a line of burning warships.

The leviathan lunged forward until most of its scaled form shot into the air. It brought its body down and a torrent of water erupted as waves rolled into the shore. The water enveloped the ships and the serpent convulsed again. This time the volume of water was even greater: a mighty inundation that doused raging flames in a heartbeat.

Dion watched as the huge serpent traveled along the shore, sending surging water at the burning ships with every leap of its body. It worked tirelessly to control the fires, and after their initial shock, the men at the harbor realized what was happening and redoubled their efforts as they cheered it on.

This was no wildran, Dion realized, but an eldran. Somehow, Solon had enlisted an eldran into his service. And in its changed form it made even the gigantic serpent that had cleared the narrows look small.

Dion shook himself. He realized he was still standing in the gate where he could easily be seen. He had to go back to the House of Algar to fetch his bow. Then he would find the *Calypso* and sail as quickly as he could to Xanthos. He had destroyed a great portion of the Ilean fleet. But the attack would still come.

He had to warn his people.

44

The stench of wood smoke now drifted into the palace. Triton had just altered his shape, flying from the terrace in the form of a dragon. Kargan had left the palace by the front, several hastily gathered soldiers in tow.

Chloe still hadn't moved a muscle. She stood in front of Solon's throne. The men who guarded the audience chamber were in disarray: some out on the terrace watching the harbor fire, others running with courtiers in the same direction as Kargan, and the remaining few uncertain, milling around without orders. Solon was in the midst of a coughing fit. A single guard held Chloe's arm twisted behind her back. The second man in her escort stood nearby, his mouth open and brow furrowed as he wondered what to do.

Tomarys suddenly spoke in Chloe's mind, as clearly as if he were standing right next to her.

'Winning means choosing the right moment. You want your enemies to be distracted. Then, when you take action, be bold. Be strong. Be confident. Nothing is more powerful than the warrior who will achieve his objective or die trying.'

Chloe let her body continue to be limp as she drew in a slow, steadying breath. She closed her eyes and opened them. She resisted the urge to try to move in order to test the strength of the guard's arm lock.

'*The key is to use surprise. You are a woman, and surprise is your main strength, for they will not be expecting you to have any skill or power.*'

Chloe felt her chest rise and fall and fought to keep her breath even. Blood roared in her ears. Her heart threatened to leap out of her chest.

She allowed rage to feed her and clamp down on the fear. She wondered which of the palace guards had cut off Princess Yasmina's ears and nose. How many had worked together to behead the girl? Who had held the whip as Tomarys was flayed? Which of them had followed Solon's orders to impale the big man, piercing a sharp wooden stake through his guts? She wondered if it even mattered – all of them would follow Solon's orders if he asked them to do the same thing to her.

Chloe imagined she was once more practicing with Tomarys in the arena. She felt his arms around her as he made his demonstrations. She remembered her own practice. She knew she couldn't hesitate; she had to get the move right, and get it right first time.

'Thank you, Tomarys,' she whispered.

'What did you say?' the guard snarled.

When she moved, Chloe put every bit of strength she possessed into the spin. She sent breath whistling out of her chest in one swift gust, grunting and making a savage cry she had never heard come out of her own lips.

Chloe turned in the direction of her free arm. Caught by surprise, the guard suddenly found himself releasing her, unable to fight the force of her whole body. Like an uncoiling spring she whirled, making a point with her elbow and bringing it higher than her head as she moved.

The roar was still in her lips as her elbow crashed into the soldier's face. She felt nothing but triumph as she made contact. Something broke in his face. Blood poured from his mouth and nose. The soldier cried out in agony and put his hands to his nose as his head tilted back so that he was staring at the ceiling. Her body completed the turn, and Chloe now used the elbow once more. She didn't hesitate; she jabbed it into the soldier's exposed throat, as hard as she could.

He crumpled, and she doubted he would move again.

'*Nothing is more powerful than the warrior who will achieve his objective or die trying.*'

Her second guard's eyes were wide open with shock. Rather than turn to run, and have him grapple her from behind, Chloe charged. She went for his hand as he reached for his sword; at the same time she smashed the top of her head into his nose.

Tomarys had always said this was a useful move, given her shorter height. He'd said it was exceptionally painful, but that she couldn't allow herself to feel sympathy; she must be like stone. Chloe brought her head up and pushed with her legs, feeling the guard's nose crunch like gravel beneath a boot heel. When he cried out she made a knife-edge with her hand and struck his wrist at the joint.

His hand came away from the sword.

It was now her sword.

She drew it in a single movement and ran the guard through, immediately withdrawing the blade as blood poured out. The soldier moaned and fell down.

Chloe didn't wait to scan the room or give the other soldiers time to attack. She had thought this plan through and taken her bearings. She knew that there were no more guards between her and the exterior courtyard.

Still carrying the sword, wondering at the heavy blade that for some reason felt as light as a feather, she started to sprint.

A ragged voice called after her – Solon was still in the throes of his coughing fit. 'Stop her!'

Cries followed her as she left the throne room and traveled along corridors she knew well. She passed a steward who dashed to the side with a cry at the young woman with the blood-drenched sword rushing past.

Running through the palace's main portal and reaching the courtyard, she crossed the area of paths and gardens in seconds.

On the far side, three soldiers guarded the wide gate. Two stood out in the street, shielding their eyes from the late afternoon glare as they looked down at the harbor. The third saw Chloe coming. His mouth opened as he started to speak.

Her sword point found his throat. He clutched his hands around his neck and fell to his knees.

Chloe speared the next guard in the back, directly between his shoulder blades. The last one turned and raised his sword to block. Weaving to the side, she kept her sword point up and then when he moved to intercept, she did something he wasn't expecting.

Chloe knew more about fighting without a sword than with one. Giving up a weapon would be unthinkable to a swordsman. But she wasn't like them.

She threw the sword like a knife. It made for a clumsy throw, but he was forced to prevent sharp steel striking his body by moving himself. With his attention distracted she shifted around him and then with his back to her she brought her clenched fist into his kidney.

He grunted with pain. When he turned to face her, she brought her knee up between his legs. He dropped like a felled tree, tilting to one side and tumbling to the ground. She bent to pick up the sword she'd thrown, then hacked at his neck.

She now had to find fresh clothing and the sword would only get in the way. Tossing the weapon, just a girl, weak and defenseless, she ran away from the palace.

Chloe was free.

45

Dion rushed up the stairs to his room high in the House of Algar. He was covered in soot and his throat was burning from exposure to the dense black smoke. A different kind of fire burned within him. He had destroyed many of the sun king's warships, but the eldran had put out the fires, saving many more. He had to quickly get his bow and quiver and flee.

He was out of breath by the time he reached his room. He pulled aside the entrance curtain and stopped in his tracks.

Chloe, daughter of Aristocles, sat on his bed.

Her long blue-black hair framed a triangular face that was pale as death. The brown eyes above her arched, upturned nose, were filled with fear. She was covered in blood. Anoush sat beside her. Dion saw that she was clutching his arms in a white-knuckled grip as he whimpered.

'Let him go,' Dion growled.

Chloe nodded and released the boy. He leaped up and ran to hide behind Dion.

'I got your message,' she said as she slumped.

Dion towered over her. 'I risked my life for you. We could both now be on our way home. Instead you stood by as your guard beat me nearly to death.'

'He's dead now,' Chloe said morosely, looking up at him. 'He was a friend.'

Through the open window Dion could hear cries in the street. He didn't know if there was a connection to the harbor fire or to Chloe's escape, but he knew they were both in terrible danger.

'I'm grateful to you, I really am. Can explanations wait?' she asked.

Dion scowled. 'We need to go. Anoush – can you get some women's clothing?'

Anoush nodded and ran out of the chamber while Dion went to the basin and began to wash his face and hands. When he finished he glanced at Chloe. 'I suggest you do the same.'

By the time Chloe had finished cleaning off the blood Anoush had returned, carrying a yellow chiton and veil.

'Good lad,' Dion said. He crouched to look into the boy's eyes. 'Do you know how we can get out of here, without going into the street?'

Anoush nodded. 'The roof.'

'Thank you,' Dion said. 'Will you be safe?'

'You have given me plenty of silver, master. It has been an adventure.' He grinned, creases forming on his round cheeks. 'If you ever come back to Lamara, I'll be here to be your guide.'

Dion gave him a rough embrace, surprising the boy. 'Now show me the roof.'

Chloe changed her clothing while Dion inspected their exit route, and a moment later they were slipping out of a window, Dion exiting first and then helping Chloe onto a flat roof. He scanned the area and saw the buildings were close enough to jump from one roof to another.

'Goodbye, Anoush!' Dion called.

The boy gave him a quick wave and then Dion led Chloe to the edge of the rail. He saw that the next roof was three feet lower and with an effort he clambered down. Chloe slipped off and then the pair ran to the next.

They passed from roof to roof until there was a gap in front of them; they had come as far as they could. Looking for a path down, Dion saw a doorway leading to the building's interior and pointed. 'This way.'

A surprised old woman carrying a basket in her arms cried out as they entered a wealthy house with carpeted floors. Ignoring her, Dion and Chloe descended the stairs and ran out onto the street.

'Where are we going?' Chloe asked. She was breathless, but had no problem keeping up. He couldn't see her face through the veil, but he was surprised at her fortitude.

'I have a boat just outside the city,' Dion said. He took a moment to get his bearings and then pointed to the left. 'This way.'

They walked rather than running, striding with skipping steps as they both fought to move quickly without drawing attention. Each set of stairs they descended brought them closer to the lower city and the gates. Each narrow alley kept them hidden from watchers. Each broad avenue made them feel exposed.

Then the gates were just ahead. Compared with the harbor on the other side of the city, the area here was a scene of normality as wagons carried bushels of wheat into the city and herders brought tethered goats in for the slaughter.

'As soon as we're through,' Dion said. 'Run.'

He kept her close as they passed between the gates. Soldiers glanced down at them from high perches on the towers at both sides.

Suddenly they were through.

'Run!'

Dion and Chloe moved from a walk into a sprint. He checked over his shoulder to see if she was keeping up and led her away from the road, skirting the walls and towers, keeping a hundred paces between them and the city until they finally left Lamara behind.

'Keep . . . running . . .' Dion panted.

The terrain here was treacherous and rocky. They weaved around spiky shrubs and leaped over clefts in the rock. Chloe fell and grazed her palms but she climbed back to her feet without complaint and continued to follow, her jaw clenched as she ran.

Dion was confused for a moment, but then he found the steep-walled stream and breathed a sigh of relief. He took Chloe along the high ground until they reached the place where the stream joined the river.

'We're going to have to get down to the bottom. Be careful,' he said.

He slid down on the seat of his trousers, calloused palms breaking his fall. When he reached the base of the gully he turned back and saw Chloe climbing down much more gracefully than he had, facing the opposite direction.

Dion stood with his feet in shallow water and pulled at the bushes, and there was the *Calypso*.

As he freed the vessel, he realized he had forgotten how beautiful it was. Sleek and rakish, with horizontal blue and gold stripes on the hull, it begged to be out and riding the open seas.

Dion began to breathe freely for the first time as he brought the boat bobbing to the shore of the river.

'I could use your help mounting the mast,' he said to Chloe.

'What do you need me to do?'

'Firstly, get in.'

She waded through the river and clambered awkwardly into the boat as Dion held it fast. Together they mounted the mast and then raised the sail to halfway so that it snapped and billowed in the steady breeze.

Glancing up at the sky, Dion saw that it was late evening and would soon be night. He nodded to himself. He had sailed through the night to reach Lamara, and he could do it again on the return journey. The lighthouses would guide him out of the inlet and into the open sea.

'Are you ready?' he asked Chloe.

'I've never been readier.'

'Sit up front.' Dion pushed the boat and hopped in. He raised the sail all the way and heard it crack like a whip as it pocketed the wind. The rakish boat heeled over, and Chloe looked at Dion with alarm.

'It's normal,' he said.

He rubbed his hand over the polished grain of the interior. The *Calypso* skimmed over the little waves, sending a surge of joy into his breast as he headed for the channel and saw the stone statue of the sun god ahead.

Dion glanced back at the city. Plumes of smoke rose in trickling curves from the direction of the harbor. He could no longer see the pyramid, and finally even the rust-colored walls and hexagonal towers were gone from sight.

The first stars came into the sky overhead as Dion and Chloe left Lamara behind.

46

A rising sun glittered from the distant pyramid, sparkling at the edges and traveling like golden flame toward the summit. The glimmer, however, stopped just short of the triangular peak. Standing at the harbor with sand beneath his sandals and the tang of wood smoke in the air, the sight of the unfinished pyramid filled Solon with anger rather than joy.

He tore his gaze away from his incomplete tomb and instead scanned the scene in front of him. There were places where only black ash marked where proud biremes had once lurked, ready to be launched at his command. At other points along the line warship after warship was completely unharmed.

Standing with him were Triton, once more a striking one-eyed eldran with the ridges of his skull uncovered by hair, and Kargan. The barrel-chested overlord of the empire's fleet was incensed, despite the fact that Triton's intervention had saved a great number of his vessels.

Solon felt his own rage echo the visible fury on Kargan's face, but he was the king of kings, and so he kept his expression impassive. Only the narrowing of his eyes would betray his emotions.

'Only twenty ships are still able to make the voyage without extensive repairs,' Kargan said.

Solon coughed and touched a white cloth, already smeared with red, to his lips. He nodded for Kargan to continue.

'However the number of marines and oarsmen we must carry means we won't have enough men for the land force. We can't simply carry more men – we'd be too heavy in the water for effective naval power.'

Triton turned his one eye on Solon. 'Let me worry about the enemy ships. Fill your vessels with soldiers. I will clear the sea.'

'And all you want is what is inside the ark?' Solon asked.

'That is all I want.'

Kargan frowned. 'What is it that you want so badly?'

'To you, a trifle – but to me something of great value. It is the symbol of my kingship. Without it, only some of my race will accept my rule.'

An officer approached. 'King of kings,' he said, keeping his gaze lowered. 'We have made inquiries.'

'And what have you discovered?'

'We believe that one of the men, a foreigner, started the fires. He fought by our side but now can't be found.'

Solon scowled. 'A foreigner? From where?'

'A Galean. From across the sea. It seems clear that he's from Xanthos.'

Kargan scratched his beard as he looked at Solon. 'He will be off to warn his people. The secret route through the Shards won't give us an advantage if they know we're coming.'

'Triton?'

The eldran king nodded. 'I'll leave to summon my forces. It will take time, but if you depart now we will join you on the way. We can scour the Maltherean Sea for your spy.'

'Wait—' Kargan held up a hand. 'Sire. This plan—'

'Kargan,' Solon interjected. 'Your orders are clear. Fill your ships full of soldiers. Make comfortable arrangements for me on the *Nexotardis*, for I will be joining you.'

'Are you sure that is—?'

'You will do your duty.' Solon turned the full force of his glare on his commander. 'And I will be with you to see it done. We leave immediately. Triton, go to your people. If the spy gives warning our plan may fail. Speed is our ally. Kargan, summon your men. Prepare to depart. I will soon return to this very shore with the ark of gold in my possession.'

47

The towering waves of the open sea rolled forward, sending the lean sailing boat up each crest before it plummeted down the far side. The relentless motion rocked the vessel from side to side and up and down, giving the impression that she would fall over at any instant. But Dion knew that the *Calypso* could hold her own. The only thing he didn't know was if he would have the fortitude to keep going for hour after hour.

Chloe sat on the timber bench in front, clutching onto the underside of the seat for support. Her face was grim and her skin was yellow. She had slept the previous night, but Dion had been given no choice but to keep going. The lids of his eyes felt like heavy weights were dragging them down.

'Chloe,' Dion called. 'I need your help.'

She nodded and slid on the seat until she was sitting close by, across from Dion at the stern with their knees touching. 'What can I do?'

'I need to rest, if only for an hour. Have you ever steered a boat?'

'No.'

He nodded. 'It's easier than it looks. The wind is coming across our beam and we're heading due north, so we won't need to tack for a long time. I want you to take hold of the tiller.'

She looked at him white-faced. 'I can't.'

'It's fine,' he soothed. 'I'm going to pass it to you, but I want you to keep it at the same angle it's at now. Can you do that?'

Chloe swallowed, but she nodded.

'Here goes.' The two of them were facing each other across the small gap between the two benches at either side of the boat. The tiller was at Dion's right and Chloe's left. Dion took her left hand with his and guided it to the polished wood of the handle. He released and she wrapped her hand around the timber. He then folded her hand in his.

'I'll guide you like this for a time,' he said. Her hand felt small and smooth inside his calloused palm. 'Keeping us on course won't be difficult, but the important thing is to keep us heading into the waves like we're climbing a mountain by the shortest path. Understand? Good.' He kept her hand moving, steering the vessel up the next wave. She gulped as they rode the far side. They climbed the next. 'I won't make you do it on your own until you feel ready.'

They continued for a time, and Dion realized it was the first close human contact he'd had since he'd said goodbye to his family at the harbor of Xanthos. He glanced at Chloe, realizing that she was looking at him also. She was pretty, he decided, and stronger than he'd thought, although he found her upturned nose irritating for some reason.

'Why are you looking at me like that?' She scowled.

Dion frowned. He didn't take his hand away from hers, but now the contact felt ice cold. 'I was wondering when you were going to tell me why you saved that villain's life in the abandoned arena. You almost got me killed.'

'He wasn't a villain,' she bit off the words. 'He was—'

'Watch out!' Dion cried. He shoved her hand, held in his; they'd been about to angle over a curling crest. There was silence for a time.

'He was what?'

'He was my friend,' Chloe said. 'I couldn't let you kill him.' She looked away. 'He taught me how to fight, and that's how I escaped. I killed four men, perhaps five, to get free of the palace.'

Dion looked at her with renewed respect. 'I tried to help,' he murmured. 'I came for you at the arena.'

'Why you?' she asked.

Dion explained about the Assembly's hesitation and her father's request. 'He will be anxious to have you back.'

'You sailed all the way to Lamara, alone?'

'No,' Dion said sadly. He thought about Cob, his old friend, who had taught him everything he knew about sailing. 'Not alone. We got into trouble. Wildren. The Oracle at Athos gave me this boat.'

When he mentioned the Oracle, a shadow passed over Chloe's face. She changed the subject. 'What did you do after you got to Lamara?'

'I enlisted as a marine. I learned about the sun king's ships.' Dion explained about Roxana. 'I looked for you.' He turned away. 'I set fire to the sun king's fleet.'

Chloe's eyes widened. 'That was you?'

Dion nodded. 'It wasn't enough, though. An eldran helped them put out the flames.'

'Triton,' Chloe said. 'He says he is their king, although I've never heard of him, and Zachary never mentioned him.' She told him about Triton's bargain with the sun king. Triton believed there was something inside the ark that was his by right. 'There's something else.' She hesitated. 'The reason they are sailing for

Xanthos . . . Dion, there is a traitor in your father's court. He told Solon about a safe route through the Shards.'

Now it was Dion's turn to be shocked. 'Only the royal family knows about it. And a few old fishermen.'

'Anyone else?'

Dion felt a cold grip clutch hold of his chest. 'There is another. My father's first adviser. But he has always been loyal.' He didn't mention the enduring conflict between Peithon and his mother.

'It's true then? About the safe passage?'

He nodded grimly. 'It's true. If they get there before we do, Xanthos will fall.'

The two worked in silence for a time. Dion kept his hand over hers, but relaxed his pressure, letting her do all the work. He decided she was learning the knack of it.

'So how did you let yourself get captured?'

She was suddenly furious. 'Let myself?' She wriggled her hand until he let her go. 'I can manage now.' He removed his hand as if he'd burned it. 'I didn't *let* myself get captured, whatever you think,' she said. 'I was prepared to die. They questioned me time and again, and I never gave away anything that might endanger my people. I saw my only friend impaled, in front of my eyes. I was thrown into a cell. I—'

Dion held up his hand. 'Bad choice of words.' He yawned so wide that his jaw cracked. 'I'm tired.' He looked over the *Calypso*, checking that all the lines were secure and seeing that Chloe was managing with the tiller. 'I need to rest. Are you sure—?'

'I can manage,' she said coldly. 'I rescued myself. Don't forget that. Look at yourself, second son of a warrior king. You don't even carry a sword.'

Dion gritted his teeth and shuffled up higher in the boat. He glanced back at her. 'The waves are getting bigger. There are two blankets. I recommend covering yourself.'

'I'm fine,' she said.

At that moment the bow smashed into the peak of an oncoming wave, sending a torrent of water over the entire vessel. Looking back at the tiller, Dion saw that Chloe was completely soaked through.

She was wearing only a thin chiton. The water made the material transparent, and he could see through to the body underneath. The wet yellow fabric clung to her breasts.

Dion swiftly looked away, but not before she saw his glance and gave him a horrified stare. He passed her a blanket, keeping his eyes to the front as he handed it back to her.

'I'll rest now,' he said gruffly. 'Wake me if you need me.'

'Dion!'

He woke groggily and his instant impression was of rolling movement, fiercer than before. Black clouds were gathering over the sun, bringing shadow to the world. Glancing at the approaching storm, Dion knew he was looking at terrible danger.

But when he turned back to Chloe, a blanket now wrapped around her, she wasn't looking at the storm.

She met his eyes with a terrified stare and then once more looked up at the sky.

A dark bird wheeled in the distance. Its immense wings flapped up and down with slow, leisurely movements. It grew closer with every passing second, and Dion realized that no bird was this big.

He reached for his bow and quiver, tucked into the storage compartment at the vessel's front. As he nocked an arrow he didn't take his eyes off the creature. The wings stopped moving as it coasted for a time, high in the sky, the triangular head on its sinuous neck craning as it scanned the sea.

Its purposeful movements told Dion that this was no wildran. The reptilian creature with shining silver scales wheeled as it lost height. The veins in its bony wings throbbed. Clawed talons grasped at the air.

'Take us into the storm,' Dion said quietly.

'But the waves—'

'You've got the feel for it by now. Just make sure we don't roll over. There's a greater danger in the sky.'

The dragon suddenly plummeted, like a falcon making a strike at a smaller bird. In this case the prey was the small boat and its two occupants. All the eldran had to do was see the *Calypso* sunk and they would never make it out of the open sea alive.

'Triton's acting for Solon. The dragon has two eyes, but he must have sent it,' Chloe said, white-faced.

Dion judged his moment as he watched the dragon grow ever closer in his vision. He could now make out the crests that swept back to form horn-like protuberances behind its head. Eyes glared balefully. Incisors the size of knives were visible in its parted jaw. Its body was entirely muscular, but at the same time it was all bone and sinew, a creature of nightmare.

As day turned swiftly to the darkness of night, though it was still midday, he risked a glance over his shoulder and saw that the storm was on them. He heard the crack of thunder and forked lightning shot down to strike the sea.

Fighting the motion of the ship as Chloe turned into the storm's heart, Dion stood with both feet far apart and thanked the gods that the motion was as natural as riding to a horseman.

He held the bow high and drew the arrow to his ear, his arms straining with effort. The dragon came on swiftly, shrieking as it descended, closer with every heartbeat. At fifty paces, Dion loosed.

The arrow plunged into a near-transparent black wing and went through the other side, opening a hole with its passage. The dragon's jaws opened wide as it screamed, but it didn't halt its swooping trajectory.

Dion drew and sighted, immediately firing a second arrow. With the dragon now twenty paces away he couldn't miss. The shaft sprouted from the back of its open maw, and this time it roared in agony, wheeling away before he could loose another.

He had to remind himself that it was an eldran as it rolled to the side. This gave him an advantage. If it remained too long in changed form it would risk turning wild. If they could hold out for long enough, it would be forced to leave.

Dion cried out as he pointed at the darkest clouds. 'Take us right in!'

Chloe nodded, showing him a face full of terror.

He watched and held onto the mast with one hand as the dragon wheeled around. But the storm appeared to be causing it problems: The creature was being tossed around in the unpredictable gusts and flurries.

It turned its back to them and fled.

But the danger was far from over. They now had to survive the storm.

'Face us into the waves!' Dion roared.

The waves towered over the small boat, and unless they kept a direct line to the crests they would be rolled in a heartbeat. Dion rushed to the mast and unhitched the rope holding the sail aloft. He hauled hard, yanking the sail down with both hands as his arms groaned with effort. He could no longer worry about their course, or wonder which way was north and which south. He dashed to the tiller and sat across from Chloe. Once more he placed his hand over hers as it shuddered in their combined grip.

Working together, they straightened the *Calypso*'s angle until Dion was satisfied. Then the bow plunged through the top of a wave and emerged out the other side as water poured into the interior.

'Bail!' Dion shouted. 'I'll take the tiller!'

Chloe threw herself into her task and, working together, they struggled to stay alive.

48

'We're heading north,' Chloe said.

'Yes, but just because we're heading north now doesn't mean we have been the whole time.'

'Which way would you have us go, then?'

'North,' Dion said. 'We'll come to Galea eventually.'

Chloe scowled, but rather than reply, she scooped another bucket of water out of the bottom and threw it over the side. She filled bucket after bucket, working ceaselessly even though her shoulders and back ached.

She saw that Dion appeared comfortable enough, holding the tiller with one hand while shielding his eyes with the other as he scanned the horizon. He seemed to think she was only good for bailing out the rapidly filling vessel, even though it was her hand at the tiller that first guided them through the worst of the storm.

As her eyes narrowed he suddenly called out. 'Here,' he said. 'Come and take the tiller. You've worked hard enough. You deserve a rest.'

For some reason his words only made her angrier. How was it that he was the one who decided when she could rest? She rose to her feet and stumbled as she passed him but he grabbed her around the waist and steadied her. Chloe muttered her thanks and got out of his way while she made her way to the stern and Dion went to the place she'd just vacated. Settling herself at the tiller, she felt relieved that the waves had now subsided, though the wind still occasionally sent heavy gusts that made the boat list to the side alarmingly. She watched Dion work, and had to admit that he was managing to get more water out of the bottom than she had, but she frowned when she saw more water well up to take its place.

Dion looked back at her and spoke gravely. 'There's a leak somewhere, and it's getting worse.'

Chloe could see concern written in the lines of his forehead, along with the fatigue she felt gnawing at her own senses, dulling her wits and blurring her vision. They'd been sleeping in shifts, but with water in the bottom of the boat they were both needed at the same time more often than not.

Dion glanced back at her as he bailed, and suddenly spoke to fill the silence. 'Tell me something about yourself.'

'Ever the curious sailor?'

He gave a slight smile at the reference to his secret message. 'What do you miss most about home?'

'My family,' Chloe said, staring out to sea. The sun sparkled off the blue water, but all she could think about was how deep it was, how much water there was between the hull and the ocean floor far below. 'My sister and my father.'

'How old is your sister? Sophia, isn't it?'

She nodded. 'She's eleven. I've taken care of her since . . .' She trailed off.

'Since?'

'Since my mother died of fever. It was three years ago. She just . . . wasted away. I learned healing arts at the temple, and I took care of her. But even the priestess said that sometimes there's nothing you can do.'

'I'm sorry,' Dion said. 'I . . . I didn't mean to bring up old wounds.'

'Not so old,' said Chloe, still watching the waves. 'I still think about her.'

Another silence grew, broken only by the splash of the bucket, the snap of wind in the sail, the groaning of the vessel's planking, and the waves pounding at the *Calypso*'s hull.

Chloe glanced at Dion when he wasn't looking. The constant wind had blown his sandy brown hair into complete disarray and his time on the sea had tanned the skin of his face a deep brown. His lips were burned and there was stubble on his chin, but it was a square jaw, and his body was lean and toned. He didn't have the build of a swordsman but he looked strong. He wasn't a warrior, but he was a fighter.

He moved tirelessly as he bent down, filled the bucket with water, and tossed it over the side. He looked like he would keep going for hours, and she knew he could.

When she had been captured, taken from her home, Dion was the only one who had come looking for her. He had sailed across the great expanse of the Maltherean Sea, to a place he had never been to, for her.

'And you?' Chloe asked. 'Do you miss your family?'

He turned to her as if surprised she'd asked him a direct question. 'I do. My older brother, Nikolas, was always good to me. He gave me that bow, and without it I'd be dead many times over. He tried to teach me to fight with a sword, but'—Dion shrugged—'I never could master it. So he introduced me to the bow.'

'You use that bow as if you were born to it,' Chloe said.

'Plenty of practice.' Dion grinned. He hauled another bucket of water over the side. 'But my father doesn't think archery is a fitting skill for the son of a king. So I searched for something else to do. Once again, it was Nikolas who gave me into the care of someone, an old sailor. I found I liked the sea. No'—he shook his head—'I love the sea.'

Chloe thought again about the vast open space they were in, at the mercy of the remorseless weather, waves, and wind. 'Even when there's a storm bearing down and a dragon on your tail?'

He laughed. 'Even then. We made it, didn't we? And despite what you may think, we wouldn't have made it without the both of us.'

Chloe felt color come to her cheeks. 'Tell me about your mother,' she said.

'Her name is Thea and she's a strong woman, as strong as you. At first she and my father were strangers, but that was long ago. Now it's clear how close they are.' Dion hesitated. 'Her story's quite sad.'

'Go on.'

He continued in between scoops of water. 'Nikolas's mother died in childbirth and with just the one heir, the king needed a new queen. For a long time a suitable bride couldn't be found, and the search continued far from Xanthos. Finally, a marriage was arranged with a minor king's daughter from a distant place called Azeros.'

'Azeros,' Chloe mused. 'I've heard of it, I think.'

'It lives on in no memory but my mother's,' Dion said. 'The day she left her home a band of wildren descended on the town. Giants. They slaughtered everyone.' Chloe turned her wide eyes on him, but he wasn't looking at her as he continued to bail. 'Then, as they hunted down any stragglers, the giants came across my mother and her escort. The soldiers hid her and drew off the wildren. She somehow made her way, alone, to Xanthos.'

Dion finally looked across at her. His eyes were sorrowful, but it wasn't for himself; he was thinking of his mother.

'She told me it was difficult, settling in among a new people. She hadn't even met my father. But like I said, she's strong. He wanted to send out the army, to hunt down every eldran and wildran within a thousand miles of Xanthos. But my mother's also compassionate. She protected the eldren from his wrath. Though we don't have quite the relationship between our two races as you do in Phalesia, we no longer kill each other.'

Chloe let out a breath. 'She sounds like quite a woman. I'd like to meet her.' She thought about the raging debates at the Assembly. 'A lot of Phalesians despise the eldren, but I've known Zachary since I was a girl, when my father took me into the Wilds to introduce me to him.' She paused as she remembered Zachary emerging from the trees, frightening her with his ancient eyes and silver hair until he'd crouched in front of her and opened his palm to reveal a shiny green frog. 'He's always been kind to me, and he saved my sister's life.'

Dion nodded. 'If there was only something we could do about the wildren, perhaps our two races could be at peace.'

'Even Zachary says that when they're too far gone to bring back, they must be hunted down. He says they're dead to him as soon as they pass the point of no return.'

'Yet now they have a king,' Dion murmured.

'Yes . . .' Chloe trailed off. She gazed into the water and thought about serpents, giants, and dragons. 'Now they have a king.'

Chloe watched as they approached the dark blur on the horizon, seeing it rise out of the sea like an immense black wave. She made sure it was definitely land before she woke Dion.

Despite lying in a growing pool of water, Dion was asleep. His chest rose and fell with every breath and he twitched now and then as he dreamed.

'Dion,' Chloe said softly. 'Wake.'

He spluttered as he shot up, seeing that his body was half submerged. Immediately, he began to bail. 'Why didn't you wake me sooner?' He scowled.

Chloe felt her ire rise. 'I was letting you sleep.'

'We could have sunk!'

She gestured to the open sea as her eyes narrowed. 'The water is calm. I was judging my moment, trying to let you rest as much as possible.'

Furiously, he tossed bucketful after bucketful over the side as he tried to evacuate the water. 'Don't do that again.'

'Look ahead of us, you fool,' Chloe said.

Dion stopped what he was doing long enough to see the growing silhouette of mountains rising out of the sea ahead. 'Land.'

'Yes, land. Where do you think it is? Athos?'

'No,' he said instantly. 'Athos is low lying, and this place is too high. My guess is Orius or Parnos.' He turned back to her, and now there was light in his eyes. 'We might be able to get help. Perhaps another boat. If this is Orius then we're not far from Xanthos.'

He continued to empty out the water, but it took an eternity before he'd made a noticeable difference. He checked the sail and then hauled on the rope to bring it in on a closer set. The *Calypso* leaned over and noticeably increased speed.

'Head directly for land,' Dion instructed. 'This boat won't last much longer.'

Chloe bit off a rejoinder; she didn't have the energy to point out that she was already moving the tiller. Instead they both watched as the landmass grew larger.

She frowned as she looked to the left and saw a second landmass, separate from the one that lay ahead. But unlike the place they were heading for, this was a solitary mountain, a towering peak with a broken summit and a thin stream of smoke trailing into the sky. Chloe looked again at the dark clouds clustering above the long escarpment they were heading for.

'Dion,' Chloe said. 'Dion!'

'What?' he said, looking back and frowning.

'Look, to the left.' She pointed.

Dion swore. 'Mount Oden. Which makes the land we're heading for . . .'

'Cinder Fen.'

Without asking permission Chloe turned the vessel so that they were approaching at an oblique angle, heading for the channel separating Mount Oden from the main peninsula. They passed the volcano on their left and then the island began to grow distant, but on their right they were now close enough to see the crystal white sand of the shore and the cliffs that climbed to the line of peaks at Cinder Fen. Dion fearfully scanned the water all around, occasionally looking for threats in the sky. Chloe prayed the vessel would hold.

But the timbers of the *Calypso* groaned, and Chloe saw that the water was coming in faster than Dion could bail it out.

'What do I do?' she asked.

'We don't have a choice.' He swallowed. 'Take us in. At least we know where we are. If we can make it past Cinder Fen we'll soon be at Phalesia.'

Chloe turned them in to shore as Dion bailed furiously. They were both searching the sea and sky constantly. The beach was empty; she couldn't see any creatures flying through the ominous clouds. Cinder Fen appeared barren, utterly devoid of life. They crossed into the light blue water. She could now hear the waves crashing on the sandy shore.

'Let's just hope the Ilean fleet was delayed by the storm,' Dion said. 'We'll be making the rest of our journey on foot.'

49

Solid ground felt like the sea, rolling under Dion's feet and giving him the impression of motion, but he was familiar with the sensation and managed to ignore it. He and Chloe walked side by side on the beach, satchels over their shoulders containing the last of their food and water. As morning became midday the sun blazed from overhead, emerging from behind the clouds that hung over the row of high peaks.

'I still think it's safer if we walk on the rocks, in the shadow of the cliffs,' Chloe said.

Dion sighed in exasperation. 'We've already been through this. It might be safer, but we'll walk three times as fast on the sand.'

'And as for hiding the boat—'

He'd known he was wrong to insist on it, but the *Calypso* was the finest boat he'd ever sailed in. She had brought him across the sea and back again, through storms and dark nights.

'I hope to get her back one day,' he muttered.

Hours passed as they followed the shore, a long stretch of pure white sand that seemed to go on forever. Dion wondered if their quest was hopeless, but he had to keep going. It would take time for Kargan to assemble the fleet, particularly after the destruction he'd wrought at Lamara's harbor. He increased his pace while Chloe struggled to keep up. But he couldn't slow. Not now that they'd crossed the Maltherean Sea, with his destination so close.

He scanned the shore ahead and the cliffs above, leading to the mountainous heights, but so far he'd seen no sign of wildren. Even so he remembered the furies that took Riko and Otus, and used the memory to remain vigilant. Glancing at Chloe he saw that she was also performing her own inspection. Dion had his quiver over his left shoulder, his satchel on his right, and the composite bow in his hand, ready to draw at a moment's notice. He had to be ready for anything.

He frowned as Chloe suddenly ran to the water's edge, but then realized what she was doing when she returned with a stout piece of driftwood she could use as a cudgel. 'Good idea,' he said softly.

They continued to walk in silence.

The beach suddenly ended. Cliffs ahead rose directly from the water, blocking all further access. Dion followed them with his eye and saw a broken cleft in the escarpment.

'There.' He pointed. 'We're going to have to climb.'

Chloe nodded as her shoulders slumped. 'And then?'

'If we can make it to high ground, my guess is there'll be a plateau on the other side.'

'No,' Chloe said. Dion frowned as he looked at her. 'Not a plateau. A swamp of ash. That's what Kargan called it. He said that past the ring of mountains is the heartland that gives Cinder Fen its name.'

'Perhaps there's a better way,' Dion muttered as he continued to examine the cliffs ahead.

'There is no other way. I can climb up if you can. Come on, it will be dark before long. The sooner we start the better.'

Chloe led the way to the cleft, placing one foot in front of the other as she began to climb. Dion followed her foot and hand holds, realizing she was a better climber than he was. There was no continuous path to follow; the slope climbed and then leveled off, becoming easier to navigate, then it rose again, steeper than ever.

Soon they'd gained an appreciable height, and looking back Dion could once again see the island of Deos and cratered summit of Mount Oden. He stopped when he saw that the way ahead was impassable, but Chloe found a path around the jagged peak. Darkness crept over them as they climbed around to reach the far slope, the peak behind them now blocking their view of the sea. The strange clouds were directly overhead, and although there were still some hours before sunset, it was almost as dark as night.

They descended into a gully and then climbed the far side, ascending yet another slope. There were cliffs and ridges all around; they were in an eerie landscape of jagged black rock, desolate and forbidding.

Dion and Chloe now traveled along a thin defile, following a path between two immense boulders slightly taller than waist height. The gap between the opposing walls of rock was narrow enough that they had to walk in single file, with Chloe leading from the front.

'Look,' she said, pointing. 'This next peak is the last summit we'll have to climb. There's low ground on the other side.' She started to rush forward. 'I'll scout ahead—'

'Wait,' Dion said, grabbing her hand.

He suddenly pinned her arms at her sides, wrapping her in a rough embrace, and hauled her to the ground.

'Wha—?'

'Shh,' Dion hissed.

Silence ensued. He continued to hold her tightly in his arms, shoulders hunched to keep their bodies hidden by the gap between the two rock walls. Dion began to wonder if he'd seen the dark plummeting shapes at all.

They both froze as they heard a strange sound.

It was the flapping of large wings, and it was close. Dion raised his head just above the boulder, then ducked as quickly as he could, his heart beating rapidly as he hoped he hadn't been spotted. The image of what he'd seen on the slope that Chloe was about to climb stayed with him.

The two furies were standing on the rubble-strewn slope with their wings folded behind them, evidently just landed. In most ways their faces were like those of eldren – almost human – but they no longer had an eldran's leanness. They stood seven feet tall, displaying a powerful size and musculature, and had reptilian legs and scaled torsos, but the scales became patchy on their arms and shoulders. Fingers were like claws and sweeping wings grew from shoulder blades. Their silver-haired heads were big, like those of ogres and giants, and tapered, with enlarged jaws and long incisors. Their eyes were wild, like those of beasts.

Chloe turned and looked at Dion; he shook his head. As they shrank further into their hiding place he could hear hoarse breathing, accompanied by the occasional sweep of wings. Smaller bits of gravel rolled down the slope; the furies were moving and their breathing was growing louder.

He heard a great snap of wings, like a sail gusting in the wind as it was raised, and then a thump as two clawed feet came down.

Dion tilted his head back; he was staring at the toes, ten inches from his head, hanging over the edge of the defile he and Chloe were cowering in. Each claw was curled and had no trouble gripping the hard rock. The fury was directly above them.

With his arms wrapped around Chloe he could feel her heart beating as her chest rose and fell. Blood throbbed in Dion's ears and his palms sweated. He pictured the fury leaning forward and looking down. It would see the tops of two human heads. A shriek would summon its friend. They would scrabble and claw at the rock until they had wounded their prey, and then Dion and Chloe would be devoured.

He thought about his bow, but it was on the ground, while his quiver was on his shoulder. He had to rely on not being seen.

The hoarse breathing overhead slowed; the fury was settling in. Dion couldn't imagine what its purpose was. He hadn't heard it talk; when wildren became wild they evidently lost the capability for speech.

Time dragged on. Keeping his breathing as silent as possible was taking its toll. Dion felt cramp in his legs and lost circulation in his feet and hands.

Still the fury's claws clutched hold of the rock, just above his head.

Dion glanced around to see if there was a rock or stick close by, anything more readily employed than his bow. Chloe's piece of driftwood lay across her lap. But when he looked at it he felt a shiver run up and down his spine.

A hairy black spider the size of his palm was clambering slowly along the breadth of the wood. It had a white stripe across its back, spikes on its long legs, and angry red eyes. The spider took three steps, then paused.

Dion felt Chloe tense in his arms. Her head was frozen in place as she stared at the spider as it moved along the wood, just inches from the exposed skin of her arms. The spider took four more steps and now it was heading to the edge of the driftwood, in a direct line for Chloe's leg.

Black legs scrabbled as it came forward; the spider gingerly stepped off the wood completely. Now it was on the thin yellow fabric of Chloe's chiton. Dion knew she would be able to feel its movements as it crawled toward the exposed skin of her knee.

Chloe's breathing now came labored. She was so tense that he wondered she could stay so rigid.

The spider now moved from the fabric onto her pale skin. She trembled and it froze on the spot, each stick-like leg arched and something fierce in its posture. Dion saw the stinger hovering over Chloe's knee.

She gave an involuntary whimper.

Dion swept his hand forward and knocked the spider off her leg; at the same time he grabbed Chloe under the armpits and stood, bringing them both to their feet. He prepared to take hold of the fury by its legs, although he didn't think that in an unarmed struggle he could defeat the larger creature.

But the fury was gone, as was its companion.

Dion whirled when he heard a sudden thump. He saw the lump of driftwood come down as Chloe swung it like an axe at something on the ground. He could guess what it was she'd just killed.

'I hate spiders,' she said.

Dion traveled with an arrow always nocked to the string. Even Chloe brandished her piece of timber like a club as she climbed. They passed the final peak, heading up the rock and around the summit, and then, as Chloe had predicted, they were on the other side of the escarpment.

The ground evened and dropped away in a gentle slope. Dion now had black earth under his feet rather than rock. Hardy shrubs grew in clumps on the hillside. The land here was a great bowl, and they were on the bowl's rim. Despite his urgency he looked down into the wide valley that nestled in the embrace of the mountainous perimeter.

'Cinder Fen,' he said softly.

At the base of the valley was an immense swamp. Gnarled trees emerged from a continuous stretch of dark murky water interspersed with the occasional muddy bank. Every second tree was blackened as if burned by lightning or flame. The quagmire went on and on, filling an area larger than Xanthos and Phalesia put together.

'The ancient homeland of the eldren,' Dion said. 'They say that when King Palemon drove them out he intended to take their lands. But then it became like this.'

'Come on,' Chloe said. 'We need to keep moving.'

The sky was still filled with dark clouds and they walked in shadow. The hazy sun had now passed to the escarpment's far side and would soon be dropping into the sea. The going was easier now as they traversed the high side of the valley, but they were exposed and Dion knew they would soon need to find shelter. They passed the skeleton of a goat – its bones picked completely clean – reminding them both of the danger posed by furies and dragons, ogres and giants.

They searched as they walked, but by the time complete darkness came they still hadn't found shelter. Eventually they could go no further, and they hunkered down behind some spiky bushes with dark leaves and thorns.

That night, Dion couldn't sleep. He stared up into the darkness and tried to ignore the eerie shrieks and growls that seemed to come from everywhere. But despite the danger, one fear was strongest of all.

How far behind them was Solon?

50

More than a hundred oars rose and fell in unison, while the hoisted sail snapped and crackled in the gusting wind, causing the timbers of the mast to groan. Solon was aboard the *Nexotardis* as it carved through the waves, leading a flotilla of two dozen similar vessels. Soldiers filled the decks of every ship; they were heavy in the water and Kargan constantly fumed at the loss of power and maneuverability. Many of the oarsmen had been replaced by soldiers, who were both inexperienced and struggled in the harsh conditions. For once, the lash couldn't overcome their fading energy: whipped soldiers wouldn't be the best men to lead an attack on a strong city.

Solon understood these problems, but he also knew enough to leave them for Kargan to solve. He had his own struggle to manage.

The pain now filled his chest, sending stabbing needles into his bones and heart. The torment he'd once thought was more than he could bear was nothing compared to the agony he felt now. His soul was being drawn through the jagged gates of Ar-Rayan on its passage to the afterlife. He was being tortured on the way.

Yet as he paced on the upper deck of the *Nexotardis* he applied the iron control that had seen him through the difficult situations of the past. He allowed nothing of his agony to show. His limbs were filled with urgency and fire. His eyes burned with intensity as he kept his mind firmly on his prize. He had committed deeds that might weigh heavily against him when judged by the sun god, but he had brought the nation of Ilea to a new, golden age. He fixed his thoughts on the prize. When he died, his body would enter the pyramid and his magi and sun priests would perform the necessary rites. He would wake in paradise.

He visualized it now. A palace in the clouds would make his crude home in Lamara look like the dirty mortal residence it was. His carnal desire, which the pain had taken away, would return with force. He would have countless women in his harem, a different consort for every time the mood came upon him, some with the high cheekbones and ebony skin of faraway Imakale and others with the ethereal complexion of the Galean nations. He would have small-breasted girls with narrow hips and buxom women as tall as himself but with strong feminine curves.

His appreciation for food had also diminished, but in paradise his appetite would be insatiable. He would eat until he could eat no more, but unlike in the mortal world, he would suffer no ill effects. Rare birds and roasted meats would fill his stomach. Colorful fruits would sizzle on his tongue, tart and sweet.

The finest wines would trickle into his mouth, held in the hands of the gods. Solon would look down at the mortal world he'd left behind and bathe his radiant smile on the citizens of the great empire he had formed, who would worship him as a god. The other gods would raise him among them.

He had climbed as high as it was possible to climb in this world. He now planned to rise in the next.

Solon's musings were distracted when the soldiers on deck suddenly cried out. They scattered, running to clear a space at the front as a huge one-eyed dragon swooped down from above to hover over the deck. The instant it landed, the creature shimmered as white smoke covered it in a cloud. When the cloud disappeared, Triton stood in its place.

Seeing Kargan cross the deck to the eldran king, Solon joined them.

'No sign of the spy since the storm. The sea is clear. If there was a boat out here, we would have found it,' Triton said.

'How are your people faring?' Solon asked as he approached.

Triton's one good eye turned to the line of ships. The distance was too great to make them out, but there were a few silver-haired eldren on every ship, although Triton was the only one of his race to sail aboard the *Nexotardis*. The men always gave them a wide berth. The eldren didn't seem to care.

'Well enough. We are ready for the fight, if that is what you are asking, sun king. Just remember our—'

'Serpent!' a sailor at the bow suddenly cried. 'Dead ahead!'

'We will deal with it,' Triton said. 'It will cause you no problem.'

Without another word he ran to the rail bordering the deck and leaped over the side, plunging into the water.

Kargan turned his dark gaze on Solon. 'A useful ally.'

'That he is.'

'But what is it he wants? What's in the ark that's so important to him?'

Solon shrugged. 'We won't give him a chance to find out.'

Kargan uncharacteristically reached out to grip Solon's arm. The sun king's eyes narrowed as he stared at his commander, but the big man wasn't to be deterred.

'He would be a powerful enemy,' Kargan said. 'Perhaps we were better off when he was safely collared and behind iron.'

'Never fear,' Solon said. 'As you say, metal interferes with their abilities. They cannot even willingly touch it. If we keep whatever it is he wants confined, we will be able to control him.'

Kargan released Solon and watched as, in the distance, the leviathan that was Triton easily dispatched a smaller serpent, clouding the blue water with red.

'I hope you're right,' Kargan muttered.

The days blurred together as Solon struggled with his soul's steady passage to the afterlife. They beached at hidden coves on islands whose names he neglected to discover, then set off early each morning to continue the voyage.

He husbanded his strength; he knew he would need it in the coming confrontation.

Then Kargan joined him at the rail and pointed to a rising cliff ahead. 'Look. The island of Coros. And there.' He indicated a passage to the left of the island. Solon saw a dozen huge, sharp rocks poking their tops above the water. 'The Shards.'

Solon tugged on his beard. The decks bustled with activity as the crew lowered the sail and the oarsmen reduced their pace to a crawl. 'Remind me of the plan,' he said finally.

'The army of Xanthos is at Phalesia. Xanthos has no navy. Our objective is to seize the city and push immediately for the pass, the Gates of Annika. With our men at the pass our enemy will be forced to confront us. That's when we strike from the sea, with their forces divided.'

Solon watched as the looming rocks grew closer. He couldn't help but feel a growing sense of danger. 'And you know the way?'

'I have the directions memorized. The fleet is falling in behind us and we travel slowly, in single file. We also have help.'

Solon saw the sinuous shape of a one-eyed serpent slinking through the water to draw ahead of the *Nexotardis*. Triton would see them safely though.

'It is time,' Kargan said grimly. He looked over his shoulder and called out.

'Advance!'

51

Dion and Chloe lay on their stomachs just behind a rocky rise. Ahead of them, on the other side of the hill, the slope gently descended until it reached a dusty road.

'The Phalesian Way,' Chloe said. 'Heading west leads to Phalesia while to the east lies Tanus. The road follows the high ground, passing above Phalesia before continuing to the Gates of Annika.' She glanced at Dion. 'On the other side of the pass is Xanthos.'

Dion felt he could almost reach out and touch the road. They had crossed the Maltherean Sea. They had made it out of the wasteland that was Cinder Fen.

But there was a problem.

At the point where the road came closest to the dangerous land where wildren roamed, a giant sat hunched over a recent kill.

He was a big one, the largest Dion had ever seen. His bony head was devoid of hair and in profile his reddened teeth were visible even from this distance. Crouched on legs the size of tree trunks, he held a horse's head in the air as he tore at the neck with savage bites. The bodies of two men lay near a second dead horse. The giant didn't look like he would be moving on for a long time.

Dion cursed. They were so close. As soon as they were on the road they could leave caution behind and make a dash for civilization.

'I can fight,' Chloe said.

'A giant?'

'Time is against us.'

Dion hesitated. 'I'll fight. You wait.'

'I'm not waiting.'

'Stay here,' Dion ordered.

He rose to his feet and slowly approached, an arrow fitted to the string as he walked cautiously toward the feeding wildran. Circling around, he came at the giant from the side, so that if the creature charged, he would be drawing him away from both Chloe and the road. When he'd reached eighty paces, the limit of his bow's range, he stopped.

Dion made a swift prayer to the gods. His heart hammered as he drew the string to his cheek. He sighted along the shaft, taking note of the wind and angling the bow into the sky. It was the most difficult shot he'd ever tried. He pictured the arrow plunging into the giant's neck.

His muscles strained with effort as he held the shot for a moment, and then he released.

The arrow flew through the air, sailing in an arc, but plunged into the ground by the giant's foot. The creature continued eating, turning the horse head in his hands and gnawing at the bloody flesh at its base, taking no notice.

Dion drew in a shaky breath and looked for Chloe as he fitted another arrow to the string. His eyes widened as he saw her circling on the giant's other side. She was already closer to the site of the kill than he was. She had no weapon.

He swiftly drew on his bow again and this time hardly thought about the shot as he released. He immediately nocked another arrow and sent it straight after the first; for a heartbeat both shafts were in the air at the same time.

The first arrowhead sliced into the flesh of the giant's shoulder, then fell away. The giant roared and wheeled, trying to find the threat as it threw the horse head to the ground.

The second shaft would have missed if the giant hadn't moved. It struck the creature squarely in the center of its chest, sinking deep in the area of its sternum.

The monster rose to its full height and bellowed. Faster than Dion would have thought such an immense thing could move, the giant saw him and charged.

Dion forced himself to stand firm as he loosed yet another arrow, aiming for the giant's eye. But the shaft went wild, flying past its shoulder. The distance between them narrowed to twenty paces.

With shaking hands he fitted an arrow to the bowstring, knowing it would be his last opportunity. He pulled and released. A heartbeat later the shaft sprouted from the giant's shoulder.

But it wasn't a kill shot.

Dion threw his bow to the ground and ran. He weaved from side to side and felt a meaty hand grasp at his tunic before he slipped free. The giant swiped and a second fist scraped the back of his head, shattering his thoughts and making his senses reel.

He tripped over a defile he hadn't seen and his vision sparkled with stars as his forehead cracked into hard stone. Dion retained enough of his wits to roll to the side as fists the size of his head pummeled the dust where he'd been a moment before. He continued to roll and then felt the ground drop away beneath him. Suddenly he was on his back, wedged in the cleft.

The giant loomed over him, crouching and reaching into the defile. A hand went around Dion's throat, fingers clutched his neck, and with his arms pinned there was nothing he could do. He felt himself lifted forcefully out of his wedged position and then the hand holding his throat began to squeeze.

Dion's vision narrowed. His chest heaved as his lungs desperately tried to suck in air. He felt his consciousness ebb away. Darkness encroached.

The giant's eyes suddenly widened. It opened its mouth to roar but instead blood gushed out. The hand around Dion's neck released and Dion tumbled to the side, coughing and gasping. The giant toppled forward, falling face first into the cleft that Dion had just vacated.

Looking up, Dion saw Chloe standing behind the giant, a blood-drenched sword held in both hands. He wondered where she'd found it, but then remembered her circling toward the bodies of the two men.

He tried to thank her, but could barely speak. Chloe simply smiled, lowering the sword. 'It was a good plan,' she said.

Dion recovered his voice and they now traveled the road with speed, heading west for Phalesia, with mountains on their right and the sea a distant blue expanse on the left.

An hour into the journey they came across a horse.

It was alive but the dead rider lay diagonally across its back, tangled in the reins. The sturdy mare watched with sorrowful brown eyes, skittish as they approached.

'He must have been part of the same group,' Chloe said, looking at the dead man. His head was twisted to the side and half the skin was torn from his face.

They exchanged glances. 'We need this horse,' Dion said.

He walked slowly toward the mare, his arms spread peacefully as he made soothing sounds. He'd always been good with horses, and the horse allowed him to carefully take the bridle. Chloe came to join him and together they untangled the rider. The body fell to the ground with a heavy thump, startling the horse, making the ears go back and nostrils flare.

'Shh,' Dion soothed. 'She's thirsty,' he said to Chloe.

Leaving Chloe holding the bridle, he found a depression in the stone and poured the last of his water from the skin.

'Bring her over.'

The mare drank greedily. Glancing up, Dion saw Chloe watching him.

'We both know you should take her,' she said.

Dion tried to protest, but Chloe held up a hand. 'Xanthos is further than Phalesia. We're past the threat of wildren now. You need to warn your father. I'll get to Phalesia and we'll send out the fleet.'

'But you—'

'We don't have time to argue. The road continues for a time and then forks at the city. The right-hand path continues along the high ground to the Gates of Annika.' She met his gaze with a steady stare. 'Go.'

'Chloe . . .' Dion said. He hesitated. 'I—'

'There is a traitor in your father's court. If Xanthos is not yet under attack, it soon will be. Solon has eldren fighting with him. Go!'

Dion looked at the mare; the horse's spirits had improved with the slaking of its thirst and the removal of the dead rider. Taking a deep breath, he nodded and hoisted himself up onto the saddle of cloth spread over its broad back. From his new height, he could see that the road stretched on and on.

'Good luck,' Chloe said.

'And you. Get to your father as quickly as you can.'

Dion dug in his heels, urging speed into his mount. He glanced over his shoulder once, seeing Chloe growing smaller and smaller, her hand raised in farewell.

And then she was gone from sight.

52

Dion had never ridden so hard. He gave both himself and the mare no respite, kicking her ribs every time she flagged and keeping his eyes focused on the road ahead.

He passed way stops for travelers and watered the horse twice more, but always he pushed on, never taking food himself or allowing his mount to graze. The mare's entire purpose was to get him to Xanthos as swiftly as possible. If he killed her as a result, it didn't matter. The promise of saving his homeland and his family's lives would be worth it.

He rode all through the day and night, and early on the second day he came to the fork in the road. Gazing at the city of Phalesia below, spanning the wide curve of its harbor, he saw a scene of utter normality. Fishing boats dotted the blue water and galleys headed out on a day's patrol. The walls on the landward side showed little activity, while within the boundary the clay-tiled roofs of the houses clustered around the winding streets and alleys, obscuring the everyday movements of the city folk. He could see the agora hugging the embankment and the glistening structures of white marble around it. The largest of them – the lyceum – stood proud and tall. The peaked roof of the library crowned rows of sturdy polished columns. The sight of the city made him finally realize he was back in Galea.

Tearing his eyes from Phalesia, Dion took the right-hand fork, following the high ground. As he passed farmland on sloping hills at his left and rugged pastures with clusters of milling goats on his right, the ground began to climb.

Two farmers stood by the roadside ahead. Rather than working, they were grumbling, arms folded over their chests as they looked at something below.

Reaching them, Dion suddenly reined in. He felt the blood drain from his face.

The farmers were looking at a large military encampment, evidently muttering about the rapacious appetites of soldiers. Taking in the size of the camp, Dion saw red pennants flying above tents.

He realized he was looking at the army of Xanthos.

Nikolas had brought his army where it would be close at hand if it was needed in Phalesia. With the Shards protecting Xanthos and the sun king's desire for the Ark of Revelation, everyone thought the Ileans would come for Phalesia.

After all, Xanthos could be assaulted only if Phalesia fell first.

Dion could even make out his brother's flag, crimson bordered with black, rippling in the breeze as it flew above a large tent. Down in the city he realized he could see red-cloaked soldiers manning Phalesia's walls, side by side with warriors in blue.

Xanthos was undefended.

Fear taking hold of his heart, Dion slipped off the horse and cried out to the farmers. They turned, surprised, and saw a haggard young man in foreign clothing, dragging a horse by the bridle as he ran toward them, calling out and waving.

'You have to send word to the army, to Nikolas, son of Markos! Can you hear me?' Dion's voice rose in urgency. 'Xanthos is under attack! You have to do it now!'

'Eh?' said one of the farmers, an old man with a pinched face. 'Who are you?'

'Dion, son of King Markos, the brother of the commander of that army down there. Do you hear me? Xanthos is under attack!'

The two farmers exchanged bemused glances.

'How do we know you are who you say you are?' the old man asked, while his younger companion scratched his head.

Dion thought furiously. He had a sudden idea, and ripped the silver chain from around his neck, with the trident of Silex bound by a circle of heavy metal.

'Here,' he said.

The old farmer came forward and took the silver necklace and amulet. His eyes widened, and Dion knew the thoughts that were going through his mind. He could sell it in the city for a great deal of money.

'Show Nikolas this, he knows it's mine. Do you understand? Do you think I would just give this to you if the need wasn't urgent?'

'Why don't you give it to him yourself?' the younger farmer spoke for the first time.

'Because I have to get to Xanthos. Please,' Dion said in frustration. 'This is urgent. All of our lives could depend on it.'

The old farmer made a swift decision and then turned to his younger companion, handing him the necklace. 'Troi, go! Run like the wind!'

The younger man nodded and started to run.

Dion leaped back into the saddle. He spurred the horse forward, leaning forward on its back, his brow furrowed as he hoped desperately that he would get to Xanthos in time.

Dion cut the journey to the pass down to hours. He knew the horse was weary to the core, and that if he kept up at this pace she would collapse beneath him, but with Nikolas in Phalesia and his family exposed to the sun king's imminent attack he pushed harder than ever before.

The steep stone walls of the Gates of Annika went by in a blur. He exited the pass and emerged into the land of hills and forest that led down to Xanthos.

He rode recklessly on the downward slope, galloping where he should be walking carefully, holding the mare by her halter.

He tried to ignore what he was seeing as he plunged down the winding hillside, wheeling around groves of olive trees and sliding on rolling gravel. His jaw was set so tightly that it ached. He kicked his heels into his mount's ribs again and again.

The city drew ever closer in his vision. He lost track of all time as the mare scrabbled down the treacherous terrain. The walls could now be seen as separate from the structures within. The Royal Palace rose from behind, surrounded by its own walls. Dion could now make out the Flower Terrace, facing the surrounding countryside, where his mother often went to be alone. It was her favorite place.

Five hundred paces from the city walls, Dion heard a snap like the crack of a whip as the mare's leg broke.

He catapulted forward, flying through the air as he tucked in his shoulder to break his fall. Rolling and tumbling, he felt the hard ground battering his body until he finally came to a halt.

The mare screamed.

Dion shakily climbed to his feet, ignoring the cries of distress coming from the horse behind him. He looked up at the palace, distant, yet so clear in his vision that he felt he could reach out and touch it.

His family was out on the Flower Terrace, gazing out at the city and the surrounding hills, where they could be easily seen by anyone below.

He saw his father, readily recognizable in his purple toga. The gold circlet of his kingship no longer crowned the white curls on his scalp, but his equally white beard was just the way Dion remembered it, although it was now flecked with ugly splotches of red.

Beside King Markos was his queen, Thea, Dion's mother, small in size compared to the towering king. Her black hair looked neatly combed. Her white silk chiton was stained with crimson.

Next in the line was Helena, Nikolas's wife. Her blonde hair framed a face stretched wide in an expression of utmost agony.

All of their mouths were open in endless screams. Sharp wooden stakes jutted from their jaws.

They had all been impaled.

The horse screamed again.

The animal's cry of pain shook Dion out of his trance, making him realize this wasn't a nightmare, it was actually happening.

He now took in what he'd been seeing as he made the frantic descent. Ilean soldiers with yellow cloaks and triangular shields were rapidly assembling in front of the conquered city. Officers bawled orders as rank after rank formed up. Spears held in right hands, shields on their left, they prepared to march. An officer wearing a steel helmet crowned with a vertical spike pointed at the distant pass and called out.

The wounded horse moaned in agony.

Dion saw his bow and quiver on the ground nearby. He picked them up and walked back to the horse as he drew an arrow to his ear. A moment later the mare's cries were silenced.

Only then did he turn to look once more at Xanthos. Smoke rose from several quarters of the city, but the attack had come swiftly; Dion's place of birth had been seized with barely a struggle.

Just below, outside the walls, a trumpet blared. The soldiers in yellow began to march.

Shaking himself, he realized they would attempt to take the Gates of Annika. With the thudding rhythm of the marching soldiers forming a counterpoint to the pounding of his broken heart, Dion left behind the dead mare and climbed the hillside, finding the road and focusing on his footsteps.

He walked in a daze. If it weren't for the soldiers on his heels he would have collapsed, but their relentless march spurred him on. Finally, he picked up his pace, beginning a shuffling run. Dion suddenly realized that he was sobbing as he ran, hot tears burning in his eyes and spilling down his cheeks, carving a path through the grime on his skin.

Hearing a whinny, he looked up and saw two soldiers on horseback carefully making their way down the hillside from above. He recognized the light armor and red cloak of a Xanthian mounted scout, but the two riders rode past him without a glance and drew up further below, watching the approach of the Ilean army. A moment later they were heading back toward the Gates of Annika.

Dion knew his brother and the army of Xanthos wouldn't be far behind. He realized with a sense of desolate abandonment that Nikolas was now the only family he had left. He'd come from Lamara as quickly as he could.

But he was too late.

———⌣———

Nightfall was approaching when Dion once more reached the pass, weariness in every limb, but knowing that he needed to give his brother one vital piece of information.

He was relieved to see that Nikolas had his men in good order. Red-cloaked hoplites in disciplined formations blocked every approach to the pass. The terrain was unsuitable for horses and cavalry were generally absent, but hundreds of archers stood gathered behind the heavily-armored hoplites, side by side with columns of javelin and sling throwers and the common infantry.

As Dion approached they soundlessly parted, turning dark eyes and fierce scowls on him. These men knew that their city had fallen. They could only hope that their wives and children had survived the attack, that with their enemy moving so swiftly, there had been little time for razing, rape, murder, and pillage.

Dion was in foreign clothes, which explained their glares. But he also knew many of his brother's comrades by name and was pleased to see their faces. Passing an officer he recognized, he nodded a greeting.

The soldier hawked and spat on the ground at his feet.

Too stunned to react, Dion decided to quickly leave the area; perhaps the soldier hadn't seen his face. But he now saw more grimaces and snarls on others that he knew were close to his brother.

Then Dion found Nikolas.

Half a foot taller than Dion, burly and as strong as an ox, Nikolas filled every inch of his leather armor with brawn and muscle. The bushy black eyebrows under his curly black hair were arched over his dark eyes as he issued barking orders to an officer twice his age. His red cloak was trimmed with gold and he wore a steel helmet with a plume of crimson horsehair, the vertical cross guard plunging from the rim to cover his nose.

Dion felt his ragged nerves calm as soon as he saw his older brother. Nikolas had almost been a father to him. Among all the horror, he would know what to do.

Men clustered around their commander, waiting their turn to speak and to get their orders. First one face, and then another turned to Dion, eyes widening when they saw him. Suddenly they all went silent. With his back to Dion, it was Nikolas who was the last to turn around.

'Dion,' he whispered.

Nikolas's eyes were as red as the embers of a fire, and burning with the same intensity. Although they were dry, he'd obviously been weeping. Dion's heart reached out to him. Dion had lost his parents. Nikolas had not only been closer to their father than Dion ever was, he had lost his wife, and perhaps also little Lukas, his son.

As Dion approached, he felt tears gather at the corners of his eyes. In his Ilean clothing, with the composite bow his brother had given him in his hand, dirty and bloody, he waited nonetheless for his brother's embrace.

But when Nikolas spoke, it was the last word Dion ever expected him to utter.

'Sword,' Nikolas said. He opened his palm and looked at one of the soldiers nearby expectantly.

The whisper of drawn steel filled the air. The soldier proffered the sword, and Nikolas gripped the hilt tightly in his palm.

He suddenly raised the weapon to strike.

Eyes wide, shocked into frozen silence, Dion didn't move to stop him.

Nikolas gritted his teeth, grunting with effort as his arm twitched, high in the air. His muscles were bunched, tensed to breaking point.

'I can't do it,' he whispered.

Nikolas lowered the sword. A sob erupted in his chest, but was swiftly suppressed. He spoke in a voice of torn emotion Dion had never heard before.

'You gave us away . . .' he whispered. 'They came through the Shards.'

'Brother—' Dion struggled to speak.

Nikolas raised the sword again and Dion's voice fell away. Once more Nikolas tried to slash down at Dion's neck. Once more his muscles tensed and wrist trembled until he lowered his arm.

'Though my parents are dead, and my kingdom has been seized by invaders; though my wife has suffered in ways I can't bear to think on, and I have no news of my only son . . . still I can't strike you.'

Nikolas visibly held himself in a state of suppressed emotion. His chest heaved up and down like a racehorse at the gate.

'Brother, it's me—'

'Go,' Nikolas said. He turned his back on Dion. 'Get out of my sight!'

'Why?' Dion asked, trying to force himself to understand.

Nikolas whirled, rounding on him. 'How would men from Ilea know about the passage? You went to Ilea, to Lamara. Look at you.' His burning gaze traveled up and down Dion's body. 'You told them.'

'It wasn't me,' Dion protested. 'It was a traitor!'

'Who, Dion? Who was this traitor, if not you?'

'It could only have been Peithon.'

'Peithon?' Nikolas grunted. He called out. 'Peithon, where are you?'

Dion's eyes went wide as Peithon stepped forward into the circle. The brow of his large face was curled into a scowl and his eyes were narrowed over his hooked nose. The fine tunic around his paunch was white and clean; he had taken no part in the fighting.

'You accuse me?' Peithon's voice rose.

'Peithon was in Phalesia when the attack came,' Nikolas said. 'Today I cannot see another member of my family killed. I may not feel the same tomorrow. Now get out of here, Dion, before I change my mind and kill you.'

53

The hills swarmed with the sun king's soldiers. The army of Xanthos blocked the pass. As night fell over a day of utter anguish, Dion went to the only place he could go.

He left the Gates of Annika and walked north, into the Wilds.

Leaving civilization behind completely, he climbed into the forested mountains and soon felt the heavy presence of trees on both sides and thick branches ahead. He crested a hill and entered a valley, with a fast-flowing river tumbling over a bed of smooth white stones.

The darkness was complete but still Dion kept walking. He followed the river until it became sluggish, with grassy banks at both sides. Entering a tranquil clearing within an almost perfect circle of surrounding evergreens, he stopped in the very center and looked up at the night sky.

Stars shimmered in the heavens, scattered pinpricks of light that clustered in strange formations. In the distance he could hear the roar of a waterfall. Something about the place calmed his ragged emotions.

Gazing at the firmament, Dion scowled up at the gods, who had all deserted him; he thought he'd come here to pray, but now the words escaped him. Who would he pray to? Aldus, the god of justice, who had caused Dion to be cursed with treachery? Helios, the sun god, whose name was uttered with supreme reverence in Ilea? Edra, the fertility goddess? Balal, the god of war? Silex, the god of the sea? Aeris, the goddess of healing?

He sank to his knees and then fell onto his back as he cursed them all, still staring up at the night's sky.

He remembered his family giving him the gift of the bow on the beach. He tried not to, but he couldn't stop himself thinking about his mother's final hours. He remembered her saying goodbye to him as he sailed away, the last person standing to see him go, her hand raised.

He wished he'd known it was the last time he would see her alive.

It took a long time, but blessed sleep finally came.

'Dion.'

He heard his name spoken by an unfamiliar voice.

He opened his eyes and saw swaying treetops, a brilliant shade of emerald green. The rushing sound of water combined with the buzz of insects to provide a soothing melody of nature. The air was crisp and fresh, and although the sky above was bright and blue, the glade was cool, filtering the strongest rays.

He sat up.

A tall, lean man with arched eyebrows was crouched on his heels nearby as he watched Dion. He wasn't a man, Dion realized – he was an eldran. He wore well-fitting garments of soft deerskin – a vest and loose brown trousers – but nothing on his feet, appearing completely comfortable on the soft grass.

He had pale skin, nearly white, and a crescent-shaped scar on his left cheek. His brown eyes were flecked with gold and appeared ancient, making Dion feel like a young child, insignificant beside someone wiser and greater. Lustrous silver hair hung to the eldran's shoulders.

Thinking of Triton, Dion reached for his bow, but then remembered that Chloe said Triton was broad-shouldered, with one eye missing and skin tight on his bald head. This eldran was slim, with long hair; his face was gentle, weathered like parchment by the passage of time.

'You won't need your weapon, Dion. My name is Zachary. You have nothing to fear. You are in our lands, but I won't harm you.'

'How do you know my name?'

'I know you well, young prince Dion of Xanthos.'

'How?' Dion climbed to his feet, and the eldran slowly rose with him. Though he was extremely thin, Zachary was taller than Dion by a full six inches. 'How do you know me?'

'Through your mother,' Zachary said softly.

'My mother is dead.'

'I know.' He spoke simply, but his voice carried a sense of loss and sadness. 'I grieve with you.'

'Leave me be,' Dion said, hanging his head. 'I came to pray to my gods, not to talk to eldren.'

'Dion,' Zachary said as he gazed down at him. 'Look at me.'

Despite himself, Dion tilted his head back to meet the eldran's gaze.

'You will want to know what I have to say. What she never wanted you to know.' Zachary paused, and then spoke clearly and succinctly, so that Dion could not mistake his words. 'Your mother was one of us.'

'She cared for your people, I know. You are all most likely alive because of her. She—'

'It's the truth,' Zachary said. 'Although I can understand why you find it hard to accept. I always thought she should tell you, but she wanted you to be completely one of them, rather than partly one of us. You should know the truth.'

Dion wondered if he was still lying on his back, dreaming as his closed eyelids banished the light of the stars. 'Truth? What truth?'

'Long ago Markos, your father, King of Xanthos, had a tragedy. His wife died giving birth to his firstborn, a son.'

Dion frowned. 'Nikolas.'

'Yes, Nikolas. Your half-brother.' Zachary nodded. 'Markos grieved, but after some years his advisers pressed him to bear another child to ensure the succession. They found him a young wife, a noblewoman named Thea, from a tiny far away kingdom called Azeros, to the north and west of here, in a valley between two mountains.'

'I know all this,' Dion said.

'Then humor me and allow me to continue.' Zachary's ancient eyes suddenly blazed, and Dion felt a stab of fear. He remembered the crescent scar on the face of the serpent that cleared the narrows . . . and then realized that he was looking at the very same eldran.

But all the eldran did was fix Dion with a steady stare.

'Out of duty, the king agreed to the marriage,' Zachary said, 'in order to father a noble son, more than to build an alliance with a small kingdom he knew little about. The young bride, Thea, and her retinue set off for Xanthos.'

Zachary's voice changed in character. The brown eyes that never left Dion's face became penetrating.

'We discovered her just outside her homeland,' he said.

Dion started. 'What did you just say?'

'She was badly wounded but still alive, the only one of her retinue to escape harm, for her escort had fought for her to the last man. We took her in and tended to her wounds, discovering the nature of the wildran attack on her homeland. I sent some of my people to Azeros and we discovered that it was destroyed by the giants, completely and utterly.'

Zachary's voice became sad. 'We tried, Dion, we tried. We tried to heal her but her body was as broken as her heart, for she knew that her home was gone, and she would never see anyone she knew again. Our best healer spent a great deal of time tending to her, sharing in her life, doing all she could for her.' He paused. 'But even so, despite the healer's efforts, the woman died.'

Dion wanted to tear his eyes away from Zachary's, but there was such strength in his stare that he couldn't look away. He didn't believe it, couldn't believe any of it.

But, at the same time, he knew it to be true.

'We eldren began to fear for ourselves. For at that time there was no peace between Xanthos and our people. We knew that if the king of Xanthos's new bride was killed by wildren, his wrath would come down on all of us. There aren't many of us, Dion. It is your race that won the war, long ago. We only want to live here in peace.'

Zachary reached out to take Dion's hands. His touch was strange, and then Dion realized why. It was no different from the touch of any other person.

'Your mother, who was the healer, came up with a desperate solution. She dyed her silver hair black and went to Xanthos. That healer became Thea. And from then on, until she died, that is who she was.'

Dion's breath came in gulps. It must have been a terrible secret for his mother to carry.

'When she reached Xanthos she was comforted by the king and given time to acclimatize to her new world. If she acted strangely, all forgave her. They put a golden chain around her neck, as is your people's custom, though it must have hurt her every day.'

Zachary's eyes moved down slightly to Dion's neck, bare ever since he gave his necklace to the farmer. 'I see you do not wear your chain. Did it ever cause you pain?'

Dion started to shake his head, but then slowed and finally stopped. He thought about the naming ceremony of Nikolas's son Lukas, and his own naming ceremony. When the magus called him to silver, he hadn't come.

'Your mother married the king, who, as is tradition, asked what gift he could give her. She asked her husband to hunt the wildren as he must, but not to seek revenge on the eldren. Over time she brought about peace between us, and together we cleared Xanthos of the wild ones.'

Dion remembered his mother dyeing her hair. She'd always said it was to cover gray, but now he knew the truth.

'My mother was an eldran?'

'She was.'

He remembered his difficulties learning swordsmanship. The only iron present in archery was in the heads of the arrows. Sailing was about rope, cloth, and wood. He felt strange.

'But I'm only part eldran. It doesn't change anything. I'm the same person I've always been.'

'Of course you are,' Zachary said.

He had a sudden thought. 'When the attack came, why didn't she change? She could have helped, couldn't she?'

'I believe that if she had asked to have her golden chain removed, and changed, your father would think he had been betrayed, right to the end. She loved your father, Dion. She died with him, rather than lose his love.'

Dion felt his eyes burning, but Zachary's steady expression kept him strong. He removed his hands from Zachary's and turned away as he thought about all he had lost.

There was still something he could do to help.

And it was standing right next to him.

Dion turned to Zachary and the eldran tilted his head to the side, waiting for him to speak.

'You know what the Ileans did to my mother. Will you help us against our enemies?'

'This is a dark time for your people.' Now it was Zachary who looked away from the fire of Dion's gaze. The eldran stared into the trees in the direction of Xanthos, as if seeing the blood that would soon be shed dripping from the low branches. 'But it is not our war.'

Dion knew Nikolas. He knew his brother would lead the army down from the Gates of Annika and try to retake the city.

For Nikolas was now the king of Xanthos.

'But eldren are fighting on the side of the sun king,' Dion persisted. 'That makes it your war. Triton—'

Zachary's eyes narrowed as he interrupted. 'Did you say "Triton"?'

Dion nodded.

'I have not heard that name in a long time.'

'He says he is your king.'

'Untrue,' Zachary said as his wizened features curled in a scowl. 'He has the blood of Marrix, but many can make that claim. He may lead those from the Waste, but only if he reclaims our homeland can he call himself our king.'

The pieces fitted together in Dion's mind. Only now did he understand the truth. There was more at stake than the survival of Xanthos and Phalesia.

'Triton needs the horn of Marrix,' Dion said. 'The horn is inside the Ark of Revelation, at the Temple of Aldus in Phalesia.'

Zachary drew back and his eyes went wide. 'How do you know this?'

'The two myths,' Dion said. 'They overlap. The story of King Palemon says he stole a magical horn and put it in an iron box, for eldren magic fails when confined by metal. The Ark of Revelation is said to contain holy tablets, and must never be opened or all will suffer.'

Dion waited for Zachary's reaction, but it was a long time before he spoke.

Finally, the eldran nodded. 'We know this. We've known this for a long time, and we've watched over the ark. But we did not know that Triton knew.'

'He only just discovered the ark's location,' Dion said, remembering Chloe's story. He hesitated. 'The one thing in common with both tales is that if the ark opens then humanity is lost. What does the horn do?'

Zachary's eyes stared into the distance, unfocused as he watched the surrounding forest, seeing something else altogether. 'It would give Triton control over the wild ones. There are many more wildren than eldren. It would give him power over them all. Long ago, our people and yours fought. For Triton, that war never ended.'

'And you?'

He looked at Dion. 'We have no wish for more war between humans and eldren.'

'If you help my brother retake Xanthos, together we will be able to save Phalesia. Nikolas has thousands of men under his command.'

Zachary's expression was pained. 'Some of us will die. We are barely a hundred.'

'If Triton gets the horn he'll bring about total war. Many more eldren will die then.'

Zachary's face was inscrutable, but Dion knew he was deep in thought.

Then the tall eldran came to a conclusion.

'Stay here,' he said. 'I will return.'

54

The sun climbed the sky ponderously, casting burning rays on countless steel helmets and making sword hilts hot to touch. The hills around the Galean city of Xanthos reverberated with the sound of thousands of boots marching on the rocky ground. Six phalanxes of hoplites – each five hundred strong – kept rigid formation as they advanced, despite the dips and rises. These crimson-cloaked soldiers were grim-faced and silent, standing shoulder to shoulder, carrying spear and shield. Progressing closer and closer to the city they sought to liberate, there wasn't a man who didn't mutter a prayer for swift victory to Balal, the god of war. Other prayers were spoken soundlessly, private pleas for family to be safe and well.

Behind the army's center, adding supporting strength and a wide arc of firing range came the ranks of lightly armored archers, with javelin and sling throwers at either end of the line.

The army of Xanthos had lost its kingdom without a fight. Not a man bore the scar of a battle wound. Their few comrades who had stayed behind were undoubtedly dead. The bodies of their king, queen, and their commander's wife, were still on display.

A mile from the city the ground leveled off, providing ample space for the men to tighten ranks as they marched. Three hundred paces from the high city wall, their commander, a broad-shouldered warrior with a red-crested plume of horsehair on his helmet, called a halt.

The throbbing rhythm of boots on the dusty plain fell to silence.

Nikolas knew his city, and he knew the strength of the gates. He had two battering rams with him, formed from the mightiest trees and hardened by fire. The enemy commander had seen the rams, and rather than wait for an inevitable struggle in the city streets had elected to arrange his forces in front of the walls.

The two armies now faced each other.

Nikolas estimated their numbers: There were at least five thousand swarthy soldiers with triangular shields and yellow cloaks.

But not only was he outnumbered; he would face a foe that would strike terror into the bravest of his men.

For at the front of the enemy line were scores of ogres and giants. The shortest was seven feet tall while the largest stood taller than three of his men one on top of the other. They carried thick clubs and immense wooden spears. Some of his men had fought wildren, but these were eldren. They would bring intelligence to the fight, not just animal savagery. Legs as thick as a man's waist stood wide apart as they waited. Muscled chests and shoulders rose to thick necks and bony heads, covered in silver hair. Huge hands gripped weapons, patting them in meaty palms.

Nikolas forced himself to look up at the palace.

The sight of his wife's body just a few hundred paces away filled him with more rage and agony than he'd thought it was possible for a man to feel. He let the fury feed him, bringing fire to his heart, making him thirst for vengeance.

As he gazed at the terrace, a tall man walked out from the palace's interior to watch the proceedings below.

He wore a robe of yellow silk and a spiked golden crown on his head. His hair was shoulder-length and dark and his pointed beard was curled in front of his chin.

Their eyes met and Nikolas knew he was looking at his enemy, the man who had ordered the execution of his family.

Nikolas drew in a slow breath. His son's fate was still unknown. He would retake Xanthos or die trying.

He had no words of encouragement for his men, nor did he need them. Tearing his eyes away from the three corpses and the passionless gaze of the sun king, he turned to his men and raised his iron spear in the air.

The army of Xanthos roared.

Nikolas thrust his arm forward, and the men began to march once more. The march became a shuffling jog, and then the jog became a run.

Across the field, the sun king's army commenced its own charge. Giants and ogres led the way, followed by rank after rank of Ilean soldiers.

Nikolas was swept up in the charge of his men; they surrounded him on all sides. The distance between the enemy armies narrowed to two hundred paces, then one hundred. At fifty paces swarthy archers poked their heads above the city wall and loosed a hail of arrows that arced through the sky.

The hoplites knew their business and shields went up overhead, even as they ran. Cries and grunts filled the air as shafts found their mark, but the running never ceased. Now only twenty paces separated the two forces.

'Javelins!' Nikolas roared over his shoulder.

He saw the long spears fly overhead. They plunged into the bellies of the rushing giants and sprouted from the chests of the yellow-cloaked shoulders. Nikolas set his sights on a twelve-foot tall giant directly in front of him as a soldier on the creature's right suddenly fell with a javelin in his throat, blood gushing from his mouth.

The two armies collided, and everything fell into chaos.

Nikolas ducked a swipe of the giant's club and charged inside its reach. He jabbed his spear up and into the creature's throat, grateful for the weapon's length. Crimson liquid erupted in a torrent, covering him from head to toe. The monster fell and Nikolas turned to face the new threat of an Ilean soldier. The man's spear came forward but Nikolas took it with the shield on his left arm, then quickly thrust in and out of his opponent's upper chest.

Arrow shafts flew in both directions as Nikolas's archers sought to clear the walls. Reacting with hardened instinct, Nikolas dipped his head and raised his arm as a shaft clattered against his shield.

He heard a throaty growl as a female ogre with a spear that dwarfed his own thrust her weapon at his head. Nikolas weaved and aimed his spear at her chest, but the creature was quick and moved to the side. Her strong hand pulled his spear away from him, throwing it to the ground.

The ogre's spear thrust again and Nikolas narrowly deflected it with his shield, taking the shattering force of the blow on his left arm as he gritted his teeth. He drew his sword in one swift movement, leaping high and slashing down, striking the exposed place where the neck joined the shoulder. The sharp steel bit deep and the ogre fell.

The two forces shifted back and forth as each struggled not to give any ground. The arrows overhead had now lessened to staggered volleys as Nikolas's men cleared the walls.

'Link shields!' he cried.

There was a hoplite on his left and another on his right. His army's training came to the fore as the Xanthian soldiers formed a long line – shield to shield, shoulder to shoulder.

'Forward!'

He felt the strength of a second rank of men at his back, holding him fast as the hoplites took a step forward in unison. The enemy charged, but came up against the hard wall of the shields and every man's right arm thrust, whether he held a spear or a sword.

Ilean soldiers fell screaming, only to be trampled over and replaced by the next rank of yellow-cloaked fighters behind. Bodies now littered the landscape. Nikolas's men dispatched the twitching wounded.

'Overhead!' someone behind him cried.

A dragon surrounded by a clutch of furies swooped down from above, but Nikolas's archers were prepared and shafts peppered the monsters' bodies, halting the attack before it began. The winged creatures fell to the ground in the midst of the Xanthian soldiers. The eldren would not try an aerial attack again.

Nikolas saw expressions of fear on the Ilean soldiers opposite, as each time they came forward they met the solid wall of shield and spear. He began to think that he could win the battle. Leaving the line and allowing a man from behind to come to take his place, he looked for somewhere he could gain a vantage and spied a small hill.

'We have them!' he shouted to his men, who roared back their support.

Soon Nikolas had a view of the battle. He saw that his line was thinner, but that was as it should be; his officers knew their business and needed to keep the line extended to prevent their forces being outflanked.

The organized chaos of the battle showed two masses of infantry facing each other, milling as they cut each other down, but the army of Ilea was giving ground.

Then, hearing a cry and seeing one of his men pointing, eyes wide with fear, Nikolas looked up.

A dozen winged creatures, three dragons encircled by a clutch of smaller furies, flew high in the sky, well out of bowshot. They didn't lose height until they were far from Nikolas's archers, well behind the fighting, then they swiftly landed.

A shimmer of smoke went around them as they shifted.

The gray clouds cleared and now he was looking at a dozen giants and ogres. They charged down from the hills, heading directly for the archers behind the center of the line.

Nikolas saw the immediate danger.

But for once, he didn't know what to do. Such a thing would not be possible with an army of men.

With relentless momentum, the snarling monsters struck the back of his army. The occasional arrow shaft plunged into leathery hide, but the lightly armored archers were completely outclassed. Gnarled fists hammered into skulls, splintering them into bloody pulp in a heartbeat. Meaty hands tore apart one man after another.

The archers broke, leaving the backs of the hoplites exposed. As the dozen creatures reached the infantry the soldiers turned to face this new threat, reducing the massed force that supported those in front. The line wavered.

Nikolas knew that in moments the ranks would shatter. The soldiers of the sun king would advance and the center of his line would break, splitting his army neatly in two as the giants and ogres reached the soldiers in yellow.

When that happened, it would all be over.

He signaled an officer on the flank, where the fighting was less relentless. He pointed at the army's rear with his sword, desperation in his movements. The officer called out and a score of soldiers broke away, pushing through to join him, but in the confusion of battle they would arrive too late.

Knowing he had to do something, Nikolas left the hill and ran toward the creatures smashing through the back of his army. 'Hold the line!' he cried to his men in front.

Those in the back were struggling against the long arms that could smash through two men at a time, knocking aside spears and shields and crushing bodies in a single blow. A Xanthian spear in a giant's hand thrust into a red-cloaked soldier's abdomen and then tossed his body into the air behind him before penetrating another warrior's chest; the man gasped in agony, writhing as the wooden spike tore at his innards.

Nothing could prepare Nikolas for the carnage as he reached the scene. Setting his jaw he leaped over a body and raised his shield to block the overhead swing of a pair of fists. The blow, from arms as large as a big man's leg, shattered his shield into pieces, nearly breaking his arm in the process.

Stars sparkled in his vision as he barely managed to evade the next blow by lunging to the side. He struck the ground and rolled onto his back. The giant snarled as he loomed over him. Nikolas knew he was a dead man.

But something huge swooped down from overhead. Wings the size of a boat's sails framed a lithe body that was all bone, muscle, sinew, and scale. A pair of reptilian jaws clasped over the giant's head, biting down hard, crushing the creature's skull. The wings flapped and the dragon tore the giant's head from its body, once more rising into the air. Nikolas saw it had a scar on the side of its face in the shape of a crescent.

The giant fell to the ground, toppling like a tree. Nikolas climbed back to his feet as he saw another dragon plunge down on the enemy with claws outstretched to grab an ogre, claws rending its shoulders and jaw turning sideways to tear open its victim's throat. Two furies picked up another giant by the armpits, flying high into the sky. Nikolas followed them with his eyes until they were distant figures, the ogre struggling in their grip. They finally let go and the ogre came crashing to the ground with earth-shattering force.

Flying creatures were suddenly everywhere, ripping into the once-indomitable force at the rear of Nikolas's army. He watched in wonder, uncomprehending how or why they were here. Then he shook himself and turned back to the line.

'Reform!' he cried. 'Shield to shield!'

With the threat from behind gone, the discipline of the Xanthian hoplites' training came to the fore. Nikolas ran to join them, pushing through the ranks and roaring for them to hold.

The line came together. But the sun king's men sensed victory and pushed on relentlessly. Nikolas had lost his spear and shield and now had only his sword. The enemy pushed forward. The Xanthians gave ground. The tide would turn one way or another at any instant.

A screaming warrior came at him, thrusting a spear at Nikolas's head. Ducking under it, Nikolas lunged forward and slashed at his opponent's unprotected knees. The warrior's screaming changed pitch as he fell. In a momentary lull, Nikolas saw that there were no longer any giants or ogres fighting with the sun king's men. He looked up. Winged creatures were fighting each other in the skies, writhing and rolling as dragon fought dragon and fury fought fury.

Bodies were everywhere. The ground was stained red with blood. Nikolas suddenly found himself fighting two men at once, and when he looked for help he saw that every man around him was occupied as each force tried to make one final surge and achieve victory.

He pushed a spear away with his sword and lunged, feeling the blade bite deeply as he struck a stocky Ilean's throat. But then his second opponent, a man as muscled as Nikolas himself, slashed down with a curved sword. Nikolas managed to avoid the blow, but he felt sudden fire as sharp steel sliced the back of his sword hand.

His sword dropped from his fingers. Seeing his enemy without shield or weapon, the big warrior's eyes lit up with triumph as he prepared to make a final killing strike. Nikolas waited for the end.

Then, swift as a bird, an arrow flew past Nikolas's ear. The Ilean cried out and put his hands to his face, trying in vain to clutch at the shaft that sprouted from his eye. As he fell and another enemy took his place, a second arrow tore into the next Ilean's face.

'Forward!' came the cry from one of the officers.

'Forward!' The men took it up.

'Forward!' Nikolas roared as he raised a fist to the sky. 'Counting march!'

Linked shield to shield, the men started to count.

'One!' They took a step forward, pushing back the enemy line.

'Two!' They grunted as they moved again.

'Three!' The enemy fell to spears and swords.

Finally, the army of Ilea broke.

They ran for the city and Nikolas saw that the gates were wide open as their yellow-cloaked comrades helped them flee. With savage joy the hoplites chased after them, cutting them down from behind.

A rearward guard held the gates for a time, and then the first of Nikolas's men swarmed through, followed by a flood of crimson-cloaked men, rushing to reclaim their city.

Nikolas looked up and saw that the skies were clear. Like a flock of frightened birds, the enemy eldren were retreating, flying over the city and beyond. On the battlefield, a group of silver-haired eldren, those who had fought on the Xanthian side, were now searching for the bodies of their fallen.

Only then did he realize that the battle was won.

An archer behind him was panting as he clutched his weapon. Nikolas turned to thank the man who had saved his life, and his eyes widened.

Dion was covered in blood, looking up at the palace as his chest heaved. He lowered the composite bow that Nikolas had given him.

'We need to get to the harbor,' Dion said.

Together the brothers rushed through the open gates and into the streets of the newly liberated city. Red-cloaked soldiers were everywhere, desperate to find loved ones and to ensure there wasn't a single man in a yellow cloak left alive. Reaching the grassy bank near the palace, where an unfinished wall barely a foot in height did nothing to protect the city from the sea, Dion cursed as he saw that they were too late.

Already the enemy warships were growing distant, their cargo of soldiers now embarked for a new destination.

An officer came forward. 'Your orders, sire?'

Nikolas wiped a hand over his face, and then looked at the palm, seeing that it was entirely red, the blood dry and sticky.

He glanced up at the palace. 'Send some men to take care of the bodies of the king, and the . . . those with him.'

The officer nodded. 'Already done.'

At that moment a regular soldier ran forward, white-faced as he gasped for breath. 'Commander—' He corrected himself. 'Sire.'

'What is it?'

'Your son,' the breathless soldier said. 'He's . . . He's in the palace.'

Nikolas felt a terrible dread sink into his chest.

'Nikolas—' Dion said.

'Clear the palace!' Nikolas called out to his men. His voice lowered to a whisper. 'Let me go in alone.'

55

Dion stood in the middle of the deserted agora of Xanthos, a shambles of broken market stalls and blood-stained marble steps. Toward the sea, the huge bronze statue of a hoplite was toppled over. The temples had been looted and the priests murdered. Many of the city folk had survived the destruction, but not all were so lucky.

He tried to tell himself that soon Xanthos would be as it had once been, but the thought seemed impossible. His parents were gone, and now he was on his own. He tried to blot out the horror of the battle to free his homeland. Xanthos was once more in the hands of its people. But Triton's eldren and the sun king's fleet had left mere hours ago, heading for Phalesia. The fight was far from over.

Though the few surviving priests had more work than they could handle, King Markos and his queen had been given their final resting places, with the army arrayed in front of the Temple of Balal and the black-robed magus chanting sorrowfully as they were interred. Dion's parents would now sleep together in the deep royal crypt beneath the temple. He vowed to himself that his mother's secret would die with her.

Nikolas had requested that he be alone for the burial of his wife. Dion had tried to provide the right words as his brother exited the Temple of Edra, but Nikolas would not be comforted. The new king of Xanthos still wouldn't let anyone into the Royal Palace.

Despite the scene of carnage at the battlefield, already the bodies of the fallen Xanthians were growing few and far between as their families gave them their last rites and buried them with honor. Dion had spoken with Zachary and the eldren with him, who were waiting outside the city walls. Fearful for the fate of the ark, the eldran had asked Dion when Nikolas would lead the army to Phalesia. Dion had told him soon.

But he was worried.

Dion's own emotions were ragged, but he needed his brother to keep going, just for a little longer. Chloe would by now be in Phalesia. The Ilean warships were on their way.

Finally, Dion could wait no more.

He left the agora and traveled to the palace's main gates. As he approached he could see the courtyard, the gardens, and the servant's quarters and stables. The gates were open, but guarded by six soldiers.

As Dion walked toward them their spears came up and their leader, a veteran soldier with thick black eyebrows, raised a warding hand to hesitantly bar the way.

'Let me see my brother,' Dion said softly.

'He is now the king,' the soldier said, uncertain. 'That is how you should refer to him.'

'He is also my brother, and a soldier. If what I think is true, though I hope to the gods it isn't, I am now his heir.'

The guard scratched his chin and then nodded to his fellows. The spears came up and the men drew aside.

Dion crossed the courtyard and entered the palace.

He went immediately for the broad stone steps leading up to the first floor. Trepidation in every footstep, he climbed them one after the other. He emerged into the banqueting hall, where little Lukas had been proudly given his name, scanning the wide room but seeing that the hearths were cold and the hall was empty.

He glanced at the Flower Terrace. His mother's favorite place would now haunt him forever.

Dion walked through the corridor and entered the audience chamber. He slowly approached the high-backed wooden chair that had been his father's throne, and was now his older brother's.

Nikolas sat on the throne with his head in his hands. He heard Dion's footsteps and looked up.

Dion approached the throne and turned to face his brother. He sank to one knee and placed his hand on his heart.

'Brother,' Dion said softly. 'You are now king.'

Nikolas's face bore the marks of grief in every line. The dark, twisted expression on his usually jovial face was one that Dion had never seen before. His reddened eyes were weary and uncaring.

'Father said this chair was never comfortable,' Nikolas said. He paused for a moment, as if he was finding speech difficult. 'By the gods, I never thought I would inherit in this way.'

'Brother . . . Sire . . .' Dion said. 'We need to talk—'

'There is something I must show you,' Nikolas said. He tugged on his thick black beard, before sighing and climbing off the throne to join Dion on the floor. 'Come.'

Feeling growing concern, Dion followed Nikolas out to the Orange Terrace. Dion's brother led him to the half-circle of stone benches, where so many times the family had sat in council with the crashing waves on the shore below the palace forming a backdrop to their conversation.

Nikolas waited expectantly at the circle for his brother to arrive. Dion followed his gaze and put his hands over his face before taking them away, forcing himself to see what his brother wanted him to see.

Seven-year-old Lukas sat composed on the central bench with his back leaning against the stone, staring sightlessly out at the endless blue horizon of the Maltherean Sea. He wore a clean white tunic, low at the neck, making the neat slice across his throat clearly visible.

'I'm so sorry,' Dion said. He didn't know what else he could say. His mouth was dry; he struggled to form words. Lukas was an innocent. Who could kill a child?

Finally, he recovered himself enough to say what had to be said. 'But, brother, this is no time for grief. You are king now and the struggle is not over. We have to help our allies. We must go to Phalesia to drive away the enemy forces. Then we can grieve.'

Nikolas turned his stricken eyes on his younger brother. 'What do I care if the sun king seizes the Ark of Revelation? Or Phalesia itself? Phalesia didn't defend us or fight with us. I owe them nothing.'

'We were victorious only with the help of Zachary and the eldren who follow him,' Dion said softly, but clearly. 'He helped us because of what is in the ark. There are things I need to tell you. You saw that a larger group of eldren fights with Solon. They are under the command of one called Triton, who calls himself their king. Inside the ark is an ancient relic, a horn that he can use to summon the wildren. Think about it. All of them at his command. Out to destroy all humans. That includes the people of Xanthos, those you are duty-bound to protect.'

Nikolas was silent. He ran his fingers through Lukas's short black hair. The child stared directly ahead, facing the sea.

'Brother,' Dion tried again. 'I did not betray us.'

'I know,' Nikolas said.

He walked to the stone rail and Dion frowned as he followed. Nikolas looked down, and Dion drew in a sharp intake of breath.

Peithon was dead, impaled on a wooden stake erected on the grassy bank below. The point of the spear rose from his shoulder blades; he hung limply, with his head lolling to the side. He wore his fine silk tunic, though it was bloody and red, and the large fingers of his hands still had heavy silver rings encrusted with jewels.

'He fled soon after you named him traitor,' Nikolas murmured. 'When we retook the city the men found him hiding in his villa, clutching onto a pouch of silver coins and throwing them at the soldiers who seized him, begging them to let him go.'

Dion realized with a start that Lukas wasn't looking out to sea. Nikolas had arranged the boy's body so that when Peithon had been impaled, his blank eyes would be able to watch.

'Brother . . .' Dion began.

'Fight for Phalesia if you want. Take your eldren. Let me bury my son.'

56

Chloe held her breath as she gazed out at the sea from the edge of the Phalesian agora. Just a dozen paces in front of her the stone dropped away in the sloped defensive embankment. The horseshoe wings of the harbor curved left and right, so that she was at the apex of the curve. She had rarely left this position since her arrival.

Her long dark hair was combed until it shone, and she had washed away the grime of her journey, although the lines of care in her forehead had deepened. She now wore a white chiton fastened with copper pins and leather sandals on her feet. A new amulet bearing the symbol of Aeris hung from a copper chain around her neck. Aeries was the goddess of healing, yet what Chloe truly wanted was a sword or a dagger in her hand. She wanted to fight.

Chloe remembered standing at this very place when Kargan had climbed the narrow steps and been welcomed by her father. The sun king's naval overlord had cast his eyes disdainfully over the city. He had then insulted her father in his own home. He had made no attempt to hide his desire for the golden ark at the Temple of Aldus. Then he had kidnapped Chloe and taken her to Lamara.

Kargan had gone and now he would return. This time he would be thirsty for conquest. This time the sun king himself would be with him.

Chloe looked to her right, at the cliff that was home to the ark, the object of the sun king's desire. She frowned as she looked at the first steps cut into the cliff, leading up from the embankment, at the edge of the harbor's arc. She followed them with her eyes, tilting her head back as her gaze finally rested on the temple at the flat summit.

The eternal flame flickered and danced. The white marble columns of the roofless temple glistened. The golden chest sparkled, reflecting the afternoon sun's slanted rays.

Solon wanted the gold and Triton desperately wanted what was in the ark. The people of Phalesia had to do everything they could to protect it.

Hearing shouted orders and barked commands, Chloe now looked down at the shore. Every soldier in Phalesia was waiting on the white-pebbled beach. She saw Captain Amos bawling orders as he ran up and down the ranks. There seemed too few men to defend an entire harbor. She had already counted them, praying for the gods to give strength to each man in turn. The long stretch of soldiers was over eight hundred soldiers long and two deep. They stood three feet apart, stretched thinly to encompass most of the shoreline, which made their line over a mile long.

There simply weren't enough defenders; Chloe could see that without knowing anything about military strategy. Phalesia's strength was in her navy, which had placed her as one of the strongest Galean nations, until the arrival of the Ileans had made them realize their vessels were outclassed.

Out in the blue water, the Phalesian fleet waited expectantly, a wall of ships guarding the entire harbor between the rocky promontories at either end. There were fourteen war galleys with sails down and oars at the ready. Like the biremes they would be facing they had bronze rams jutting from the bow, just below the waterline. Thirty rowers to either side of the open-decked vessels framed a central complement of a dozen archers and marines, standing tall and proud with blue cloaks fluttering in the wind as they prepared to defend their homeland.

Chloe wasn't alone on the embankment and stood in the middle of a long line of consuls. Flanking them on both sides were a few dozen archers and a score of soldiers.

She heard her father beside her let out a breath. 'Daughter,' he said quietly. 'You should go and hide in the villa with your sister and the servants.' His eyes were moist as he looked at her. 'I don't want to regain you only to lose you again.'

Chloe once more scanned the long arc of blue-cloaked Phalesian soldiers on the shore. 'I came too late.'

Aristocles shook his head. 'Your warning gives us a chance. The men are equipped and deployed. The fleet guards the harbor. If we survive the day, Phalesia has you to thank.'

She sighed as she looked up at her father. 'Any news from Xanthos?'

'All we know is that the city fell. Nikolas departed through the Gates of Annika with the Xanthian army and did not return.'

Aristocles looked every day of his age. His high forehead and balding pate revealed the worry lines on his face.

'Are you going to find a safer place?' Chloe asked.

The first consul shook his head. 'My place is here.' He indicated the line of consuls, standing along the embankment as if they were the city's last line of defense, although to a man they were unarmed and too old to fight, even if they had the skill. 'This is where we will all make our stand. Amos will hold them on the shore, and then if he must he will fall back to this embankment. If the enemy makes it to the agora, then we know the city has fallen.'

'Then I will stand with you,' Chloe said, her jaw set.

Suddenly, Aristocles gripped Chloe's arm and she saw him scanning the sky above and behind them. The sound of heavy wings filled the air. Dozens of dragons and furies in a range of sizes plunged down from overhead, approaching from the city's landward side. Winged shapes filled the air, arranged in a V-shaped formation behind their leader.

'Archers!' roared an officer with a blue crest on his helmet nearby.

The cluster of archers ranged around the consuls on the embankment nocked arrows to bowstrings and drew.

'Wait!' Chloe cried. She ran to the officer, waving her arms. 'Hold your fire!'

Aside from a few abandoned market stalls framing the edges, the agora was completely deserted. The foremost dragon flapped its silver-scaled wings to slow its momentum and Chloe's eyes widened as she saw a rider on its back. The lean young man with sandy brown hair was hunched forward as he gripped onto the dragon's neck with an expression as grim as death. Chloe recognized the crescent scar on the side of the angular reptilian head. The archers lowered their bows as she ran forward.

Dion slipped off the dragon's back, white-faced and staggering as he found his feet. Behind him, clouds of gray smoke enveloped Zachary and the other eldren, shimmering as each changed back to his normal form.

In a heartbeat Dion stood in front of several dozen silver-haired men and women. They were all tall and lithe, with sharp features and pale skin, and wore clothing of deerskin and animal hide. Their hair was in a variety of styles: Zachary's lustrous shoulder-length hair was short compared to some of the slim women, and several of the men's hair was close-cropped and spiky. They were an attractive people, but grim and sober-faced.

'What are they doing here?' muttered a consul.

'They're here to fight alongside us,' Dion said, sweeping his gaze over the gathered consuls.

'The gods have no wish for them to be near our temples—' began Consul Harod, his red face scowling as he stood near Chloe with his arms folded over his chest.

Chloe's eyes blazed as she rounded on him. 'Perhaps they were sent by the gods.'

'Enough!' cried Aristocles. He came to stand beside Chloe and Dion and turned to challenge the others. 'My daughter is correct. Any man who suggests turning away the eldren who are our friends is no true patriot of Phalesia.'

Under his gaze, Harod tugged on his thick beard and was pensive for a time, before he finally nodded. 'If they want to fight for our city, let them.'

'They do—' Dion said.

'Zachary?' Chloe interrupted. She saw that the eldran was trembling as he stood with his fists clenched at his sides. Remembering the time he had nearly lost himself in giant form, she once more saw that there was wildness in his eyes.

Zachary wasn't the only eldran who appeared to be having trouble. He drew in a slow, shaky breath and then nodded. 'I have been shifting form too much. I feel my identity slipping away. My people will not be able to change for long.'

'Anything you can do to help will not be forgotten,' Aristocles said. He bowed deeply. 'I thank you, on behalf of all my people, for coming to our aid at this dark hour.'

Zachary merely nodded a weary acknowledgment as Chloe's father turned to Dion.

'Dion of Xanthos,' Aristocles said warmly. 'It appears my daughter is not the only one to have changed.' Chloe could see her father take note of the bow Dion carried in one hand and the sharpened wooden spear in the other. 'I see you no longer wear silver.'

Chloe realized it was true; Dion no longer had the silver symbol of Silex around his neck, nor the chain it hung from. 'You are ready to take up iron, the materia of the warrior?'

Dion glanced at Chloe, then back to Aristocles. Chloe saw a strange expression on his face.

'I suppose this is a time of change for all of us,' Dion said.

Aristocles' expression was quizzical, but he reached out to clasp the young man's shoulders. 'I must take this opportunity to thank you for the return of my daughter.'

Dion smiled slightly as he turned to Chloe, and now it was as if he were speaking to her. 'She made it out on her own. Your daughter is a strong woman.'

'That she is,' Aristocles said. His expression then turned grave. 'What news from Xanthos?'

Dion hesitated. 'My brother took back the city. I last saw him yesterday. He remains there as king.'

Aristocles was stunned. 'He is not coming to our aid?'

'No, First Consul,' Dion said sadly. 'I'm afraid he is not. He lost his whole family. Father, wife, son . . . And all because of a close friend's betrayal. The shock is too much; he's withdrawn into himself.'

'But'—Aristocles struggled to comprehend the news—'our alliance. Surely he knows the Ilean attack was none of our doing?'

'First Consul!' the officer with the indigo crest on his helmet cried. 'The enemy approaches!'

Chloe heard a chorus of gasps; her father went rigid. Everyone's eyes turned to the sea.

It was time.

A long line of Ilean warships filled the horizon, evenly spaced and approaching the harbor with speed. Oars rose and fell, their tempo increasing with every sweep. Soldiers swarmed on every deck.

Chloe watched the line of warships loom larger in her vision as they grew ever closer to the wall of Phalesian galleys.

'So many ships,' she whispered.

Her heart sank as she saw sinuous serpents lunge out of the water before plunging back into the sea – a deadly force of Triton's eldren. She swiftly counted; there were two dozen biremes facing the Phalesian fleet of fourteen war galleys. With the serpents aiding them in the sea, the defeat of the Phalesian fleet was guaranteed.

'First Consul.'

Aristocles tore his eyes away from the harbor as Zachary spoke.

The eldran indicated the others with him. 'We have all decided we will fight in the sea. The more ships we sink, the fewer soldiers will reach the land.'

Aristocles swallowed. 'Do what you can but no more,' he said. 'Don't push yourselves too far. We all know the risks you are taking, not only to your lives but also to your sanity. Remember, the eldren fighting for the sun king will also suffer the same fears, and our navy will fight with you.'

Zachary nodded. As he led his people to a cleared space in the agora away from people, Chloe saw the eldren meet one another's eyes.

And then smoke clouded the air around them.

57

The *Nexotardis* was just in front of the line of biremes, leading the charge. The drum pounded so quickly that the oarsmen could barely keep up. At ramming speed the ships traveled in a direct line for the Phalesian fleet arrayed against them.

Solon and Kargan stood close to the bow, where they had a view of the wall of Phalesian war galleys ahead and the biremes arranged at either side. The sun king saw Kargan frowning as he looked down into the water, where one-eyed Triton, now in the form of a mighty serpent, lunged in and out of the water.

'Our allies are powerful,' Kargan muttered.

Solon glanced at his commander and smiled with thin lips. 'Speak plainly, Kargan. No one else can hear you.'

'I will.' Kargan scowled at Solon. 'I fear this alliance has been made in haste.'

Solon spread his long-fingered hands. 'Triton is desperate for the ark. Once we have it, and what is inside, we will be safe from any treachery.'

Kargan nodded, but Solon could see he was unconvinced. 'Not all goes to plan,' the barrel-chested naval commander said.

'You are speaking of the attack on Xanthos,' said Solon. 'I place no blame on your shoulders. The spy who burned our ships evidently provided enough warning for their army to seize the pass. But it was always a gamble, and look'—he nodded in the direction of the city—'the true prize awaits.'

The Phalesian galleys now plunged their oars into the water and commenced their own speeding attack. The distance between the two forces narrowed to five hundred paces, then four.

'I will get the gold for myself,' Solon said. 'We can put whatever we find inside the ark into an iron box, and we will have control over the eldren forever.'

'And if we don't get the ark?'

Solon turned his feverish gaze on Kargan. 'We must get it, mustn't we?'

Kargan didn't reply. 'I must see to my ship,' he said, leaving Solon alone at the bow.

Each vessel, Phalesian and Ilean alike, now chose a target, angling to approach with a glancing blow. The *Nexotardis* skimmed over the water as she flew like a spear at a Phalesian war galley, which came in to meet her as the distance shrank to fifty paces.

Kargan suddenly bawled orders to his crew and the *Nexotardis* sharply turned to the right. The Phalesians attempted to change their galley's trajectory, but with her greater speed and power the *Nexotardis* began to draw away; the gap between the two vessels increased.

Then Kargan roared again and the *Nexotardis* cut a sweeping turn to the left, heading into the Phalesian galley's side. Arrows flew through the air on both sides and Solon ducked under the rail as a shaft skewered the air where he'd been a moment before. He felt a lurch and heard a sickening crunch as the *Nexotardis*'s ram raked along the side of the Phalesian galley, scraping a hole in the opposing ship's side. Poking his head over the rail he saw the Phalesian ship tilt to the side as water rushed in. The galley sank swiftly as Kargan's archers loosed arrows at the next closest enemy vessel.

Looking along the line, Solon saw more of his captains making contact. Two ships met head on, the collision shattering both vessels as the rams tore gaping holes in their opposing bows. Another bireme captained by a stocky woman with short bleached hair struck a Phalesian ship with a perfectly executed attack.

Cries filled the air as ship after ship went down, the Phalesians taking heavy losses but inflicting few casualties of their own. Ignoring the danger of whistling arrows, Solon stood at the bow and watched with his heart racing. He cursed each vessel of his own that went down, taking hundreds of his soldiers with it, men who were needed to seize the city.

The waters around the ships boiled like a cauldron as thrashing gray serpents battled, their scaled bodies coiled one around the other, making it impossible to tell them apart. Merfolk grappled and gasped as well-matched opponents sought to drown each other. With the eldren under Triton's command facing an opposing force of their own race, perhaps traditional tactics would determine the confrontation between the warships.

But then Solon saw a leathery wedge-shaped head with a silver frill lunge at the *Nexotardis* from the left side. The serpent struck the vessel hard, attempting to push the bireme's bow to the right and open her up to two approaching Phalesian galleys. Arrows flashed down from the ship's rail, bouncing off the tough hide, but the serpent merely roared as it continued to push. Solon found himself unable to look away from the monstrous jaws and the crescent scar on the side of its face.

He realized the creature's tactics were going to be successful. The two war galleys were so close he felt he could reach out and touch them. When they struck the side of the ship Solon was currently standing on, the bireme would shatter into pieces. There was nothing he could do but hold on with a white-knuckled grip.

As the danger grew another larger serpent lunged out of the water and smacked down on top of the monster with the crescent scar; Solon had seen Triton in serpent form enough to recognize the eldran king. The two became embroiled. Kargan bellowed orders. The *Nexotardis* began to turn, straightening its approach to the two galleys.

They passed on either side as the *Nexotardis* slid between them. The Phalesian archers let loose a volley of iron-tipped arrows. Kargan's crew and marines either fell under the hail, clutching the shafts that sprouted from their bodies, or like Solon ducked under a rail.

Solon climbed shakily back to his feet. He couldn't believe he was still alive.

He tried to assess the battle, but the sea around Phalesia's harbor was a confusion of sinking warships and writhing eldren. At every instant vessels were grinding up against each other. With nowhere else to seek refuge, the yellow-cloaked soldiers thronging the decks of the biremes hid under the side rails.

Then two more Phalesian galleys went down and Solon saw that there were no more of the enemy's open-decked galleys remaining. Two Ilean biremes joined the *Nexotardis* on either side. The line of warships slowly reformed. Solon counted his ships and saw that only four had been crippled or sunk, leaving twenty remaining.

Blood filled the water as the corpses of serpents, merfolk, sailors, and soldiers knocked against each other, bobbing on the surface. The rest of the eldren, evidently spent, had split into two forces, one heading for the safety of the harbor, the other climbing ropes to clamber shakily onto the warships' open decks, unable to risk further changing.

The Ilean vessels now approached the white-pebbled shore of Phalesia.

And Solon saw with satisfaction that only a thin line of soldiers stood between him and his prize.

58

Dion and Chloe watched the naval battle unfold. The two forces met and suddenly it was impossible to see what was happening. Oars splashed and warships crunched together. Serpents writhed together, sending water spouting high into the air.

Dion felt Chloe lean against him, clutching his arm as an opening gap revealed half a dozen sinking Phalesian galleys. A bireme went down and the consuls and soldiers cheered. But still more Ilean warships raked the hulls of the smaller vessels, sending torrents of water into their bellies and sinking them in moments. Archers on all sides sent volleys of arrows flying at their enemies. Dion had to remind himself that every bireme sunk was a blessing to the soldiers on the shore below.

For it was obvious to everyone watching that the Phalesian fleet was being massacred.

There was nothing the eldren from the Wilds in the north could do to help their human allies, for every serpent fought another creature just like it, and every one of the merfolk on both sides was met by an equally strong opponent. Dion's heart went out to Zachary and his people, who were fighting despite the risk to their sanity.

The struggle between the two groups of eldren came to a close, as they were forced to call a mutual draw and leave the battle.

But the same couldn't be said of the conflict between the two fleets of Phalesia and Ilea. Suddenly there wasn't a Phalesian galley left afloat in the water. The line of biremes drew up once more, still at least twenty strong.

The battle for the harbor was over.

Dion took a slow breath and looked down at the thin line of men guarding the shore. When the sun king's men disembarked, the blue-cloaked Phalesian soldiers would try to stop them before they had a chance to exit the water and form up with strength. Dion hefted his spear in his right hand and clutched his bow tightly in his left.

He met Chloe's eyes. 'I'm going down there.'

Dion saw her glance up at the Temple of Aldus before she nodded. 'Dion—' She hesitated, as if she was going to say something she wasn't certain of, but all she said was, 'Be safe.'

He was worried about her, but he knew her well enough to know she would never leave her father's side. 'You too,' he said.

Dion ran down the thin set of diagonal steps that led to the beach from the embankment. He skirted the shore and joined the line close to the scar-faced Captain Amos.

Together they waited, fifty paces above the waterline, a long line of archers and hoplites just two soldiers deep.

The first to reach the shore were the eldren. They had done their utmost to save the city from the sun king's fleet but had been matched by the force under Triton. First one, then another silver-haired man or woman climbed out of the water, scratched and bleeding, shaking their heads, fighting the encroaching wildness after changing for so long. Soldiers cheered and helped them out of the water and Dion saw Amos speaking with Zachary, who had a red line of claw marks on his neck. The eldran glanced at Dion as he came over.

'It rests on you and the soldiers with you now, Dion of Xanthos,' Zachary said. 'I must take my people home and tend to their wounds, as well as their minds.' His voice turned ominous as he met the gaze of both Amos and Dion. 'You have to hold them here.'

He left, too weary to speak another word, gathering the eldren and leading them to safety.

Amos reformed his men and now they readied themselves, the long line of soldiers muttering prayers as they faced the coming assault from the water.

The twenty enemy ships passed from the blue water to the turquoise shallows. The vessels gathered momentum and then the oarsmen shipped their oars as the soldiers who manned them prepared to leave their posts to fight.

'Archers!' Amos cried. 'On my mark!'

Dion plunged his spear into the pebbled beach and grabbed an arrow from his quiver, nocking it to the bowstring.

A scraping sound filled the air as the shallow hulls of the warships struck the shore. With near-perfect symmetry, vessel after vessel climbed the beach before their momentum ground to a halt.

'Wait for it!'

The upper decks of the biremes emptied of soldiers as the officers sent their men down below. Dion tried to calm his breathing and fixed his gaze on the closest warship, just forty paces away. A torrent of yellow-cloaked soldiers poured out from both sides of the bireme's lowest deck. The men at the front entered water that was barely ankle deep, while those at the back plunged in to their waists.

Dion remembered burning the ships back at Lamara's harbor. He only wished he'd been able to destroy more. He drew the string to his cheek and picked his target: a bearded warrior with oiled hair slicked to his scalp.

'Fire!'

Dion loosed his arrow as the shaft joined hundreds of others. He struck the bearded warrior in the throat, blood gushing out of his mouth as he fell. Arrows plunged into the first wave of warriors before they had a chance to climb the beach, slaughtering them in numbers.

'Again! Draw!' Amos roared. 'Fire!'

Dion loosed another arrow, sending a shaft into a grizzled soldier who tried to raise his shield but wasn't quick enough for the point that struck his cheek. Another wave of soldiers pouring from the warship's side went down, but they were joined by still more of their comrades. The Ileans in the shallow water formed a line, their shields held high to allow more of their fellows to group behind them.

Now fewer shafts found their targets. Dion's next arrow penetrated a wooden shield but failed to strike through to its owner. He reached for yet another as Amos bellowed for his men to fire at will.

At either side of the warship a wall of triangular shields now fanned out, allowing soldier after soldier to emerge under the protection of his countrymen. Swiftly glancing along the line, Dion saw the same situation unfolding at every warship: the Ileans were gathering strength, even under the onslaught of Amos's archers. Soon they would advance.

'Forward!' Amos cried. 'Shield to shield, spear to spear!'

The Phalesian line moved forward, but Dion saw that it was too thinly spread to maintain a rank two men deep while standing shield to shield. The second rank swiftly became mingled with those in front. There was terrible danger here, he realized. A concerted push would smash through the line, and soon Amos's men would be facing enemies both in front and behind.

Nonetheless it was the only move available to the Phalesian captain. He needed to fight the soldiers of Ilea as they climbed out of the water, when they were most vulnerable. Dion grabbed hold of his spear and ran forward, finding himself standing between a young soldier barely in his teens and another archer. The boy clutched his spear with white knuckles as he waited for the enemy's approach. The archer sent an arrow at the shield wall on the warship's right, but the point uselessly embedded itself in a shield. The archer reached for another arrow but his quiver was empty. He had no other weapon.

Sticking the spear into the ground again and checking his quiver, Dion saw he had just two arrows remaining. As he drew the first an enemy arrow sped at his head. He ducked and was saved when the boy at his left managed to block it with his shield. Dion took a deep breath and drew once more and released, striking an Ilean soldier's knee where the shield wasn't protecting him. The man went down with a cry.

He prepared his last arrow as across the line, the sun king's soldiers finally charged.

Dion loosed and killed a roaring spearman with a well-placed arrow in his chest. He barely had time to drop his bow and lift his spear before the two forces collided.

The Phalesians held their ground. All along the line snarling men's faces were barely inches away from each other as shield pressed against shield and spears lunged forward as each man tried to find a gap in the defenses of the soldier in front of him.

The archer at Dion's right was protected by neither shield nor weapon, and he went down in an instant as a spear found his chest. The line began to buckle. Everywhere there were grunting men and cries of pain. A short, stocky warrior with leather armor and a yellow cloak thrust his spear at Dion's head. Dion weaved to the side and felt it whistle past his ear. With both hands he jabbed his own spear at the warrior's face but the man ducked behind the shield on his left arm.

'Close ranks!' Amos cried.

A dozen paces to his left, Dion saw Amos fighting with desperation. The scar-faced captain lunged forward to skewer an opponent's throat with his sword and then slashed down at another, but for every man he killed another took his place.

The youth turned to gasp something to Dion, but he never discovered what he'd been about to say, for an arrow suddenly penetrated the boy's shoulder and he fell with a cry of pain. Dion closed ranks with the men at both sides again. Finding a gap, he managed to spear the stocky Ilean facing him, thrusting deep into his upper torso and pulling out in a single movement, but the enemy continued to push forward.

Amos suddenly looked along the line, then wheeled his arms. 'Fall back! Back to the embankment!'

Everywhere the line wavered, then finally crumbled. Dion thrust one last time with his spear and felt the point bite into something, but whirled without looking to see where his blow had struck, barely managing to keep hold of his weapon. Every soldier in blue joined the rout as they ran for the embankment.

He faltered and nearly fell when he felt a sharp stab of pain between his shoulder blades.

Stumbling, he righted himself and continued running. At all sides hoplites and archers ran for the narrow stairs leading up the sloped embankment. Glancing back over his shoulder he saw two swarthy Ileans on his heels. One held the sword that had scored his back. He could almost feel their hot breath on his neck.

Dion spun and threw his spear, making one of his pursuers dodge to the side. He glanced up at the embankment as he reached the bottom of the steps. Risking another look behind him he saw an arrow from above strike the second Ilean's upper thigh. The yellow-cloaked soldier roared with pain as he fell.

Dion panted as he climbed the steps while arrows smashed against the stone around him. The press of men crowding behind him made him nearly trip into those in front. The short journey up the stairs took an eternity as he expected an arrow to spear his body at any instant.

Finally, he crested the steps.

The first thing he saw was a Phalesian archer dead at his feet. Barely pausing, Dion crouched and picked up the man's bow and quiver before joining the soldiers forming up along the defensive bastion.

The two forces both paused to gather themselves.

Standing with the last of the defenders arrayed along the summit of the curved stone wall, Dion saw that the fallen of both sides littered the curving shoreline, but the beach was now firmly in the sun king's hands. The last pair of survivors made it up to the embankment, joining their fellows in guarding the steps that led from the harbor to the agora.

As order gradually came to the ranks of the yellow-cloaked soldiers below, Dion saw a barrel-chested commander, who could only be Kargan, gesturing as he barked orders to his officers. A lanky man with long dark hair and a curled beard, wearing a spiked golden crown and a bright yellow robe – he must be the sun king himself – stood tall on the upper deck of a warship and surveyed the area, before descending a ramp to the shore.

The last defenders waited along the embankment. The Phalesians had lost at least half of their number. The consuls who made up the city's leadership milled behind them.

He heard Aristocles speaking loud enough for all to hear. 'No! I refuse to leave the city.'

Dion looked frantically for Chloe, but she wasn't anywhere to be seen.

Out of bowshot, the sun king's soldiers prepared to make their final assault. Rank after rank of yellow-cloaked soldiers assembled in orderly rectangles. A silver-haired eldran now stood beside Solon;

both were gazing up at the Temple of Aldus. The Ileans had conquered the Phalesian army as easily as they'd crushed the navy.

Dion swiftly assessed the defenders' numbers. He knew they would fall in the first wave.

A trumpet blared.

The attackers roared. The defenders shook their weapons.

The sun king's men began to run.

Instantly, every archer atop the bastion drew his bowstring to his cheek and released, and Dion fired with them. But the attackers raised their shields to ward off the volley and few arrows struck home. The Ileans rushed the twin sets of steps and there were suddenly so many soldiers milling below that Dion couldn't miss striking limb, torso, or shield.

The sun king's soldiers reached the top of the steps and the Phalesians cut them down. But for every man that fell, another took his place. The rush became a flood, and the flood became a torrent. There were simply too many of them.

Dion continued to loose arrows into the mob below, but he knew that despite his efforts the struggle was pointless. He tried to aim at the Ileans cresting the wall but there was too much chance of striking a Phalesian.

He reached for an arrow, but his quiver was empty.

Then he saw Chloe.

She had a sword in her hand and was high on the cliff, climbing up the steep stairway, heading for the Temple of Aldus. Realizing she planned to defend the ark to the end, Dion scanned the ground, frantic as he bent and his hand closed around the hilt of a fallen soldier's blade. He tried to push through to the edge of the embankment, striving in vain to reach the base of the steps against the surge of soldiers.

Amos and a hundred hoplites were now the last men trying to hold the wall. Scores of yellow-cloaked soldiers made it to the embankment with every passing moment. Amos fell when a shield struck his forehead. The blue-cloaked soldiers around him turned and ran.

Dion deftly weaved around the fleeing Phalesians as he reached the base of the cliff. He turned and faced the agora, feeling the iron hilt in his hand burn, and knowing the sensation now for what it was, knowing that it stemmed from who he was, what he was.

He prepared to defend the steps, protecting the ark with his life.

Protecting Chloe.

The attacking soldiers knew the sun king's desire, and as they swarmed into the agora while the consuls fled in front of them, a broad-shouldered Ilean with a plume of orange horsehair cresting his helmet saw Dion, the sole defender of the path to the Temple of Aldus.

The soldier charged.

The sword felt impossibly heavy, even though Dion held the hilt in both hands. He nonetheless lifted the weapon and knocked aside the first savage thrust of his enemy's spear. Dion raised the weapon again and attempted a fumbling thrust, but the blow was easily deflected by the shield on his opponent's left arm. The Ilean suddenly threw his spear and Dion barely managed to lunge to the side as the weapon skewered the air.

Revealing a scarred, snarling face under his plumed helmet, the enemy soldier drew his sword from the scabbard at his waist. He took his time, slashing overhead and forcing Dion to raise his weapon to block. The force of the blow made the sword fall out of Dion's hands, clattering to the stone.

Dion prepared to die.

Then a horn rumbled, deep and thunderous, overriding even the battle cries and the crashes of steel against steel. The strident note sounded from somewhere down in the city. He heard a roaring voice he knew well: 'The sun king's head is mine!'

Like a rising tide creeping up from the lower city, countless crimson-cloaked warriors of Xanthos swarmed into the agora, crashing against the sun king's men and fighting in a fury of hand-to-hand combat. Nikolas's bearded face was twisted in a fierce snarl as he led his men in the charge. The fleeing Phalesians cheered as they changed their path, turning to join the newcomers.

The hoplites smashed into the attackers before the Ileans had realized their peril. Soldiers in yellow cloaks continued to crest the wall and pour into the breach. Soldiers in red rushed the agora in greater and greater numbers to meet them. With a new danger to face, Dion's opponent turned, uncertain, then ran to the aid of his men.

Still standing on the steps to the temple, Dion watched with wide eyes as the melee in the agora became a frenzy of blood and death.

The battle could go either way.

59

Solon, king of kings, ruler of the empire of Ilea, was standing close to the water's edge, the bulk of the *Nexotardis* above and behind him. He was confident of victory: his stronger, more disciplined soldiers had crested the embankment and would soon seize the city. Beside him the one-eyed eldran king, Triton, had his fists clenched at his sides.

Solon frowned as he saw Kargan running in the wrong direction. For some reason Kargan had descended the steps; he was leading hundreds of men away from the defensive wall.

He raised an eyebrow when Kargan arrived, covered in blood. The big man gasped and wheezed as he made his report. 'The battle is lost! We must retreat.'

'Lost?' Solon's eyes widened. 'The city is yours!'

'The army of Xanthos has arrived,' Kargan panted. 'We don't have the numbers to push them back.'

Shielding his eyes as he gazed up at the city, Solon saw soldiers in crimson cloaks fighting with savagery as they cleared the embankment. The Ileans began to flee, their flight becoming a desperate retreat down the steps as the bravest among them tried to hold against the onslaught of the soldiers at their backs. Yellow-cloaked soldiers tumbled from the high wall of the embankment, screaming until they struck the ground.

Kargan barked orders at his men. 'Get the ships off the beach! Hurry or you're all dead men!'

'No,' Solon said, shaking his head. 'No!'

Kargan turned his dark gaze on his king. 'Solon, your prize is lost. If we don't leave now we'll lose the fleet.'

Solon watched in disbelief as Kargan ordered the men who'd stayed with the warships to get them afloat. As more soldiers rushed down from the city he bellowed commands and instilled order in the terror-filled men.

The newly arrived Xanthian soldiers, under the leadership of a broad-shouldered bearded warrior in a crimson-plumed helmet, poured down the steps and began to gather in numbers, preparing to make a final charge to destroy their fleeing enemies and seize as many ships as they could.

Solon realized in a daze that he would soon be leaving. But he couldn't leave. The ark at the temple remained tantalizingly in reach.

Beside him, Triton spoke. 'You can still be victorious, Solon. When next will you see enough gold to send your soul on its journey to the afterlife?'

'I . . .' Solon shook his head, at a loss for words.

'I can win you this city,' Triton said. 'But I cannot open the ark. For that I need your help.'

Solon looked from the eldran to Kargan, still bellowing orders to get his men moving.

'I can take you to the ark,' Triton continued. 'The lid is heavy but you will be strong enough to open it. Give me what is inside and I will win this battle for you. You can have the gold. You know that gold is not what I want.'

Solon saw the crimson-cloaked soldiers now had the numbers to attack. The big black-bearded commander stood just below the wall, his men ranked behind him, standing shield to shield. He held his sword in the air, then waved his men forward.

The biremes were moving off the shore as the sailors and soldiers got them moving. Once away from shore, those on board would be safe.

Solon met Triton's eyes. He nodded.

'Take me to it,' he said.

Triton smiled.

Clouds of gray smoke gathered around the eldran until his body was completely obscured. The smoke elongated and thickened, becoming dense and massive as Solon stood back.

The mist shimmered.

Triton was suddenly gone, and a monstrous one-eyed dragon now stood in his place. The dragon dipped a leg, and Solon knew what he was supposed to do. He clambered onto its back, gripping the scaly, leathery flesh just behind its forelegs with his knees and leaning forward to hold the protuberances behind its head.

With a surge of terrifying power, the wings lifted and descended, propelling them up into the sky.

Solon felt his spirits soar, as if he were suddenly released of a terrible burden. He no longer cared about Triton's plans: as long as he could bring about his successful entrance to the homeland of the gods, it no longer mattered what transpired in this mortal world. He would be the sun king no more; he would become more than a man.

After death, he would be a god.

The dragon's wings, each as big as a bireme's sail, flapped steadily, thrusting at the air as it flew high into the sky. The incredible perspective revealed the ships of Solon's fleet drawing away from the shore and clusters of fighting men on the embankment and the beach. The occasional soldier stared up at him with horror combined with fear, and Solon smiled as Triton took him above the temple, giving him a direct view of the summit. He saw the columns framing the golden ark in the center. Behind the Ark of Revelation, the eternal flame burned brightly on its pedestal.

The dragon and its rider plummeted down to the plateau.

Landing lightly on the cliff edge, the winged reptile came to a rest and Solon slipped off its back. A sudden spike of pain speared his chest, but he pushed it aside with an iron will. At such a height, gusting winds buffeted his body, slowing his steps as he walked toward the golden ark.

'You will find a horn within,' a voice behind him said. Glancing over his shoulder, Solon saw Triton had shifted back to his usual form. The eldran stood impatiently with legs astride, his brow furrowed as his expression urged Solon to haste, although he was evidently reluctant to approach the chest of gold himself.

'Give me what is inside,' Triton said, 'and you will triumph.'

Solon continued his approach to the ark. He saw fanciful designs in the gold. It was even larger than it appeared from below; he knew it would give him everything he needed and more. He inspected the lid. It was much smaller than the ark itself, embedded in the very center, just a couple of feet to a side. A long handle ran horizontally across it.

Something glittered out of the corner of Solon's eye. It was at the corner of his vision but startling enough to make him turn as he frowned.

He saw a young woman with long dark hair step out from behind a column. She carried a shining steel sword, holding it by the hilt in both hands. The sparkle of the afternoon sun on the blade had alerted him to her approach.

She had thought to surprise him, but the sun god Helios had warned him of her presence and she was unable to make her hidden strike. When he recognized her, Solon gave a dry chuckle.

'I remember you, girl,' he said. He waved a hand dismissively. 'Now get out of my way.'

'No,' said Chloe. She continued to approach him with the tip of her weapon slightly raised. 'I won't.'

Solon was unarmed, but he was unperturbed. He turned completely so that his back was to the ark, raising his voice as he called out to the one-eyed eldran king.

'Triton,' he said. He nodded in Chloe's direction. 'You know what to do.'

60

The battle was won. Dion felt the tension in his shoulders slowly relax as his countrymen cleared the agora, pushing the Ileans all the way to the embankment and finally forcing them to flee the shore.

Nikolas was at the forefront, baying for the sun king's blood as he led his men down the narrow steps to the harbor. Dion's brother had come. Phalesia had survived.

Chloe was safe.

From his vantage Dion could see the tall man with the spiked crown standing near the warship and the tall scar-faced eldran at his side. The sun king would flee. He would be forced to return to Lamara without his prize. Sweeping his gaze over the agora, Dion saw too many bodies to count, a gruesome sight worse than any slaughterhouse.

But when Dion looked back to the harbor he felt the blood drain from his face. His eyes went wide with horror.

He saw the one-eyed dragon and the sun king rise from the shore.

Dion knew that Solon had lost the fight, but for the sun king the struggle was far from over. There was only one place the pair could be traveling to.

Panic overwhelmed him as the dragon climbed high in the sky, then swiftly plummeted down, in the direction of the nearby summit.

Dion's eyes traveled up the cliff face. Chloe was up at the temple, preparing to defend the Ark of Revelation with her life. He had been too late to save his family in Xanthos, and he would be too late to help her.

The climb would take him far too long.

He thought about all he and Chloe had been through. He remembered the men he had set out with on his quest to travel to Lamara, all killed by wildren. The vision of the serpent's huge head plummeting as it swallowed Cob along with half of their boat would stay with him to the end of his days. He recalled the mermaid that saved him and the strange seer at Athos who gave him the incredible *Calypso*. Chloe's own travails filled his mind: she had been imprisoned and her only friend and protector had experienced utmost agony in front of her eyes. She had learned to fight and freed herself from the sun king's clutches.

The words they'd spoken on their frantic voyage home came to the forefront of his awareness, but along with the words were the looks and gestures. He remembered her clutching onto his arm, and his own desire to protect her as they'd watched the enemy fleet approaching the harbor.

Desperation coursed through every fiber of his body.

Dion knew he would be too late to save Chloe's life.

61

Chloe stood on the smooth floor of stone within the temple's framing columns, at an equal distance between Triton and Solon. She tried to face both opponents and keep her sword point up, just as Tomarys had instructed. Blood roared in her ears as her heart raced. Her palms sweated; the hilt in her hands felt slippery.

'Understood, sun king.' Triton fixed his stare on Solon. 'I will deal with the woman. You open the ark and give me what is mine.'

Solon frowned at the golden chest. 'I may not have the strength—'

'Then find it!'

Chloe wondered if she could reach Solon before Triton could strike. She needed to attack the Ilean king before he could open the chest that must never be opened.

In her mind, Tomarys was speaking.

'*Be strong. Be confident. Nothing is more powerful than the warrior who will achieve his objective or die trying.*'

But Chloe didn't know if she was strong enough for this.

Gray smoke suddenly misted around the eldran king. In a heartbeat his body was completely enveloped as the cloud thickened and grew to an impossible size.

The mist shimmered.

The huge one-eyed dragon roared as it flew out of the smoke. An immense silver-scaled body of muscle, sinew, and bone rose into the air as outstretched wings flapped. The jaws gaped as the beast revealed a mouth filled with white teeth the size of daggers.

Chloe saw Solon's outstretched arms as he reached for the handle on the lid of the Ark of Revelation.

She turned to face the dragon, but then moved again to face Solon, trembling with indecision. The veins in Solon's temples were clearly visible as he grunted with the effort.

A crack of light poured from under the slowly opening golden lid.

Chloe decided to charge the sun king, knowing the dragon would kill her before she came close to the tall man at the golden chest.

Then something incredible happened.

A second dragon plummeted down from the sky, but where the scales of the one-eyed Triton were glossy silver, this dragon's scales were as black as night. Until now the one-eyed dragon was the largest Chloe had ever seen.

The newcomer rivaled it in size.

The black dragon's claws were outstretched from its body as it swooped, screaming a challenge to the eldran king. It struck the one-eyed dragon with lightning speed, gripping hold of its enemy's body with muscled forelegs until both creatures tumbled one over the other, rolling over and over, smashing into one of the temple's columns with enough force to shatter the marble and break the column in two, toppling it with a crash of shattering stone. The two tumbling dragons flew up into the sky, writhing in an embrace of terrifying strength.

Solon turned at the sound, his face shocked. He saw Chloe running at him with the sword held in white knuckles as she lunged. With a snarl, he came forward to meet her.

But she realized too late: Solon was a warrior king; he would have been trained since birth in combat. He nonchalantly weaved and brought a hand smashing down onto Chloe's wrist. The sword fell out of her hands and skittered along the smooth paving stones. He pushed on her shoulder as she tumbled out of control, the shove sending her running forward until her head struck a column. A burst of pain exploded in her head as she staggered and then collapsed onto the hard ground.

Her senses reeling, Chloe was about to roll over and push herself to her feet, when Tomarys spoke again.

'*To sow the seeds of victory before the fight begins, we must play with expectations.*'

She kept her eyes closed and body still, even as part of her screamed that she had to act. Finally, she lifted her head and saw Solon return to the Ark of Revelation and heave at the handle. The lid came up. Rainbow light now bathed his face in a glow of rippling color. His expression was triumphant as he held the edge of the lid high with one hand and reached inside with the other.

High above her, the one-eyed silver dragon and its shiny black opponent flew apart, then collided again. Chloe saw torn skin on both of them, blood dripping from ugly gashes.

She saw the sword, resting on the ground between her and Solon. There would be no better time.

Chloe climbed to her feet and stumbled over, grabbing hold of the hilt and lifting the weapon. It was suddenly light in her hands and she knew what she had to do. Solon was consumed with the ark; his eyes feverish as he took hold of whatever was in there.

'*You want your enemies to be distracted. Then, when you take action, be bold,*' Tomarys whispered in her ear.

She came up behind the sun king and gazed at the thick yellow silk of his robe, at a place directly between his shoulder blades. She thought of Princess Yasmina's terrible fate. Most of all, she remembered her friend, Tomarys.

'Let me end the pain,' Chloe murmured.

Solon whirled at the sound of her voice but she didn't hesitate, she thrust in hard, plunging the sharp blade into the center of the sun king's back, feeling the steel make contact and then slide in with little effort. The point emerged out the other side as he screamed in pain. The lid of the ark crashed closed and the rainbow light immediately vanished. He clasped his hands over the blade as if trying to pull it out through his chest. Chloe let go of the hilt as he stared at her with eyes so wide she could see their whites.

The sun king opened his mouth to speak. He staggered for two steps, clutching the sharp steel as he glared at her. Crimson liquid spurted from between his lips.

Finally he fell to his knees and then toppled to the side. Solon shuddered and then died, eyes gazing sightlessly as his lifeblood welled around his body. Chloe looked at her shaking hands. The Oracle's prophecy had been fulfilled. The sun king had died in the thirty-first year of his reign. But it hadn't been the sickness in his chest that killed him.

Hearing a roar of frustration, Chloe saw the one-eyed dragon release its grip on its enemy and fly away. Unable to open the ark himself, Triton's plans had been defeated. The black dragon came down from the sky, flying unsteadily to the cleared space between the temple's columns, one of its wings moving with jerky movements. It shuddered as it finally landed a short distance from the cliff edge.

The creature's chest heaved as the angular eyes regarded Chloe with strange sorrow. Despite the fact that it had saved her life, she felt a shiver of fear as she looked at it.

Mist suddenly clouded the black-scaled dragon, thickening before it began to shimmer. She forced herself to approach. She didn't know which of the eldren it was who had saved her, but she had to thank him.

But when the mist cleared, Chloe felt her entire world crashing down around her. She knew her face was filled with horror. She refused to believe what she was seeing.

Dion lay facing her with his head on his arms. There were gashes on his face and lower arms, and his tunic pressed up against more wounds on his body. He shivered and trembled.

He had his eyes closed, but then they opened wide.

He was looking at her.

'Dion . . .' Chloe said. She didn't know what she was going to say next.

He clambered to his feet. His white tunic was red with blood. His dread-filled eyes met hers and then he looked at the cliff edge.

'No!' Chloe cried.

He ran to the precipice and leaped off. Chloe told her muscles to move but she stood transfixed. She waited for the splash as his body struck the surging sea far below.

But it never came.

62

The journey from the Temple of Aldus to the base of the stairway embedded in the cliff seemed to take an eternity. Chloe was forced to pause every few steps, gasping for breath and fighting a trembling in her limbs that wouldn't stop.

When she completed her descent she put a hand to her mouth.

Bodies lay scattered around the agora and along the summit of the sloped bastion, too many for her mind to encompass. Soldiers of three nations littered the city's main square, their faces twisted in final expressions of agony. Phalesia had survived, but at a terrible cost. Chloe wondered if the horror would ever end.

She stumbled to the embankment and saw Captain Amos, an ugly swelling on his forehead, issuing orders to his men. Concern filled his face as he saw Chloe approach.

'The sun king's body is up there,' Chloe whispered.

'Chloe . . . Are you all right?'

Taking a deep breath to steady herself, Chloe finally nodded. She straightened and took hold of herself as Amos called out to some of his men, sending them up the cliff.

'What happened?' he asked. 'How did the sun king die?'

Seeing a familiar figure, Amos beckoned, and Chloe saw her father rushing forward.

'Daughter!' Aristocles cried, alarmed when he saw Chloe's blood-drenched chiton. 'Are you well? You're unharmed?' He looked at her quizzically.

'Where is the sun king?' a rough voice called as a man who must be Nikolas approached. He scowled, his eyes dark under his bushy black brows, the expression fierce on his broad face.

'He is dead. He tried to open the ark. Something . . . was in there.' She drew a slow, shaky breath. 'An . . . eldran saved me. It's over.'

'We must thank him,' Aristocles said, looking around. 'All of them.'

'They've all long gone,' said Amos. 'But we'll find a way.'

'They don't need thanks,' Chloe murmured. 'They just want peace between our races.'

Speaking these last words, her thoughts turned to Dion. She tried instead to focus on her father and her home.

'Nikolas—' Aristocles began.

'King Nikolas,' Amos admonished.

'Of course,' said Aristocles, bowing smoothly. 'King Nikolas of Xanthos. We thank you.'

Nikolas nodded, but his eyes were turned to the sea, where the enemy warships were scattered across the waters of the harbor as they drew away. Chloe saw several captured vessels on the shore.

Noting his gaze, Aristocles spoke. 'Kargan still lives. We should consider sending out a boat under a white flag to conduct talks . . . give them a chance to retrieve their dead.'

'No,' Nikolas countermanded. He glared at Aristocles. 'My men will burn their dead. We'll burn the sun king with them.'

Aristocles hesitated, but the army of Xanthos was in his city, greatly outnumbering the Phalesian soldiers, and he nodded.

There was silence for a time as they all watched the departing ships.

'Do you think they'll be back?' Chloe's father asked.

'They'll be back,' Nikolas said. 'The war for the Maltherean Sea has only just begun.'

Chloe shivered.

'Sire! This prisoner wants to speak with the king of Xanthos.'

Turning, she saw two crimson-cloaked hoplites escorting a stocky woman with short sun-bleached hair. The woman wasn't in armor, instead wearing a loose tunic that was almost manly on her muscular frame. Her skin was weathered to a dark tan.

Nikolas turned and impatiently waited for the prisoner to approach.

'Well?' he asked. 'If you want to say something, speak quickly.'

'I . . .' she hesitated and then spoke again, more firmly this time, meeting his stare with a steady expression of her own. 'My name is Roxana. I am . . . was . . . captain of the bireme *Anoraxis*. I am also a shipbuilder. I have no wish to die or be taken as a slave. In fact, he said you would give me a villa if I built ships for you.'

'Who said?' Nikolas frowned.

'Dion.' Chloe realized who she was. 'Roxana. He spoke of you. He said you're a good person.'

'Right,' Roxana said wryly. 'Dion of No-land, the man from a small village on a tiny island with no name.' Perplexed expressions met her words.

'Xanthos,' Chloe said softly, looking away. 'Dion of Xanthos.'

'So are you the father who thinks archery is for commoners?' Roxana addressed Aristocles. 'Will you give me my villa?'

'A villa?' Aristocles' eyebrows rose. 'Well, I'm not sure if the Assembly—'

'Wait.' Nikolas held up a hand. 'My brother always said naval power would determine the fate of the world, something I think we've all learned first hand.' He smiled grimly at Roxana. 'Roxana, if you build me more of these ships, I will give you a villa.'

'What of my men?' Roxana persisted. 'There are many with skills who were captured. Most were enslaved by the sun king. If you name them free they will serve you well.'

'Any who wish to serve under you may live, but they'll still be slaves. The rest?' He shrugged. 'We're not usually in the business of taking slaves.'

'I'm sure most will serve.' Roxana grinned. 'Dion—' She looked around. 'He burned two thirds of the fleet. If he hadn't we might be facing each other on different terms today. Is he here?'

When silence met her words Chloe left the group. She walked to the edge of the embankment, following the summit of the wall, heading left until she was in a place free from death, provided she didn't look down at the shore.

She kept her gaze firmly on the blue horizon. Kargan's biremes were now distant specks. The nation of Ilea, proud center of an empire encompassing most of Salesia, had been humiliated. The sun king was dead but his position would be fought over by his heirs and commanders. The golden pyramid in Lamara would inspire the same greed that had led Solon to the Ark of Revelation.

Nikolas was correct. The war for the Maltherean Sea had only just begun.

As if on cue, Chloe heard heavy footsteps as Dion's older brother came to join her. She examined his features as he approached. Nikolas and Dion were completely unlike each other. Nikolas was a full head taller than his younger brother and had black bushy hair with a thick matching beard. Dion spoke softly, while his older brother spoke with the rough voice of a soldier.

They shared the same father, but they were half-brothers, with different mothers. Dion had always spoken about Nikolas with love and respect; his older brother had guided and helped him for as long as he could remember.

But when she looked at Nikolas, Chloe saw a dark shadow in his eyes. Recent events had changed all of them.

'Chloe. About my brother . . . I saw.'

'You know?'

'I wasn't the only one. I know now what he is.' Nikolas hesitated. 'Where is he now? Is he dead?'

It was some time before Chloe spoke. 'He threw himself off the cliff. But I don't think he is dead.' She turned to him. 'Will he return?'

'The question is, should he? He's not one of us. His mother was always strange . . . I suppose it all makes sense.'

'He is your brother,' Chloe said with force.

'He is,' Nikolas said softly. 'But perhaps he is better off now. Perhaps, away from all this, he can be happy.'

Chloe opened her mouth to speak, but then faltered as she saw her father approach, his arms wide and his shadowed eyes glancing from face to face with an expression of forced warmth.

'It is good to see the two of you together. To survive the coming days our two nations must be strong. Our alliance must be a marriage between us.'

Chloe's mouth dropped open.

Nikolas glanced at Chloe, then at her father.

He slowly nodded.

'I see the wisdom,' Nikolas said. His voice was filled with sadness and regret as he spoke. 'I must mourn my beloved wife and son, but as king I must also think about the future. My brother is gone and may not return, nor do I think it right that he should. He is certainly not fit to be my heir.'

Chloe turned pleading eyes on her father, but he carefully kept his face turned away from her as he gazed at the new king of his neighboring nation, the man who had saved Phalesia.

'First Consul,' Nikolas said. 'When I have finished grieving those I have lost, I will marry your daughter.'

Chloe whirled away, her chest rising and falling and her gaze fixed sightlessly on nothing, nothing at all.

The prophecy of the Seer of Athos thrust itself into her consciousness. The words, spoken in a sibilant hiss, burned as they entered her mind.

You will kill a man you pity.

She remembered Tomarys, her loyal bodyguard.

You will marry a man you do not love.

Chloe couldn't fight the inevitable. The Seer had prophesied the sun king's death. Her own fate was sealed. Nikolas was to be her husband.

You will desire a man you fear.

She thought of Dion. He had given everything for his homeland, and now he had lost everything he'd fought for. Out of two strong nations, he was the only one who came for her.

Chloe heard a soft voice behind her. 'Chloe, are we safe now?'

Turning, she saw little Sophia staring up at her with wide eyes. She bent and pulled her sister into a close embrace, rotating so that Sophia wasn't looking at the gruesome scene at the harbor.

Chloe's own vision misted as she watched the waves crash into red foam on the shore.

63

North of Xanthos, in the land called the Wilds, a tall, lean man with silver hair entered an emerald glade.

The music of creaking insects and tumbling water mingled with the crash and roar of a distant waterfall. The glade was at the base of a valley, near a clear river that flowed over smooth white stones. Grassy banks at both sides gave way to an encircling perimeter of evergreens that swayed in a gentle breeze.

The eldran, clad in deerskin and bearing a crescent scar on his cheek, entered the clearing and stopped. The blue sky overhead was clear and bright. The sun's slanted rays glowed on the high branches.

Despite the beauty around him, Zachary sighed as he resumed his soft tread.

In the middle of the clearing, an immense reptilian creature with shining black scales watched his approach with sad eyes. The dragon wheezed and raised its angular head before lowering it back down to the ground. Its monstrous form was muscled, its long body coiled with pent-up power. The wings folded on its back stretched out and elongated, fluttering for a moment before the creature appeared to lose will and its motion stilled once more.

Zachary made soothing sounds and kept his hands carefully visible with arms spread. He saw the animal docility in the black dragon's eyes and knew the danger he was in. It was on the very edge. Once it became wild, there would be no turning back.

The dragon allowed him to come so close that Zachary could reach out and touch the angular ridges on its wedge-shaped head.

Then Zachary spoke. He knew he would have only this one chance. He knew he was risking his life.

'Your name is Dion,' he said softly. 'Your father was Markos. You grew up in Xanthos. You have a brother, Nikolas.'

The dragon growled and the head came up once more. The huge eyes stared at Zachary, filled with sorrow.

'Your name is Dion,' Zachary said again, willing the creature to understand. 'Remember who you are.'

He felt his pulse race as the dragon's growl became a rumble. The midnight scales rippled as its body tensed.

Then Zachary's shoulders slumped and he breathed a sigh of relief as smoke misted the air around the creature. In moments the cloud enveloped it entirely, and then the mist wavered in his vision, shimmering like a mirage in the desert.

When the smoke cleared, Zachary was looking at a young man with sandy brown hair, his head tilted, raised on his arms with his abdomen on the grassy floor of the glade. He wore a blood-soaked tunic and shivered with pain and exhaustion.

Dion's gaze met Zachary's, and the eldran felt his heart reach out. The wildness slowly vanished from the young man's eyes.

'Come, Dion,' Zachary said. 'Come with me. I will introduce you to your people.'

The eldran helped the young man to stand and then Zachary looked away, in the direction of Xanthos.

'There is no longer anything for you in that world.'

ACKNOWLEDGMENTS

Huge thanks go to Emilie, Eoin, Sana, Neil, and all the team, both in the UK and the US, for simply being so wonderful to work with.

I'd also like to give special thanks to Ian for trimming and tightening where it was needed, and for straightening out the wobbles in this ship's course.

Thanks to all of you who reach out to me and take the time to post reviews of my books. Your feedback matters. In this day and age, we're in this together.

ABOUT THE AUTHOR

James Maxwell grew up in the scenic Bay of Islands, New Zealand, and was educated in Australia. Devouring fantasy and science-fiction classics from an early age, his love for books translated to a passion for writing, which he began at the age of eleven.

Inspired by the natural beauty around him but also by a strong interest in history, he decided in his twenties to see the world. He relocated to London and then to Thailand, Mexico, Austria, and Malta, developing a lifelong obsession with travel. It was while living in Thailand that he seriously took up writing again, producing his first full-length novel, *Enchantress*, the first of four titles in his internationally bestselling Evermen Saga.

Golden Age is the first novel in his highly anticipated new series, The Shifting Tides.

When he isn't writing or traveling, James enjoys sailing, snowboarding, classical guitar, and French cooking.